Hands of the Order Book One

# A Kiss of Glass

## J.D. Brubaker

Hands of the Order

Book One: A Kiss of Glass

By J. D. Brubaker

Copyright © 2023 J.D. Brubaker.



ISBN: 979-8-9882196-0-6 (Paperback)

ISBN: 979-8-9882196-1-3 (Hardcover)

Library of Congress Control Number: 2023907435

This book is a work of fiction. Any references to historical events, real people, or real places are used fictitiously. Other names, characters, places and events are products of the author's imagination, and any resemblances to actual events or places or persons, living or dead, is entirely coincidental.

Front cover image and book design by Angelee van Allman.

Printed by J.D. Brubaker Books

First edition printed 2023.

jdbrubaker807@gmail.com

www.writingasajourney.com

UTARA
FIRE'S HEARTH
PASSING'S END
ARMISTICE
TERRACE
GARDEN'S HEM
SUN RIVER
NEVEAN

UTARA
HEVEAN
NYNIVRI
LOZOR
CYBASSUS

# Contents

# Prologue

*Kyndra awoke suddenly and sat up in bed. She was breathing heavily, her chest rising and falling in swift succession. The room was dark. The fire in the hearth had gone out some hours before and left behind only a faint, orange glow from the still crackling embers. She could hear nothing at first and wondered what had awoken her. Perhaps she had been dreaming again, she thought as she ran her fingers over her face. She shivered and wrapped her arms across her chest. It was cold now in the late autumn months. Snow had already covered the pass leading to the fortress and more would surely fall as autumn gave way to winter. She grabbed a shawl and climbed from underneath her covers and walked to the stained glass window to her left.*

*The silver moon shone brightly in the night sky surrounded by millions of stars sparkling against the dark canvas. It was beautiful up here, but she often wondered if the isolation was good or bad for the recruits. Or for any of them, for that matter. It was the one thing she never could agree upon with the others. They wanted the isolation, the treacherousness around them. They said the silence of the mountain pass was like a guardian shielding them from those they did not wish to meet. And though she understood this,* she still could not escape the thought that there might be a different way, a better way.

Kyndra looked around at her room. It was a sizeable room made of stone and wood, but it was not what she would consider comfortable. The furniture was old. The mattress she slept on was thin, allowing the boards of her bed to push through the straw and feathers. Her blankets were made of wool and, though thin and somewhat ragged, at least offered some warmth against the frigid temperatures of the mountains. The room, like the fortress, was practically empty save for the few personal items like books and candles she had brought here to personalize the space. But it never could quite feel like home.

She never would have even considered the isolation if not for Rhaean, her daughter. Only fourteen years old, she was already wise beyond her years. Kyndra smiled at the thought. It was for Rhaean that she wanted to do what was best for all of them. Rhaean was a strong student, but it was clear that she took the remoteness of this place hard. It was, perhaps, even a hindrance to her ability to learn and grow.

"I feel so stifled here," she had said some months before, "as though I don't belong."

"You've been here since you were born, my darling," Kyndra had replied, "If anyone belongs here, it is you."

Rhaean sighed and shook her head. "You don't understand. This place...it is alive in its own way. So much resides here, so many spirits and other beings, and they don't want us here. They don't want me here."

*Kyndra's skin had tingled as Rhaean spoke. Everyone knew the fortress was haunted. But no one had ever indicated that the spirits might be malevolent. As far as she knew, the spirits were nothing more than that: the souls of people who had died here, and now, for whatever reason, couldn't or wouldn't pass on into the next life. They had never been problems before, and it worried her to hear her own daughter explain it. She had given Rhaean as much encouragement as she could, promising to take her concerns to the council. She had done so and the council had rejected her concerns outright. She had fought. They had dug in their heels and threatened her and Rhaean with expulsion, an unprecedented action. Recruits were sent away often enough, but a Mother never had been. Not in the entire history of The Order's existence.*

*It was no use thinking on it, she told herself as she turned to walk back to bed. She had voiced her concerns and they had been taken under advisement. There was nothing else for her to do but trust that all would turn out well.*

*That was when she sensed it. Magic. A great deal of it coming from down the hall. A moment later, screams erupted and a chill went down Kyndra's spine. She took a step towards the bedroom door when it suddenly flung open and one of the students stood before her, eyes wide with fear.*

*"Mother Andromeda, come quick," she said.*

*"What is it, Fyona?"*

*"It's Rhaean, Mother."*

*Mother Andromeda's heart skipped. "What about her?"*

*The girl grabbed her hand and they rushed down the hallway towards the dining hall. The screams intensified, filling Kyndra with a dread that she had never felt before. As they neared the dining hall, she could smell the horrifying stench of burning stone and ash. She felt tears welling in her eyes and she lifted up a prayer to any and all gods that might be listening for her daughter to be safe. She resolved in that moment that she would take Rhaean away from this place. They would leave and never, ever, return. They would be safe. Rhaean would be safe. She swore it to herself and to all the gods.*

*The moment they entered the dining hall she knew her promise had been made in vain. She was too late. It was all far, far too late.*

# Chapter One

*Town of Terrace*
*Country of Utara*

Embers crackled in the stone fireplace. Eight year old Nasya and her younger sister, Maiah, sat as close to the fireplace as they could, absorbing the last remnants of dying heat that emanated from the hearth. It was October and already the air was cold, bitingly cold. The two girls wore their warmest garments with some of their other clothing underneath, and still they shivered. Nasya eyed the pile of logs in the corner of the room, wishing she could add a log or two to the almost-dead fire, but she had been given strict instructions not to. Her parents had said something about needing to make the firewood last as long as possible.

Next to her, Maiah whimpered. Nasya scooted closer and

wrapped her arms around her sister's small shoulders. It didn't help that it was well past supper time and neither of them had eaten since breakfast. And that meal consisted of nothing but some stale bread and one cup of milk each. At the mere thought of food, Nasya's stomach rumbled. She looked over her shoulder towards her parents, wondering when they would set to making their next meal. If there would be a next meal. Her mother and father sat on the opposite side of the room. They were conversing with a guest, a woman who had arrived about an hour before and who had done most of the talking since. Nasya had not caught her name.

The woman was tall from Nasya's perspective, and elegant. She wore a gown made of a fabric Nasya had never seen before, but she could tell it was expensive. It had no tears, no stains, and was well kept. The woman's skin was brown, her hair was black and braided, and her eyes were a bright blue. She kept her voice low, so Nasya was unable to hear any of the conversation, but judging by the looks on her parent's faces, she assumed the woman had brought upsetting news.

"I'm hungry," Maia whimpered, laying her head on Nasya's shoulder.

Nasya rubbed her hands up and down Maiah's arms and nodded. "I know. I am, too."

Suddenly, the woman stood to her feet. So did Nasya's parents.

"You will be given adequate compensation, of course," the woman said, no longer speaking softly as she clasped her hands together in front of her body.

Nasya watched as her mother let out a heavy sigh and looked at her husband. She seemed to be close to tears. To drive her point home, the woman took out a large coin purse. It was heavy with money. Both of her parent's eyes widened.

"There is enough here to feed, clothe, and warm you all for years to come," the woman said.

Nasya's father sighed. "When do you need an answer?"

"Immediately," she replied. "I am here now. I will not pass this way a second time."

Nasya's parents looked at each other helplessly, wordlessly. A moment of silence passed between them.

"I will take a lack of a choice as 'No,'" the woman added. "I will give you three minutes before I leave, and the offer is revoked."

"I don't like this, Galen," Nasya's mother said.

"I know, Lisla. But we need the money. And a life with us is no life at all. Not when we're starving, freezing, and have no means to improve our situation."

Lisla was crying now. Nasya stood to her feet and faced her parents, suddenly filled with fear and anger. Who was this woman? Why had she come? What had she said that would cause her parents this much grief? A moment later, Lisla nodded and collapsed into a heap of sobs. Galen looked at the woman and also nodded. He took the purse from her.

The woman faced Nasya.

"Come here," she said.

Nasya walked over to her hesitantly.

"What is your name?" the woman asked.

"Nasya."

"And your age?"

"Eight."

"Can you read?"

Nasya nodded.

"Can you write?"

She nodded again.

"Good. When I leave here, which will be in only a few moments, you will be coming with me. My name is Mother Corvus. That is what you will know me as."

Nasya looked at her parents and shook her head. "No. I don't want to go with her!"

Lisla couldn't even look at Nasya. Only Galen knelt before her, his eyes distant and dark.

"Nasya, listen to me. You are going with this woman. She's taking you...to school," he said, his eyes lowering to the floor for a brief second before lifting back up to meet her gaze. "You will learn. You will train. And you will live." He held onto her arms. "And you won't make a fuss. Yeah?"

Nasya's eyes were full of tears. She didn't understand. Why was she being sent to school? Wasn't her place with her family? It didn't make any sense. But her father's eyes were filled with so much emotion, she couldn't defy him, no matter how badly she wanted to stay here, in their home, with them. So she nodded slowly, but didn't speak. In the corner, her mother still sobbed, refusing to turn and look at her. She didn't even say goodbye to Nasya.

It was all over in a moment. Mother Corvus took Nasya outside where a plain carriage was waiting. She motioned for Nasya to get in, gave her parents a final nod, and then climbed in herself. Nasya stuck her head out the window as the carriage drove away, finally allowing herself to cry. She watched, desperate for a final wave or glance from either of her parents. But there was nothing to see. They didn't even watch her ride away.

Nasya sat back in her seat. Tears streamed down her face. She didn't understand most of what had happened, but this much she knew: her parents had been paid to give her up, and they had done so with little hesitation. She hoped her impression was wrong, that she had missed an important detail that would explain why her parents chose money over her. Deep down she knew, even if she had missed something, it wouldn't be enough to erase the pain of having been sold away by her own kin.

"There's no use in crying," Mother Corvus said. She sat across from Nasya and stared out the window of the carriage as the countryside passed by in silence. "Tears won't change anything."

"I want to go home," Nasya mumbled through her tears.

Mother Corvus sighed and looked over at her. "You don't have a home anymore," she said, her voice firm, but not unkind. "You don't have a family anymore. Your parents sold you to us, to The Order. Whoever you are now, whoever you were back in that hovel, is dead and gone. And truthfully, it was only a matter of months before you either starved or froze to death, so you would have been dead either way." She leaned forward. "This way, you will have a life. A great life. A powerful life. An important life."

Nasya watched as the woman's blue eyes sparkled. There was passion, excitement, even joy in the piercing blue of her eyes, as well as a coldness that Nasya envied. It wasn't a lack of emotion that fed the coldness, but a distance, a disconnect that came from experience. If she remembered her own family and felt pain at their memory, it didn't show.

"You will also be fed, clothed, and housed throughout your training, which is more than I can say for what your parents offered you."

Nasya felt anger flare in her chest. "They loved me," she said defiantly.

Mother Corvus looked at her. "Love would not have kept you alive through the winter, fledgling."

They were going to a place called Passing's End, Mother Corvus said. It was a fortress that had been built at the base of three different mountains. The pass, according to Mother Corvus, was one of the best places for their training to be conducted because it allowed them to exist, live, and learn in complete privacy. The pass had not been utilized in some decades, she explained.

"How long will it take us to get there?" Nasya asked on the second day of their journey.

"Another three days, provided the weather holds."

The first day of their travels had been horrible for Nasya. Hours of riding in the carriage with very little rest had been exhausting. She had spent the bulk of it in tears and silence. Mother Corvus must have sensed the heavy heartbreak that weighed over Nasya, because she let her cry openly without expressing any irritation or shaming her into suppressing her emotions. Eventually, they had stopped near a river for a light meal of cold ham, some sharp cheese, and some bread. Nasya had forgotten how hungry she had been, and after the first bite of bread had touched her tongue, her stomach came alive with hunger and she ate ravenously. Mother Corvus gave her a second portion that was even larger than her first, and Nasya ate it up in mere moments.

"Gods above," Mother Corvus said, "when was your last meal?"

"This morning," Nasya said, her mouth full of food.

"How much did you eat?"

Nasya shrugged. "A slice of bread and some milk."

She nodded slowly. "But you had dinner last night?"

Nasya looked up at her and shook her head. She didn't elaborate, didn't explain how most days she and her sister were given one meal and it was usually in the morning. She didn't explain how her parents only ate one meal every other day. Mother Corvus stared at Nasya for a moment. She didn't say anything, she just watched as the eight year old ate more food in one sitting than she'd eaten the rest of the month put together.

They climbed back into the carriage and continued on the

road towards Passing's End. Nasya sat back in her seat, her stomach full for the first time in longer than she could remember. It was almost painful, feeling this much food in her body at once, but it was a pain she reveled in. And for a moment, she forgot the sadness she'd felt earlier that day. She simply sat with her head resting against the back of the seat, her eyes closed, as she let her body adjust to the sudden influx of food. She was jostled out of her repose when she felt something placed in her lap. She opened her eyes and looked down. More ham, bread, and cheese had been given to her. She looked up at Mother Corvus questioningly.

"Eat your fill, fledgling," was all she said.

Nasya did just that. They were in the carriage for several more hours and any time she felt even the smallest cry of hunger in her stomach, she grabbed from the food she'd been given and allowed herself to eat until the hunger faded. It did not curb the loneliness she felt, or the confusion that still wracked her mind, but it fulfilled a more primal need. And in the uncertainty that had now become her future, it was enough to lighten the darkness she felt closing in around her.

That night, after what seemed like hours riding in total darkness, they came to an inn that seemed to be in the middle of nowhere. As Nasya emerged from the carriage, she looked up at the large building made of wood and stone. It was three stories high with tall windows and a sloped roof. Mother Corvus led her inside. There was a dining area to the left with a kitchen in the back, and to their right was a wide staircase leading up to the rooms. Upon entry, they were greeted by the smell of many different foods. Roasted chicken, fresh baked bread, stew with venison broth and large chunks of meat, and cheese pies. Suddenly, Nasya's stomach was again ravenous.

Mother Corvus booked them a room with two beds, and then sat at an empty table close to the large hearth in the center of the dining area. Nasya looked around at the other guests. Were they all travelers like her? Without a home? Without family? Their futures, blank pages waiting for pen and ink? She had never been outside of her hometown before. She had seen very little of the people of the world and didn't know what made anyone leave their home, their comfort.

A woman walked over to their table. She wore a blue dress with a stained apron around her waist.

"What can I get the two of you?" she asked.

Nasya didn't know what to say. She looked over at Mother Corvus for any indication of what she could order, but Mother Corvus ordered for her.

"A loaf of sourdough with butter. Two large bowls of stew. And a roasted chicken."

The woman nodded. "Anything to drink?"

"A flagon of wine for me. A pint of ale for the girl."

Nasya waited for the woman to walk away before saying, "I'm not supposed to drink ale."

Mother Corvus kept her eyes up, watching the other patrons as she spoke. "You haven't drank anything all day, and the water here is little better than piss. The ale will also help you sleep."

Nasya nodded. They were quiet for some time. Their food was brought out after only a few minutes, and they both set to eating. Nasya paid no heed for the mess she was making, nor for any pretense of manners. She tore off chunks of bread and dipped them into the stew. The rich, almost creamy broth soaked into the bread nicely. She wasn't sure she'd ever tasted something so delicious. It was only after she'd eaten half the bread and half of her stew that she saw Mother Corvus watching her, a faint smile on her face.

"I'm sorry," Nasya said, her mouth full. She wasn't sure why, but she felt as though she had made a great error, despite the humor in Mother Corvus's eyes.

"It's alright," Mother Corvus said. "I remember when I stayed here with the Mother who was sent to bring me to Passing's End. I must have scarfed down three full bowls of stew in less than an hour."

"You stayed here?"

She nodded. "I did. In the same room you and I will be."

Nasya watched as the woman ate. It, like everything else about her, was elegant and effortless. It was slow and methodical, almost rhythmic, the way she cut her food and brought it to her mouth. She had never seen anyone look so lovely as they ate their dinner.

"So...you were taken from your family, too?"

The woman's eyes stared into Nasya's. She waited a moment and then shook her head. "No. I was picked up off the streets. But I had been starving for days and was close to wasting away into obscurity. The Mother who traveled with me offered me food, clothes, and shelter, and I would have done anything to have those things provided to me."

Mother Corvus leaned forward until she was closer to Nasya. "You are grieving what you think you've lost. You'll eventually see that this is where you were always meant to be." She sat up straight. "Your first lesson is this: eating is not a race, there is no reward for finishing your food first." She pointed to the utensils next to her. "Have you ever used those before?"

Nasya blushed and shook her head.

"Well, you will now."

Mother Corvus picked her own utensils up and held them in her hands. She held a fork and knife for the chicken, a spoon for the stew. She buttered the bread and laid it next to the bowl of stew. "It may seem frivolous, eating this way, but it is the proper way. And as a recruit training to be part of the Sisterhood of The Order, you will only do things the proper way from this point forward. Is that understood?"

Nasya nodded. She picked up the spoon (it was the least daunting of the items) and began scooping broth, vegetables, and meat into her mouth. Mother Corvus let out a grunt of disapproval. "Do not hold your spoon like that," she said, slowly demonstrating the correct way to hold it. Nasya tried to copy her, and it took a few moments to get it right, but she did eventually hold the spoon the same way as Mother Corvus. She began to eat again. Mother Corvus nodded. "Yes, much better. Remember to also sit with your back straight. Good posture will separate you from the low born citizens."

"But I am low born," Nasya replied.

"No one else needs to know that."

Nasya continued to eat. She finished her stew and bread, and then was given several large slices of roasted chicken. Mother Corvus demonstrated how to use the fork and knife and Nasya found them far more difficult to use than the spoon. But she tried and by the end of the night, she had noticeably improved.

When the food was gone, Mother Corvus grabbed her wine and Nasya's ale and walked up the stairs to their room. There were two beds fully made with what looked like the most comfortable blankets Nasya had ever seen. A fire had already been lit in the hearth, so the room was wonderfully warm. And on the table were two other loaves of bread, a dish of butter, a bowl of fruit, and two wheels of cheese. Nasya felt as though they were royalty to be given such treatment, but Mother Corvus acted as though it was typical and entirely expected.

Mother Corvus closed and locked the door behind them.

"Sit and drink your ale," she said as she removed her heavy cloak.

Nasya sat at the table and took a sip from the large goblet. She winced as she swallowed. "Does all ale taste like this?"

Mother Corvus grinned. "More or less. But it will help you sleep after today's excitement, so drink as much as you can."

Nasya listened and, even though she hated the taste, she drank every ounce of ale she'd been given. And quickly, her head began to swim. Mother Corvus told her to crawl into bed and sleep, for they had an early morning. Nasya climbed under the covers of the mattress that was unbelievably comfortable in comparison to the bed she was used to. The blankets were as warm as she had imagined and, for the first time in her life, she felt she understood what luxury was. In mere seconds, she was asleep.

The next day was much the same as the first. It began with a breakfast Nasya could only have ever imagined: sausage links, thick slices of bacon cooked crispy, large biscuits with butter and jam, boiled duck eggs with salt and pepper, and thick slabs of ham. Nasya ate as many helpings as she was given, suddenly aware of just how starved she had been up until now. It was as if her body recognized the abundance of food before her and, fearful that it wouldn't last, took in as much food as was physically possible.

Once they had eaten, Mother Corvus led them back to the carriage and they continued riding towards the mountain pass. Today was a much less emotional journey. It wasn't that she no longer missed her family (she did, with an ache she didn't think would ever lessen), but it was hard to mourn her current plight when it brought with it as much food as her little body could stand. She didn't know what kind school she was being taken to, nor did she really understand what kind of learning she would be given, but one thing that was clear was that she would never starve again. And that, on its own, was enough to dry her tears.

They stopped only once before nightfall, and that was to break for supper, like they had the day before. Nasya was given more ham, bread, and cheese, and she ate her fill. Mother Corvus was not talkative today, but Nasya didn't mind. She was content to travel in silence. There was something different about her today, something Nasya couldn't quite name. She seemed distracted, even on edge, as though waiting for something to happen. She was always looking around them; if they were in the carriage, she would frequently look out the window in all directions, and when they stopped for supper, she hardly ate anything. She kept looking around in an almost paranoid frequency. Nasya nearly asked if anything was wrong, but decided not to. She didn't want to know if anything was wrong because, for the first time in as long as she could remember, the number of things wrong in her life fit on one hand.

That night they came to another inn, though this one was much smaller. It was on the edge of a hamlet. The inn was also attached to a public house. The two companions took a seat near the hearth and waited for the kitchen wench to take their order. A young woman approached them a few moments later. Mother Corvus, again, ordered the food. It was clear she had been to this place before and knew the food they served. The meal consisted of two bowls of lentil stew, two trout filets, boiled potatoes, and a loaf of bread with butter. Mother Corvus also ordered two cups of mulled wine and another pint of ale for Nasya.

This time, Nasya remembered to use the utensils she was given. She still struggled a bit with them, but it was easier than the night before. The food itself was delicious. Nasya couldn't believe that in the world outside of Terrace, people ate so well and so fully. She didn't know if this was the kind of food she would have at Passing's End, but right now she was grateful for all of what she was being given.

They slept in another room similar to the one the night before. They broke the fast there and then continued on their journey. They would be at Passing's End by nightfall, she was told. The other recruits would be arriving in the next few days, and starting next week, their training would begin. Nasya still wanted to ask questions, but she dared not break the silence between them unless she was spoken to first. It wasn't that she was afraid of Mother Corvus, for the woman had not been unkind in their short acquaintance, but she was worried she would do something to enrage her, and that she did not want to do. Not when her wellbeing likely rested on this woman's shoulders.

It was late when they finally reached Passing's End and much colder than Nasya had expected. At least two inches of snow covered the ground for miles leading up to the fortress. Nasya was taken from the courtyard into the stone building. She was shown to the room that was to be hers, given a tray of food, and left to herself. The room was small but cozy. There were two beds, two desks, and a closet. A fire roared in the hearth.

Nasya looked down at the food she'd been given. It wasn't as large a portion as she'd eaten at the two public houses, but it was hot and smelled appetizing. She had a bowl of some kind of stew with large chunks of potato and a meat that tasted like mutton, as well as some bread with butter and another pint of ale. She still hated the taste of the beverage, but she couldn't deny that it gave her a deep, warm sleep that she now coveted.

She sat on the floor near the fire and ate her dinner. She practiced using the spoon again, and this time it felt a bit more natural than before. The stew was good, though not as mouth watering as the others she'd had. But Nasya wasn't going to complain. Ever since leaving with Mother Corvus, she had lived three days without extreme hunger. If her stomach grumbled, it was simply a reminder for her to eat rather than an expression of her body slowly shutting down. She couldn't recall the last time she hadn't gone hungry.

When she had finished her food, she set the tray on one of the desks and climbed into the bed closest to the window. The bed wasn't fancy or large, but the mattress was soft and the blankets were thick and warm. The air outside was cold, but her room was well heated by the fire. The last few days felt like luxury in comparison to what she'd left. Though, if she was honest, now that she was alone, Nasya felt a deep ache to see her parents again. She missed their routine, their voices, the smell of her mother's hair. She missed playing with her sister. It had been a hard life, but it was the one she knew. And now it was gone.

Nasya cried herself to sleep that night. Some of the emotion was sadness, a deep regret that she had been taken from her family. Some of it was fear, the uncertainty of what her life would become. But the bulk came from exhaustion. It had been three hard days of travel. Three hard days of confusion. Three hard days of new places, new people, new experiences. And there was something about the newness of her circumstances that drained her of all energy and simply allowed the tears to flow. In mere minutes, she had cried herself into a lazy stupor that quickly slipped into a deep, restful sleep.

Morning came the way it always did. Cold rays of sunlight fell through the window of her room, waking her softly. Nasya stayed under the covers for several minutes, content to bask in the warmth of her bed. The fire in the hearth had died in the night, but the room had held onto the heat. When Nasya did emerge from under the covers, she saw that a pile of clothes had been left on the foot of her bed. A second pile had been placed at the foot of the other bed. Nasya assumed it was what she would be wearing since her own clothes were nearly falling apart.

She changed into her new clothes and then left the room in search of food. She hadn't taken two steps out of her room before she nearly ran into Mother Corvus.

"Ah, so you are awake," she said, looking down at her. "It is nearly time for breakfast with some of the other recruits." She motioned for Nasya to follow her. They made their way down a long corridor lined with lit torches. Nasya was impressed at the vastness of the fortress. It had looked large when they'd arrived last night, but she hadn't seen the bulk of it in the darkness. Now, it struck her that this building was large enough to house everyone in Terrace.

They came to the dining hall and Nasya spotted six girls sitting at a table in the center of the room. Nasya was taken over to the same table and sat down. It was then that breakfast was served. Large pots with a thick porridge were brought out along with pitchers of milk, loaves of bread, jars of butter and jam, and bowls with different types of fruit. The girls were given leave to eat to their heart's content. No one spoke.

Nasya looked around at the faces at the table. Mother Corvus sat at the head of the table, and another woman sat at the opposite end. She was dressed in the same robes as Mother Corvus. The girls were all dressed alike, too. They wore plain frocks made of wool and cotton. Nasya studied the girls around her. They looked to be close to her age and, if she had to guess, had been sold from other poor families across the country. And like her, they seemed focused entirely on the abundance of food before them. Nasya turned her gaze to where Mother Corvus sat and found the woman watching her. Nasya wished to know what she was thinking, but knew better than to ask.

After breakfast, the girls were instructed to return to their rooms and begin reading the first chapters of the books that had been left on their beds. Nasya walked into her room and found a fire had been lit in the hearth. She smiled, glad to be warm with a full belly. She grabbed the pile of books and sat on the floor to read them. There were five books in her pile, all of them old and falling apart. One was a book on geography; one was a book on botany; two were on the histories of the three great dynasties of the world, and the last was an introduction to the primary religions of each country. Nasya was intrigued as well as intimidated. How was she supposed to understand any of this? She decided to start with the geography book since it would be easier to absorb. She held the book in her lap, leaned her back against the foot of her bed, and started to read.

She didn't know how long she'd been reading when the door to her room opened and a girl was brought in. The woman with her was clearly unhappy. She was scowling, her eyebrows furrowed downward, and her lips were pursed.

"Here is your room," she said. "Change your clothes, then get to reading."

With that, she closed the door, leaving the two girls alone. The girl turned around and looked at Nasya. "I don't think she likes me," she said, her eyes sparkling.

Nasya grinned. The girl was slender with dark skin and dark, curly hair.

"I"m Scarlet," the other girl said, grabbing the clothes that had been laid out on her bed.

"I'm Nasya."

"Have you been here long?"

"Since last night."

Scarlet nodded. "Hopefully you had a better time than I have," she said, changing into her new clothes.

Nasya watched her, fascinated by how nonchalant she was about the situation. Had she been taken from her family, too? Or had she been given a choice to be here? It was odd for Nasya.

She couldn't imagine being unaffected by this place, the people. Granted, Nasya enjoyed the warmth and the full belly, but she couldn't deny that she was afraid, confused, and homesick. Scarlet didn't seem to be any of those things.

"Did they tell you anything about why we're here?" Scarlet asked, sitting on the floor with her pile of books.

Nasya shook her head. "Mother Corvus said something about training."

Scarlet raised her eyebrows. "That's all she told you?"

Nasya nodded.

"But you don't know what we're training for?"

Nasya shook her head. "Do you?"

Scarlet shrugged. "I know that this isn't an ordinary school." She motioned at the building they were in. "What kind of school hides its students up in the mountains?"

"Mother Corvus said solitude allows students to learn without distraction."

Scarlet snorted. "Or they bring us here to keep from being found?"

"Who...who would want to find us?"

Scarlet didn't respond. She started looking at the books, her eyes scanning the pages at a quick pace. Nasya returned to her own reading, but her mind couldn't focus. She kept thinking about what it was they were there to learn. Deep down she had known from the beginning that this wasn't a typical institution, but she allowed herself to believe that it was while she was traveling. It was easier to imagine lessons, tests, and books than it was to think about what she was really going to be taught. Even now, looking down at the books they'd been instructed to read, all Nasya could think about was why she'd been given these particular books. Why did she, a low born girl, need to know the histories of the great dynasties? Why did she need to study plants? And what did those things have to do with one another?

The two girls read in silence for the rest of the morning. There were still recruits that were on their way to Passing's End, so their training wouldn't begin in full until everyone had arrived. They were given permission to wander the fortress, so long as they didn't go beyond the second floor. And they were expected to complete the first three chapters in all five books before their training began in earnest. Otherwise, their time was their own.

It would be another three days before all of the recruits arrived. In that time, Nasya became very attached to Scarlet. They stayed by each other's side as often as they could. As the girls were given their daily chores (making their beds, sweeping and mopping the floors in every room, washing their clothes, and learning how to cook), Nasya and Scarlet did their utmost to be paired together. They got on well together. Nasya was quiet and reserved; Scarlet was outspoken and vivacious. She loved to make Nasya laugh and would frequently do and say things to elicit even so much as a smile from Nasya.

Eventually, the recruits were all assembled and it was time for their training to begin.

# Chapter Two

*Fortress of Passing's End*
  *Country of Utara*

The primary classroom was large and rectangular with two fireplaces, one at each end. Like the rest of Passings End, it was constructed entirely out of stone with thick wood beams to reinforce the ceiling and walls. Lit torches lined the walls on one side while the other wall held four stained glass windows. Tables lined the outside of the room, leaving the center open for training. The girls were seated at the tables where they were given pieces of parchment, quills, and bottles of ink. At the front of the room stood six women. They all wore the same robes, similar to how the girls all wore the same dresses. Uniformity, they were told, was the basis of discipline.

"We are Mothers Cassiopeia, Fornax, Lynx, Phoenix, Corvus, and Hydra, Mothers of The Order," said Mother Phoenix, a woman of medium height with long black hair, amber skin, and bright blue eyes.

"The strength is in the blood," the six women said together.

"We will be your teachers, your trainers, your leaders, and your advocates," said Mother Lynx. She was also of medium height but had shoulder length black hair, almost sickly pale skin, and lavender eyes. "We will not be your friends. You will not like us, and we will not like you. But you will respect us, you will learn from us, and we will support you here during your training, as well as out there once you've graduated."

Another woman, Mother Fornax, stepped forward. She had short blonde hair, brown eyes, and light skin. "There are fifteen of you here now, but only six will graduate and become Sisters of The Order."

"The strength is in the blood," the women said again.

"You are the blood. The future of The Order, of our way of life, rests in you," said Mother Cassiopeia, a short woman with pale skin, long, wavy brown hair, hundreds of freckles all over her face, and light brown eyes. Nasya didn't like the tone in her voice, though she didn't know why.

"You will read," said Mother Lynx, "you will memorize, you will write, and you will grow. But you will also run. You will climb. You will navigate. You will fight."

"You will fight with swords," said Mother Corvus, "you will fight with bows and arrows, you will fight with poisons, and you will fight with your fists."

"You will be an extension of us just as we are extensions of The Elders," said Mother Hydra, a tall woman with bright red hair, dark brown skin, and the greenest eyes Nasya had ever seen. "You will devote your lives as Hands of The Order, as Sisters of The Great Movement, just as we have done."

"The strength is in the blood," they all murmured in unison. "The strength is in the blood. The strength is in the blood."

Nasya felt her skin go cold. She had questions, so many questions, but didn't know how to ask them. And even if she had, did she want to know the answers? The Mothers divided the girls into groups, each one led by two Mothers. The lessons primarily revolved around discussing the first chapters of the books they'd been given. Nasya had completed the reading, but she had understood very little and retained even less.

Nasya's was a group of three girls led by Mothers Cassiopeia and Corvus.

"Who can tell me the first of the great dynasties?" asked Mother Cassiopeia.

Nasya thought carefully, feeling the answer close to her memories. She remembered that the first dynasty had come forward over a thousand years ago, but the name of the dynasty escaped her. She wracked her brain and wished she had paid more attention to the history books. Geography was the subject that most excited her out of the materials she had been given. And while the history books connected to geography, she had an easier time remembering places than she did people and timelines.

"The first dynasty was the Song Dynasty, Mother Cassiopeia," said a recruit in Nasya's group. Her name was Florynce Lyric.

Mother Cassiopeia nodded. "And why was it called the Song Dynasty?"

"There are two reasons," said Florynce. "The first is that it bears the same name as the primary family within the Dynasty: the Song-Rise family. The second reason is that the members of this dynasty were incredibly musical and wrote the bulk of the hymns we sing today."

"Who was the head of the Song Dynasty?" asked Mother Corvus.

Nasya wanted to answer. She wanted to contribute, but she could not think of any names from her reading the night before. With so many books to read, how was she to know what details to focus on? Was she to memorize the books, word for word? She thought as quickly and as hard as she could, but still nothing came to her.

"Bandon the Great," said another recruit named Kassra Fiber.

Nasya took notes, desperate not to miss a single piece of information.

"And where did the Song Dynasty hail from?" asked Mother Corvus.

Nasya felt a jolt of excitement. She looked up from her parchment and said, "The Reedsport Province, which is now part of the country of Hevean."

"Where did they settle?" Mother Corvus asked again.

"In the grassy plains of Gearheart, which is now a county in the heart of Lozor," Nasya replied again.

"And why might these locations bear importance on the Song Dynasty?" asked Mother Cassiopeia.

"International relations," said Kassra.

"Explain," said Mother Cassiopeia.

"The Song Dynasty was not from Gearheart, and yet they took the land, built palaces and settled their own kin as lords and ladies of the plains. This must have angered the locals, the people who had lived there from the beginning of humankind." Kassra added.

"And why is that significant?" asked Mother Corvus.

The girls were quiet. The Mothers waited for an answer, letting the silence marinate between the recruits. Nasya's head spun with information. She had read every chapter she was supposed to, presumably the same pages as the other girls, and yet she could not think of an answer to Mother Corvus's question. And truth be told, she really didn't understand why one piece of land should be more important than another to a large, powerful family.

"Come on," said Mother Cassiopeia. "Think. Why might the anger of the locals have been significant to the Song Dynasty?"

"Remember the chapters of the other books, too," Mother Corvus said. "There's a reason we're having you read all five books simultaneously."

"Different cultures?" asked Florynce.

The Mothers nodded. "Good. And?"

"Different religions?" asked Kassra.

"And what role do these things play in the histories?" asked Mother Corvus.

The girls fell silent once more. Nasya scribbled more notes, not even sure if she would be able to understand them later. The Mothers sighed.

"The anger of the locals is what caused the Early Rebellion," said Mother Cassiopeia. "The uprising of various clans against the Song Dynasty. This was mentioned in the last chapter of the first history book."

The girls made note of their error. The lesson continued in much the same way, with the Mothers asking questions about the readings, and the girls giving as many answers as they could. Nasya was mostly quiet, except when a geography question was asked. Unfortunately, her knowledge on geography was not enough to earn her any esteem from the Mothers. Mother Cassiopeia made her irritation evident, always casting her gaze towards Nasya to see if she would answer a question that was asked. Every time Nasya remained quiet, Mother Cassiopeia's glare narrowed.

The lesson continued for several hours until they broke for dinner. As the girls left the classroom for the dining hall, Mother Corvus pulled Nasya aside.

"Did you read all of the chapters assigned?" she asked.

Nasya nodded. "Yes."

"Yet you could only answer the geography questions."

Nasya didn't respond.

Mother Corvus sighed. "You must apply yourself more intentionally," she said, "Take notes as you read. Ask questions when you need assistance. Try to answer the questions as they come up in the lesson, even if you are not sure if what you're saying is correct or not." Her eyes darkened in the way Nasya had seen when they were traveling to Passings End. It was the same disconnect, the emotional distance Nasya had envied. "You do not want to be removed from training, fledgling."

The girls went into the dining hall where dinner was served. Breakfast and supper were the largest meals of the day. Dinner was of lighter fare, but the girls were encouraged to eat their fill. Plates and bowls were passed from the Mothers, who sat at one end of the table, down to the recruits. Dinner that day was lamb stew with carrots and cabbage, bread with melted cheese, and cups of milk. The girls waited until they were given permission to eat, and then immediately began spooning stew into their mouths.

Nasya remembered to sit up straight and held the spoon as Mother Corvus had shown her. She ate carefully, if not quite gracefully, her mind preoccupied with the warning Mother Corvus had given her. Nasya hadn't known that they could be removed from training until that morning. Of the fifteen recruits, only six would graduate. That meant that nine girls who were here now would not be here at the end. Nasya wondered if this meant they would be sent back home. Something told her it did not.

The meals were prepared by three permanent cooks and two

of the recruits who had done the best during their lessons. While the others cleaned, they got to cook in the kitchens. It was meant to signify what happens when recruits do well, and when they don't. All of the girls were within a year or so of each other's age. This was intentional on behalf of The Order. They trained the girls as one cohesive entity.

"You will train as a group, learn as a group, and succeed or fail as a group," Mother Lynx had said in their first lesson. "You will move, think, breathe, and live as almost one person so that when you are released from this place as Sisters of The Order, you will be practically interchangeable."

Nasya still didn't understand what it meant to be Sisters of the Order. They were serving a legacy, the Mothers told them, but what was the legacy? Why had these recruits been chosen? Surely within her hometown of Terrace, there had been other girls her age belonging to families as poor as hers who could have been brought here. Why did Mother Corvus choose her and not them?

As the days went by and their lessons continued, she began to sense that there was something lurking behind what they were told by the Mothers. Something nefarious and dark. As the days went by, this feeling only increased. More and more, the Mothers eluded to their lives after graduation, what they would be doing once they completed their training. They weren't giving explicit details, so Nasya couldn't put the pieces together just yet, but she knew they were being trained for a specific purpose.

That purpose, whatever it was, hung like a shadow over Passing's End. Nasya sensed it. She knew Scarlet sensed it, and she was certain the other girls were aware of it, too. What it was, they didn't know. And all Nasya could think about was how this purpose would define the rest of her life, and she didn't even know what it was. She was angry. It wasn't that she wanted to leave; she was homesick and she missed her parents, but she didn't want to lose the safety of Passing's End. She was angry that she had never been given a choice. Whatever her life would amount to after this would be decided here, and yet she had been given no choice in the matter of her own existence. She'd been thrust into this place against her will and that gnawed at Nasya. It felt wrong, even if she couldn't explain why. It was in the back of her mind almost constantly, tugging at her thoughts, pulling her attention away from her studies. Yet, she had no recourse, no means of addressing her worries without bringing them up to the Mothers, and that she knew she would never do. Where Scarlet was able to abide their foul moods and their rigidity with humor and a carefree spirit, Nasya could not. She could not stand their harshness, their impatience, their inflexibility. It filled her with dread. It made her long for home, for her family, even for starvation and the cold because at least that suffering was familiar, a dread she understood. But here at Passing's End, nothing made sense.

Every evening after their usual training, the girls would spend time studying. Some of the girls studied alone. Others studied in groups. Nasya and Scarlet studied together every day, both of them huddled on the floor near the hearth in their dormitory.

Nasya did as Mother Corvus instructed and scribbled notes on parchment to try and retain the information she read. Since geography came more easily to her, she spent the bulk of her studying hours on the other books. As the days passed, she saw some improvement in her ability to retain and recall the information, but she still struggled.

"You're overthinking," Scarlet told her one afternoon. "You've grown so anxious that you can't focus when you read."

Nasya sighed and covered her face with her hands. "I don't know why it's so difficult," she said, on the verge of tears.

Scarlet shrugged. "Everyone has their skills, and everyone has their struggles."

"You don't have struggles," Nasya muttered. She envied Scarlet's ease with her studies, the ways she let the Mothers' harsh words roll off of her without so much as a second thought.

Scarlet grinned. "Yes I do. I'm just better at hiding them."

Nasya looked up at her. "How do you hide them? The Mothers see completely through me. Nothing escapes them."

"I wish I could explain it. It's just...something I've always done."

Nasya groaned and stretched out on the floor. "I hate botany!"

"It hates you too, apparently," Scarlet said.

Nasya gasped and turned her face towards Scarlet, who was grinning from ear to ear. "You think you're very funny," Nasya said.

"I *am* very funny."

Nasya grabbed one of her dirty socks and threw it at Scarlet. Both girls giggled. It was moments like this that Nasya really was grateful to be at Passings End. Despite the hardships, there were moments of beauty that filled her with warmth. Most of those moments revolved around Scarlet, the first real friend she had ever had. They weren't in the same training groups, but they spent all of their other time together and often stayed up late in the dark hours of the night whispering back and forth. They didn't speak much of their pasts, their families, their former lives. But the here and now was ripe with conversation. And before long, Nasya found herself growing more attached to Scarlet than she had been to anyone else, including her own family.

The months passed slowly. And Nasya struggled. Each day was a reminder of how difficult it was for her to perform even the simplest of tasks. The cleaning she could do, the reading and writing she could do, and as far as behavior was concerned, she was never out of line. But everything else was nearly impossible for her. She lived each day in constant fear that she would be removed from training. And this fear, as Scarlet told her often, only made her studies that much more difficult.

There was one afternoon almost three months into training that gave Nasya some much needed reassurance. The morning lessons had been completed, the cleaning was done, and the girls sat in the dining hall eating their dinner. They were part way through the meal when Mother Fornax stood to her feet.

"Today, we will not have our usual afternoon lessons," she said. "Instead, we are going to take a brief walk to a favorite local spot. Dress warmly, but also bring a change of underclothes with you." The girls murmured among themselves, curious as to what this local spot was that would require a change of clothes. Mother Fornax held up her hand and the girls quieted. "You will understand once we arrive. Finish your meals, ready yourselves, and meet us by the main entrance."

Nasya and Scarlet were the first to clear their plates. They scurried off to their dormitory and grabbed a change of underclothes. They put the clothes in small sacks they could carry on their backs, and then made their way to the main entrance. All of the Mothers were already waiting. Only one other recruit was there, a tall girl named Syra. They stood in formation, silently waiting for the others.

"Nasya," said Mother Cassiopeia, "how are your studies?" There was an air of mockery in her voice that plucked at Nasya's feelings in a way she hated.

"I am taking notes as Mother Corvus suggested," Nasya replied, trying to keep her voice even, "and I reread the sections that most confuse me."

"Then you are still struggling, I take it?" she asked, the sound of a satisfied grin dripping off her voice.

"In some ways, yes, Mother." Nasya didn't see the need to lie or bend the truth.

"You seem to struggle more than any of the others. I wonder how long you will last at this rate," Mother Cassiopeia added.

Nasya didn't respond, nor did she need to. Mother Hydra, a woman who was silent far more often than she was talkative, spoke up.

"Book lessons are only one part of training, Mother Cassiopeia," she said, her voice even, but pointed. "Nasya might do better in the physical training."

"And the physical training is the most important," added Mother Corvus, who gave Nasya a soft, almost undetectable smile of reassurance.

Mother Cassiopeia grunted but did not respond. Nasya felt the weight of the exchange. It was no small thing for one Mother to openly contradict another in front of recruits. And two Mothers had come to Nasya's defense. It gave her some comfort, but also added a degree of anxiety. Her success or failure would reflect back on Mothers Corvus and Hydra, and she didn't want to let them down. She could only hope that what they said was right, and she would be much better at physical training than she was with books.

The girls were all eventually assembled at the main entrance, and their walk to this unknown location began. They were not told how far this location was. They simply set off through the cold and the snow. They walked in silence for some time before the girls began to whisper to each other. The Mothers did not quiet them, and so the girls became more comfortable chatting casually as they walked. Some speculated as to where they were going. A couple thought they were going to a nearby village. Another thought they weren't going anywhere at all and that this was just a test to see how long the girls would follow.

Nasya had studied the map of Passings End and the surrounding areas. She knew there were no villages within walking distance unless the Mothers planned to scale down the side of a steep ravine. The only other options, then, were nature based. Rivers, lakes, and the like. The change of undergarments narrowed down the options to a hot spring hidden in the side of a mountain.

"We're going to a hot spring," she whispered to Scarlet.

She was right. The Mothers eventually came to a large cavern where the hot spring was. The girls all smiled and Scarlet gave Nasya a proud look and a nod. The girls stood and waited, staring at the water that was steaming. Their winter clothes were already too warm for the cave.

"Well, don't just stand there," said Mother Phoenix. "Strip down and jump in."

The girls wasted no time. They took off everything but their chemises and jumped into the steaming water. It felt glorious. Nasya closed her eyes and let out a slow sigh, the warmth of the water soothing her sore, stiff muscles after the walk through the snow. The Mothers also took off most of their clothes and climbed into the water. The girls were given a long time to soak, to play, to be kids. No lessons, no quizzes, no books. Just clean, hot water away from the winter cold.

Scarlet stayed close to Nasya, her eyes wide and full of life.

"I didn't expect we'd be given something like this," she whispered.

Nasya nodded. "Neither did I. But I'm loving every bit."

Scarlet grinned. "Did you know your eyes change color when

you're in the water?"

Nasya furrowed her eyebrows. "What? They do?"

"Yeah. Usually they're this dark green, but in the water they're much brighter. Almost turquoise."

Nasya smiled. "That sounds...pretty."

Scarlet nodded. "They are."

Flutters filled Nasya's stomach. Beauty wasn't something she thought about much, though she did often wonder if there was anything beautiful about her. Her hair was a deep red, thick, and fiercely curly. Her skin was olive toned, and her eyes, as Scarlet had said, were a dark green. Her features were striking, that much she knew. But whether or not she held the markers for beauty, she didn't know. Her eyes – Scarlet had called them pretty, and that filled her with an emotion she couldn't explain. It was more happiness than she had experienced since coming to Passings End. And from Scarlet, the most important person in Nasya's life, only made it even more valuable.

"We brought you here because, in the last three months of training, we have been particularly impressed with your improvements," said Mother Lynx.

Nasya watched as Mother Cassiopeia's eyes flitted to her, glaring hard. Mother Cassiopeia clearly did not believe Nasya's improvements were impressive.

"And we know the cold can be hard to manage up here, so close to the mountains," said Mother Phoenix. "You are welcome to come here as often as you like, so long as you never walk through the woods alone."

"To be clear," said Mother Cassiopeia, her deep, raspy voice echoing against the walls of the cavern. "Anyone caught in the woods going any other direction than to this place will be removed from training. And we *will* catch you."

"This place was a refuge for us when we were recruits," said Mother Corvus. "And we hope it will be the same for you."

They were given another hour or so before they were told to change into their dry undergarments. Once all were dressed, they walked back through the snow to the fortress where they were told to study until supper was served. Nasya and Scarlet retreated to their room, sat near the hearth, and read quietly. Nasya's mind was alive with energy. She tried to focus, but she was restless. Something gnawed at her, like a finger plucking the string of a lute. It was subtle but constant and made Nasya's mind wander. More than once she found herself just staring at the flames in the hearth, her thoughts scattered. But no matter how hard she tried to focus, her thoughts drifted away from books and studying. She couldn't describe it, but it was as if something was pulling her thoughts away from everything else.

After almost an hour of struggle, Nasya decided to simply let her mind wander for a moment. Perhaps she needed to give herself room to think, to daydream, before she could really commit to her studies. She stared at the flames and listened to their soft crackle in the quiet room. Scarlet was deep in her reading, the gentle sound of pages turning every so often moving like ripples through the air. The rhythm was enough to almost lull Nasya into a half-sleep, a kind of waking daze that was neither restful nor energizing. Her eyelids began to feel heavy, but they didn't quite close. The warmth from the fire felt like a tingle against her skin.

Suddenly, Nasya found herself staring down a long corridor. It was dimly lit by torches with small flames lining the stone walls. It reminded her of Passing's End, and yet she knew instinctively that she was elsewhere. She also knew she needed to walk down the corridor. Something was waiting at the end, something she needed to see. Nasya placed one foot in front of the other and walked down the hall. It was so quiet, she could hear the drops of rain pouring outside.

She didn't know how long it took for her to reach the end of the corridor, but when she did she saw a door. A plain, wooden door with an iron handle. She needed to go through the door. Nasya reached out her hand and grabbed hold of the handle. She pushed open the door. She walked through the threshold.

At first, she saw only darkness and heard only silence. Then in the distance, a whisper. It sounded like wind, but as it built, she realized someone was saying her name. She reached out into the darkness and a moment later, a cold hand grabbed hers, hard. Nasya gasped and tried to pull away, but the other hand was too strong. The whisper grew loud and raspy and continued to call her name. Nasya braced herself by putting her other hand on the door frame and tried to pull free, but to no avail.

"Scarlet!" Nasya shouted, but her voice was muffled.

In the darkness, a gray light began to shine. It started small and then grew out from where her hand joined with the other until she could see skin. It was pale, almost blue, and translucent. As though frozen. The gray light continued to expand and the more it did, the harder Nasya tried to break free. She continued shouting for Scarlet, but her voice remained muffled, as though she was screaming underwater. The light grew until Nasya could see everything before her. She was held by a fearsome creature with bluish skin, a large mouth with long, pointed teeth, no eyes or nose, and wisps of silver hair.

"Welcome Nasya," it said.

The gray light then began to spread up Nasya's arm.

"No!" Nasya shouted, tears streaming down her cheeks. "Let me go! Let me go!"

The creature only laughed. Nasya felt the light underneath her skin, crawling, its legs against her muscles, her bones. She didn't know what this was. She didn't know what was happening. Only that she wanted to be back with Scarlet in the safety of their room.

"Please let me go!" she cried.

"Nasya!" came the echo of a familiar voice in the distance.

It was Scarlet. Nasya called for her. The creature continued to laugh as the gray light consumed all of Nasya's body, lighting up her skin from underneath it. Her veins were like silhouettes against the light.

"Until next time," said the creature before letting go of her hand.

Nasya fell backwards onto the stone floor of her dormitory. Tears stained her cheeks. She was dripping with sweat. Scarlet sat over her, her eyebrows furrowed and her eyes wide with fear. Nasya breathed heavily and looked around. She was back.

"What in the name of all the gods happened?" Scarlet asked, helping her sit up.

Nasya cried and shook her head. "I don't know."

"You were convulsing," Scarlet said, wrapping her arms around her. "And you kept saying my name over and over in this harsh kind of whisper."

Nasya let herself cry and buried her face in Scarlet's shoulder. Once she'd gotten over the worst of the shock, she tried to explain to Scarlet what she saw. As she gave each detail, her hope of it all being some kind of daytime nightmare dwindled. Scarlet listened quietly and only asked a couple of questions. When she had finished, Scarlet tucked Nasya's hair behind her ears.

"It was a nightmare. That's all," she said.

"I wasn't asleep. It couldn't have been a nightmare."

"Then what do you think it was?"

Nasya shrugged. "I don't know."

"When I first looked up at you, you seemed to be asleep. Your eyes were closed and your chin was resting against your chest."

Nasya looked at the flames. She didn't know how to explain to Scarlet how she knew that it wasn't a dream – it could not have been a dream. But somehow she knew that it wasn't. What she'd seen, what she'd heard, where she'd gone, it was all real. Somehow.

"The convulsions...they must have been brought on by the walk in the snow," Scarlet said. "And what you saw was part of the convulsions. You said the hand was cold when it grabbed you, so that would make sense."

Nasya nodded briefly. She wanted Scarlet to be right because then that meant she could forget the whole thing. She wanted to forget it very much. She ran her hands over her face, still feeling the light beneath her skin. Scarlet, who was in the middle of saying something, suddenly stopped mid-sentence.

"Gods above..." she muttered.

Nasya looked at her. "What is it?"

Scarlet motioned towards Nasya's hands. Nasya looked down and gasped. A chill slid down her spine. There was no light beneath her skin like there had been in her vision, but her veins were dark like silhouettes, just as they had been in her vision. It went all the way up her arms and down into her chest. It was as though the light she'd seen had been absorbed by her blood, its illumination reversed.

"I don't understand..." Nasya said, her voice soft.

# Chapter Three

Twenty-eight year old Nasya Ember woke early to the sound of a rooster's call from the farm next door. She let out a sigh and moaned, rolling from one side to the other. Normally, she would have ignored the bird and continued sleeping, but she had work to do. She opened her eyes slowly, her lids heavy with the comfort of sleep in a warm bed. It was a sensation she'd come to love since the first time she experienced it as a child. She reveled in it. Whispered small prayers of thanks for it.

The room was mostly dark, save for the still crackling embers of the fire from the night before. Even in the twilight, she took in the face of the woman lying next to her. Nasya grinned. The woman's olive-toned skin was bare and her gorgeous brown curls outlined her face. Her eyes were still closed in sleep. Nasya laid still for a moment and watched her breathe steadily.

She thought of the night they'd spent together and felt her body begin to tingle. The passion had been palpable, the connection between them strong and unlike anything Nasya was used to. The woman, a traveler, had only intended to stay one night in the town of Armistice. She had paid for Nasya's company that night, and then the night after, and the night after. It had been nearly two weeks and still she had not moved on from Armistice.

Nasya scooted closer to her and pressed a gentle kiss to her shoulder.

"Beth," she whispered. "Wake up. I have to leave soon."

Bethlaine moaned and opened her eyes ever so slightly, giving Nasya a tired smile.

"But the bed is so warm with you in it," she mumbled, moving closer and kissing Nasya on the lips. "If you leave, who will I sleep next to?"

Nasya grinned and pressed a kiss to the tip of her nose. "We're in a brothel, Beth. There are at least eight other whores to keep you warm."

She rolled over and climbed out of bed. The wood floor was cold and sent a shiver up Nasya's body. She draped her wool robe around herself and stoked the fire in the hearth. There were enough embers that a small flame began to lick at the remaining pile of wood, adding a little more light to the room.

Beth sat up. "I don't want to be with any of the others."

Nasya didn't say anything as she began to dress. This was a conversation she wasn't prepared to have. She knew what Beth was going to say, and a small part of her might have even wanted her to say it. But Nasya knew better. Her life was not conducive to attachments. Nasya tightened the strings on the back of her dress and began to tie them, hoping that Beth would drop the subject. She didn't.

"We could stay here," she said. "You could keep your clientele and I'm sure there's a farmer nearby who could use assistance."

Nasya let out a slow breath. "I think you're running away with yourself," she said, avoiding Beth's gaze.

"No. I'm not."

"Yes, you are," she replied, finally looking at her. "I've enjoyed your company. It's been fun, truly. But I'm a whore. A traveling whore. There is no life for me that includes stability and a proper home."

Beth crawled from under the covers and sat at the foot of the bed.

"Then I'll travel with you," she said. "I'll find other means of earning a living."

"You want me to continue fucking other people to make some coin while you find odd jobs as we travel across Utara together." She shook her head. "It's madness, Beth. It...it just isn't done." She sat and began to put on her thick socks. That wasn't the real reason she couldn't be with Beth, but she wasn't about to tell the truth when she could hardly even admit it to herself. "Besides, you came to Armistice for your own reasons. I won't pull you away from your duties, whatever they may be."

"Is that supposed to be noble?" Beth asked, an edge in her voice that Nasya had never heard before. "Am I supposed to feel grateful?"

"I don't think you're supposed to feel anything. It's just the truth."

Beth looked down at her hands for a moment, and then climbed from the bed and began to dress. Nasya felt wretched. It was this sort of thing that made her profession less than ideal. She knew she was hurting the woman she had come to think of as a friend over the last two weeks, but it couldn't be helped. And even if Nasya had been able to make such a choice, she knew she wouldn't. At least, not with Beth.

Beth finished dressing and pulled a bag of coins from the pocket of her trench coat. She counted out six gold florens and placed them on the table.

"For your services," she said.

Nasya shook her head. "I don't expect you to pay me."

"You've made it clear that everything between us is to be kept strictly transactional. I took up an entire two weeks of your time, and so you should be paid accordingly."

"Beth," Nasya said, standing to her feet. "I cannot bring you with me, but that doesn't mean I want the last two weeks to come to this."

"I know that this isn't all you do, Nasya."

"What are you talking about?"

"Your...profession, or whatever it is you call it. I know that whoring isn't all there is to it."

Nasya's skin ran cold. She frowned. "I still don't know what you mean," she said, trying hard to keep her voice from trembling.

"You talk in your sleep," Beth said. "Pretty loudly, I might add. I know that this is just hiding whatever it is you really do."

"They're dreams, Beth. That's all."

Beth shook her head. "They're real."

Nasya ran both hands through her red hair. "If they are, you'd have to realize why I wouldn't be able to bring you with me. It wouldn't be safe."

"I'm trying to tell you that I know, and I don't care. I'll take the risks, knowingly and intentionally."

Nasya shook her head. "You think you know what this is, but you don't. You cannot understand the extent of the risks you'd be taking by coming with me." Beth went to speak but Nasya spoke over her. "Make no mistake, Bethlaine, my life is dangerous and it would only be made more so if someone was with me."

Beth looked crushed. Nasya walked over to her and ran a finger down her cheek.

"It's because I care that I have to leave you behind. I couldn't live with myself if something happened to you because of me."

Beth didn't say anything. She looked at Nasya for a moment, gave a brief nod, placed the florens on the table, and then left the room. Nasya cursed. It wasn't how she'd wanted things to go. As hard as The Mothers of The Order had tried to crush her compassion, Nasya clung to it with a fervor that surprised even herself. She had been trained well, and she performed her duties with the flare of an artist, but she was not cruel. She made sure that was a line she never crossed.

She didn't have many belongings with her, but she packed what little she had into her satchel and made her way down to the public house attached to the inn where she lived. She paid for a breakfast of eggs, pork sausage, and boiled potatoes before covering her rent for the month. Then she left and began walking towards Terrace, her hometown. It was a day's and a night's journey there, and she would be walking the whole way.

# Chapter Four

*Fortress of Passing's End*
  *Country of Utara*


Six months had passed since Nasya arrived at Passing's End. Winter had settled over the mountains, its grip tight on the high elevations. Snow dumped constantly for weeks at a time. It was beautiful, but horribly cold. The girls were all given ample clothing to keep themselves warm as the temperatures dropped below freezing, and fires were lit in every hearth every single day to keep the stone fortress heated. Still, the girls were cold. The Mothers made sure to provide them hot meals three times a day, as well as steaming baths throughout the week. Despite the rigorous and often unmerciful lectures and studying, the Mothers took the recruits' health seriously. It was one of the only good things about being at Passing's End.

Eventually, winter gave way to spring. The temperatures rose slowly. The snows lessened and then ceased altogether. Rain melted the snow. The sun began to shine warmer everyday. And little by little, spring moved ever towards the summer months. Leaves and blossoms bloomed on the trees, lighting everything in an emerald hue. The forest during spring and summer was the most beautiful sight Nasya had ever seen. She had never known that the color green could fill her with so much warmth.

Nasya had adapted to the intense learning schedule. She was completing her reading assignments with more ease, taking what notes she needed as she went. But when it came to retaining information and using it to answer questions during the lectures, she was no farther along than when they first began. She didn't know what held her back. Nor did the Mothers. Mothers Corvus and Phoenix had even tried teaching her one-on-one to see if that was what she needed, and still she did not progress.

It wasn't that she was unintelligent. All of the Mothers saw that she was clever, particularly in specific subjects like geography, reading, and writing. She thrived in these studies, surpassing even those students who were best in other subjects. But botany, history, mathematics were all lost to her. She did her best. She put in as much study time as she could, and the Mothers saw it. In fact, she overheard the Mothers commenting that she was the hardest worker of all the recruits, and that had to count for something.

"Hard work is all well and good, but we need recruits who

can do what we're training them to do. All the hard work and motivation in the world will not turn a recruit into a Sister of the Order," said Mother Cassiopeia. "The power is in the blood."

"The power is in the blood," repeated the others.

Nasya knew that Mother Cassiopeia hated her far more than any of the other Mothers. It didn't bother her much because the feeling was entirely mutual. But it was hard to know that she had the work ethic but lacked the actual abilities necessary for her to succeed. She didn't know what else to do, how to better learn what she was being given to study. Nor did she know what she needed to be successful, so it wasn't as though she could ask for assistance, either. Scarlet helped her as much as she could, and though she saw herself making some progress, it was slow going and far too minimal to satisfy the Mothers.

"You will get there eventually," Scarlet assured her.

Nasya snorted. "Getting there years after everyone else won't make any difference," she said, laying on her bed. "Coming in last place here means that I won't become a Sister."

Scarlet shrugged. "I'm not so sure. I overheard the Mothers talking a few days ago about two other recruits and how they likely wouldn't make it through the first year of training."

"Are you sure I wasn't one of them?" Nasya asked sarcastically.

Scarlet shook her head. "Your name was not mentioned. If you can outlast nine of the recruits here, then you'll graduate."

"That's a big 'if,' Scarlet." Nasya sat up. "My diligence can only take me so far. I have to start showing greater improvements or my days here are numbered."

Scarlet offered a soft smile of reassurance. "Keep working as hard as you are, and it will all fall into place. I really do believe that."

Nasya didn't respond. She tucked her knees under her chin and wrapped her arm around her shins. It was times like these that she missed her former life. Not the cold and the starvation, but the simplicity and the ease of existence. She had chores around their hovel, but they were easy. She had studies (her father made sure of that), but they weren't so complicated and she wasn't expected to memorize so much at once. More than anything, she missed her family. Her mother's gentleness. Her father's humor. Her sister's rambunctious nature. She would never see them again.

"It would help if I could get a good night's rest," she muttered, stretching back out across her bed.

"The nightmares are almost every night now," Scarlet said.

"I wish I knew what caused them."

"Have you talked to Mother Hydra yet?"

Nasya shook her head. "I don't think I can."

"But she'll have answers, and perhaps a remedy to help you sleep without dreaming."

"At what cost, though? They already dislike me enough. If I go to them complaining about nightmares, they'll laugh me all the way back home."

"These aren't typical nightmares, Nasya. Once you explain what you see in them, I'm sure they will understand the situation." Scarlet moved from her place on the floor to sit across from Nasya. "If I had the dreams you do, I'd be absolutely petrified. Any of us would."

Nasya knew there was truth in that. She knew what normal nightmares were supposed to be. And these were not like that. They'd begun the night after she'd had the vision and convulsions and they had continued every night since. They weren't the same dream, they were all different, and they were all terrifying. She saw shadows, glowing gold eyes in the darkness, beasts with black and silver fur, hands reaching up from the ground. And cemeteries. So many cemeteries.

"What's the worst that could happen if you tell Mother Hydra?" asked Scarlet.

"I'm not taken seriously. I'm mocked and disliked even more than I am already."

"What's the worst that could happen if you don't tell?"

"The nightmares continue. I don't get the sleep I need. I don't improve in my studies. I'm removed from training."

Scarlet shrugged. "It seems an easy choice to me."

Nasya sighed and then groaned. Scarlet was right. She was always right. The idea of telling anyone else of her dreams was almost as terrifying as the dreams themselves. But she knew that she couldn't just do nothing. It had been months. Something had to give. She resolved that she would tell Mother Hydra that night after supper. She didn't even know how she was going to explain any of it, but she was going to try.

Supper was served at six o'clock. Now that the cold was gone and early summer had settled over Passing's End, their meals consisted of fresh fruits, vegetables, and some kind of protein. They were given large helpings of delicious salads with servings of chicken, pork, mutton, and sometimes fish when they could be caught in the nearby lakes and ponds. Bread, butter, jams, and cheese were always staples of every meal, and the girls were given as much as they desired. The smaller girls were especially encouraged to eat heartily. Nasya ate her fill and, just when the girls were released for their evening recreation time, she approached Mother Hydra.

"Forgive me, Mother," she said, "but I request an audience with you."

Mother Hydra was a formidable woman. She was stern and rarely smiled, and yet Nasya felt as though she, more than any of the other Mothers, except Mother Corvus, cared deeply about Nasya's success.

"What is it?" Mother Hydra asked.

"I...I need your help with something," she said, her nerves heightening.

Mother Hydra raised her eyebrows. "Yes?"

"I've been having horrible nightmares, Mother," she said, trying not to stammer or sound too ridiculous. "They're not typical nightmares and they've been keeping me up at all hours."

Mother Hydra frowned. "What kind of nightmares?"

"Dark ones. Terrifying ones."

"You have them every night?"

Nasya nodded.

"For how long?"

"Months."

Mother Hydra was quiet for a moment. "What do you want from me? To understand them? Or make them stop?"

Nasya hesitated. "Both?" she asked. "If that's possible?"

"Before I can help you understand them, I need to know what's in them. Keep track of each dream you have. Write down every detail you can. Return to me in a week and I will see if I can help interpret them. If I can't, then I'll give you something to help you sleep."

Nasya nodded and rushed away to her room. She had hoped Mother Hydra would simply give her a sleeping aid without any other questions, but it was also exhilarating to think that she might actually get answers as to what the dreams meant. She ran to her bedside bureau and pulled out her quill, ink, and some pieces of parchment. She wanted to be ready to write down her dreams when they inevitably haunted her sleep that night. If there was any chance of her finding actual rest and peace in the darkness of slumber, this was it.

Passing's End was cold. Frigid, filled with the icey bite of the January air. She stood in the middle of a hallway. It was dark. The torches that lined the walls were unlit. Only the pale twilight of early morning falling through the windows offered any light by which to see. It cast a blue pall over the stone and glass. She listened for the sounds of any movement, but all was silent. No voices. No footsteps. It was as though the fortress had been abandoned.

She blinked, her eyes adjusting to the darkness, and realized that the windows on the left side of the hall were all broken. Shards of glass littered the ground. Gusts of wind blew through the windows, caring flurries of snow into the fortress. Her heart began to pound in her chest. What was this? What had happened that she had missed? She started to move forward, stepping carefully around the shards of glass so as not to cut her bare feet. Every room she came to was empty and dark. There were no fires burning in the hearths.

"Hello?" she said, her voice echoing against the walls.

There was no response. At least, not at first. When she had made her way up the stairs to the second level, the darkness deepened and the silence seemed to hold its breath. The air was thicker up there. No warmer, but not nearly as biting. And she could smell faint hints of something on the air, something sweet but rank, like rotted food. She stepped quietly down the second floor hallway looking for any signs of life. There was nothing. Only darkness. Only silence.

Until the echo of a woman's laughter reached her ears. She spun around, her eyes wide. It had come from behind her, but there was nothing there. Only the rest of the hallway. Could the voice have come from one of the closed up rooms? She didn't know. She didn't think she wanted to find out.

"I'm not afraid of you," she heard herself say.

The laughter filled her ears again, this time much louder. "Yes you are," it said in a sing-songy voice. It moved from behind her to overhead to somewhere further down the corridor.

"I'm not," she said, her voice sounding much more assured than she felt. "Show yourself to me, if you dare."

More laughter. "You're not ready."

She let out a deep breath and continued walking down the corridor. She didn't know what, but something urged her forward. Her eyes were wide. Her mind was alert. Her body was cold and stiff, but she knew she would be ready for the strike when it came. Though what was striking and from where, she didn't know.

Wind from below rushed up to the second floor and blew her hair around her shoulders. Still, she met with only darkness.

"You say I am not ready, yet I am not the one hiding," she said, her voice loud and harsh in the eerie silence.

There was no laughter this time. A new voice greeted her. "Why are you so angry, child?"

She gasped. "Mama?" she asked, her voice no louder than a whisper. She spun around, her eyes frantically searching for whomever had spoken. "Is that you?"

"You've always been so angry..." the voice said, fading as though the speaker was moving away from her.

"No, mama, don't leave me here!"

She rushed forward, breathing heavily, and pushed open a large wooden door. She was suddenly outside in the snow. She stopped and gasped as the cold sucked away her breath for a moment. She looked over her shoulder. Passing's End and the door she had just run through were gone. Only ruins stood where the fortress once was. She furrowed her eyebrows.

"You're just like your father," the second voice said, carried on the wind.

She turned back around and searched urgently for the voice and to whom it belonged. Her heart raced. "Mama!" she shouted. "Please, mama!"

A loud, vicious growl came from her right. She turned and saw a large beast, wolf-like in appearance with silver fur and bright red eyes. It snarled and bared its fangs at her. She stood, too frightened to move, her feet buried in the snow. The wolf's mouth was stained with blood. She felt a hand rest on her shoulder. She turned and looked and saw a woman with dark brown eyes staring at her. On the left side of her neck, a chunk of flesh was missing. Blood stained her neck, her chest, and dripped all the way down her left arm.

"Mama!" she gasped.

"Anger will not save you, child," the woman said. "Like teeth, it can only rip apart and destroy."

The wolf leaped at them. It landed on the woman with the dark eyes and bit into her neck again. The crunch of bones and the tearing of flesh filled her ears. Blood stained the snow covering the ground. And the woman cried out in pain.

Nasya screamed and sat up in bed. Tears streamed down her cheeks. Scarlet was next to her. She wrapped her arms around Nasya's shoulders and ran her hands through her hair.

"Shhh," she said soothingly. "It was only a dream, love. Only a dream."

Nasya shook her head, crying loudly. "My mother! It killed my mother!"

Scarlet held her tighter. "It was a dream. It wasn't real."

Nasya shook her head again, burying her face in her hands. "You don't understand…"

Scarlet didn't respond. She let Nasya talk. She let her cry. And Nasya couldn't stop thinking about the sounds of death she'd heard at the end: the bones, the teeth. How the smell of blood mingled with the crisp of snow and winter. It was vivid in her mind. She could practically smell it now, even in the waking darkness of her dormitory. She cried for a moment longer and then took up her quill and parchment. It had been a week of the most horrifying dreams yet, and she recorded each of them for Mother Hydra. She wrote down every detail. When that was done, she climbed back under her covers and cried quietly into her pillow.

Scarlet layed next to her and held her. Nasya's dreams had been full of her mother for a whole week. Every dream featured something to do with her.

"Tell me about your mother this time," Scarlet said softly.

"She was attacked by a large wolf," Nasya said, her voice hoarse from crying. "It was silver with red eyes."

Scarlet's body stiffened. She didn't respond, so Nasya continued. She gave Scarlet all the details of the dream. When she still didn't respond, Nasya sighed. "I'm sorry you have to share a room with me."

Scarlet held onto her even tighter. "I'm not."

The girls stayed in Nasya's bed. They fell asleep holding each other until the morning light woke them.

Nasya stared out the stained glass window to her right. It was a beautiful day outside. The sun was shining. The sky was a bright blue filled with fluffy clouds. The trees were so green and bright in the sunlight, their leaves cast an emerald hue over the courtyard. Nasya felt almost driven to run outside and bask in the warmth of the late morning. But she couldn't move from her place inside. Not until she'd completed her test.

She stared down at the papers in front of her. She had completed most of the test, but now was faced with the issue of writing out lengthy answers to the questions being asked, on subjects she still did not quite understand. Her head ached. She had not slept well. Again. It had been two weeks since she'd taken the details of her dreams written down to Mother Hydra, and still she had heard nothing. Been given nothing. She didn't understand what was taking so long. She only wanted something to help her sleep. Was that really so complicated?

"Nasya," Mother Cassiopeia snapped, "write. Now."

The woman's eyes were filled with anger and annoyance, something that Nasya had become increasingly accustomed to. She bent over her papers and forced herself to think through her pounding head. It took some time, but she was able to write out a two-page analysis of what she'd understood from the readings. It wasn't good writing. It wasn't an original analysis. But Nasya knew she'd given it all she had. She turned in her papers and made her way out of the classroom. It was time to do her chores, and today it was her turn to sweep and mop the large hallway on the first floor of the fortress.

She grabbed her buckets, one empty into which she would dump the dust and dirt, and one filled with water and soap, her brush, her broom, and an extra bar of soap, and made for the hall. It was long, but straight and easy to clean. Down the hall were various rooms, most of which were where the Mothers slept. Nasya set to work with her broom, carefully sweeping up as much dirt and dust as she could. This work she didn't mind much. It was easy. She could be alone with her thoughts. And she didn't feel quite so out of place, so under scrutiny.

It was times like these that she allowed herself to daydream. She didn't think of anything in particular most of the time, but simply let her mind wander to wherever it would lead. Usually, this meant imagining her life outside of graduation. The recruits now knew what they were training for, and it was both an exciting and unnerving prospect. The Order, they were told, followed an ancient way of life set up centuries before. It had taken many forms over the years, but their primary purpose never altered. They were a group disconnected from all political, religious, and personal affiliations and ambitions. They served no one and nothing other than the preservation of The Order itself, and the good work they sought to perform. They were called many things: Hands of The Order and Sisters of The Order would be their official titles.

They would be assassins.

Fighters upholding peace and balance in the world. Nasya didn't quite understand how that would be, but it thrilled her down into her very toes to think of herself as someone with that much power. She thought of all the places she might go, all the people she might meet. She thought of a life away from Passing's End and out of sight of The Mothers, especially Mother Cassiopeia. She thought of the change she might bring about in the world. It was as Mother Corvus had said when she took Nasya from her home: she would live an important life. The likes of which would never have been available to her outside of The Order.

Nasya's mind continued to wander as she swept. It wasn't until she had gone all the way to the far end of the hallway that she heard the voices of the Mothers coming from one of the rooms. At first she paid no mind to them. It was common for them to meet together to discuss lessons, recruits' improvements and struggles, and other things. But she quickly heard her own name mentioned and stopped to listen to what was being said.

"I must give Nasya something," said a voice that Nasya recognized as Mother Hydra's. "It has been two weeks. I know she will ask me about it soon."

"For god's sakes," said another voice that Nasya knew to be

Mother Cassiopeia. "It was a damn dream. If the girl cannot handle a bloody nightmare, how will she ever survive what she must do if she graduates?"

"Forgive me, Mother Cassiopeia," replied Mother Hydra, "for not making myself clearer. These nightmares," the faint sound of papers rustling reached Nasya's ears, "are not the dreams of a scared child struggling to adapt to her surroundings. They are...eerie. Specific. Almost omen-like."

"What are you saying?" asked one of the other Mothers. Nasya thought it was Mother Phoenix.

"I believe these dreams of hers are pointing to something bigger. Something inside of Nasya that we haven't yet seen."

Mother Cassiopeia laughed. "How many times have we heard this exact story before? You are incapable of seeing the worst recruits for what they are. You have to make them different, special. It's pathetic."

"And because of you, Mother Cassiopeia, those recruits were all rejected from training and never reached their full potential. You act as though I was proved wrong, but you saw to it that they were removed from Passing's End before their abilities manifested," replied Mother Hydra. "Remember that I am the only Mother here with magic. I am, therefore, the only one qualified to comment on whether or not Nasya's dreams are typical nightmares or something more."

"And you think they are something more?" asked Mother Lynx.

"I do."

"What is this something more?" asked Mother Corvus.

"That, I do not know. But this last dream, especially, is dripping with foresight. Dare I even say prophecy."

"Prophecy?" exclaimed Mother Fornax. "Are you certain?"

The sound of papers rustling met Nasya's ears again, and a moment later Mother Hydra was reading from one of the pieces of parchment in her hands. "'Passing's End was filled with little more than snow and shadow. Windows were broken, pieces of glass scattered across the stone floor of the great hall. Torches lined the walls, but were unlit. No soul but mine walked the halls. No eyes but mine witnessed the destruction. The fortress had become a ruin.' What is that if not a prophecy?"

"Forgive me, Mother Hydra," said Mother Corvus, "but I think that is quite a stretch."

Another rustle of papers came from the room. "That was an excerpt from Recruit Rhaean's dreaming records," said Mother Hydra.

"Rhaean? From when we were recruits?" asked Mother Lynx.

"It matches Nasya's account of her nightmare word for word." said Mother Hydra.

Nasya felt a chill crawl up her spine. The hair on the back of her neck stood on end.

"And there have been three other recruits since Rhaean who have recorded similar dreams, all of them featuring some form of Passing's End in ruins."

"What is your point?" asked Mother Cassiopeia, annoyingly.

"There is something special about Nasya, just as there was

about the other recruits. They struggled, too, just as she has done. These dreams may reveal their true message in time. Nasya herself may provide us answers to these questions, if given the chance."

Nasya suddenly felt that she had heard too much. She did not want to be caught standing so close to the room, so she quickly swept up the remaining debris, put it in the bucket, and then went down to the opposite end of the hall where her other bucket was, knelt down, and began to scrub. This would take her longer to complete, crawling around on her hands and knees, scrubbing into every nook to keep the floor clean. Her mind was not with the cleaning. It was possessed by the words she'd just heard Mother Hydra speak before the other Mothers. Her skin tingled. It had never occurred to her that she was having these nightmares for a reason, that she had been chosen to see things. She never thought it could mean she was special. She'd never been special before.

Nearly fifteen minutes later, the Mothers emerged. Nasya kept out of their way as they passed by her. Mother Hydra was the only one who stopped to speak to her. She was told that, while Mother Hydra could give her something to aid her sleep, she thought it best for Nasya to continue having her dreams, and documenting them as clearly as possible. She would meet with Nasya every morning to discuss them. And if needs be, she would be given a sleeping aid every other night to ensure her sleep was restful. There was kindness in Mother Hydra's eyes, and it filled Nasya with warmth.

Things changed for Nasya after that day. Mother Hydra was much more involved in her lessons, sometimes going so far as to teach her one-on-one. She was still learning what the other recruits were being taught, but at a different pace. And within a matter of days, she was improving. It was still slow progress, but it was noticeable and that made her proud. Mother Hydra had also added a pile of books to her reading list, all of them literature written about magic.

"You may not have magical abilities," Mother Hydra said when she gave her the books, "but you are clearly connected to some form of magic. It is not the typical person who is given the gift of dreams."

Nasya ran her fingers over the covers of the books. "I wouldn't call these dreams a gift," she mumbled.

Mother Hydra grinned. "They may not feel like it now, but when you finally understand them, you might feel differently."

Nasya began to read them every night. Mostly they were written as fables, lore, and myths, but Mother Hydra encouraged her to make note of anything that stood out. And so she did. Little by little, she wrote down words, phrases, questions, and page numbers for cross referencing later. And with each day that she continued her studies with Mother Hydra, her dreams became more interesting rather than terrifying. She still wrote them down whenever she awoke, making sure to include every detail she could remember. Over time, they changed. Sometimes in small ways. Other times in large ways, to the extent that they were almost completely different dreams entirely. The weeks turned to months and her nights were almost constantly bombarded with the most vivid nightmares.

Every other night, Mother Hydra gave her milk mixed with some herbal remedy that allowed her to sleep dreamlessly. Nasya clung to these nights, retreating to her bed far earlier than the other recruits so that she could be sure to get a long, restful night's sleep. Her exhaustion began to lessen. Her focus strengthened. And things became easier, little by little.

# Chapter Five

*Fortress of Passing's End*
  *Country of Utara*


One full year had passed since Nasya had been brought to Passing's End. She was taller now, though not by much, and her hair had grown down to just below her shoulders. It was winter again, though the mountains had been engulfed in snow and frigid temperatures for well over a month and a half. Their lessons were still taught in full force, only now they were also given physical exercises as part of their training. Every day they were told to run up and down every flight of stairs in Passing's End. It would improve their endurance, the Mothers told them. Nasya was among the most agile recruits, able to run for long periods of time without tiring. In fact, she enjoyed running, stretching, and strength training. For her it was like another form of meditation and helped her clear her mind of unwanted thoughts and distractions.

Her dreams continued and, therefore, so did her one-on-one lessons with Mother Hydra. By this point, Nasya had read through one of the books on magic she had been given and was just beginning a second. The first book had been primarily about the history of magic on earth. According to the book, magic created the world. Dragons, the purest and most raw form of magic incarnate, had breathed fires so hot that hundreds of stars melted together to form the earth, thereby weaving threads of the most powerful magic into the very fabric of the world. The water, the flowers, the roots of trees, the daytime and the night all existed as they did because of dragon fire. And every being that lived upon the earth or in the sea was connected to this magic. Some races, like the fae, were born with the ability to manipulate the magic in and around them and could do so with ease. But most people, being mortal, were not given the same abilities.

Though there were some, Mother Hydra told her, who, through decades of study, found themselves in possession of magical abilities beyond their comprehension. They were known by many names depending on their abilities. Witches. Warlocks. Mages. Druids. Enchantresses. Nasya studied them all. She learned of their powers, their abilities, and their down-falls. The magic might be pure, but the people wielding it were not always. Magic mixed with cruelty, greed, and selfish ambition, was a deadly concoction.

Mother Hydra still collected Nasya's records of her dreams. As far as Nasya could tell, this was a practice she would continue to keep up as long as she was at Passing's End. Her position so far was safe. Mother Cassiopeia clearly did not want Nasya to remain and any time there was a counsel meeting to determine which of the recruits would be dismissed, she always put forth Nasya's name, and no one else's. But the other Mothers, especially Hydra and Corvus, did not share Mother Cassiopeia's opinions, and so others were chosen instead. In this first year of training, a total of three girls had been sent away. Nasya reveled in the fact that she had made it this far, and hoped that she would continue to persevere.

She had also made another friend among the recruits. A girl two years older than her called Barbarella – they called her Bell – had taken a liking to Nasya. They weren't as close as Nasya and Scarlet, but Bell had begun spending time with both girls and they quickly became thick as thieves. Bell was one of the more skilled recruits. It seemed as though she picked up any subject as quickly as she did breathing. All forms of study were natural to her. She spent time helping Nasya with some of her more difficult subjects, and Nasya found herself continuing to improve.

"What did you read in the first chapters of The Magical Histories volume two?" asked Mother Hydra one morning during their lessons.

"The book jumped ahead by several decades from the end of

volume one, which was surprising," Nasya said.

"Why was that surprising?"

"Volume one ends with detailed descriptions of how mortals first obtained any magical abilities and the impacts this had on the earth, and then volume two begins by explaining that the dragons had all disappeared. It seemed odd that in all that time, as dragons began to disappear, no one thought to write down the specific events that caused it."

Mother Hydra nodded. "It is odd. Why do you think there was such a gap of time between the two volumes?"

Nasya thought for a moment. "I'd say it's because something happened, something cataclysmic, and everyone was preoccupied with responding to the event that they forgot to record the specifics. And then by the time someone did sit to write it all down, the events were little better than lore."

Mother Hydra nodded again. "Very good, Nasya. This is important to keep in mind any time you're reading about magic. Not every book should be taken literally. There will always be inconsistencies, gaps in time, questions unanswered. But that doesn't mean there aren't still threads of truth to find among the fiction."

"I also wanted to ask about the different magical factions," Nasya said, flipping open the second volume to a page in the first chapter. "Here. If this is supposed to be a list of all magical groups, then why are not the fae listed?"

"Because the fae are born with inherent abilities that they don't need to learn how to use, while the groups listed here are born with magical abilities, but they must learn to use them."

"But werewolves, vampires, and changelings are listed here, though they are born with magical abilities they don't need to learn how to use."

"It's true that weres and vampires are born with abilities that are inherent to who they are, but they still must learn to control them. Weres, like other changelings, will shift once they're old enough for the magic to awaken inside them, but when it comes to controlling this shift and controlling what they do in their non-human forms, that takes time to learn. They are minor differences, but they change quite a bit."

Nasya nodded slowly, absorbing what she'd been told. "Then, witches and warlocks and the like have to learn how to use their magic, too?"

"Yes. And it takes a lot of time for them to do so."

"So...where do I fall into this?" Nasya asked, looking up at Mother Hydra.

"Dreamers are a different sect altogether. Your dreams come from magic, but they are not an ability that you can learn to control or manipulate. You are simply a vessel for what you are meant to see."

Mother Hydra did not meet her eyes when she said this, and something about her tone troubled Nasya. It was sharp, curt, almost like it was what she had been told to say. Why she would say something she did not believe to be true was beyond Nasya's thinking. She decided not to press the subject. She was told to read the next few chapters and write out a summary, and so she set to work doing just that.

A couple of hours later, it was time for physical training. The girls changed into their trousers and tunics, their bare feet cold against the stone floor. Each day the number of rounds they took on the stairs increased. The day before had been nine rounds; one round meant they had to run from the ground level up five stories to the top floor, down the long attic corridor, and down the back stairs to the ground level. Today, they were told to do this twelve times with as few breaks as possible.

"Endurance is one of the most important aspects of being a Sister of the Order," shouted Mother Phoenix as the girls began to run up the stairs.

"The power is in the blood," said the Mothers in unison, and the girls all repeated it.

All of the Mothers were scattered on different levels of the fortress, lining the path that the girls would take to complete their circuit.

"You must be able to push through all physical and mental exhaustion," shouted Mother Fornax. "You will not be able to anticipate every circumstance, every unexpected turn of events that may arise as you're completing your assignments."

"You may find yourself in situations that require hasty evacuation," shouted Mother Lynx, "and you may not have an easy way out."

"Ignore your body's aching," said Mother Cassiopeia, "ignore the rapid beat of your heart, ignore the burning in your lungs. Place one foot in front of the other. Breathe deeply and steadily and you will find yourself adapting to the speed."

Nasya's small frame was conducive to running. She moved swiftly without tiring as easily as some of the other girls. In fact, only Scarlet and a girl named Ynora could match her speed and endurance. Nasya grinned at the two girls as they neared the completion of the first round, and took the stairs without slowing down. Her feet were cold, especially her toes, but still she ran. Up the stairs, down the hallway, and down the back stairs. Over and over. Scarlet and Ynora managed to keep up with her for the first six rounds, but then began to fall behind. Ynora fell back with the rest of the girls who, by the sixth round, were mostly walking up the stairs, jogging down the hall, and then going as fast as they could down the back staircase.

It wasn't that Nasya felt no exhaustion. She was tired like the others. She breathed heavily, her lungs aching for air. And by the seventh of the twelve rounds, her legs felt heavy, like they were made of water. But she refused to slow down. She would not stop. She drowned out any thoughts of her lessons, the Mothers, the other recruits, and focused on nothing more than her body. Her goal was to speed up with each round, instead of slowing down and losing momentum. She ignored Mother Cassiopeia's glares every time she passed by her and simply breathed, cleared her mind, and focused. By the eighth round, she felt as though she wasn't in control of her body any longer. It was like she was witnessing her movements being made, rather than being the one making them.

She was the first recruit to finish the exercise. It wasn't until she stopped running that the real pain and fatigue took her body. Her side felt like it was split open as her breathing became more erratic. Her muscles ached. Sweat poured down her face. She immediately started to stretch to keep her body from becoming too stiff. One by one, the other girls completed the exercise. And while it wasn't timed, the first half of the girls that finished were given clear smiles of recognition.

Once every girl had completed the twelfth round, they were given several moments to rest and stretch before dinner would be served. Then they were told to change for the afternoon meal, after which they would be sent to their rooms to study.

Snow fell in thick clumps of large flakes. The air was beyond cold. Almost unnaturally cold. Early morning twilight cast an icy blue hue over the landscape. She stood up on a high point above Passing's End, a lookout made of stone, and stared at the woods and the mountains buried in the heaviest days of winter. Below her, the ruins of Passing's End lay quiet. Only sounds of the wind and the everyday scurrying of forest creatures could be heard.

To the left, somewhere deep in the forest leading to the mountain pass, she saw curls of smoke ascending into the clouds. Someone was camped out within only a few miles of the dilapidated fortress. And though she didn't know who it was, something in her gut told her they weren't friendly. She needed a closer look.

She suddenly found herself on the forest floor, crouching low, sneaking towards the sound of a crackling fire. Hushed voices murmured. She could see them through the branches of the evergreens. There were six. Their faces were blurred, obscured, unrecognizable.

"They never even had a chance," said one, laughing.

Over the fire was a pot filled with something cooking. It smelled like stew.

"Of course not," said another, biting into a chunk of bread. "Never expected the problem to be among their own."

"All that training, and for what?" said a third.

"Hush," said a tall, womanly looking figure. Her eyes were a stark, metallic gold color. "Do not gloat yet. Others are still out there."

Silence fell over the group. A moment later, she was walking through the ruins of Passing's End, her heart thundering in her chest. Something had happened. Something horrible and unforeseen, but what? And to whom? She walked carefully, climbing over logs and stones and other debris, her eyes scanning the snow for any clues. But she found nothing aside from the crumbled stones that used to make up the building that was once her home.

Then, to her right, she saw it. A splash of bright red on the white snow. She froze. It was in what used to be the courtyard. Blood. A lot of blood. And from it, deep imprints that appeared to be drag marks. She followed them, worried about what she would find at the end. The drag marks led out of the former courtyard and into the woods to the west, but they did not lead far. She came to a body covered by a bright red cloak.

Somehow, she knew who it was.

Her heart stalled in her chest. Tears filled her eyes. She didn't want to believe it. Didn't want to confirm it. She could walk away. She could forget about this place and the blood and the drag prints. She could forget about the fire in the woods. She could. But she knew she wouldn't. She leaned forward slowly, bending at the waist, and reached for the red cloak.

"Do not ask the questions you do not want answers for," said a voice over her shoulder.

She gasped and spun around. No one was there.

"The dead cannot be haunted," the voice said again, from behind her.

She spun around again. "Show yourself or be silent!" she shouted, her voice echoing on the cold wind.

When the voice did not speak again, she bent over and reached for the cloak. She pulled it back, and from her belly came a loud scream. Tears fell down her face. She backed away, unable to stop the screams. After a moment, the only sound she heard was the echo of her own screams as grief took hold of her and squeezed, like an iron grip in her chest.

"Nasya! Wake up!"

Nasya opened her eyes. Scarlet stood above her, looking down on her face.

"There, there," Scarlet said, helping Nasya sit up. "It's alright."

She was still crying. Her hands shook violently. She looked around; she was in her own room, wrapped in her own blankets. She was safe. It had been nothing more than a dream. A horrible dream. One she wanted to forget. Gods, that she could erase this dream from her memory.

"You've awoken the entire fortress," said Mother Cassiopeia

It was only then that Nasya realized all of the Mothers and most of the other recruits stood in her doorway. Scarlet was to her left, sitting on the edge of her bed, and Mother Hydra sat on her right. Mother Hydra stared at her with wide eyes.

"What did you see, fledgling?" she asked.

Nasya shook her head. "Do not make me repeat it, Mother. Please."

"How long was she screaming?" Mother Hydra asked Scarlet.

"At least five minutes, Mother. The longest of any nightmare yet, and definitely the loudest." Scarlet ran her fingers through Nasya's hair. "She must have seen something truly horrible."

"It was a nightmare, for god's sakes," said Mother Cassiopeia. "The more you coddle her, the worse they will get."

"Mother Cassiopeia, that is quite enough," said Mother Corvus, stepping into the room. "Please take the other girls back to their rooms and see to it they're given a mug of ale to calm their nerves. Mother Phoenix, please get some wine for Nasya."

The people dispersed. Nasya managed to slow her breathing, though she still trembled and cried.

"Nasya, I must know what you saw in your dream," said Mother Hydra. "It is of the utmost importance."

Nasya only shook her head. She couldn't speak it. Couldn't give it life, not even in the darkness of her dorm with Scarlet and Mother Hydra on either side of her. She would forget. She would let it go, let it slip out of her mind and away from her consciousness. This was not something she would carry. It was not something she would give a voice to.

Mother Hydra sighed. Wine was brought to Nasya and she swallowed the whole goblet in two gulps.

"Here," Mother Hydra said, pouring another half goblet of wine and placing three drops of liquid from a blue vial into it. "Drink this. It will help you sleep. Tomorrow, I would like for us to talk about this."

Nasya nodded slowly and drank the wine. Mother Hydra gave instructions to Scarlet to look after her the rest of the night, and then the room was empty, save for Nasya and her friend. Scarlet crawled under Nasya's covers and held her close.

"I'm so sorry," Scarlet whispered, pressing a kiss to her forehead.

Nasya knew she didn't need to speak. Scarlet wouldn't ask about the dream, either. She gave Nasya her space, respected her privacy. And while Nasya wanted to help Mother Hydra understand her dreams, this was one she didn't think she could write out or discuss. Not after what she'd seen. The blood. The certain death of the body. The mangled, almost completely disfigured face. She shuddered just at the recollection.

"You're safe. I'll stay awake until you're asleep, but I'll be right here with you all night," Scarlet said, running her fingers through Nasya's hair. "You're safe. I won't let anything happen to you."

83

# Chapter Six

*Village of Terrace*
  *Country of Utara*

Winter had taken hold of the land with a strength that was surprising. By mid-November the leaves had all been blown from their trees, frost had given way to thick slabs of ice that covered the ground, and a fierce wind had settled in the valleys of Utara. But for twenty-eight year old Nasya, the cold was merely a reflection of the direction the country was taking. It used to be that Utara was an economic leader in the region. They'd boasted more trade and prosperity than any other country in the west. Even the common folk lived prosperous lives and local leaders, like mayors and sheriffs, had been vigilant in ensuring that the poorest members of their communities were taken care of. Utara had been so well known for its prosperity that citizens from other countries saved up all they could to move there and begin new lives. But that had been decades ago. The country now was nearly unrecognizable to what it had once been.

This was never more apparent than when she walked through the village where she had lived for the first years of her childhood. Terrace had also once been a thriving community. They grew wheat, barley, and a multitude of beans. There had been several livestock farmers who provided milk, eggs, and cheese to the markets. Hunters had traveled through the village frequently to sell slabs of venison as well as smaller game like racoons, squirrels, and rabbits. In return for the meat, the farmers of Terrace traded bread, rice, and fruit.

As Nasya walked into Terrace, she remembered some of her younger years living in a small hut with her parents and sister. While they were not rich, they had not gone hungry. At least, not at first. In fact, her mother had always made such delicious meals, Nasya could remember the taste even now, decades later. Her vegetable and barley stew was a particular meal that Nasya recalled with fondness. Her mother would always make larger portions than she needed and distribute the extra to their neighbors. Her cooking had made their family a favorite among the town of Terrace, and was precisely what inspired her parents to build the public house that her father and sister still managed.

But those years had been few. By the time Nasya had reached the age of five, Terrace had already felt the heavy blow of poverty and scarcity. Now, walking through the village as a grown woman, she hardly recognized the place that once was her home.

Huts and hovels had grown into disrepair due to the increasing costs of lumber. And those who had once found and cut their own wood for building could no longer do so without paying a massive fine. The mayor and sheriff acted as extensions of the king's guard, inflicting severe punishment on those who broke the law. Families lived outside in the cold. Children starved. Parents sold their children into servitude so as to spare them freezing to death in the frigid winds, just as her own parents had done. It was all due to the King's war with their neighbor to the north, Hevean. That and his youngest son's extravagance. Rumors had it that the war was just a ruse to distract from the prince's inability to be frugal, and his father's inability to hold him accountable. The population had been cut by half, if not more, due to starvation and succumbing to the elements. Many of those who could do so had moved to larger cities where there were more opportunities. But the farmers whose livelihoods were tied to the land did everything they could to keep growing food that would keep them, and those who stayed in Terrace, from starving.

Nasya couldn't help but feel guilty as she walked towards the hovel where she was born. She was not richly dressed, but she wore warm clothes that were not torn and ratted. In her purse was more money than most of them had seen in their entire lives. As she walked by, she dropped several coins into the empty cups and bowls of those begging for charity, making sure not to miss a single person. It wasn't much, but she could afford to give up most of the money she carried, for she had consistent employment that paid her well. And though this would likely draw some attention to herself, she didn't care. She couldn't turn away from people in need when she had the means to lessen their suffering, even if just a little.

She came to a halt as she neared her family's hut. It was attached to a larger building, the village's only public house. The hut's roof had caved in long ago and had not been lived in for some time. After her mother had died, her father and sister moved into the public house to save money on firewood. They could not heat the pub and their hut at the same time. And as customers began to dwindle and the pub made less and less each year, any money they had was spent keeping the pub open, rather than rebuilding their hovel.

Nasya chewed nervously on the inside of her lips. She wasn't supposed to be here. When The Order purchased her, she had to leave her former life and identity behind. She had agreed to this. But it was an agreement she had been unable to keep. Risking severe punishment, she had, on her first return home since she left it many years before, introduced herself back into their lives. She had been anxious to know that they were well, despite her promise to The Mothers never to make contact. And that was when she'd officially learned of her mother's passing. It was also when she saw the horrific state of her father and sister's home, and resolved to do whatever she could to help them. They might not have taken care of *her*, but she would give them what she'd been denied. If there was one thing she had fought to hold onto, it was her capacity for compassion and forgiveness. The face-to-face visit was a risk she had only been able to afford once and would not risk again. But they would always know they could count on her to look after them.

The meeting had not been the loving reunion she'd imagined. It came about thirteen months after she graduated from training with The Order. She had been passing through Terrace on her way to complete an assignment and, seeing the horrendous state of the rest of the village, had been unable to pass by without stopping to see her family. She observed them from a distance, her heart aching to see her father looking so old and so in pain. He walked with a heavy slouch and a cane. His hands shook. He was bald and his skin was sallow and sunken. And Maiah, her younger sister, was so thin, Nasya was surprised she could walk at all.

Then her father had tripped and fallen to the ground, and before she knew what she was doing, she was at his side, helping him to stand. He didn't know her when his eyes, red and puffy from sickness, looked up into her face. He had frowned and pulled away, mistrustful. It was Maiah who had gasped and said, "Nasya?"

The recognition passed over her father then, but instead of embracing his eldest daughter, he had backed away. It was as if he thought of her as a ghost, and in a way she was. Nasya wasn't his daughter any longer. The hovel wasn't her home. Terrace wasn't her village. She was little more than a stranger, a reminder of what had been before destitution and desperation made he and his late wife sell their eldest girl to a woman they'd never met before, and without any understanding of what would become of her. And she couldn't explain any of it; where she'd been, what she'd done, who she was.

The coldness of their stares, the irrevocable distance that divided them, made Nasya's eyes fill with tears. She had said nothing. She merely grabbed her coin purse and emptied half of its contents onto the chopping block to her left, and then walked away. They didn't call her back. They didn't run after her. They'd said nothing. Nasya thought that such a meeting would have rid her heart of the rest of the love she felt for them, filing it away with her other memories of her former life, but she'd been mistaken. Months later, she still couldn't get them out of her mind. That was when she'd written to them and promised she would send money whenever she could. They had not written back.

Nasya shuddered at the recollections. Somewhere deep inside her, beneath the hard shell she'd wrapped herself in, a little girl still cried for her family. It was that girl who now took most of the remaining coins from her purse and placed them just inside the partially open window near the front door of the public house. Her father and sister were likely in the kitchen preparing for dinner and wouldn't hear her. That was imperative. She would continue sending as much financial assistance as she could, just as she had promised, and that would have to be enough to satisfy her longing for their company. She blew a kiss into the window, turned away with tears in her eyes, and walked out of the village towards Sun River, the Utaran capitol.

# Chapter Seven

*Fortress of Passing's End*
*Country of Utara*

Twelve year-old Nasya's skirt was filthy. She had spent the better part of two hours sweeping the stone floor of Passing's End, only she had not been given a proper broom to sweep with. Instead, she held a brush with bristles, and she crawled on her hands and knees back and forth across the foyer, sweeping all of the dirt and dust into piles to be tossed outside. All the girls were now old enough to be responsible for heavier chores throughout the week. They cycled through them, each one given a different task every day. The foyer was the hardest of the chores. People moved through it almost constantly; she would have the entire floor nearly swept and ready to be scrubbed, when one of the Mothers would come in and disturb a pile of dirt, requiring her to begin again.

When she finally did have the foyer swept, she filled a bucket with water and soap, cleaned off the brush, and used it to scrub the stone floor. This, too, was an arduous task because, rather than disturbing piles of dirt, the comers and goers would inevitably trail dirt and mud onto the now wet floor. Nasya would have to work extra hard to remove them.

All of the girls hated cleaning the foyer, but it was Nasya who was given the task more often than any of the others. It was the one chore reserved for those who failed to learn during the morning hours of their education, and Nasya was still frequently behind. It didn't seem to matter how hard she studied, even if it was twice as hard as the other girls; what mattered was how much she retained.

Nasya had already been sweeping for at least two hours and had not yet been able to start scrubbing. It was a rule that no one could eat their dinner until they finished their chores for the day.

"You will learn discipline," the recruits were told daily, "You will learn to ignore things like thirst and hunger until every task you've been given is completed. You will learn the importance of urgency *and* patience, for you will need both as you advance in your training."

At the thought of food, Nasya's stomach grumbled. She hadn't eaten since that morning's meal several hours before. It had been a bowl of porridge with milk and, while not delicious, it was filling. But dinner she could not have until the floor was clean. She worked quickly, sweeping up as much dirt as she could, hoping she would be able to eat her afternoon meal within an hour or so.

Just then, the double doors of the entrance opened and Mother Cassiopeia walked inside with two other recruits behind her. Dry summer dust trailed behind the three as they entered and settled on the floor. The girls cast apologetic looks her way and tried to walk carefully so as not to disrupt the piles of dirt she'd already swept up. Mother Cassiopeia, however, paid no such mind.

"Still sweeping?" she asked, glaring down at her. "If you moved any slower, I'd think you were part snail," she said with a mocking grin. It was then she noticed the other girls were intentionally avoiding the piles of dirt Nasya had already swept up. Mother Cassiopeia heaved a frustrated sigh and began to spread the dirt around with her toes. Nasya sat up, astonished. The other two recruits gave Nasya sympathetic glances. When she was done, Mother Cassiopeia looked down at Nasya.

"Work builds character and gratitude," she said. "Two things you are entirely without. Move with a sense of urgency, and you might actually finish this floor before supper."

"But what about dinner?" Nasya asked.

Mother Cassiopeia laughed. "It was served an hour ago. What about it?"

Nasya stood to her feet. "An hour? But I didn't get anything to eat!"

"And why might that be?" Mother Cassiopeia asked angrily.

Nasya sighed and looked down at the stone floor. "Because we must earn the meals we're given," she muttered.

"That's right. Now, sweep! And be glad you still have a place here at all."

Mother Cassiopeia and the other two girls moved away, leaving Nasya to herself. She worked for another two hours sweeping and, finally, scrubbing the floor. She completed her chore, showed the progress to Mother Corvus, and was given permission to go to supper, which was just being served. Nasya made her way to the dining hall and sat down. Her stomach growled with hunger.

She sat next to Scarlet and filled her plate with as much food as she could. Scarlet leaned over and whispered, "Where have you been?"

"The foyer," she responded.

Scarlet sighed. "Again? Did you not do that yesterday?"

Nasya nodded as she took a bite of a turkey leg.

Scarlet shook her head. "Gods above! They really define the word unforgiving, don't they?"

The girls ate the rest of their meal in silence, neither of them willing to incur any more wrath than they did on a daily basis. Scarlet was excellent at her studies and in all other areas of training, but her love for Nasya marked her as an outlier. Indeed, Scarlet had stood up for Nasya more than once to all the Mothers, including Mother Cassiopeia, and they made no secret of their dislike of that. Scarlet's life had, therefore, become much like Nasya's; unnecessarily harsh. Nasya hated to see it and even told Scarlet to distance herself from her, but Scarlet wouldn't hear a word of it.

Most of the other recruits intentionally kept their distance from Nasya. Even Barbarella, the only other recruit she considered a friend, had begun spending less and less time around her. It didn't bother Nasya much. She didn't want anyone else punished over her failures. It was hard enough to see Scarlet punished, however stubbornly the thirteen year old faced the Mothers' retaliations. Nasya didn't want to see anyone else subjected to the same treatment. Bitterness grew inside of her. Resentment festered. And from them sprouted a stubbornness and determination that Nasya clung to with all her might.

After supper, the girls were given time to themselves. Nasya used these few hours to practice the subjects she found the most difficult. Most of their informational studies were completed, though Nasya continued to practice them so as not to forget anything important that might come up again later in training. Her struggles now lay primarily in the running, climbing, and strength training. Where she once thrived, the intensity increased to such an extent that now she struggled with all of it, much to the detriment of the rest of the recruits. Whenever she fell out of a hike or couldn't complete a run, the rest were given extra exercise. And though none of the recruits had explicitly blamed her, for they knew she was trying, Nasya still was determined to do everything she could to hold her own.

Unfortunately, she wasn't nearly close to where she needed

to be. Aside from Scarlet, she was left to struggle alone while her future Sisters were punished for her mistakes. Nasya could sometimes taste the resentment building between her and the other girls, and she couldn't blame them. She didn't blame them. None of them had asked for this, had chosen this, had any say in their being brought to Passing's End. All of them had been torn from their families, and on that footing, they held common ground. It was enough to keep the other girls from retaliating on their youngest companion, but it wasn't quite enough to quell the building resentment.

As the summer sun began to set behind the mountains, Nasya made her way out into the courtyard and stretched. It was a meditative practice that kept the girls limber and reinforced self-control. Sometimes The Mothers used it for discipline, forcing the girls to balance cups on their heads or outstretched arms. "Giving in to exhaustion is not an option among The Order!" the Mothers said, "If you cannot even hold a cup on the end of your arm without growing tired, how will you defend yourself in the field or fight back against an assault?"

Most of the time, meditation was simply for maintaining movement and flexibility. Nasya used it to concentrate before giving herself a physical challenge to try and overcome.

"The mind is where all discipline begins," Mother Phoenix would always say. "The stronger the mind, the better the discipline."

Nasya chose to give herself these extra hours to strengthen her body, but she always began with long, heavy meditation to strengthen her mind. What her body couldn't do, her mind would make up for. At least, that's what she hoped would happen eventually. If what the Mothers' said was true, her failures in training were the result of an undisciplined, weak mind. And that, only she could change.

As she stretched, her movements were slow and intentional. She kept her eyes fixed straight ahead on one of the trees just outside the courtyard and breathed slowly in through her nose and out through her mouth. Focus was the key. One of the reasons she struggled so much with the physical demands of training, Mother Hydra had told her years ago, was because she was too scattered, unable to focus her attention. Her thoughts would distract and discourage her. Meditating helped to reinforce the importance of intense focus and steady breathing. The movements themselves looked more akin to dancing, her arms and legs always in motion.

Nasya breathed in slowly, filling her lungs with the warm summer air. Passing's End was situated deep in an old forest. Surrounded by trees on all sides, the castle was almost always shaded. It kept the courtyard cool in the summer, for which Nasya was grateful. She was not fond of the heat.

"Focus," she told herself, forcing her thoughts to return to her breathing.

She stared at the spot across from her and continued to consider her breathing, her body, her skin, her feet connected with the earth; her mind wanted to wander, but she brought it back to the same tree over and over. She thought of how the stones felt beneath her bare feet, and of how the breeze around her smelled of honeysuckle from the grove just outside the courtyard. "Breathe in, breathe out," she thought as she cleared her mind of all thoughts other than her body and its movement, its tightness, its stiffness, its response to the warm air. She tried not to think about what her life had been like only a couple years ago. These were the most pervasive thoughts she struggled to ignore. It did no good to dwell on the past, on lives that would no longer be lived, on identities no longer available to her.

"Nasya."

The voice was barely even a whisper, hardly detectable if not for the quiet around her, and yet it made the hairs on the back of Nasya's neck stand on end. She looked around, wondering if it was one of The Mothers trying to get her attention, but the courtyard was empty. Though the evening was warm as the sun set below the horizon, the air suddenly became cooler. The breeze blew a little more strongly. The courtyard wasn't dark, though it was on the cusp of twilight with pink wisps of cloud illuminated by the fading sun. Everything was silent. She furrowed her eyebrows, confused. Had her mind been playing tricks?

When everything remained quiet for a moment, she went back to focusing on her breathing. "Ignore the distractions," she thought and recentered herself. She moved slowly through her forms, clearing her mind of everything, including the voice she told herself must have been a trick of the ears.

"Nasya."

The voice was louder this time and sounded familiar. She looked around, her heart beginning to beat harder. It had to be one of the Mothers calling her, but she didn't see anyone; no one had entered the courtyard, no one was at the door to the castle, and no one was at the gate. She was alone, and yet she knew for certain now that she had heard someone call her name.

"Hello?" she said as the courtyard continued to grow dark. "Is anyone there?"

Only the rustle of the wind through the trees answered back. She tried to think of an explanation that made sense. She didn't see anyone in the courtyard with her, but that didn't mean she was alone. Perhaps this was a trick being played on her by the other recruits? Or maybe one of the Mothers was trying to distract her intentionally to help her learn to focus? Both seemed possible. She let out a huff of frustration, and then centered herself again. She would not be deterred.

Several minutes went by. Then an hour. Nasya had not heard the voice again. She finished stretching and immediately began to train her strength. She practiced balance, she practiced pushing through the pain of exhaustion, and she practiced ignoring how tired she was. This more than almost anything else was of utmost importance for the recruits to master. They could not allow themselves to be weak. They could not reveal their limitations.

Nasya was dripping with sweat under the darkening sky after only a half an hour of strength training. Her small body struggled to keep up the speed and enthusiasm with which she'd begun, and it seemed the more she tried to push herself, the more her body continued to break down.

Suddenly, she heard the voice again, only it didn't say anything. It just laughed. It was a woman's voice. Nasya stopped and began looking around, breathing heavily. The laughing started out quiet and then gradually built to a menacing cackle.

"I hear you, whoever you are," Nasya said loudly, "I know you're there and you don't frighten me."

"I should," the voice said again in a whisper, only this time Nasya felt breath on her neck as though they had spoken directly into her ear. The scent of peppermint filled her nostrils, the exact scent of the oil her mother used to rub into her fingers and knuckles after a long day of planting.

Nasya gasped and spun around, her eyes wide. Still no one was there, but now the hair on her arms stood on end and her heart was racing. Where had they gone? How had they moved so quickly? Why had she smelled peppermint? Someone had been close enough to touch her – how had they managed to hide quickly enough that she hadn't seen them?

While she wanted to be brave and discount what had happened, something deep in her gut told her this was not at all what it seemed. She decided she was done with her extra training for the night and returned to the castle. She moved quickly and entered the foyer, shutting the large oak doors behind her. She tried to ignore how fast her heart was racing. She tried to tell herself she wasn't frightened, even though she knew she was. She made her way to the room she shared with Scarlet, who looked up as Nasya entered.

"Done already? You never come to bed this early." She must have seen a look on Nasya's face because she frowned and closed the book she was reading. "Are you alright?"

Nasya moved away from the door, poured herself a goblet of water, and gulped it down. "Yes," she said, "I'm fine."

"You're as white as a sheet," Scarlet said, moving from her bed to where Nasya stood by the window.

"I said I'm fine," Nasya responded, angry at herself for being such a failure. A real recruit would have stayed outside and finished their training. A real recruit would have been able to face the voice without hesitation.

"Nasya," Scarlet said softly. "You're shaking."

Nasya looked down at her hands. She couldn't hold them still. She put down the goblet and walked to her small wardrobe. She opened it and took out her nightgown.

"I..." she began, and then hesitated. She slipped out of her dirty dress. "I heard someone calling my name in the courtyard," she said, sliding her nightgown over her head and placing her dirty clothes next to her bed. "At first I thought it was one of the Mothers, but no one was outside with me."

Scarlet listened intently.

Nasya climbed onto her bed. "The voice sounded like a woman. Called my name twice, but I didn't see anyone. I thought it might have been some of the recruits trying to scare me, but no one was there."

She did not mention the peppermint.

"We all know this place is haunted," Scarlet said, sitting at the foot of Nasya's bed and taking Nasya's hands. "Some of the other girls said they saw a ghost out there in our first week of training. I'm pretty sure it was a woman. That's probably what the voice was." Scarlet slowly and methodically began to rub Nasya's hands. It made Nasya's skin tingle everywhere. Scarlet must have seen that Nasya was still unnerved. She smiled softly. "They can't hurt us, Nasya. At least, not any more than the Mothers do already," she said, chuckling.

She continued to rub Nasya's hands as the two girls sat in silence. Nasya's attention was torn between how surprisingly soft Scarlet's hands were in comparison to her own, and the ringing of the laughter she'd heard in the courtyard that still filled her ears, even though she couldn't hear the voice anymore.

"You're safe, Nasya," Scarlet whispered before climbing back into her own bed and continuing to read the book she'd been immersed in.

Nasya nodded and climbed under her covers. Normally, she'd have washed herself off after such a long day, but she was stiff and tired. Nasya laid down and rolled onto her side. She wasn't sure she believed her explanation, but it was comforting to see how unconcerned Scarlet was. Maybe she didn't have to be either? Ghosts were known to be tricksters, playing on people's minds and fears. And Scarlet had said that other girls had seen a ghost, so it wasn't as though she was the only one who'd experienced something strange. She let out a slow breath, decided that she would put the incident out of her mind, and within moments had fallen into a deep sleep.

Nasya didn't tell anyone else about the ghost. Not only did she have no idea how to even bring up such a subject, but she was wary of saying anything that might be used against her later. She had listened more intently than usual to the idle chatterings of the other recruits and, while some of them did mention seeing a ghost, none could give any particular description of what they'd seen, nor had the ghost spoken to them. It was enough to give Nasya doubt as to the truthfulness of their stories.

As for her own experiences, they continued, but always when she was out in the courtyard on her own. Sometimes months would pass and she would hear nothing, and then all at once for days in a row, the voice would return, and always with the scent of peppermint. It was the peppermint that troubled her most. She had no explanation for it, no idea from whence it came. There was nothing in or around the fortress that gave off such a fragrance and none of the Mothers wore it. It troubled her deeply.

Whenever the voice did speak, Nasya simply made her way back inside and kept to her room. She did not acknowledge it, did not speak to it, did not exhibit any signs of even hearing it. She hoped that whatever it was would grow tired of her and move on to bother someone else. Moreover, she never mentioned it to anyone else again, not even Scarlet. It was as if she'd heard the voice only once. It bothered Nasya that she would keep something like this from Scarlet, the one person who had always been safe, the one person who was most likely to believe her. But somehow, she simply couldn't speak the words. Even when she tried to, planned to, was about to do so, something held her back.

Months passed. Seasons came and went. Training continued. Everyday the girls were told of the increasing political dangers existing between the countries of Utara and Hevean. The two countries were on the brink of war and had been for some time. The Mothers asked if anyone knew what might cause this schism between countries that had been allies for decades.

Scarlet was the first to speak. "The current King of Utara was married to a royal from Hevean, was he not?"

Mother Lynx shook her head. "Not him. His younger brother."

"Would this not strengthen the ties between the two royal families?" asked Mother Fornax.

"Did not the Hevean Princess die?" asked Scarlet. "Could that be at the root of this increasing hostility?"

Barbarella nodded. "Yes, especially if someone from Hevean suspects foul play in her death."

"Did she not die in childbirth?" asked Ynora. "As did the baby?"

"That was the official story," said a recruit named Cecilee. "It does not follow that it was a truthful one."

"But there would have been physicians and servants attending her," said Florynce, "all of whom would have seen her giving birth, and would have been present at her death."

"Think more broadly," said Mother Cassiopeia. "What causes rifts between allies?"

"Money," said Kassra.

"Resources," said Briony.

"Betrayal," said Nasya without thinking.

All eyes suddenly turned to her, and she blushed fiercely.

"Explain what you mean," said Mother Corvus.

"Well..." Nasya said, trying not to stumble over her thoughts and her words, "alliances are made for money, resources, political support, but they aren't usually broken over those same things. Betrayal, whether real or imagined, however, is considered a great grievance between allies."

"What kind of betrayal?" asked Mother Hydra.

Nasya couldn't believe the words that were coming out of her mouth, nor did she know where this knowledge was coming from, but she didn't stop them. "Could be personal or political. One ruler wants the other to help them wage war on a neighboring country, or perhaps one has made a separate allegiance with an enemy of the other, or maybe someone has planted a rumor in the ears of one specifically to unravel the alliance between them. Regardless, even an imagined betrayal is like a backhand to the cheek, and it can be enough to demolish the closest bonds."

The silence that followed the last echo of her voice against the walls of the room was heavy. It loomed over Nasya's head like a beacon. She felt incredibly small and silly as all eyes bored into her. Only Scarlet's was full of love and pride.

"What made you think of all this?" asked Mother Phoenix.

"The histories we read in our first years here," Nasya said, her voice much quieter than it had been. "Gareth the Gallant of house Crescent and Martha the Magnificent of house Evergreen broke a bond that had existed between their two families for nearly a century, and all because of a rumor that was later proven to be nothing more than the idle gossip of servants."

"You remembered all that from your first years of study here?" asked Mother Cassiopeia suspiciously.

Nasya nodded briefly, her gaze cast down to the stone floor.

"What do the rest of you think of Nasya's idea as relates to Utara and Hevean?" asked Mother Lynx.

"It fits, Mother," said Maeve, another recruit.

"Why?" asked Mother Lynx.

"Because Hevean is ripe with rumors, especially as regards the queen. Rumors travel fast. One of them could easily have reached Utara and spread to the King's ears. If it was the right rumor, it could cast a shadow on their alliance."

Silence filled the room once more. Hardly anyone even moved, and Nasya felt as though it would be better to disappear entirely than sit in that heavy, oppressive quiet. A moment later, it ended.

"Nasya's instinct is a good one," said Mother Corvus. "As of yet, no one can quite ascertain what has specifically happened to sour the bond between these two royal families, but there is a great deal of chatter and speculation. This means that when it comes to the political, personal, and even religious states of the countries we live in and move through, we cannot trust in any alliance. They may crumble at a moment's notice, and for seemingly no reason whatsoever. Why is this important to us?"

"Because we have no ties, no alliances, no connections to anyone but ourselves," the recruits said in unison.

"And?" asked Mother Fornax.

"And the atmosphere can change, even as we're in the middle of an assignment," said Scarlet. "But our objective will always remain the same."

The lesson continued, but it was obvious the Mothers were pleased with the discourse. Nasya saw brief looks of pride cast her way by Mother Corvus and Mother Hydra, and it filled her with relief and gratitude. She knew it wasn't enough to change the circumstances around the rest of her struggles, but at the very least, she had proven that she was more than what they observed in their day to day instruction.

The longer the recruits were in training, the more the Mothers had overt influences on the girls. Nasya, being the youngest of them, was also the easiest one to tease, mock, and bully. The first couple of years the girls all got along, but the more they grew and the more they saw how much some of the Mothers despised Nasya, the more their attitudes began to change towards her. Scarlet, Barabella, Florynce, and Ynora were the consistently supportive and encouraging recruits Nasya could count on, but the others slowly pulled away from her. Some of them, anxious to ingratiate themselves to Mother Cassiopeia, went out of their way to make Nasya's existence at Passing's End even more miserable than it was currently. And though the Mothers didn't outright support this behavior, neither did they put an end to it. More than once, Nasya even saw Mother Cassiopeia smile or wink at the girls when they shoved Nasya to the floor or tripped her in training to make it look like she had stumbled.

As the months went on, Nasya found her own growth to be filled with conflict. She wanted, more than almost anything, to prove herself to the Mothers and the other girls, and she worked hard to do so. But time carried with it the deepest truth of her spirit, and she found herself thinking of Terrace and her home more often than before. At times, her feeling of homesickness was so heavy, she had to hide in the privy chamber to cry. She considered running away, sneaking out of the fortress at night and making her way home, but the distance was too far to make on her own. Not to mention, she had no idea which way to go in the first place.

Ultimately, it was her connection with Scarlet that kept her going at Passing's End. She loved her dearly and respected her more than anyone else she'd ever known. Scarlet was her inspiration, her motivation, and her guidance. Nasya never shared with Scarlet her thoughts of leaving, but something told her Scarlet already knew them. It was the way Scarlet's eyes filled with tenderness whenever Nasya was struggling the most, the way she smiled and placed a gentle hand on her own. It was as though she could smell Nasya's internal turmoil. Nasya hadn't known she was capable of so much love until she met Scarlet, and she wasn't prepared to leave that behind, not even if it meant returning to her own family.

# Chapter Eight

*Fortress of Passing's End*

*Country of Utara*

Five years had passed since Nasya had come to Passing's End. Somehow, she managed to keep her position as a recruit. She was thirteen now. Their basic book lessons had been completed, and they advanced to more complicated studies of current and recent social, political, and religious divides. The rest of their training focused on hand to hand combat, the use of different weapons, and more stealth-focused instruction. If they graduated, they would each be given their own profession to use as a cover, a means of building a fake life for themselves as they took on and completed assignments in secret. They might be political advisors in different countries, or servants in prestigious families, or owners of an inn, or any number of identities.

Regardless, they needed to know how to live both lives without calling unwanted attention to either one, and that would take time.

Nasya was still dedicated to her training, but she questioned this devotion more often than she had done before. If it didn't matter how hard she worked, why push herself? Why care? Why try? At best, she was ignored by most Mothers, and at worst she was the primary object of their hate and anger. Even Scarlet's kindness was beginning to lose its sway over her in the shadow of the increasing intensity of training. Where Scarlet's words used to encourage and revitalize her, now they merely added to the tenderness Nasya felt for her friend, but they did not motivate her as they once had.

It didn't help that she was still hearing voices; the one had turned into multiple, and she heard them everywhere in Passing's End, not just the courtyard. What began as voices speaking her name grew into voices calling to her, telling her to run away, asking her to come to them, and myriad other things that made her skin crawl. She knew she needed to tell someone what was happening, but she couldn't bring herself to do so. Not when she felt her position at Passing's End was so precarious. Though she was beginning to think that being rejected from The Order might not be such a horrible idea. It wasn't as though the voices were anything other than voices; she hadn't seen anyone or anything; had only ever heard voices on the wind like echoes in a long hallway. They were distracting and it unnerved her that no one else seemed to hear them and that they only ever spoke to her when she was alone, but aside from that, they posed no threat and caused her no real alarm.

It seemed she had been filled with nothing but conflicting emotions and desires, and she had no idea how to resolve them. She felt as though she was already a burden to the few who supported her and didn't wish to add more to their shoulders. This was something she would carry on her own, regardless of how heavy it became. She could do that much.

Besides, for some weeks now, Scarlet had not seemed like herself. She was pale and tired, and even her smiles of encouragement felt like shadows of her former vivacity. Where before she studied for hours after training, she had, for some time, been going to bed incredibly early, and still every morning she looked as though she hadn't slept at all. Nasya asked her if she was alright, and Scarlet assured her it was just fatigue. Nasya didn't believe her. Every evening when she normally would have been devoted to her own studies, Nasya tended to Scarlet; she grabbed her water, went to the kitchens and fetched cups of broth to give her, drew her hot baths, and made sure she was warm and comfortable. Most of the time, Scarlet was so tired, she noticed very little of what went on around her. It was a good thing too because if she had known how hard Nasya worked to take care of her, she would have put a stop to it. Scarlet hated being fretted over.

But Nasya wasn't about to watch her suffer. Not when she could do some small things that might make her friend more comfortable. Even Mothers Phoenix and Lynx came to check on her periodically. Scarlet was the favorite among the recruits, and the Mothers all worried about the girls getting sick. Being so isolated in the mountains, any physician who could possibly help was days away, and the sick didn't survive. Two recruits had already succumbed to sickness since training had begun, and the Mothers weren't about to let that happen to Scarlet. Surprisingly, they gave Nasya free reign over whatever was needed to ensure Scarlet's full and quick recovery.

However well tended she was, no one knew what ailed her. She had a fever that came and went continuously, sometimes by the hour, and she frequently complained of a headache. These were the only symptoms they perceived, and on their own were not enough to make a diagnosis, or provide specific medication. All they could do was give her tonics to relieve her headache and combat the fever. Mother Hydra did so three times a day, and after a week or so, they started to see improvements. She was awake more often than she was asleep. She could walk around without feeling dizzy. The light didn't make her headache worse. And, after a full three weeks, she began to return to her normal self.

Still, no one knew what had made her ill. The Mothers considered perhaps it had been the food, but when none of the other girls were sick, they decided against it. They thought maybe it had been a prank gone wrong, another recruit slipping something into her drink, but that seemed unlikely. Scarlet was well liked by the other recruits. She had never had any problems in the five years they had been at Passings End. Ultimately, they gave up trying to resolve her mysterious illness. She was on the mend and, so long as she continued to improve, they decided they didn't need to know the cause.

The night sky was clear and dark. There was no moon and the light from the stars was not enough to see by on the dense forest floor. Which was, of course, the lesson: there would not always be the conditions wanted or needed to complete an assignment, but it was still a Sister's responsibility to work through or around the conditions she'd been given.

The darkness was thick and quiet as Nasya ran through the underbrush of the northern woods. She held a compass pointing her westward and, as she ran, she stopped briefly and checked her coordinates. She was still going in the right direction, though she felt she should have come to her marker by now. Unless this was a new navigational course, and one much larger than they'd practiced on earlier that day.

Nasya looked around and listened, breathing steadily to heighten her senses. She could hear hardly anything other than the soft patter of footsteps to her right and left. The other recruits were following the same instructions she had been given, only Nasya was certain they were doing so more successfully.

"Nasya," a voice behind her whispered.

She turned and saw the face of her roommate, Scarlet. Sweat poured down her cheeks. Nasya offered a smile, genuinely glad to see her. For three days, Scarlet had seemed fully recovered from her sickness, and Nasya was relieved. Scarlet motioned with her hands for Nasya to keep going.

"Don't stop," she whispered, coming alongside her.

"I'm not," Nasya said. "Just checking coordinates."

"You're a little too far south," Scarlet said, holding Nasya's hand in her own and moving it so the compass pointed in the actual right direction. "Remember to make sure the compass is pointing to true north or you'll miss the marker entirely."

Nasya's skin tingled at Scarlet's touch. Only thirteen years old, and she was far too aware of what it meant to be starved of human contact. Any and all affection built flutters inside of her and chiseled away at the walls she'd begun to build around herself. Scarlet was the only person who affected her in this way. Nasya wasn't sure if it was because she was her only friend, or if it was because they had gone through these horrible last five years together, but for some time now, Scarlet's touch impacted her in ways she couldn't describe. Scarlet's black skin was almost impossible to see in the nighttime darkness, but Nasya could feel the gentleness seeping into her fingers as though Scarlet was made of nothing but kindness.

"Nasya," she whispered. "Did you hear me?"

Nasya nodded. "Yes, keep true north." She grinned. "If you know which way to go, why are you down here?"

Scarlet smiled. "To keep an eye on you, of course. Now hurry, before they see you've stopped."

And with that, Scarlet scurried off into the night, disappearing behind the trees.

Nasya let out a deep breath. Her head swam and her focus was jarred. Scarlet was different for Nasya. Special. It was a kind of kinship she couldn't explain, and after Nasya had tended her through her mysterious illness, she felt even more bonded to her. It was not only friendship she felt now, but something stronger, deeper, more urgent. She hoped Scarlet felt the same way for her, but didn't know how to ask, nor did she know what it was she would be asking. She also didn't want to risk losing her only friend by imposing her own feelings onto their friendship.

This was their first full night away from Passing's End. That morning, they had been given satchels with flasks of water and some small rations of food, a compass, and a map of the landscape around Passing's End. They were to hike all the way to their navigation training course, and they had to do so before nightfall, or else would be forced to start the process over. During the day, navigation had been simple. Most of the recruits had made the hike in five to six hours. The terrain through the woods had been mostly downhill coming from the mountain fortress, and being early autumn, the weather had been clear.

Once they had all arrived at the course, for no one had been sent to start over, they were allowed to eat as the Mothers explained what they would be doing throughout the night.

"There is a series of markers positioned in these woods. Your job is to use your compass to find them," Mother Lynx had explained.

"It will be dark tonight. You will have nothing but your compasses and maps to guide you. The markers are identified on your maps by different coordinates," said Mother Cassiopeia. "You will have until sunrise to find every marker."

Nasya let out two slow, deep breaths to try and steady her pulse. She was having a hard time focusing. She had made the hike from Passings End in a little over six hours, and as of now had found two of the seven markers identified on her map. At this pace, she knew she would not complete the exercise before dawn, and that filled her with dread. Her focused breathing was the simplest task, the one meant to keep her grounded, steady, and even that she struggled to do. It was as though something in her body and mind filled her with an energy she couldn't control. It was an odd sensation that made her palms sweat and her heart race. She gave herself two moments of breathing, and then shot back into the forest. This was not something she could afford to fail. It wasn't just a matter of completing the course, it was also how she completed it, and in what kind of time.

"Nasya..."

She gasped and stumbled over her feet for a moment, but did not stop running. This voice was not Scarlet's. It was one of the many she pretended to no longer hear, only she hadn't expected it out on the navigation course. She had never heard it or any other voices outside of the fortress.

Until now.

Ghosts haunted specific places. Rooms. Buildings. Landmarks. Even individual items. She had read about them a great deal in the last few years, curious as to how to make the voices stop without needing to go to the Mothers for help. And while she hadn't found any solutions to the voices she heard, the research had afforded a lot of helpful information in understanding different forms of hauntings.

But none of what she read had prepared her for this. Ghosts didn't travel away from the places they haunted. And that could only mean the voices she heard weren't ghosts at all. It was an odd revelation, but she wondered if, perhaps, it was something reaching out to her? This time, it felt less like she was being called *to* and more like she was being called *for*. The way her heart continued to quicken, how her hands grew clammy and her mouth was suddenly very dry, indicated an urgency akin to the expectation that she should respond...somehow. There was something thick behind the voice, something unexpected and veiled in mystery. She had heard this voice several times over the last year in varying degrees of intensity. She had dreamt of the voice, even, always only seconds away from seeing their face, but never quite able to make the connection.

And now it called to her at a time when she most needed to concentrate. She couldn't afford to be distracted. What if, after all the confusion and fear, this was still just a ruse created by the Mothers to get under her skin? Test her dedication to The Order? Challenge her? What if that was why the voice was now reaching out to her outside of Passing's End? It didn't seem likely, but she couldn't deny that it was a possibility. She told herself to stay focused, to use her anger as energy, to remember her breathing, and to push through every distraction, whether internal or external.

A moment later, everything changed. The voice, which had never been louder than a harsh whisper, suddenly began to shout her name over and over, ringing shrill in her ears.

"Nasya! Nasya! Nasya!"

It was a piercing cry that sounded as though many voices were screeching all at once. As the voices grew louder, the forest around her began to change. She saw eyes staring at her from the darkness. She saw faces appearing in the leaves of the trees and in the shrubs and logs on the forest floor. Her heart was racing faster than it had ever beat before. Somehow, she managed not to cry out, not to scream. Somehow, she managed to keep planting one foot in front of the other.

She looked down at her compass and saw she had been running in the wrong direction again. She adjusted her course, found true north, let out a shaky breath, and forced herself to continue. She had to be close to the marker now. Just a few more yards.

It was only then that she heard the sound of heavy feet behind her. She looked over her shoulder and saw three beings running towards her, but they weren't other recruits or the Mothers. There was something ominous about them, something she strained her eyes to see.

"You belong to us, Nasya!" they said in unison, and it sounded as though she was surrounded by voices, people, beings.

She stopped running and scanned the trees and forest for anything familiar, anything safe. She was shaking. Partly from exhaustion, but mostly from the terror that took hold of her body. Whatever the Mothers were trying to accomplish, it was working. 'This isn't the Mothers,' she thought, and she immediately knew it to be true. This was something altogether new and otherworldly. As she stood facing the shadows following her, the forest continued to morph into something unrecognizable. Hands reached out of trees. Eyes and faces appeared against the dirt, the leaves, the boulders. Things seemed to climb out of the very ground. They all said her name over and over. The eyes moved in her direction. The hands extended towards her, reaching, grabbing, trying to get as close to her as possible.

Nasya scrambled away, but everything around her metamorphosed. Nothing was safe. She crawled on her hands and knees, practically going in circles to try and escape as every plant, every leaf, every patch of moss changed form and came to life, laughing, wheezing, calling her name on an endless loop. It was as though the forest was shrinking around her, closing in, eliminating the space between her and utter chaos. Nasya put her hands over her ears and tucked her knees under her chin.

"What do you want from me?" she shouted, feeling long tendrils of tree bark playing at her hair and brushing her skin.

They laughed.

"Why do you keep calling to me?"

They laughed louder.

"It is not us who call to you," they hissed. "It is you who calls us."

"Nasya!" another voice shouted, snapping the girl back to

reality.

With only a few blinks, the forest went back to what it had been before. No fingers. No faces. She was crouched in a small glen. Before her was Mother Cassiopeia, eyes wide and filled with anger. Nasya's head swam. She retched into the dirt. She felt as though her heart would explode inside her chest, she was breathing so heavily. Sweat ran down her face and soaked her clothes. She tried to ignore the exhaustion of her body and stand up quickly, but her legs felt like liquid and she collapsed to the ground again.

"What in the fucking name of - " said Mother Cassiopeia, but Mother Hydra cut her off as she came into view.

"That will do, Mother Cassiopeia."

Nasya didn't know from where she'd come in the darkness, or how she'd gotten there so quickly.

"I...tried...to focus," Nasya said between heaving breaths. "Tried...to ignore...the illusions..."

Mother Hydra frowned. "Illusions?"

Nasya nodded. "The ones...you sent...to distract me." She didn't know why she said the words when she knew they hadn't been illusions, but something in her mind wasn't ready to accept that fact yet. Something in her needed the Mothers to confirm what she knew to be the truth.

"Those did not come from us, and they weren't illusions," said Mother Phoenix.

The other Mothers and recruits came into view, and they all stared at Nasya with wide eyes. Nasya frowned. "I...don't understand..."

"They came from you, fledgling," Mother Corvus said as she stared at her with eyes so penetrating, Nasya was sure the woman could see her very organs. "Or rather, you awakened them."

Nasya shook her head. This wasn't happening. Couldn't be happening. Tears streamed down her cheeks and her body shook with violent convulsions. "S-Sc-Scar...let..." she said, turning to find her friend, desperate for comfort.

She couldn't see Scarlet anywhere.

"It seems our most problematic pupil contains magic," said Mother Lynx.

Nasya could no longer speak. Her body had not recovered from whatever had just happened. She still could not stand and remained on her hands and knees, sucking in large breaths of air. Her stomach churned and she retched again and again until she could only dry heave against the pressure in her gut. It couldn't be true, what they were saying. She couldn't have magic. She didn't. She was just a girl, barely more than a child still.

"Regulate your breathing!" Mother Cassiopeia snapped.

"I am trying, Mother," Nasya sputtered, her vision blurry and dark around the edges. She felt she would pass out.

By now, Mother Cassiopeia was only a foot from Nasya. She swung her hand and slapped the thirteen year old across the face.

"You know I despise that word!" Mother Cassiopeia exclaimed.

"It's hard, Mother," Nasya found herself saying.

She didn't know why she'd spoken, but she could not unsay the words. She watched as anger turned to fury in Mother Cassiopeia's eyes.

"Hard?" Mother Cassiopeia said. "You think remembering a simple breathing technique is hard?"

"Mother Cassiopeia," said mother Corvus, "now is not the time for this!"

But Mother Corvus was ignored. Mother Cassiopeia brought up her leg and kicked Nasya in the chest. She fell backwards, barely catching herself on her hands. "*Try* remembering your breathing techniques as you're facing off with your opponent!" Mother Cassiopeia said, kicking her again. "*Try* remembering to regulate your breathing when a man is forcing himself into you!"

Nasya choked on her need for air as she crawled away from Mother Cassiopeia, but she couldn't put enough distance between them to miss Mother Cassiopeia's boots. Each blow to her chest was like fire in an already infected wound.

"Please, stop," she said, her voice raspy from the lack of air.

"Mother Cassiopeia!" shouted Mother Hydra.

"Begging will not save your life when you fuck up an assignment! When your target waits for you! When it is you against a fleet of soldiers! When they take turns raping you over and over and over!" Mother Cassiopeia shouted, continuing to berate and beat the child.

By now, all of the other Mothers stood and watched as one of their own went after the youngest girl and, to their eyes, moved with the intention of utterly breaking her. It was true that Mother Cassiopeia's dislike for Nasya was well known, but this had unraveled the usually stoic woman. The other recruits wanted to step in and help, but none wanted to risk facing Mother Cassiopeia's wrath. And Nasya still could find no trace of Scarlet.

"You've been here for how long and have not improved? It's exactly girls like you who endanger our entire existence! And in the end, it will not be you who pays the price for your incompetence!"

"Stop," Nasya said, her hands shaking from the adrenaline and rush of emotions coursing through her veins.

"You are a waste of time and instruction. You do not deserve our dedication, our experience. You aren't worth a fraction of what we paid for you!"

"Mother Cassiopeia, that is enough!" exclaimed Mother Corvus.

"Is it any wonder your parents so easily parted with you?"

"Mother Cassiopeia!" shouted Mother Phoenix.

"Even they could see they were getting a better deal!" Mother Cassiopeia said, raising her hand to strike Nasya again.

"I told you to stop!" Nasya screamed, rage suddenly overcoming her fear and exhaustion.

Everything slowed. Her breathing and heartbeat steadied. She stared at Mother Cassiopeia as the woman's hand swung in the air. Nasya sucked in a deep breath, her muscles beginning to tingle. She let out a scream, keeping her eyes always on Mother

Cassiopeia. It was a high pitched cry that reached from the depths of Nasya's very essence, and carried out across the woods, shaking the branches, bursting out against every living thing. The Mothers and the recruits covered their ears. In the distance, Nasya thought she heard the sound of a wolf howling, and it only made her scream louder.

Suddenly, her ribs felt as though they were being stretched inside of her body. Heat emanated underneath her skin and in a single second, two enormous wings released from her back, covered in black, luminescent feathers. In the next second, several large feathers shot from the wings towards Mother Cassiopeia. Everything seemed to work slowly. Nasya watched as the black of the feathers shifted, turning to sharp blades of steel in midair. The older woman ducked quickly, the blades barely missing her.

Nasya didn't even realize what she'd done at first. It was as though she was suddenly two people, a little girl too tired to stand, and another who carried wings in her back. And yet, she knew she was both simultaneously. The wings were hers. They had always been hers. She turned and looked over her shoulder at them. They were enormous, both of them as large as her, and heavy. She looked around and saw the faces of the Mothers, the faces of her fellow recruits, and she felt a surge of emotions all at once. Fear was the first to land in her temples. It sent a thunderous chill down her spine, erasing every other emotion, every other feeling.

Her eyes eventually landed on Mother Cassiopeia who stood still, her eyes wide. Hot tears fell down Nasya's cheeks. It took only a few seconds for her to realize that she had very nearly killed Mother Cassiopeia. Her body trembled violently as the fear overtook her entirely.

"Wh-what...what's happening to me?"

Mother Cassiopeia moved towards her slowly now.

"You are of the fae," she said, reaching out and running her hands along the feathers.

Nasya felt her touch and started, stumbling backwards. It was the most intense sensation she had ever felt. It reached from the feathers down into the hollow bones that stretched from her back, as though Mother Cassiopeia had dipped her fingers into the bones themselves. But it was more than touch; as Mother Cassiopeia's fingers slid along the almost fabric-like feathers, Nasya's mouth filled with the taste of dirt and sweat, and something she thought was moss. Her nostrils filled with the smell of lavender, the scent of Mother Cassiopeia's body oil. And she suddenly could hear the rhythm of her heartbeat, its pace and its speed, its strength. It happened in seconds, her body overwhelmed by the influx of her senses, and all from a mere second of contact between her new wings and Mother Cassiopeia's long fingers.

"Th-these are p-part of me?" Nasya whispered.

She was shivering now as her body readjusted to the cool temperature of the midnight forest. And though her surroundings had settled into something resembling peacefulness, everything within her screamed not to trust it. It was a trick. It had to be. A cruel trick designed to torture her, confuse her, pain her.

But Nasya knew this wasn't true. Not when she saw the eerie calmness that had settled over Mother Cassiopeia, something that she had never seen before.

"They are not *part* of you, child. They *are* you."

Mother Cassiopeia looked into Nasya's eyes and stared. She said nothing, but Nasya felt distinctly that this meant so much more than it seemed. And for the first time, she felt as though Mother Cassiopeia saw her; instead of looking to criticize, there was something behind her eyes that made Nasya feel acknowledged. She felt understood.

"Mother Hydra shall be responsible for your training from now on." Mother Corvus said from her left.

Mother Hydra stepped forward. "You and I will leave this place tomorrow morning."

"L...leave? Where?"

"Teaching you here is no longer safe. We must go where you can train in a place equipped to handle magic. You and I will leave for the fortress of Fire's Hearth, high up in the mountains."

Nasya looked around her and met the eyes of the other recruits. She couldn't tell if they were envious, or if they pitied her. She didn't know which one was better, which one she wanted them to feel the most. She searched desperately for Scarlet, anxious to know that at least with her, things would remain the same. Scarlet was her only confidant, her only companion. It took nearly two glances at the faces around her before she spotted her. She stood almost completely behind the others, nearly out of sight. Her face was pale and her cheeks sunken. She looked ill again and Nasya's heart thudded with worry but she did as she was bid, wanting more than anything to speak to Scarlet. The other girls would be starting the training course over. They would continue what Nasya had unintentionally interrupted while she packed her few belongings.

Mother Hydra opened a portal with magic, allowing them to return to the castle in mere moments instead of hours. She gave Nasya a bowl of hot broth once she had packed her things, and taught her to retract her wings.

"They are you and you are them," Mother Hydra said. "When you want them to expand, they will, like they did tonight when you accessed your magic for the first time. Likewise, when you want them to retract back into your body, they will."

Nasya couldn't understand how such large wings fit inside her tiny frame, and yet when she thought about them folding up and retreating inside of her, they did just that, leaving no trace behind. She started to ask questions, but Mother Hydra cut her off.

"You need to sleep. You've had a taxing evening. We will talk on our journey to Fire's Hearth, and I will answer your questions."

She then told her to get as much sleep as she could. They would be leaving after the morning meal. But she wasn't able to sleep. Not after the night she'd had. Not after everything she'd seen and heard and felt. Her body hummed with heat and weight and an energy she couldn't possibly control. She wanted to run, to feel the wind in her hair and on her arms.

No.

She wanted to fly.

Nasya didn't get to see Scarlet before she and Mother Hydra left for Fire's Hearth. None of the recruits had returned from their night navigation course, and Mother Hydra wasn't going to wait around for them. Nasya wanted to insist that she be allowed to say goodbye to her friend, but she was still too overwhelmed by the happenings of the night before to ask for much. Instead, she contented herself with leaving a written note for Scarlet on her bedside table. It was brief, but honest. She thanked Scarlet for her ever consistent friendship and kindness, expressed her deepest and most heartfelt love and respect for her, and then asked that she write to her while she was away. She signed her name and pressed a kiss to the parchment before leaving the room.

Mother Hydra and Nasya ate their morning meal in the dining hall. Neither spoke. Nasya knew the focused look on Mother Hydra's face well. It meant that she was in no mood to be interrupted or spoken to. Nasya had many questions, but she decided to wait until they were well on their way before bringing them up. Once the two had completed their meal, they packed their belongings into a carriage and began the journey to the fortress that lay even deeper inside the mountain pass. Fire's Hearth was said to be one of the oldest fortresses in the world. It had been built centuries before by the fae as a place for people to study magic and learn to wield it.

The morning passed slowly. Nasya stared out the window of the carriage, her mind and heart heavy with feelings she didn't know how to process. Everything she knew about herself was now different. She could feel it. Her mind was more open than it had ever been and her body was charged with an energy that smelled of pine trees. She could feel these changes in every thought, in every movement, in every inhale and exhale. It was as though something deep inside of her body was slithering to the surface, biding its time, waiting to consume her entirely. It frightened her.

It had been several hours of their journey when Mother Hydra finally spoke. "Last night, did you understand what was meant when we said you are of the fae?"

Nasya shook her head. Her heart began racing. She wasn't sure if she was ready for these answers yet, wasn't sure she could handle their weight.

"It means you have fae blood in your veins."

"My parents were both human," Nasya said, unsure how she could be part fae when neither of her parents had ever exemplified resemblance to them.

Mother Hydra nodded slowly. "The man and woman we bought you from were both human, yes." She looked at Nasya with an intense stare. "But...they may not have been your actual parents."

Nasya frowned. "I don't understand."

The older woman bit her lower lip and sighed. "Typically when these things occur, the magic comes in smaller bursts, indicating that the connection to the fae is many generations back in the family line. It may not even manifest in every generation, going dormant so to speak, until it finally does manifest in a member of the same bloodline." Mother Hydra turned her eyes towards Nasya, their hazel color not breaking contact with Nasya's gaze. "But your burst last night wasn't small at all. In fact, I think it's one of the greatest amounts of magic I've ever seen come from someone of your age."

Nasya didn't respond, but the words spoken to her made the hair on the back of her neck stand on end.

"The amount of fae blood needed to manifest power like that is..." she shook her head, "frankly, astronomical."

Still, Nasya did not speak. Tears stung her eyes. Not only was her very existence completely different from everything she'd previously believed, but now the people she thought of as family were, more than likely, not her family at all. How was she to reconcile these revelations? What was she to think? To feel? To do?

"What I'm saying is that the people who raised you could not have been your real parents, fledgling. You are, at least, half fae."

Nasya raised her eyebrows. "Half?"

"At least. You most likely are not full fae; you don't have long, pointy ears and you've clearly only just come into your magical abilities, whereas full-blooded fae are born already able to do magic. But the amount of fae blood in you is potent. The wings alone are evidence of that much."

"What...what does this mean?" Nasya asked. "Am I still going to be a Hand of the Order?"

"If we can teach you to control your powers and access them at will, then yes, I believe so. But, Nasya, you must understand that this magic you possess is no little thing. You could very well be the most powerful member The Order has seen in decades. Even centuries."

Nasya's head began to swim. Her vision was blurry. Her heart was still racing. This was beyond anything she had anticipated.

"I do not understand. You have magic too, Mother?"

"Yes, but I was taught to use it. You were born with it." Mother Hydra adjusted her sitting position so that she was leaning forward with her elbows on her knees. "I am what is known as a Mage, a mortal being with the ability to access the magic of this world. I had to be taught how to access magic, how to harness it, and how to control myself while under its influence. The fae *are* magic. It is inherent. They are not taught how to access it, but rather how to control what already exists inside of them. That is the power you have, and it is very different from my own."

Nasya shook her head. "But I thought you were going to teach me?"

Mother Hydra sighed, a faint smile tugging at the corners of her lips. "I am, yes. But I will be teaching you how to use the magic you already possess, powers you were born with. More than anything, I will be teaching you how to control what flows through you. More bursts like the one last night could prove fatal to yourself or those around you."

A chill went down Nasya's spine. "Fatal? I could accidentally kill someone?"

She nodded. "It has happened before. You do not yet know your own strength or abilities. Right now, your magic is fueled by emotion. We need you to learn to recognize when you're nearing the zenith, and reel yourself back before you tip over the edge."

"What's...what's the zenith?"

Mother Hydra looked out the window. "The point when so much magic is flowing through someone, that it permanently alters their physical makeup. This almost always results in death for the person wielding magic, and can mean death for anyone near them." She let out a shaky breath. "It is to be avoided at all costs, fledgling."

They both fell into a thoughtful silence, neither of them willing to expand on the words that had already been spoken. It was now that Nasya understood why so many people turned to prayer in their darkest moments. She wished that she believed in a deity, any deity, so that there was someone who might ease her fear and dread.

# Chapter Nine

*Capital City of Sun River*
  *Country of Utara*

Sun River was only four miles from Terrace. Nasya had walked the distance in one day as the terrain was flat and easy. It was also a well-frequented route both into and out of the capital, which meant it was clear of debris and well maintained. The city sat on a hill overlooking the rest of the valley and could be seen from the streets of Terrace.

Sun River was vast and bustling with activity. Many people had left their homes in smaller towns and come to the city hoping for a brighter future. And under normal circumstances, this would have been possible, but considering how many people were moving to the capital en masse, the brighter futures were looking dimmer and dimmer. The town square was littered with merchants of all kinds selling their goods, none of whom were making much money. In fact, most fared no better here than they had in the smaller towns and villages, for even though there were more customers, the importance of the city meant higher living costs and, due to the volume of people flocking to it, a shortage of space. However, the ball that night meant an increase in wealthy visitors, and everyone was hoping to make a little extra money as guests arrived.

Nasya walked slowly through the town square, eyes scanning everyone and everything. Where she had stood out in her hometown, she now blended in. Her clothing was clean and well kept, but plain. She looked as though she was nothing more than the daughter of one of the merchants, or a merchant herself looking for a stall to set up. Of course, she had also been trained in the art of avoiding attention, even when in plain sight. It was necessary in her line of work to access important places and people without detection. And today was her only chance to observe the city and its occupants before the masquerade that evening.

As she wandered the square, she listened to the chatter among the citizens. King Tavin was hosting an extravagant ball, one he could not afford, presumably to honor his youngest son, Prince Xaran's, twenty-fifth birthday. Most considered this to be a ruse for King Tavin to invite as many wealthy guests as he could to try and raise funding for his continued war with Hevean. It was well known that the war had not only cost an enormous amount of money, but was also an absolute failure. Whatever had been his reasons for declaring war in the first place, they no longer satisfied his citizens. If they ever had.

"He says the war is to free Hevean's slaves," said one merchant.

The woman he spoke to who ran the cart next to him, snorted. "They 'aven't 'ad slaves in decades. It's one of the few good things the queen 'as accomplished in her reign."

"This is clearly King Tavin's attempt to secure a marriage between his eldest son and the Princess of Hevean...oh, what's her name..." said the first.

"Sadie," replied the second and they both laughed.

"Right. The one no one can remember."

"The one no one 'as seen in ages. I 'eard she was locked in a tower or somethin'."

"Wouldn't surprise me, what with all that kerfuffle about the Queen being jealous of her beauty and all that."

Another merchant joined into the conversation.

"Didn't the queen keep the princess from marrying? Sent her beau off to war?"

The other two shrugged and the third nodded his head. "Yeah, I'm pretty sure I heard somethin' about it. Beau was a knight, I think, and the queen had him killed."

"Wouldn't surprise me," said the second merchant, "though why she keeps the Princess so close to 'ome is a mystery. 'Specially if she's jealous of 'er."

"I dunno," said the first. "Hard to say what really goes on with royal folk."

"What I don't understand is why the queen of Hevean don't just attack Utara and take out the king," said the third.

The other two shushed him loudly.

"You want to lose your 'ead?" cried the second.

It would be best for Utara, Nasya thought to herself as she hovered around the carts, taking in as much information as she could. It was not uncommon for royals to get themselves into wars they had no business fighting. But something was different about this one, something that piqued Nasya's interest. Perhaps it was how long the war had gone on. Or perhaps it was King Tavin's lack of transparency with his people regarding why he continued to wage the war against. Regardless, it didn't make sense, and that was something Nasya couldn't ignore.

The Order had always been knowledgeable regarding the wars and skirmishes throughout the world. It was a necessary part of The Order's very existence, keeping track of all polit-ical proceedings and using them to their advantage. But King Tavin's justifications for the war and the continued increase of taxes was odd to everyone. Why couldn't he simply strike a treaty with the queen of Hevean? What compelled him to keep fighting a war he didn't have the money to fund, especially when he had been losing for some time? And what kept the queen from attacking, as one of the merchants had suggested?

# Interlude: Kyndra

*Kyndra stood at the entrance to the dining hall, her eyes wide with disbelief. Ygritte, one of the other recruits, was crouched down on her hands and knees, crying, screaming, begging for Rhaean to stop. And Rhaean...if Kyndra had not been told that she was in trouble, she wouldn't have recognized her own daughter. She was floating in midair. Her dark curls had turned a deathly white. Her eyes were completely black except for the bright orange pupils at the center. Underneath her skin moved fractals of light, presumably pumping through her veins with each heart beat.*

*"Scarlet!" Rhaean screamed. "Scarlet! Where is Scarlet? Bring her to me!"*

*Kyndra's heart panged. Scarlet was no longer in training. She had not improved enough, had not retained enough of her training to maintain her position. She and Rhaean had been very close, and now the pain of losing her friend was sending her over the edge into something Kyndra didn't know how to face. She didn't know what to do, or if there was anything she could do. From beside her, the recruit who had burst into her room was pleading with her to do something. And though she knew there was little chance of stopping what was taking over her daughter's body, she had to try.*

*She stepped forward and began to call to Rhaean, her voice gentle at first. Soon, she was speaking in an unnaturally loud voice. It was deep and raspy.*

*"Rhaean, daughter of Kyndra, be still!"*

*The girl stared at her and smiled wickedly. It sent a chill down Kyndra's spine. "You have come at last," Rhaean said, in a voice not her own, "I wondered when you would."*

*"You are in pain, my child," Kyndra said as she moved towards her, "but I can help you. You just must stop this madness."*

*Rhaean laughed. "This madness is the only thing bringing your daughter comfort."*

*Kyndra's legs began to tremble. Something foreign had taken over her daughter's body, mind, spirit. Something malevolent and bitter. Did it know the danger it posed for her and everyone else in the fortress? Was that, perhaps, its intentions?*

*"What can I do to convince you to let my daughter alone?"*

*Rhaean laughed again, her voice dipping very low and then raising high to something akin to a screech. "Your daughter does not want to be let alone, Mother Andromeda," the voice said mockingly.*

*"She has been crying out for her friend," Kyndra retorted, "not you!"*

*"She has been crying out for weeks, and I am the only one who has listened!"*

*Around them, the flames that lit the torches of the dining hall and the fires in the two hearths at either side of the hall blazed even more strongly. Kyndra knew what was happening, and if it didn't stop, this being would use Rhaean to destroy the fortress and everyone in it. She had to think fast.*

*"You're right," Kyndra said, moving forward ever so slowly. "No one else has listened to her. I tried, but it was not enough." The dark eyes that had replaced Rhaean's stared down at Kyndra. "I failed. I tried telling the council, I tried convincing them to leave, but they did not heed my words. And instead of pushing the issue, I dropped it. I was wrong. So very wrong. But I'm here now, my darling. I can take you away from this place."*

*As she spoke to her daughter and the spirit within her, Kyndra had been casting a spell over the fortress. It was a wordless spell cast only with the use of very specific movements of her fingers, which she hid behind her back. She hoped Ygritte could see what she was doing and join in. It would make the spell stronger, more effective.*

*Rhaean laughed again. Her body lit up with more orange light beneath her skin. "You think you can make a little promise after everything and she will just forgive you?"*

*"Give her a chance," Kyndra said. "Let her choose for herself."*

*"You do not understand, Mother Andromeda, Kyndra of the western ocean. I see into your daughter's mind, heart, and soul. I know her desires, her secrets. I know her better than she knows herself, and I see the truth." She stared down at Kyndra, eyes wide and filled with anger and hatred. "I am not the malevolent one he re."*

# Chapter Ten

*Fortress of Fire's Hearth*
*Country of Utara*

As she and Mother Hydra made their way down from the heights of one of the mountain passes, the building came into view. Nasya counted nine different wings in total, and more than half of them were in ruins. It looked as though it had been abandoned and unused for decades. Yet, as they approached, Nasya began to see something in the air around it, something that almost looked like a shimmer of some kind. Mother Hydra saw her squinting out of the carriage window.

"What you see are the smallest indications of the wards around the fortress. They are invisible to anyone without the ability to use or access magic, and to the likes of you and I, they let off a golden shimmer in the daylight and silver at night," she had said.

"Why are there wards around the fortress?" Nasya asked. "It's already treacherous enough to get there."

"This place is different than Passing's End," Mother Hydra said. "Fire's Hearth was built to contain magic and to maximize its effects. As such, there is a power here that must be protected. The wards are strong and it would take time to unlock them. And only then could someone who is unwanted here gain access to the fortress itself."

Nasya nodded slowly. "Then the wards are a kind of magical moat, so to speak, intended to keep unwanted people out?"

Mother Hydra nodded as they pulled into the courtyard. "Yes, essentially. Although they have, at times, been used to keep things inside of the fortress, too."

Nasya cocked her head to the side. "I don't understand. What could possibly need to be kept inside the fortress?"

A haze clouded Mother Hydra's eyes. She averted her gaze away from Nasya and looked out the carriage window. She was quiet. Introspective. Reminiscent. She cleared her throat and blinked twice. "Magic is unpredictable, fledgling. It has been known to...make things happen that are unexpected and, potentially, dangerous. Sometimes the things it does, creates, or awakens must be contained for everyone's safety."

It was all she said. And Nasya wasn't about to press for any more information. When the carriage finally stopped at the center of the courtyard, Nasya stepped into the cold air and looked up at the tall towers of the fortress. It was covered in snow and ice. The windows were dark. The courtyard itself was quiet. No birds or other sounds of wildlife were heard. It was strange for the forest around the palace to be so quiet, even in the middle of winter.

"Why are there no birds?" she asked.

Mother Hydra had already walked up to the large, double doors of the entrance. She turned at Nasya's question, looked around at the sky above them, and then turned her gaze back towards the twelve year-old.

"The wards keep out every unwanted being, including animals. In the past, birds and squirrels and even mice have been used as a means of breaching secure buildings. The earliest members of The Order didn't want to risk this. When they cast the wards, they ensured that absolutely nothing that wasn't already approved would get into this courtyard." She opened one of the large, metal doors. "Come."

Nasya followed her inside. It was dark in the foyer, though it was midday and the pale, gray light of the winter afternoon shone brightly in the courtyard. She followed Mother Hydra through the foyer, up a short flight of stairs, and into a large room lined with torches and candles. Mother Hydra gave a single snap of her fingers and they came to life with flames.

"This is the training room," she said. "It holds an extra layer of wards around it to ensure the safety and the integrity of the building against anything that might happen in here."

"Like what?" Nasya asked.

Mother Hydra looked at her and a similar haze crossed over her eyes. "You are a fae just now stepping into your full magical power. You do not yet know your full strength, nor how to control it. Whether intentional or not, you could unleash potentially fatal magic and, however capable I am, I may not be able to intervene. The wards ensure that any damage from this room is minimal to the fortress and surrounding nature."

Fear creeped up Nasya's spine. "Am...Am I really that dangerous?"

"You might be. There's no way of knowing until we start training."

Their first weeks in the fortress were spent acclimating Nasya to the power of her newly manifested abilities. Mother Hydra led her through several different meditative exercises to try and ascertain how many different abilities she possessed. Could she wield fire? Wind? Any of the other elements? Did she possess psychic abilities? Could she levitate objects? Turn herself invisible? Shapeshift? If a fae had ever presented a certain kind of magic, Mother Hydra tested it against Nasya's skills, and to no avail. She could see nothing of the primary arcane in her at all.

When they weren't working on magic, she continued what lessons she would have been learning at Passing's End. For the first time since she had come to The Order, Nasya began to make real progress. Mother Hydra explained that repressed magic in the quantities she possessed was likely taking up enormous reserves of energy, making even the smallest of tasks like reading and memorization far more difficult than they otherwise would have been. Those words filled Nasya with a vindication she could almost taste. It had never been her fault; she wasn't a failure; it had always been entirely outside of her control. She wished she could see the look on Mother Cassiopeia's face when that realization struck.

Nasya's progress was so swift, that in only a matter of months, she was actually ahead of the learning schedule for the recruits at Passing's End. She passed the night navigation course, she passed her hand-to-hand combat forms, and she passed every test of knowledge she was given. Mother Hydra's pride and excitement were easy to see, and Nasya reveled in it. She wished she could see the look on Scarlet's face when she saw how much she had improved.

But there were other changes that emerged as they spent more time at Fire's Hearth. The awakening of her magic had removed whatever physical and mental barriers had held her back in her studies, but they had also opened her up to dreams even more vivid than she'd had in years prior. Almost from the first week, Nasya began to sleepwalk. She had never done so before. At first, she would find herself awake, standing in her own room near the hearth. She didn't know if she had gone anywhere else in the palace and then come back, or if she had simply climbed from bed and stood still, but it happened often enough that she told

Mother Hydra of it.

The look in her eyes as she listened was alarming to Nasya.

"Is...Is that...abnormal?" she asked.

"Not entirely," Mother Hydra replied, "but it is worrisome."

"Why worrisome?" Nasya asked.

"There's no telling what kind of spells you might accidentally cast," she said, looking away from Nasya, her eyebrows scrunched together.

"Magic can be cast in one's sleep?" Nasya asked. "It doesn't require consciousness?"

Mother Hydra shook her head. "Not in someone who is of fae blood. We must be careful."

"What will you do?" Nasya asked, her heart racing.

"I will have to think about it," was all the response she gave.

This was not exactly comforting. Her young mind understood that Mother Hydra wouldn't have the immediate answer to every question or problem, but she didn't understand how one as experienced as her could have worked with magic for so long and never seen someone sleepwalk because of it. Moreover, it was particularly concerning learning that she could accidentally cast magic in her sleep and wreak havoc on the fortress.

"Isn't there something you can do to control the magic while I'm asleep?" she asked.

Mother Hydra gave her a strange look. She was thinking deeply. "Such things have been tried before," she said after several moments, "but I'm not sure they're successful enough to be worth the time. Repressing magic, even temporarily, in one born to wield it carries its own dangers."

Nasya's fear grew. "So I shall exist as a danger to myself and everyone around me until I learn to control my powers?"

Mother Hydra looked at her, eyes wide with a mixture of amusement and compassion. "Oh fledgling, you are already a danger to yourself and everyone around you and you will become even more dangerous still. You must get accustomed to this knowledge if you're to succeed."

The weeks passed and Nasya still awoke in the middle of the night and found herself standing in her room. It didn't happen more than once a week, but it was enough to make Nasya unnerved and anxious. Mother Hydra gave her a strong sleeping concoction to try and limit the sleepwalking, and it worked for a time.

Nearly four months passed and Nasya never once awoke standing up. And though she was relieved, there was a look in Mother Hydra's eyes that told Nasya she was not as satisfied. Whatever still worried her, she kept to herself.

The smell of ash filled her nostrils. She could see nothing. She could hear nothing. She stretched out her hands to find her way, and met only air. But the smell of ash and something burning was overwhelming. It filled her lungs and she began to cough. It seemed hours passed in total darkness. She tried moving, lifting her feet to take a step or two, but her foot caught on something and she tripped. She landed on her hands and knees and suddenly, an orange light engulfed her.

She looked up but her vision was too blurry to see anything beyond dark silhouettes against an orange sky. And always, the smell of burning and ash and death. She didn't know where she was but something rang in the back of her mind to get up, to get to her feet, to move quickly. She tried to steady her breathing. It was difficult with the ash filling the air, but she eventually managed to find her breath and her vision steadied. She stood to her feet. She was in a fortress made of stone stained black. Somewhere, there was a fire. She could hear screams and her heart stalled in her chest.

"Scarlet," she whispered.

She turned and looked around frantically. Something was wrong. Where was Scarlet? She tried calling for her, but her voice was muffled. She stumbled around, still unable to see very clearly, and tried to orient herself. She heard someone shouting and she tried shouting back, but she couldn't even understand her own words.

Suddenly, a bright light flashed in front of her and a woman's voice called out, "You will not take another step!"

"Where is Scarlet?" she heard herself scream and suddenly she was filled with immense anger.

A staff made of obsidian swung in her direction, a blue light glowing through it from top to bottom. Something wrapped around her hands. She tried to pull herself free, but the grip was too tight. She growled.

"Let me go, you fiend!" she shouted.

Her wings unfurled and she began to flap. The staff swung at her again and something wrapped around her ankles.

"I said let me go!" she shrieked, her voice suddenly high pitched and scratchy.

"Nasya!" the person wielding the staff shouted, "Nasya, stop this!" Her voice was pleading, full of panic.

"Bring her to me!" she screamed, "Bring Scarlet to me!" She wrestled against her bindings, but they were strong. The smell of ash and scorched stone was stronger now.

"Nasya, wake up! Please, you must wake up!"

Light formed under her skin. A fire burning from the inside out. It might break her free of her bindings, so she focused on it and it grew in heat as well as illumination.

"No! Stop! Nasya, don't!"

The staff swung once more and an enormous gust of wind exploded outward, sucking the breath from Nasya's lungs. She fell onto her hands and knees, choking and sucking in air. The orange around her was gone. The ash disappeared. The stone beneath her was gray and unburnt. Nasya looked up and found Mother Hydra standing across the room from her. She held an obsidian staff in her hand that glowed blue. Nasya looked down at her hands. The light beneath her skin was fading away like the last remnants of burning embers. She looked back up at Mother Hydra. The woman was breathing heavily. Her eyes were wide and filled with terror. Nasya had never seen the woman scared before.

Neither of them spoke for several minutes. The first to break the silence was Mother Hydra.

"What did you see?" she asked, her voice hoarse.

Nasya looked down at the stone floor. The light in her hands was gone, but every part of her body tingled. She felt as though she could breathe fire, so much heat ran through her.

"Nasya," Mother Hydra said, walking towards her slowly. "I must know what it is you saw."

Nasya crawled backwards, tears filling her eyes. "No, stay away!"

Mother Hydra held up her hands and stopped moving. "Listen to my voice, fledgling. What did you see?"

"What happened?" she asked, so hoarse, she could speak only in a whisper.

"What did you see, Nasya? I must know. Tell me. Now."

Nasya heard the fear in Mother Hydra's voice and forced herself to focus. She thought back to the images of her dream, if, indeed, that's what it had been. They were confusing and convoluted, almost as though they were out of order. "I saw ash. A blood red sky. Fire. Stone burnt black."

Mother Hydra's eyes were ever on her as she spoke, wide and unwavering, unblinking.

"I heard screaming. I saw your staff. Heard your voice. But didn't know it was you." She licked her lips. They were suddenly dry and chapped. Her skin no longer tingled, but started to sting. "Someone bound my arms and wrists."

Mother Hydra cursed under her breath and looked away.

"I was trying to find Scarlet. You stopped me."

Nasya felt fear wash over her. She began to shiver and it was then she realized she was entirely soaked in sweat. No part of her was dry, not even her nightgown. She looked up at Mother Hydra and saw her watching closely.

"What is happening to me?" Nasya asked, a new wave of tears falling down her cheeks..

"Your power is growing," Mother Hydra said, her voice soft, "at a faster rate than I have seen before."

That wasn't the whole answer and Nasya knew it. Something about this filled Mother Hydra with a terror she could not hide, and Nasya saw it. Felt it. Smelled it on her skin like perfume. And though Nasya wanted the truth, she couldn't bring herself to ask what else this meant.

Mother Hydra approached Nasya and held out her hand. "Come, we must draw you a hot bath."

Nasya took the woman's hand and followed her back to her room. There was a brass tub near the enormous hearth. Mother Hydra filled it with hot water and told Nasya to undress and step in. She did as instructed. She washed herself as Mother Hydra stood at the window and stared out into the night.

Nasya could barely think at all, she was so tired. It was hard to believe that a dream and sleepwalking could exhaust her; it was even harder to believe that what she'd seen had been a dream at all. It was so vivid, she could still taste ash in the air. How could she have had such a dream when she had taken the sleeping concoction? After months of uninterrupted sleep, it was all undone. Hot tears continued to spill onto her cheeks and she did nothing to stop them.

"Your dream tonight was a blending of two worlds," Mother Hydra said suddenly, not turning around. "Part of what you saw was the past, and part of it was the future. Or, at least, a potential future."

Nasya didn't respond. She just waited.

"We've known for some time that you might have the gift of foresight, but your prior dreams never came to anything, and so the other Mothers dismissed them. What they don't understand is that all magic is, by nature, deceptive and uncertain."

Nasya climbed from the tub and put on a fresh nightgown. Mother Hydra turned away from the window and met Nasya's gaze.

"The other Mothers wanted your dreams to be more consistent, more predictable, and when they weren't, they discounted their validity. Tonight has proven that your ability to see beyond this present world is, in fact, quite powerful."

"But how can I see the past and the future at the same time?"

Mother Hydra shook her head. "I cannot explain that, fledgling. What I know is that the fire you saw happened decades ago when the last of the magical recruits were here. It was when I was learning to control my own abilities." She swallowed and cleared her throat. "A pupil younger than I was prone to sleepwalking. Usually, it came to nothing serious, but one night she managed to sleepwalk into one of the larger wings and cast a fire curse. It awoke the rest of the fortress, but not in time to save her."

Nasya felt the hair on her arms stand on end.

"I watched as she reached her zenith and magic consumed her

from the inside out," Mother Hydra said. "It was fire, bright and loud like wind that burned in every shade of every color as it ate through her body. It was a horrible, slow death. And all I could do was scream." She blinked. "That was part of the vision you saw tonight. More than that, I think...I think you were somehow connected to her because the words you spoke, the rage in your voice, and the fear in your eyes are exactly as I remember them." She cleared her throat.

"I was searching for Scarlet," Nasya said, furrowing her eyebrows in confusion.

Mother Hydra nodded. "Yes. And so was she. One of the girls we trained with was also called Scarlet, but she did not last through training."

"Then what was the future I saw?"

Mother Hydra stared at Nasya in silence for a moment. "I think you saw your own zenith," she said, her voice soft. "Or, at least, you saw a potential future where you reach your zenith and magic consumes you."

"But you said nearly every occurrence of this means death for the person with magic."

Mother Hydra nodded. "Every occurrence of it that I know of has been fatal."

Nasya's mouth went dry and she felt as though the air had been stripped from her lungs. "Are...Are you saying I saw...my own death?"

"I don't know, fledgling. I don't know."

In the days that followed, Mother Hydra took every precaution to ensure that Nasya was safe and in control of herself. She even began sleeping in Nasya's room so that she could wake her before any other dreams spiraled out of control. Training continued as normal, though Nasya felt herself growing more and more hesitant with every day that passed. She didn't know how to process these things she kept learning about herself. It was hard enough that the only family she had ever known could not have been her real family, but now she also possessed enough magic that she could accidentally kill herself or others. The only way to learn to control her powers was to keep training, but in the meantime, the fear she carried on her shoulders was heavy.

For one thing she was extremely grateful, and that was Mother Hydra. She was as tough and as hard as ever, but not cruel or unkind. She took care of Nasya, held space and even compassion for her struggles and her fears. The longer they were at Fire's Hearth, the more Nasya felt she could trust her. It wasn't an affectionate connection, but it allowed Nasya to breathe a little easier. With Mother Hydra in her room every night, Nasya's dreams remained in her mind, rather than took over her body. She continued to see things she didn't understand, and she took to writing them all down, like she had at Passing's End. Mother Hydra sometimes could explain aspects of her dreams, and sometimes she couldn't. Regardless, Nasya wrote them down every morning in case any patterns emerged.

Months passed. Nasya's strength continued to grow. Things that were once difficult for her were now as easy as if she had been born doing them. She could run for long distances without tiring. Her speed and agility improved. Her mind and body were more connected, more in tune, and more focused than ever before. Her magic grew as well, and filled her with both excitement and trepidation. She had felt completely powerless for so long that now, despite the dangers, she couldn't deny the immense pleasure she derived from seeing her powers unfold.

"Concentrate on the flame," Mother Hydra said one afternoon.

A lit candle sat in front of Nasya on the floor. She stared at it, her silver eyes glowing metallic against the firelight, the silver appearing molten against the illumination of the dancing flame.

"Breathe slowly and watch the flame as it flickers on the wick," said Mother Hydra, "Stare into it as though its very essence was created for your control, and when you feel the connection, snuff out the flame without blowing on it."

This was an exercise Nasya had grown used to. It was what she was taught to do to establish her connection with the elements. For months she had practiced focusing on representations of the different elements to try and manipulate them, and had seen no results. But ever since her dream of the past and the future, the exercises yielded results easily, as though she had been doing them her whole life. She had already done this with water and with earth, focusing on moisture in the air or dirt on the floor, to see what she could with them, and now had only to do it with fire and air before she could advance to more specific spells. Mother Hydra pushed their magical studies more heavily than anything else so that Nasya would have complete control over her abilities before advancing to the next level in her regular training. She called it a precaution, but Nasya felt as though it was more than that, perhaps even a strategic choice to give her a step up when she returned to Passing's End.

"Focus," Mother Hydra said softly. "Bring your thoughts back to the flame."

Nasya breathed slowly in through her nostrils and exhaled slowly out her mouth. She stared at the flame and focused on the whitest point where the flame connected to the wick. She could feel the little bit of heat emanating from it. She stared until she felt her mind begin to warm and then reached out with her thoughts, her mind stretching like fingers searching for something to grab onto. She reached until she felt a gust against her subconscious. She summoned it. From over her shoulder, a gentle gust of wind rushed by, danced around the flame causing it to bend and spin, and then extinguished it. A thin spiral of smoke rose into the air.

Nasya looked up and found Mother Hydra looking at her with a faint smile.

"Did you just connect with the wind and the flame simultaneously?"

Nasya nodded.

"Well done." Mother Hydra squinted in thought and then said, "Grow a flower through that crack in the floor there." She pointed at a nearby crack in the stone.

Nasya stared at the crack and tried to sense how deep down any roots or seeds might be. The stone floor was thick, and beneath it was hard, compact dirt filled with rocks. Nasya concentrated hard to try and find something she could use, and after a few moments, she found it. A seed. She switched her focus and began to imagine the seed sprouting, its contents growing up and pushing through the hard dirt and squeezing through the crack in the floor. And though it was a small seed, she felt it responding to her influence. The more it grew, the more of herself she exerted to encourage it. This was how she was to learn to control her abilities, by always transposing pieces of herself into each spell, each incantation, each ritual. It gave her more control over what she was manipulating.

It was also how she was to learn to identify when too much magic was flowing through her. The more of herself put into a spell, the more room there was for magic to seep in and consume her, making it necessary to always be aware of how much of herself was being used at once. This, more than anything else, was hardest for Nasya to learn because it was always subtle, almost undetectable. It required her to perform her magic slowly, carefully, and with absolute intention. As Mother Hydra said, she had to be completely aware of herself and her magic as individual entities, as well as how they interacted with and influenced one another. As confusing as it was, Nasya did her best to retain what she was taught.

Even now, doing something as insignificant as growing a seed, her thoughts were on nothing more or less than herself – her body, her breathing, her heartbeat, her connection to the stone floor that covered the dirt where the seed was growing – and the magic flowing through her. In only a few more moments, a strand of ivy broke through the crack in the stones and grew along the floor towards one of the windows where rays of sunlight lit up the glass.

The look on Mother Hydra's face filled Nasya with flutters. She was proud, and the thirteen year old could tell.

"Impressive, Nasya. Very impressive."

"Thank you, Mother."

Mother Hydra began to pace. "Do you know why magic begins with the elements?"

"Because they are the ingredients that make up the whole of the world and everything in it," Nasya replied.

Mother Hydra looked over at her and continued pacing. "That is one perspective. Could there be another?"

Nasya furrowed her eyebrows and looked over at the ivy she had conjured. It was still there, its longest tendrils reaching up towards the window for any glimpse of daylight. It was no longer winter, but Fire's Hearth still held dustings of snow and winter temperatures. She thought of how the seasons changed so smoothly elsewhere, coming and going without reference to anyone.

"Because they are what magic created first," Nasya said, looking back at Mother Hydra.

The woman nodded. "Very good. All magic begins with the elements. Even the spells that seem to be the most disconnected from the physical world still rely on the elements for their success. Without mastering the elemental spells, there can be no advancement."

Nasya nodded and made a mental note to practice elemental magic more often. If it was to be the fuel of her fire, then she needed to be as intimate as possible with them.

"Return to your room to study. Supper will be ready in a couple of hours," Mother Hydra said.

Nasya stood to her feet and walked out of the training room back to her dormitory. She grabbed her books from off the bookshelf, sat near the hearth, and began to read. The fire was large and filled her room with heat. Nasya enjoyed the heat of the fire and how it felt against her skin. As she sat and studied, she spread her wings and let them warm against the crackling fire.

Her thoughts wandered to Scarlet, as they often did. She wondered how her friend was doing back at Passing's End, and when they would see each other again. She had asked Mother Hydra if she could write to Scarlet, and she had allowed it. Scarlet hadn't yet responded. Nasya didn't know if this was because she wasn't allowed to, or if Scarlet didn't want to write back, but either way Nasya felt keenly the absence of her friend. For all that was going right at Fire's Hearth, this was the one thing that bothered her. It made her feel alone, and in that loneliness, she found herself wondering if any of this was worth the hassle and the heartache it had caused.

# Chapter Eleven

*Fortress of Fire's Hearth*
  *Country of Utara*

It had been many weeks since the last clear day had allowed Nasya the chance to go outside. The encroaching winter season meant that snow fell in large flakes almost consistently every single day, and almost always the winds blew harshly through the pass, making the outdoors treacherous at best. But today, for the first time in over a month, the sky was clear and bright blue against the silver sun. Nasya took the opportunity to go outside and hike up to the lookout above the fortress. It was the fourteen year old's favorite spot to meditate.

She would not be meditating today.

The frigid air burned her lungs as she hiked up the steep slope. If not for the snow, the walk would have been somewhat pleasant, but the snow was deep and came up to her knees, making every step that much harder. She could have cast a spell to clear away the snow, but she enjoyed the challenge. It built up her strength and endurance in ways other exercises didn't. Besides, it was the descent back to the fortress that she was looking forward to the most.

When she finally reached the summit, sweat trickled down her face. She made her way to the edge and looked out across the vast forest. Almost directly below her was Fire's Hearth. It looked like a playhouse from this height, even with its gigantic size. Extending out from it and the mountain was an endless sea of trees covered in white. Somewhere out there was Passing's End, though it couldn't be seen through the dense woods. Nasya loved the view from here. It was the only form of freedom she had ever found while training with The Order.

She inhaled and exhaled slowly. It was time for the descent. She extended her wings out as far as they could go. The wind was steady but calm, which meant she should have an easy time getting back to the forest floor. But first, there would be flight. She backed away from the edge, keeping her wings open and ready for the wind. After a final deep breath, she sprinted forward, her heart racing. Everything within her told her to turn back, to slow down, to think better of this, but she kept going.

She reached the edge.

She made the leap.

As her feet left the ground, her wings caught the updraft of the wind, and she began to soar. She smiled brightly and began to flap her wings. It was awkward at first, but she soon adjusted and even as the updraft shifted directions, she maintained her course. Her wings carried her with ease. Nasya let out a cry of excitement and pointed herself downward. She sped up and as she came closer to the ground, leveled off and flew into the cover of the trees. Flying in open space was one thing. Navigating through the trees at high speed was another. This was a newer part of her training, but it was something that thrilled her. Even now, as she flew in between the trees, her fingers and toes tingled with excitement.

It only took her fifteen minutes to make her way to her destination. She landed in the snow, retracted her wings, and grinned at the person waiting for her.

"Took you long enough," said Scarlet. "I'm only half frozen waiting for you," she teased.

Nasya shrugged. "There's a hot spring just inside that very cave," Nasya said walking towards her. "You could have gone in."

"I didn't want to risk you getting lost," Scarlet said, her eyes twinkling with joy.

Nasya and Scarlet went inside the cave and immediately jumped into the hotspring. This had become their habit and their secret: once a month, they would each find time to sneak away to the hotspring and spend one half hour together. It was all the time they could risk. Scarlet had not been allowed to respond to the letter Nasya had sent her, and when months had passed, Nasya sent one more saying that she would be waiting for her at the hotspring. She gave a date and time and hoped Scarlet would be there. She had been, and so began their monthly meetups. It did Nasya good to see her friend. They would soak in the hot water, talk about training, and then sneak back to their respective fortresses before anyone could notice they were gone.

"Your wings look stronger every time I see you," Scarlet said.

Nasya nodded. "I can go farther and faster with them every day, it seems."

"How's the rest of your training going?"

Nasya shrugged. "As well as ever. Mother Hydra has been pleased with my progress."

Scarlet cocked her head to one side. "But?"

Nasya sighed. "I'm not sure. Things are still so...uncertain with my magic."

"You're understanding the spells?"

Nasya nodded.

"You're progressing in what you can do?"

She nodded again.

"Then what's the problem?"

"I don't know," Nasya said, frustrated, "but I can tell that something's missing. Something within me still hasn't been accessed yet. I don't know what it is. But it's there."

"Have you told Mother Hydra?"

Nasya nodded. "I have. She says it's how this process works. Things come out little by little, not all at once."

"But that doesn't satisfy you?"

Nasya looked at Scarlet and shook her head. "No. It doesn't. And that frightens me." Despite the heat of the water, a chill washed over her. "More than once, I've exhibited huge bursts of magic. It's dangerous. So to feel that there's something else within me that hasn't been revealed yet, something I may not be able to control, isn't exactly comforting."

"Maybe it isn't supposed to be comforting? Maybe the point is to embrace the discomfort and the uncertainty?"

Nasya furrowed her eyebrows. "What do you mean?"

"Maybe by wanting to understand it all at once, you're keeping yourself from understanding it altogether?"

"Hmm. I never thought of it that way before."

"I'm no magician, so I could be completely wrong, but maybe try embracing the discomfort? Maybe it'll help?"

Nasya made note of Scarlet's words. There was something in them that rang true in Nasya's ears. If pushing herself this hard was only holding her back, then perhaps it was time to try a different approach. She thought of this as she and Scarlet continued to talk and soak in the hot water.

After thirty minutes had passed, both changed out of their wet clothes into something dry for their treks back. Nasya hated to say goodbye. She was lonely at Fire's Hearth. She missed Scarlet fiercely, and sometimes was on the verge of saying so when fear gripped her and she swallowed the words. She couldn't bring herself to tell Scarlet of her deepest feelings. Not yet. Not when they were only allotted thirty minutes every month to see each other.

Before they parted, the two girls shared a long embrace, and Nasya held on as tight as ever. She reveled in these moments, savored the intimacy, the kindness, and the affection. They were all she had to keep her company in the frigidity of Fire's Hearth. Scarlet held her close too, her arms wrapped around Nasya's shoulders.

"I'm always here," Scarlet whispered just before they parted. "Don't forget that."

Nasya offered a grateful smile, unfurled her wings, and took off into the air. She looked down and watched as Scarlet moved quickly through the snow towards Passing's End. As much as she loved their few moments together, the ending always filled her with sadness. She knew that any one of these could be their last time in each other's company. It was unlikely, to be sure; Scarlet was still the best recruit out of the remaining eight, but there was no telling when the tides might shift and the Mothers decided against advancing her. It wasn't something anyone expected to happen, but that didn't mean it wouldn't. If the recruits had learned anything in their years of training it was that the Mothers were completely unpredictable.

In only a few minutes, Nasya landed back in the courtyard of Fire's Hearth. She flapped her wings to shake off the cold, and then retracted them back into her body. Mother Hydra was waiting for her.

"You were gone longer than I'd expected," she said.

"There was more snow in the pass than I anticipated," Nasya responded, moving towards her. "It took me a while to get to the top of the lookout."

Mother Hydra stared at her with piercing eyes. Nasya was fairly certain that she didn't believe her story, but nor did she challenge it.

"How are your wings holding up against the wind?"

"Better every day," Nasya said, following her inside. "They still take a moment or two to adjust to the gusts, but once they do, it's as though I've been flying my entire life."

"It will take time for them to develop their full strength. The more you grow, the more weight they must carry."

Nasya nodded.

"I noticed that you haven't written down your dreams in several nights." Mother Hydra faced her. "Why is that?"

"I haven't had any dreams," Nasya lied.

"I sleep on a mattress on the floor of your room, Nasya. I know whether you dream or not. Why haven't you recorded your last four dreams?"

Nasya hesitated. She didn't have any other excuse or explanation, but she would rather have flown through the snow naked than tell Mother Hydra the real reason for not writing them down. She chewed nervously on the inside of her cheek.

"Well?" Mother Hydra asked, raising her eyebrows.

"I...I don't want to say, Mother," Nasya replied.

Mother Hydra sighed. "Was it that bad, fledgling?"

Nasya nodded.

"I cannot prepare myself or you for whatever might come if I don't know what might be coming," Mother Hydra said gently.

Nasya let out a slow breath. "I saw the deaths of all in my cohort who will become Sisters of The Order. I saw their bodies sprawled out on the ground outside of Passing's End."

Mother Hydra did not respond.

"And I saw who was responsible for their murders," Nasya added, knowing she couldn't withhold this important detail.

Mother Hydra nodded slowly. "Who was it?"

"The Mothers," Nasya said, her voice no louder than a whisper. "All six of you stood over the bodies. You held knives and swords and axes and staves. Everything was red with blood."

Nasya watched Mother Hydra's face. There was no change of expression, no sign of shock or fear or anger, and yet her eyes darkened like the night bleeding into and corrupting the day. She said nothing. She merely stared at Nasya in quiet thought.

"I was the only Sister who remained alive," Nasya added.

"And this was what you saw in all four dreams?" she asked.

Nasya nodded. "It was the same every time."

She let out a deep breath. "Well, now I know. I will write to the other Mothers and tell them what you've seen. With any luck, we can ascertain the potential cause and uproot it before it happens."

Nasya didn't understand how that could be, but she said nothing. Mother Hydra instructed her to go and read for the rest of the afternoon, and that was what she did, though her mind was heavily occupied with thoughts of what her dreams could mean. She knew enough to understand that her dreams weren't outright predictions of the future; even those with the gift of foresight were only given pieces of a potential future. Nothing was set in stone. Nothing was guaranteed. What Nasya didn't know was if her dreams were, in fact, visions of a potential future, or a premonition of something worse. She also wasn't sure she understood the difference between them, or how potential futures became definitive futures.

She decided she would read about dreams and visions to try and ascertain the truth, or at least point her to a better understanding of what was going on in her own mind. What worried her most was Mother Hydra's almost stoic reaction. The woman wasn't exactly expressive, but the look in her eyes as Nasya had revealed her dreams had chilled her to the bone. Nasya suspected that these dreams meant far more to Mother Hydra than she let on, and that was not something Nasya wanted to think about.

Nasya let out a slow, shaky breath as she lifted her leg onto the cot. She was in her room in the fortress of Fire's Hearth. It was small, confined, and without windows; she never ceased to feel isolated and cramped. But it wasn't until recently that she'd begun to feel trapped in a story not of her choosing.

Her dreams had gotten worse. Much worse. They were more frequent, occurring almost every single night, and with each one they grew more vivid, more terrifying, and more real. In the last five months, Mother Hydra had used magic to wake her at least ten times. It wasn't just that the dreams were connected to her magic, it was that each one took her deeper into her own psyche, making it that much harder for Mother Hydra to wake her up.

Beyond that, the dreams themselves filled Nasya with terror. When she awoke, it took her several minutes to realize she was safe in Fire's Hearth. More than once, her dreams had blended with her consciousness and she had attacked Mother Hydra. Nothing about her day-to-day existence was normal any longer. Sleep, when she did have it, was utterly restless. And even Mother Hydra's sleeping concoctions were losing their sway. Nasya felt distinctly that she was nearing a breaking point, and she didn't know how to prepare for it.

Nasya now fully understood what Mother Hydra had meant when she'd said training her would be dangerous. Her magic, while inside of her since she was born, was still new to her mind and her body. She had not embraced it yet, and now wasn't sure if she even wanted to. Magic was what burdened her with these dreams, and because of them she felt paranoid every moment of every day. She hated being set apart from everyone in her life. In Passing's End she had been a failure, a point of contention among the Mothers, but here at Fire's Hearth, she was a symbol of everything she might be and wasn't. And there was no one around to ease the load, to offer comfort.

Her heart panged with loneliness for Scarlet. She remembered with fondness the whispered conversations they had in the darkness of their bedchamber, how they told each other what they could remember of their families, and how they allowed themselves to dream and wish for easier futures. Many nights they crawled under the covers and gave each other the only moments of beauty they could find at Passing's End. They laughed. They cried. They held each other close, and slept side by side.

They were all they had.

Nasya's readings on dreams and other forms of visions had not produced any useful information, either. Because it was hard to pinpoint the meanings of dreams, all of the writings she found on them were generalized and unspecified. Based on what she'd read, her dreams could be literal predictions of the future, a metaphor indicating an issue in her own mind, or they could be absolutely nothing at all. Every answer was just as likely as the one before it. And as far as she could tell, they were only manifesting because of the magic continuing to awaken inside of her.

Nasya looked down at her leg and the laceration that ran from her hip down to just above the knee. There was a lot of blood, and though the wound itself was superficial, it was deep enough to require cleaning and sutures to close it. She grabbed the rag that was next to her, dipped it into the bowl of water and soap that she'd placed next to her leg, and gently began to wipe away the blood.

The flesh was irritated, but so far there were no signs of an infection. She slowly and carefully continued to clean the wound, too full of rage to do anything else. Mother Hydra had used strong magic in their training that afternoon. During one of the exercises, Nasya had done something that upset her, and before she could even blink, Mother Hydra whipped a sharp blade through the air. It had torn through her leather trousers and sliced open her leg.

Mother Hydra had ended training and left the hall without so much as a word.

Tears stung Nasya's eyes. She looked up at her small room, hoping that Scarlet would suddenly appear and she would find herself back at Passing's End. Scarlet would dry her tears and help her tend to the wound. She would make a joke about Mother Hydra that would elicit a belly full of laughter from Nasya, and the world would seem a little less bleak.

But this chamber was empty. There was no one for her to confide in, no one to distract from her suffering, no one to care for her feelings. She hated this place even more than she had hated Passing's End, and that seemed impossible. What had begun as progress and an awakening of her truest self had shapeshifted into an existence completely unrecognizable, and it all started with her dreams. Not only was she deprived of sleep, so was Mother Hydra, and the weeks of exhaustion meant that the two of them grated on each other's patience. More than that, though, was the looming sense of dread Nasya could no longer ignore. The more she learned of magic, the worse her dreams became, and the more she suffered at the hands of Mother Hydra who, until now, had been easy to work with. At least, relatively speaking.

Four more years. That was what lay ahead of her: four more years of cruelty, of failures, of struggles, of loneliness, and all to be followed by what? A lifetime of death and blood and only herself for company? She didn't think she could stand it. How could she when her entire life had amounted to nothing but suffering?

The bleeding stopped. Nasya sprinkled some lemon juice into her bowl of hot water and dipped a fresh rag into it, soaking it through. Then she laid the rag over the wound. It stung like nothing else, but this would ensure it wouldn't become infected. She let the rag sit for a few minutes, and then pulled it away to suture the wound. She grabbed a needle made of bird bone, dipped it in the hot water with lemon, and then began to close up the wound. She winced as she gently pulled the needle through her skin. The laceration on her leg looked worse than it was, but it hurt more than she anticipated.

It was moments like this when she most missed her mother. She remembered how carefully, how tenderly, she had always been when she and her sister injured themselves. It never seemed to matter how reckless her daughters had been or how foolish, the moment she saw they were hurt, she grabbed her kit and immediately went to work tending their wounds with love, kindness, and gentleness. Nasya smiled at the memory and continued to stitch the wound on her leg. She missed her family more and more these days. She wished she could see them, talk to them, and ask for their advice. It was strange how quickly she wanted to be with them again, even though they had sold her to The Order. The fear of her nightmares made her long for anything that carried warmth and love, even if it was imperfect.

If given the choice to return to them, to leave The Order, in that moment, it would have been no choice at all. Yet, it was true. The magic, the nightmares, the isolation had taken away any motivation her progress had afforded. It no longer mattered to her how close she was to graduating, how much she had improved since coming to Fire's Hearth. Nor did it even matter that her parents weren't her real parents. They were still the only parents she had known, and she missed the lives they had built with her. She wanted simplicity. She wanted safety. She wanted normalcy.

But she was different now, and normalcy wasn't a luxury she possessed any longer. That was undeniable. Nasya thought of the wings in her back. She thought of the voices she heard around her, the dreams she had almost every night. She had finally learned to quiet the voices, to hold them at bay, to somewhat control how often she heard them, but she still didn't know what they were or from whence they came. Neither did Mother Hydra. Her best guess was that Nasya possessed some form of telecommunication or psychic abilities. It was only a guess, and one that neither she nor Nasya really believed. Nasya couldn't read thoughts. She couldn't communicate to others with her mind. She simply heard voices she couldn't explain, and in moments of distress, the world around her would change; eyes would appear, hands would reach for her from stones and branches, all of them summoned by her.

If she left The Order, she would never understand the truth of who she was or what she was meant for. This she knew for certain, and it gnawed at her insides as much as her loneliness did. She was afraid of herself. Returning to her family wouldn't change that. Running from The Order wouldn't change that, either. But she simply couldn't go on as she had been. It was too much. And it was not enough.

A soft knock sounded at her door. She looked up as Mother Hydra entered carrying a tray. Nasya didn't have time to dry her eyes before Mother Hydra saw her tear streaked cheeks. She looked down and saw the laceration that Nasya had finished stitching up, and set the tray on the bedside table. On it was a plate of food and a flagon of ale. She sat across from Nasya at the foot of her bed, and held her open palms a few inches above her wounded leg.

Nasya watched as she muttered slowly in a language Nasya had never heard before. Almost instantly her leg began to feel warm, and then it tingled, and then the pain set in. It was different from the pain she'd felt when her leg was cut; this was deeper, more urgent, as though something was forcing nature to work faster than it was supposed to. Nasya winced and closed her eyes as the warmth turned into an intense burning that ran deep into her leg and moved outward. She told herself she wasn't going to scream. She wasn't going to make any noise at all, especially not after Mother Hydra saw her crying. Tears fell down her cheeks again, but she made no sound, even though her chest burned with a desire to scream as loudly as she could.

The pain in her leg was searing hot.

A moment later, the pain was gone. She looked down at her leg and saw that the wound was healed. The stitches were gone. There wasn't even a scar. She looked up and saw Mother Hydra's eyes on her.

"Are you alright?" she asked.

Nasya nodded.

"I don't mean your leg, fledgling."

Nasya looked down at her hands. How was she supposed to explain how she was? How she felt? What she wanted?

"I was once a lot like you," said Mother Hydra, moving to grab the tray and bring it over to the bed. "I was taken from my family at a young age, only four years old."

Nasya blinked in surprise. "Four? Why so young?"

"Probably for much the same reason as your family parted with you," she said, laying the tray on the bed. "They were destitute and had already watched two of their children die. The money The Order paid them was enough to clothe and feed the rest of the family for years on end. It seemed an enormous blessing for the small sacrifice of their youngest child."

Nasya felt pain ripple in her chest. She had long felt anger over her parents' ease at giving her up. She never understood how they chose which of their girls to part with, and she didn't know what it was she had done to be their choice. It wasn't that she thought her sister should have been taken instead, but rather she wished she had belonged to a family whose love for her was deeper than their desire for money.

"I struggled in my training, too," Mother Hydra said, handing Nasya the flagon of ale. "My Mothers were relentless in their pushing, their degrading insults. I spent many nights in my room crying myself to sleep."

Nasya took a sip of ale, unsure of where this conversation was going. She had never seen a moment of such kindness from any of the Mothers, and she didn't want to ruin it by speaking.

"But through all of it, I overcame," said the Mother, "and I promised myself I would become the strongest and most prolific Sister ever to be in The Order. It didn't matter how much I struggled, how much I grew to hate the Mothers, I persevered. Like you, I discovered I had the ability to wield magic, and I used it to fuel my learning. I leaned on it when I felt I had nothing and no one else." She paused and looked into Nasya's eyes. "Do you understand what I'm telling you?"

Nasya nodded impulsively, and then shook her head. "I'm not sure that I do, Mother."

Mother Hydra sighed. "I never was very good at this part," she muttered, picking a grape from the tray and tossing it into her mouth. "The point is that, however hard things are right now, you have a gift brewing inside of you that is unmatched by anything else in this world. It is what makes you who you are, and it will be what takes you to the end of your training, and beyond."

"Beyond?" Nasya asked.

"Outside of The Order. Most Sisters choose to stay in The Order, but there have been some who have gone on to do incredible things. The magic inside of you will show you the path you're meant to take. It will take time, you are still young, but the more you listen to what is inside of you, the farther you will go." She cleared her throat and stood to her feet. "Tonight and tomorrow, I want you to rest." She pulled a small vial from one of the pockets in her robe. "This is a very potent sleeping agent. I want you to take all of it tonight. It will allow you a rest-filled sleep. Tomorrow, I will begin showing you how to use your magic to heal and renew your body, mind, and spirit. You can't rely on sleeping agents forever, and until we know what's causing your nightmares, you will need another form of rest. We will pick back up where we left off today at another time." She motioned to the tray. "Eat as much of that as you can. You need your strength."

"Mother," Nasya said as the woman moved towards the door.

Mother Hydra stopped and looked over her shoulder. Nasya wanted suddenly to tell her so many things, to unleash every question she had, every thought and feeling, to keep this connection open. But she knew she couldn't. So instead, she simply said, "Thank you."

Mother Hydra's eyes glistened for a moment. She stared at Nasya unblinking for what felt like ages, and Nasya began to wonder if she had better not have spoken at all. But then Mother Hydra offered a small smile.

"I believe in you, fledgling." she said.

Then she left, and Nasya was alone with her thoughts once more.

"Gods damn you, girl!" shouted Mother Hydra. "Do you ignore my instructions just to spite me?"

Nasya was on her hands and knees breathing so hard, she thought she would choke. Blood dripped out of her nose and fell to the stone floor. The very air was frozen, and burned her throat and lungs as she inhaled desperately. She was learning how to keep warm in a place too frozen for life. Like so many things, even the simplest of magic spells seemed to take all of her effort and focus, and even then she didn't always get it right. What had originally come quite easily to her now felt like a weight around her neck. She could summon the elements to her command well enough, and she could manipulate them in small ways, but the wards and protection spells cast to protect her against the elements were much harder to master. She could feel the magic around her, sensed it in every breath she took, and yet no matter how hard she focused, she couldn't get the spells to take.

Mother Hydra's patience had run out months ago. Where before she had shown compassion and even tenderness to Nasya, now she was utterly different. She was the woman who pushed and prodded and challenged much harder than she ever had before, and with the increasing demands, her patience grew more and more thin. The woman who had brought the tray into Nasya's room only three months before was gone. Her kindness, her tenderness, her concern for Nasya's well being seemed to have been eaten up in that one evening. The only thing left running through her body was anger. It tainted the air around them with a scent of molten iron.

"Water..." Nasya croaked.

"Water must be earned," Mother Hydra said loudly, overly enunciating every word. "And you haven't done anything right since we started training this morning." She struck the end of her staff on the stone floor. "Now, stand up."

Nasya did as she was instructed. She had finally learned to use her magic to give herself strength, even when she felt weak and helpless. She was dripping with sweat. Her face was smeared with tears and blood and dirt. But she was on her feet, prepared to try again, even though she knew she would likely fail.

"Magic is the same as any other extension of your existence," Mother Hydra said, pacing slowly in front of her. "Intelligence, comprehension, speed, strength, they all communicate with magic to heighten its potency and it, in turn, heightens them."

Nasya stood still and breathed slowly. Her fingers tingled with something that felt simultaneously like fire and ice. She could feel magic inside of her in the same way that she felt emotions. At times, it was calm and simply there, and other times it was overwhelming to the point of panic. And always there was one truth that rang out in the back of her mind: as part fae, more was expected of her than any of the other girls. She would be given the hardest assignments, the most dangerous destinations, and she would be expected to execute them perfectly. None of that would be possible if she didn't learn how to keep her spells and incantations intact.

Mother Hydra glared and continued to pace.

"Magic is what?" she said loudly.

"A force. A gift. And a weapon," Nasya responded.

"You are what?"

"A force. A gift. And a weapon," she said again.

"Which means?"

"Magic and I are one and the same."

Though Mother Hydra's hands did not move, something slapped Nasya hard across the face.

"Then why..." Another slap. "Do you..." Another slap. "Still..." Two slaps. "Fail?" A final slap, Mother Hydra's voice was loud and shrill. Her staff glowed blue in the darkness of the room.

Nasya straightened her posture and looked ahead. "I don't know, Mother."

The older woman walked slowly towards Nasya, her dark eyes fiery in the fading light of day.

"You test my patience more than any recruit I've ever trained before," she said, her voice quiet, her words biting and frigid. "You are an oddity. You come here and start to succeed in your primary training in as fast a time as I have ever seen, overcoming every defeat, every struggle, every hardship. You can summon and manipulate the elements as though you have always been able to do so, but you still cannot cast a simple warming spell to keep yourself from freezing. And you say that you do not know why?"

Silence filled the inches between them.

"You do not want to be here," said Mother Hydra. "You wish to be returned to your family."

They were statements, not questions, and Nasya felt herself begin to tremble.

"I thought you were dedicated to your training? I thought you wanted this?"

"I was not ever given a chance to want or not want it," Nasya said, her voice hoarse. "I was not given the opportunity to choose any of this."

Mother Hydra thought for a moment and then nodded. "What if I told you I could send you back there? Would you go or stay, if given the choice?"

"What?"

"You want a choice? I'm giving it to you now. I can send you home, if that is what you want. But once the choice is made, it cannot be unmade. Which will it be? Stay? Or go?"

Nasya hesitated only for a moment before replying, "I would go, Mother."

Mother Hydra leaned in as close as she could without touching Nasya's face. "Then that is why you are failing," she whispered.

With a swift movement, she turned and waved her staff, lighting all of the candles in the room ablaze. She swung it again, and a roaring fire came to life in the hearth.

"I cannot train those who refuse to be trained. I will send you back to your previous life through this," she said, snapping her fingers. A mirage appeared next to Mother Hydra, revealing her family to her. "If you ask me to."

Before Nasya could reply, Mother Hydra continued.

"But you should know what it is you're giving up," she said, looking at Nasya with a stare more intense than Nasya had ever seen. "You are a skilled fighter with a strong mind. You are clever and cunning. If you applied yourself, you would find within you a power even stronger than you now wield."

Nasya felt emboldened by the closeness of her family. She heard herself sarcastically say, "So that I can become a glorified assassin?"

Mother Hydra's eyes changed. It was as though a dark cloud had been pulled away from her eyes, and something akin to awe filled their darkness.

"Oh Nasya," she said, using her name for the first time in years, "if you would allow me to train you - to really train you - you could become an unstoppable force. An assassin at first, yes, but in time, you could become an archmage. Even an enchantress."

A cold shiver traced its way down Nasya's spine. "En-enchantresses aren't...aren't real..."

Mother Hydra smiled. "Aren't they?"

Then, the cloud returned and covered her eyes. "Bear in mind that if you leave, there will be no one to help you control your powers. You will still be dangerous, perhaps even deadly, and you will be alone in your journey to self-control. But, if you ask me permission to leave now, I will grant it."

Nasya looked at her family in the mirage, her heart urging her forward. This was the moment she had wished for, a chance to return to the normalcy that had been her former life. It was a struggle, to be sure, but at least she knew there would be love. It was steps away, and she wanted to take those steps, to leave this place and all its haunts behind.

Yet something held her back. Even though she had just said she would leave if given the choice, she found she couldn't speak the words. She couldn't walk away. She wanted to, more than anything, as she watched her father and her sister work in the public house. She could practically smell the stew, the bread, the venison.

But it was just a dream. One she held close and cherished, but like the portal open before her, the life beyond it was a mirage. She was no longer part of their family. Perhaps, she had never been. She was of the fae, after all. Not born to Lisla and Galen. Adopted. Chosen, maybe, at one point to join their family, and then also chosen to be the one sold away. Never to be seen again. Never to know if she lived or died. Whatever love she remembered in her childhood, whatever tenderness and affection there had been, would it remain inside of them? Would they even want her back?

It was then she knew the truth. She could not return to them, not permanently. The little girl who missed them was no longer their daughter, their sister. She was a young woman with possibility, one they had given up and abandoned. But even beyond that, she still didn't understand the magic inside of her, didn't understand her own strength, couldn't yet control her powers. The Order was offering the only chance she had to learn who she was meant to be. And she couldn't give that up. Not when so much magic coursed through her, spoke to her, reached for her from the depths of her essence. It was shocking, to be faced with what she thought she wanted, and to let it slip away, but in the moment of choosing, her deepest desires had been revealed.

She looked away from the portal, her eyes filling with tears, and shook her head.

"I ask permission to keep training, Mother," she said, her voice cracking under the weight of emotions coursing through her.

The portal disappeared.

"What is magic?" Mother Hydra asked.

"A force. A gift. And a weapon," Nasya replied, tears rolling down her cheeks.

"What are you?"

"A force. A gift. And a weapon."

"Which means?"

"Magic and I are one and the same."

"Which means?"

Nasya didn't know the answer. Mother Hydra had never asked this question before. Nasya stood still and silent.

"It means that the magic pulsing through you is woven together with every thought, every feeling, every moment of triumph and heartbreak." She stood in front of Nasya. "Do you understand what I'm saying?"

Nasya met her gaze. "Magic comes from emotions, experiences, thoughts, pain."

Mother Hydra gave a singular nod. The candles which had been lit a moment before were suddenly snuffed out and the air in the room dropped to well below freezing. Nasya's fingers were immediately numb. She knew what she needed to do.

"Cast the fucking spell!" Mother Hydra shouted.

Nasya didn't stop her tears. She didn't ignore her feelings. She embraced them, looked down into her soul and examined everything she'd felt in the moment she saw her family and then decided not to return to them. As emotions cracked open in her chest, her body began to go numb. She thought of the longing, the loneliness, the fear, the anger. She sucked in sharp breaths as her heart ached. More tears fell. She could hardly feel the freezing air around her anymore. She knew Mother Hydra was shouting at her again, but she didn't hear the words. All she knew was the turmoil of her soul. The less she tried to bury it, the heavier it became until her entire body trembled.

From somewhere dark and deep inside of her mind, a memory came to her. It was the day she'd been taken from her home, the very moment she'd been put in the carriage and driven away. She had looked over her shoulder at her parents, tears streaming down her cheeks. She wanted to see their faces one last time, to see them watching her, to be reminded of their love. But they had been staring at the pouch with the gold they'd been given. They had been preoccupied with counting it. She remembered calling to them. She remembered they had not looked up from their gold. She remembered they had laughed for joy, even as she was still within view.

Nasya wept openly at the memory. How had she forgotten this? The family she missed, the parents she thought of in her times of greatest need, had laughed as she was taken away. Nasya cried. Then groaned. Then shouted. Then screamed with pain, releasing every wall she'd built around herself since being taken from her family. She felt the burst begin inside of her chest, and then rush through her and out of her fingertips.

She opened her eyes and every candle, every torch that lined the walls of the room, and both hearths were suddenly ablaze with flames of red and gold. Around her body, heat pulsated with every breath, every heartbeat. She looked down at her hands. They were warm. *She* was warm, as though she had created a barrier of summer heat between herself and the frozen air of the room. Nasya looked up at Mother Hydra whose eyes glimmered brightly.

"You are a force. A gift. And a weapon," she said. "Never, ever, forget it."

# Chapter Twelve

*Capital City of Sun River*
*Country of Utara*

Nasya moved on and browsed the carts and shops. She purchased a couple of items from the merchants who looked the poorest. She didn't need what she bought, but it had long been her habit of doing what she could for the less fortunate. She gave sympathetic smiles to the merchants and moved through the square, eyeing the main entrance to the palace. She needed to time her movements very carefully. She didn't want to be remembered by any of the guards. That was of the utmost importance. Anonymity was the one thing that kept The Order going.

"It's ridiculous, isn't it?" a voice near her said.

She turned and saw a man standing at one of the nearby carts.

He was tall with olive skin, a thick beard, long, dark hair pulled back, and wore brown trousers and a black tunic. He seemed to be browsing. She wasn't sure if he was talking to her or not.

"All these guests, all the extravagance," he added, looking at her and then motioning his head towards the palace. "I've lived here my whole life, and I've never seen things get this bad."

Nasya nodded slowly, unsure of what to say.

"The worst part is that this money could be put to much better use if the king would actually listen to his people," the man said, moving towards Nasya.

"Since when does royalty listen to anyone?" she said, looking around for any alleys or pubs she might use to disappear, should the need arise.

"Are you a guest at tonight's ball?" he asked.

She chuckled. "Do I look like the type who would attend a prince's birthday?"

He grinned. "You look like you've just finished a long journey," he said, eyeing the muddy hem of her skirt, "I thought perhaps you were someone's handmaiden or something."

Nasya shook her head. "Alas, I am not that lucky."

"Just here for the day?"

She gave him a pointed stare. He was asking a lot of questions. "Actually, like many, I moved here from Terrace to try and rebuild." She shrugged. "It was that or starve in the country."

"It seems more and more people are facing that choice," he said sadly. "I wish it didn't have to be that way."

"It wouldn't," a nearby merchant woman chimed in, "if that

lazy eldest son actually did something about it."

As the people around her chuckled and agreed with the merchant, Nasya moved slowly away. Too long among one group of people increased the chances that they would remember her, especially her silver eyes that stood out among everything else plain about her. She inwardly thanked the gods that the courtyard was so full of people. It lessened, but did not eliminate, the likelihood of being recognized. She took a few more steps away from the cluster of carts, but was annoyed to find that the stranger who had spoken to her was now following. "Are you a merchant?" he asked. "Or a farmer?"

"Neither, actually," she said, hoping he would take her lack of elaboration as a hint to leave her alone.

He didn't. "What is your profession then? How do you make a living?"

"Well, I'm a single woman who recently made her way into a large city. What do you think my profession is?"

He raised his eyebrows. "You're a whore," he said, and then winced as though he'd realized what he'd just spoken out loud. "That was thoughtless of me," he said. "I apologize."

She shrugged. "I'm used to it by now."

This man clearly wasn't going to be deterred by her lack of interest in his interest. It was something she'd grown to expect from most men, and it was the one thing that annoyed her more than almost anything else from the opposite sex.

"I can see why you chose to leave Terrace," he said. "I imagine business has been slow for a while."

She nodded but didn't speak as she continued to move through the town square. A room had been booked for her at an inn in the cheap part of Sun River. If this man wasn't going to leave her alone, then she would simply dull him into disinterest. It was towards the inn she decided to walk.

Merchants also lined the streets of Sun River, as the courtyard was too full for anymore. They called out to those walking by to try and gain their attention. These were mostly food merchants, whereas the others had been sellers of small gifts and trinkets. Nasya would have preferred to stay in the courtyard, but she didn't want to be seen studying the main entrance. Everything had to be above board.

"You must forgive me for following you," the man said. "I don't mean to be rude or presumptive." He hesitated. "I simply...well, you strike me as someone who is different from the other whores here."

"I didn't realize you know the other whores in town so well," Nasya said sarcastically.

The man mumbled and muttered a response that made Nasya want to roll her eyes.

She sighed. "Are you ever actually going to ask me how much I cost?" she asked, feeling somewhat annoyed. She needed to prepare for the masquerade, and this man was definitely interfering with her ability to do so, but she wasn't sure she could pass up the opportunity to make some easy coin.

He smiled sheepishly. "Was I that obvious?"

"Were you trying to be subtle?' she teased.

Nasya weighed her options. She hadn't intended on taking clients so soon after arriving in Sun River, but on further consideration, decided she needed her cover to be convincing. She was here posing as a prostitute, after all. A prostitute who had moved to a new city to make more money but turned away interested clients would look too suspicious.

"I usually charge three bronze florens per hour."

His eyes sparkled. "I can pay that."

"Seeing as I just arrived in town and haven't even settled in yet, would you be willing to wait until after midnight?"

He nodded. "Of course. Where are you staying?"

"At the King's Corral Inn. Ask for Cinders."

He smiled. "Cinders?"

"It's a nickname."

"I'll be there." He flashed a quick smile and then turned and walked away.

Nasya sighed heavily. This was going to complicate things, but not enormously. She would lay with him, and once he awoke, she would eat breakfast with him, and then look for more clients. It would be quick and easy. Most men usually were.

Once the man from the square had disappeared from sight, Nasya casually made her way up to the room that had been reserved for her by The Order. She had much to prepare for the ball that evening. When she was inside the room with the door locked behind her and the blinds of the windows shut, she sat at the table near the hearth and studied the instructions she had been given. Much like her last two assignments, this one, too, was odd. The instructions were sparse and yet, at the same time, oddly specific. The usual process was the client would give the Elders their list of requirements and then the Elders would make whatever adjustments were needed to ensure that each Sister could complete the assignment while still adhering to the rules of The Order.

This process, it seemed, had changed suddenly and without much explanation from the Mothers. Nasya's last assignment had been extremely odd in that the instructions given to her by the Elders did not adhere to the rules of The Order. Specifically, the rule that all assignments were to be completed in private so as to pose as little risk as possible to themselves and, through them, The Order. It was why each of the Sisters were given aliases. No one but the members of The Order knew their real identities. And yet, her last assignment, the client had asked that it be completed publicly, and the Elders did not object.

Nasya stared at the parchment in her hands. Her stomach churned with nervousness. She had been extremely lucky to have escaped her previous assignment and this one too was to take place during the masquerade. It was against all the proto-cols she had been taught. She couldn't help but feel as though something was going on around her that she couldn't see, some-thing untoward and secretive. Still, this was her job. It was what she had been trained to do, and if The Order was changing, she would change with it.

# Chapter Thirteen

*Fortress of Fire's Hearth*
  *Country of Utara*

Nasya sat with her legs crossed on the stone floor. Dozens of scrolls were sprawled out in front of her. She was hunched forward, her eyebrows furrowed together as she perused them all, her silver eyes scanning for specific words. She was sixteen years old. She had been a recruit with The Order for eight years and had been studying magic with Mother Hydra for three. In those three years, much of her life had changed. Especially so since the moment she was given the choice to leave, and decided to stay. That day, that one moment in time, had been the solidification of everything she had been hoping to accomplish. The struggles, the conflicting desires, had faded into renewed motivation and determination.

Everything about her life at Fire's Hearth was different than it had been. It seemed that in the act of choosing to stay at Fire's Hearth and continue her training, her mind, her body, and her magical abilities fused together and created a new sense of self. It wasn't a conscious thing; it wasn't something she actively noticed, but rather it was like an advanced state of being. She felt more at ease. More sure of herself. Her struggles in training were typical now, exacting the usual kind of effort that comes with learning something new.

These accomplishments in training translated to more control over herself and her magic. She still had visceral, vivid dreams, but she was able to control herself both in the dream and in the real world. It wasn't that the magic itself was disconnected from her, or that it was less potent. Instead, it was as though it flowed more fully and more deeply through her body, permeating every thought, every movement. And the result was that she found herself more in control of her actions, even in sleep, her subconscious not allowing her magic to push her so close to the edge. She no longer walked or cast spells in her sleep. Her magic, once a force that she felt would never be controlled, was now as much a part of her existence as anything about her.

Mother Hydra no longer had to sleep in her room to prevent catastrophe. She, too, seemed impressed at how quickly Nasya had developed this newfound control of her powers.

"Remember this lesson, fledgling," she had said. "Internal conflict is more than just a rush of emotion and confusion. It is a catalyst for magic."

Nasya nodded. "Emotions fuel magic," she said.

"Yes, the negative emotions even more so than the positive. The moment you chose to stay here, your internal conflict dissipated and your emotions focused on controlling the magic within you." Mother Hydra gave her a strong, stern look. "Be wary of internal conflicts. They may take back the control you now hold."

It was a lesson Nasya had not allowed herself to forget. Her morning and evening meditations focused greatly on studying her internal motivations, desires, and hopes to ensure she was never that conflicted again. So far, it seemed to be working.

Even more impressively, Nasya had learned almost everything she could from Mother Hydra regarding magic and how to use it. Everything she was given to practice, she retained. Mother Hydra was a powerful and talented mage, and she taught Nasya well. But for the deeper, more intrinsic parts of magic, Nasya had to teach herself.

Fire's Hearth held a vast library of writings on magic: magical creatures, magic spells and wards, magic items, and general knowledge of how magic flowed through the earth. The more she read, the more she wanted to learn. As of yet, she hadn't found where her limits were. Mother Hydra warned against such tests. The zenith was always a point of which to be wary, as dangerous as it was. Nasya took Mother Hydra's warnings to tread carefully. So she read. Everything even remotely connected to magic, the Fae, or strange occurrences that had no explanation, Nasya studied until she had the details memorized. She knew dozens of spells by heart, could name off virtually every plant, stone, or gem that contained magical properties, and she was now studying every different kind of magic that had ever been recorded.

Through these studies, Nasya found that enchanters and sorcerers were, in fact, real. Perhaps some of the tales regarding them were more mythological, but their existence was fact. Nasya couldn't help but feel excited at the idea. And though the scrolls she read held relatively little information on them, it was enough to awaken more of her curiosity.

It was here that Mother Hydra found her.

"There you are," she said, walking into the main study hall, "Everything was so quiet, I thought perhaps you'd accidentally portaled somewhere."

Nasya grinned but didn't lift her eyes away from the scrolls on the floor.

"What are you reading today?" Mother Hydra asked.

"I'm looking for information on all the different forms of magic there are to see if I can do them all, or if my abilities are limited in some way."

Mother Hydra nodded slowly. "Well, I can tell you that there is a lot more information on those like me who had to learn how to access magic than there is on those like you."

At this, Nasya looked up at her. "Is that because there are more of your kind than mine? Or is it because your magic is more contained, more consistent?"

"Those are good questions, but I'm afraid I don't know. The

only answer I can provide is that for me, there is a clearly defined limit to how much magic I can access at one time. Mages usually cannot reach a zenith because our bodies simply cannot hold that much power inside of us."

"Never?"

She shrugged. "Well, almost never."

Nasya adjusted her sitting position and cocked her head to the side. "Then witches, warlocks, and mages cannot become either sorcerers or enchantresses?"

Mother Hydra's eyes glimmered as though she had been waiting for Nasya to ask this exact question. "Not on their own, no. They would need assistance from someone far more powerful than them just to even cast the spell."

"What spell?"

"Before anyone can reach the level of sorcerer or enchantress, a spell must be cast to ensure their physical form can withstand the shifting process."

Nasya leaned forward. "I don't understand. What's the shifting process?"

Mother Hydra actually smiled. "I'm guessing you haven't read through all of these scrolls yet," she said, sitting on the floor across from Nasya and her scattered pieces of parchment. "What is a sorcerer or enchantress?"

"A being of tremendous magical power," Nasya replied.

"And what's the difference between them?"

"Well, in terms of capabilities, there isn't a difference. What they each represent, however, is diametrically opposed to one another. Sorcerers typically have been known to stand for hoarding power and using their magic to conquer and destroy, whereas enchanters work to heal and bring about peace. In simple terms, one serves dark magic and the other light."

Mother Hydra nodded. "And what are dark and light magic?"

Nasya thought for a moment. She wasn't entirely sure what Mother Hydra was asking. "As I understand it, dark magic is used for evil and light magic is used for good," she said hesitantly.

Mother Hydra shook her head. "That is a common misconception. Dark and light magic are nothing more than representations of the types of powers a person has. For instance, shadow fae, blood fae, and dark fae are not inherently evil, and yet the magic they are most often connected to is dark magic. Mages, like myself, are usually connected to light magic, and yet there have been many mages who were cruel and committed horribly evil acts. It's true that sorcerers usually manipulate dark magic, but that isn't what makes them evil. It's what they use their magic for that determines their goodness, or lack thereof."

Nasya nodded as she listened.

"What have you read regarding the amount of power sorcerers and enchanters possess?" Mother Hydra asked.

"Only that they are unmatched by any other creature known to exist, except for furies," Nasya replied.

"Correct. And do you think that a mage like myself or a fae like you could possess that kind of magic as we currently are?"

"No, Mother," Nasya said, wondering why this thought had

never occurred to her before.

"You're right. That's why the spell of shifting is cast. Before anyone can ascend to that level of magical ability, their entire existence must be transformed into a vessel capable of holding that amount of magic inside of them. It doesn't guarantee that the person will survive the shifting process, but it gives them a chance. In many ways, it's similar to when a magical being reaches the zenith, only instead of accidentally being consumed by magic, the spell is intentional and performed under strict supervision to ensure that it holds."

"Has this spell ever actually been performed?" Nasya asked.

Mother Hydra nodded. "It has, though it's been centuries since it was last attempted."

"Then...people have successfully become sorcerers and enchanters?"

Mother Hydra's expression changed. Her eyes clouded with what seemed to be regret, and possibly shame. "They have, yes. But it exacts a steep price."

"What do you mean?"

She shook her head. "Another time, perhaps."

Nasya leaned forward. "No, now. Please."

Mother Hydra was shocked at the demanding tone of Nasya's voice, but rather than chastise her, she let out a deep sigh.

"Many centuries ago, The Order wanted to solidify its position in the world by utilizing magic in every way they could. They sought out only those children who exhibited magical abilities, and then pushed those children to their breaking points. It was this that illuminated the limitations for witches and mages, and for a time, The Order only took in children with fae blood. Dozens of recruits were lost to the zenith, and those that did manage to survive their training were forever altered." She met Nasya's gaze. "It's natural for us to romanticize magic, but the truth is that it, like any other force of power, can be exacting and cruel. Not everyone gifted with the ability to harness magic is suited to its influence. The Order quickly found that for many of their Sisters, magic had turned them bloodthirsty, warmongering, and power hungry. Within only a handful of years, at least half of the Sisters who had survived the rigorous magical training had abandoned The Order and committed horrible atrocities in the name of magic."

Nasya felt her skin go cold. "You are saying that magic corrupts."

"It can, fledgling. It can very easily. I wish I could say that it only occurred in those filled with hate, or those who had been maladjusted to their surroundings, but even the best and most disciplined recruits succumbed to the feeling of power and authority that magic gave them. Of those Sisters, four attempted the spell of shifting, the spell that would transform them into a being capable of containing the most powerful magic. Of those four, only one survived. The other three perished in what is believed to be the three worst deaths ever recorded."

Nasya's heart was racing. "What became of the one who survived?"

"No one knows. Whoever helped her merely recorded that

she had, indeed, survived, and that she was so physically altered as to be utterly unrecognizable, but nothing else was written down. She's immortal, wherever she is. And she is essentially a demigoddess, not that it does any of us much good."

"She disappeared?"

Mother Hydra nodded.

"And no one else has ever successfully ascended?"

"No other record exists of someone successfully ascending, no. But that doesn't mean it hasn't happened."

A question prodded at Nasya's mind, one she wasn't sure she wanted to ask. She knew she needed the answer, but was afraid of what it might be.

"Mother," she said, her voice shaky, "why...why did you say that...that I could be an enchantress?" She didn't even know how to meet the woman's gaze, and so she kept her eyes staring down at the floor.

It took several minutes before Mother Hydra answered. "Because you're the first recruit I've trained who, when confronted with your magic ability, was afraid of it."

At this, Nasya lifted her gaze to meet the older woman.

"Even now, when you have more control over your powers than you ever have before, you shy away from embracing your full potential. That's special, Nasya. And rare."

Nasya could only blink. What Mother Hydra said was true, she was afraid of her own power, but she never would have thought that her fear was what might make her worthy of it. They sat in silence for a while, and then Mother Hydra slowly stood to her feet and walked away, leaving Nasya to the company of scrolls and the silence of the training room.

The autumn air was filled with thick flakes of snow. Nasya sat at her lookout and stared over the vast stretch of wilderness below her. It was dark. Early morning hung over the land like a baited breath. Her wings hung down behind her, thick with feathers. Since the wings had first emerged from inside of her, every autumn they took on an extra layer of feathers to shield her against the cold. And then every spring, they were shed. It was jarring to see fae wings behave like those of actual birds since the fae possessed no other similarity to fowl, and yet the process continued every single year.

It had become one of her favorite pastimes to hike up to the lookout and then sit and stare at the trees below. She had been reading about these woods and, according to the scrolls, there was a deep magic that lived among the trees and forest folk. Were-creatures lived here, as did the spirits of the forests themselves. Somewhere deep in the heart of these woods were cities of the fae. And though Nasya had never seen any of these creatures, she keenly felt their presence, their magic, their influence on each other and the land.

Hidden behind clouds, a full moon shone bright silver against the black sky. And after several moments of watching from her perch, Nasya extended her wings outward and lept from her place. She dove towards the trees and flew just above their canopy, her silver eyes scanning the forest floor for anything interesting. She flew carefully, aiming for the hot spring where she and Scarlet had been secretly meeting as often as they could manage. Anymore, it was only a few times a year, but it was better than nothing at all.

The thought of Scarlet made Nasya's heart beat faster. Things were different now from when they were younger. The two girls were still extremely close, but there was an unspoken element to their connection that hadn't always been there. Nasya didn't know how to describe it, or if she should even mention it to Scarlet. Whatever it was had been growing between them for some time, and she knew Scarlet sensed it the same as she. What it meant, she couldn't say. But it was ever on her mind.

Out of the corner of her eyes, she saw movement below her. There was a clearing and in it she saw an enormous creature running on all fours in the same direction she was flying. It was a wolf, and it was clearly headed for the hot spring. Nasya's heart skipped. Scarlet wouldn't have any weapons to defend herself with if she encountered this beast. She would need help. Nasya flew as quickly as she could to the hot spring. It took her only a few minutes. She landed in front of the entrance and watched carefully for the approach of the wolf. Judging by its size from the air, Nasya felt certain it was a werewolf. Perhaps even a lycan, the largest of the werewolves and the most dangerous, the most bloodthirsty. Lycans were often lone wolves because they tended to be too brutal, too viscous to lead a pack successfully. Mother Hydra said they sometimes made their way this far north because it provided them safety from hunters. Nasya didn't know how she would face off against it, but she knew she had to try. Scarlet would be arriving at any moment, and Nasya wasn't about to let her fight the creature alone.

It came into view and Nasya cursed under her breath. It was enormous, at least six feet tall on all fours with paws as big as her head. Its fur was a blend of black and dark red, and its eyes glowed in the darkness. Its snout was stained with blood. Nasya spread out her wings as far as they would go, trying to make herself look larger, like more of a threat than she actually was. The wolf saw her and growled for a second, and then quieted. Nasya watched as it layed down in the snow, placing its head on its paws. She frowned. What was this? Some kind of trick? It whimpered then, its glowing eyes still locked with her own.

A moment later, the wolf began to change. She wasn't sure what was happening at first, but after a moment, it was clear that the werewolf was shifting out of its wolf form. Nasya watched, fascinated. She had never seen a were before, and certainly hadn't watched as one transformed. As the shifting continued, Nasya's eyes widened. The black and dark red fur turned into a girl with dark skin and dark, curly hair.

"Scarlet!" Nasya exclaimed. "You...but..."

Scarlet stood to her feet and let out a deep sigh. "You're earlier than I had anticipated. I didn't intend for you to see this," she said, moving quickly toward the cave with the hot spring. She was completely naked and needed to warm herself fast.

Nasya followed her into the cave. "You're a werewolf?" she exclaimed.

Scarlet jumped into the pool of hot water and grinned up at Nasya. "I'm a lycan, technically," she said, motioning for her friend to join her.

Nasya stood with her mouth gaping. She couldn't wrap her mind around this. Slowly, she began to strip down to her under garments, and then climbed into the hot spring with Scarlet.

"Why have you never told me?" Nasya asked, trying not to be mad that her friend had kept something this important from her.

Scarlet looked away and shrugged. "I didn't know how."

"What do you mean? You just open your mouth and say the words."

Scarlet sighed. "I know that," she said, flashing a somewhat exasperated glance towards Nasya, "but I just...I didn't know how you would take it."

Nasya frowned. "How I'd take it?"

"Can we change the subject, please?" Scarlet asked, laying her head back to soak her hair in the water.

Nasya frowned. "You still have blood on your face," she muttered.

Scarlet splashed water on her face and the two sat in the hot spring in silence. Nasya didn't want to be the one to speak next. Scarlet wanted to change the subject and Nasya wanted answers. It seemed to be an impasse. It took several moments of awkward silence before Nasya couldn't take it any longer.

"What did you mean when you said you didn't know how I would take it?"

Scarlet sighed in frustration. "I didn't know how you would take not being the only magical recruit in training."

Her words were enough to suck the breath from Nasya's lungs. She watched Scarlet for a long moment, unsure of how to express the hurt in her chest. Nasya resented the implication that she needed to be the only magical recruit among the remaining eight.

"You didn't tell me because you thought I needed to be special?" she asked, her voice quiet.

Scarlet met her gaze and held it, but didn't speak. Her silence was enough for Nasya. The pang in her chest grew with each beat of her heart. She looked away and tried to think of anything to say, but came up blank. Instead, she turned and began climbing out of the hot spring.

"No, Nasya, don't go," Scarlet pleaded, moving in her direction.

Nasya didn't speak. She simply grabbed her clothes, put them on haphazardly, and cast a warming spell on herself so that she could make it back to Fire's Hearth without freezing.

"Nasya, please," Scarlet said. "Don't leave it like this."

Without another word, she walked out into the night, unfurled her wings, and flew into the cold winter air. Tears fell down her cheeks. She couldn't believe what had just happened. How long had Scarlet kept this from her? From what she'd read of weres, their ability to shift at will took years to master. How many years it had been, she didn't know, but it had to have been at least three. That only made the pain worse; knowing Scarlet had kept this from her for so long. She couldn't help the hurt that her feelings for Scarlet were clearly deeper than Scarlet's were for her, if she didn't trust her enough to tell her the truth. Moreover, that Scarlet thought Nasya would be upset if she wasn't the only special recruit was too much for Nasya to handle. That was what stung the most.

Months passed and Nasya stopped going to the hot spring. She'd had many opportunities of doing so, and yet she chose to remain at Fire's Hearth. Instead, she read and she trained and she practiced her magic. She flew to higher elevations and strengthened her wings and her ability to navigate while flying. She studied the greater spells and incantations, committing them to memory. In an effort to keep herself centered and focused, she increased her meditative practice to three times each day. She wanted to keep her mind alert and connected to the magic flowing through the earth. Most importantly, she wanted to avoid internal conflicts.

One night in the middle of spring, Nasya was meditating before bed. She had been meditating for close to an hour, her mind blank, her breathing steady. Most nights, this process helped her prepare for sleep, but tonight was different. She heard a voice calling her name from outside of her room. She opened her eyes and turned to look at her open door. No one was there, but that was from where the voice had come. She waited a moment, and it called again.

She stood up and walked out into the hallway. The torches on the walls had all been put out. Only the faintest of light from the partially hidden moon illuminated the hall. The voice called to her again. It was a child. A boy, she thought. She followed it down the hall and into the library, but she saw no one. The library was empty and dark.

"Hello?" she called.

The sound of crying came from one of the back corners. Nasya followed the noise and scanned every aisle for any sign of someone, but she could see nothing. The voice was fainter now. Nasya closed her eyes and began to meditate again, wondering if that would help strengthen her connection to whomever it was that called to her. She breathed slowly and focused her thoughts on the boy. She used her mind to call out to him, to ask his name, to ask what he needed.

In her mind, he came to her. He was small. Underfed. He rubbed his eyes and moaned.

"I'm Nasya," she said. "What's your name?"

"Gavyn," he mumbled between sobs.

"What can I do for you, Gavyn?"

He merely groaned and turned away from her. She called for him to stop, to come back, but he ran into the darkness. She followed. She had to follow. She called his name, but she only heard his little sobs in the darkness. Finally, he stopped and crouched down, hiding his face in his arms.

"Please," Nasya said, "tell me what you need."

He sniffled and looked up at her. "She needs to let me go," he said, large tears streaming down his cheeks. "Tell her to let me go!"

Nasya furrowed her eyebrows. "Tell who?"

"Ygritte," he said, hiding his face once more. "My mother."

Nasya was about to ask who that was when a different voice called her name and snapped her back to consciousness. Nasya blinked and found herself no longer in the library, but standing in Mother Hydra's room. She looked around, confused as to how she had come to be here when only a moment before, she had been in the library. Then she looked at Mother Hydra. Her eyes were wide and she was staring just past her.

Nasya turned and saw the boy, Gavyn, standing in the doorway. She looked back at Mother Hydra. "Do you see him?"

Mother Hydra nodded, her eyes still wide and unblinking. Nasya shook her head. She felt dizzy, her mind like liquid, as though she had just awoken from a long, deep sleep. She looked back at the boy and he stared at her and at Mother Hydra.

"I'm tired, mama," he said. His lips moved, but the words came out of Nasya's mouth in a blend of her own voice and the child's.

Mother Hydra didn't move. She didn't speak. She simply stood and stared, her mouth gaping and her eyes flicking back and forth between the boy and her pupil.

"Mama," he said, rubbing his eyes, "I'm tired and it's cold."

"How…" Mother Hydra began, her voice soft and shaky. "How do you know this conversation?" she asked, her gaze piercing into Nasya's.

The sixteen year old couldn't answer. She didn't know what was happening. Everything was hazy. She wanted to rest, to sleep, to walk away from whatever was going on and let the darkness of slumber take her. But she couldn't. A connection had been made, that much she knew. It was like an anchor in her chest, as though Gavyn had been waiting for her to reach out to him. Nasya didn't know how that could even be possible, but it didn't matter now.

"It's too dark," said Gavyn, his voice shifting slowly from the sound of a child's voice to something deeper and raspy. "It's too dark! I want light! Too cold! Too cold! Too cold!"

Nasya's heart raced. She was frozen, suspended between the past and present. In her mind she could see the hovel, the holes in the roof, the dying embers of a fire in the hearth. And all at once, Gavyn's body became engulfed in flames. Nasya heard screaming, a woman's voice, and in only a fraction of a breath, the boy was gone. He was gone from the hovel, and he was gone from Mother Hydra's room. Nasya collapsed to the floor in a heap of tears and deep breaths sucked into her lungs in sharp gasps.

Mother Hydra still did not move or speak. She stared at the place where Gavyn had stood and tears glistened in her eyes.

"What...is...happening...to me?" Nasya asked, dry heaving in between gasps for air. Every part of her body tingled as though needles were being pressed into her skin over and over. Her stomach churned in an endless tumult, sometimes making her nearly sick, and other times just producing coughs and bile in her throat and mouth.

"We have found your particular magical ability," Mother Hydra said softly, sitting on the edge of her bed.

Nasya looked up at her through vision blurred by tears. She was even more dizzy than she had been previously and she couldn't get the room to stop spinning, or to quiet the continuous pounding of her heart in her ears. It took a moment, but Mother Hydra finally saw that Nasya was struggling and she knelt next to her on the floor and placed a hand on her forehead.

"You're burning up," she said, slowly helping her to her feet. "We must get you back to your room and in bed."

The moment Nasya was standing, she finally retched onto the stone floor. It occurred to her that she had been sick on Mother Hydra's bedroom floor, and for a second she felt horribly embarrassed, but a moment later she nearly lost consciousness just by taking a step forward. This kind of reaction to magic had never happened to her before and she was suddenly frightened. She could feel her body growing hot and cold simultaneously. She felt horribly nauseated with each step she took, and barely clung to consciousness.

As they made their way towards her chamber, Nasya's mind was filled with thoughts and questions and every emotion.

Mother Hydra tried to keep her calm.

"It's alright," she said softly, "You will be alright. Your body is reacting to the new strain of magic you've connected to."

Nasya was too sick to understand. She had meditated before. She had heard voices before. She had seen ghosts before. Why was this suddenly a new strain of magic? She tried to ask, but was sick again, vomiting onto the stone floor of the hallway just outside her chamber. She mumbled an apology that Mother Hydra did not respond to. A moment later, she was laying in her bed and Mother Hydra was calling for the cook. The elderly woman came quickly into the room.

"I need pitchers of hot water and clean cloth brought quickly. Also, please bring me my kit."

It was the last full sentence Nasya heard before she began to slip into and out of consciousness. All she knew for a long time was tremendous heat and horrible cold. It seemed every few seconds, her body's need for warmth and cold shifted without warning. Voices were around her and every now and again, a blurred face would come into view, but she couldn't identify to whom it belonged. Nor did she care. Her body ached and shivered. She was sick over and over, whether there was anything in her stomach to purge or not. She couldn't keep anything down, not even the simplest of broths. Her clothes were changed several times, she was sweating so severely. At one point, before losing consciousness entirely, she heard a frightened voice say, "She's so pale."

In response, Mother Hydra said, "I did not think it would

make her this ill."

Then she knew only darkness.

Nasya didn't want to leave the darkness. It was calm there, and quiet. She couldn't feel her body at all, and it was a relief. Yet, something tugged at her mind, tugged gently, almost nudging her out of the darkness. There was something she needed to see. Reluctantly, she allowed herself to connect to the movement and slowly, light began to wax into view. It was blurry at first and took a while to come into focus, but when it did, she saw a scene she had not anticipated. She saw herself laying in bed, her face pale and her hair slicked with sweat. To one side of her sat Mother Hydra, holding her fingers against Nasya's wrist to check her pulse. To the other side of her sat Scarlet, her eyes wide with fear.

"Will she be alright?" Scarlet asked, looking up at Mother Hydra.

The woman sighed. "I do not know. I've never seen this kind of a reaction to magic before."

Scarlet's brows furrowed and she looked back down at Nasya's unconscious body. "Is it really so bad?"

"It's the worst I've ever seen," Mother Hydra said. "Typically the sickness is the worst for the first twenty-four hours, and then tapers off swiftly. Nasya has been increasingly ill for seventy-two hours, at least, and there's no sign of it tapering at all." She shook her head. "I haven't the slightest idea what it means or how to treat it."

Nasya raised her eyebrows and blinked slowly. She had been

incapacitated for three days? How was that even possible?

"Do you think it's specifically necromancy causing her body to react this way?" Scarlet asked.

"I do. I cannot think of what else it might be, and communing with the dead is known to be a dangerous feat. There's no telling how a particular spirit will impact one's mind, body, and soul."

Necromancy? What necromancy? Nasya felt a headache coming on. She heard voices and saw ghosts, but that didn't mean she could commune with the dead. What had given Mother Hydra that idea? Scarlet and Mother Hydra were quiet for several minutes, giving Nasya time to adjust to this information, though it certainly wasn't the kind she had ever thought she would have to adjust to in the first place. She wasn't a necromancer. She couldn't be. She had read about necromancy quite a bit since coming to Fire's Hearth, and she had specifically avoided any spells or incantations that might link her to a spirit of the dead because of how dangerous it was known to be. Ghosts were relatively harmless. They could walk among you and give you a fright, but they couldn't hurt you. Necromancy created a link between the dead and the living; this meant that the living soul could communicate with the dead, but it also meant the dead could possess the living person's body and mind. The souls of the dead were not always benevolent and, if given the chance, would wreak havoc on the living person trying to commune with them.

It was then that Nasya recalled a small piece of information that she had forgotten until now. There were two kinds of necromancers: those who used spells and incantations to temporarily commune with the dead, and those born with an inherent ability to connect with the realms of the dead. The former was far more common and much easier to control, while the latter was little better than an absolute curse, unless the person could learn how to control the ability. Suddenly, everything fell into place. She was the latter. It explained how she was able to hear so many voices, see so many spirits, have all of those dreams that felt like prophecy: she was not simply hearing and seeing things, she was, and always had been, accessing the realms of the dead and not-alive. And connecting to Gavyn, the little boy, was the final step in awakening this inherent ability.

"Is there anything I can do to help?" Scarlet asked.

"You're doing everything you can already," Mother Hydra said.

"It's just..." Scarlet grabbed a cloth, dipped it into the cold water by Nasya's bed, and gently wiped off the unconscious girl's forehead, "when last we spoke, we quarreled and...I don't want her to...without knowing how sorry I am."

Nasya could hear the tears catching in Scarlet's throat, and her heart panged.

"I know that you two meet at the cave of the hot springs," Mother Hydra said, "and I can tell when the two of you have argued. Nasya comes back in a huff and pours herself into her studies. It's the only way she knows how to cope."

Nasya had never seen any of the Mothers display so much kindness and compassion towards a recruit. She knew Mother

Hydra had kindness within her, and some of it had even been extended towards herself, but in this moment she was talking to Scarlet as an equal, and that was unheard of.

"I also know how much the two of you care for one another," Mother Hydra added, "which is why I sent for you in the first place. I thought having you here would make tending to her easier. I thought she might sense your presence and...push through all of this."

Scarlet nodded but didn't speak, and Nasya felt herself overwhelmed with emotion.

"The truth is," Mother Hydra continued, "I've never seen anyone as young as her possess so much power. If she survives, she will make an incredible Hand of the Order, but really, the more I see of her, the more I feel instinctively that she is meant for far more than this life. No one born of fae blood with wings like hers will be content with the life of an assassin for very long." Mother Hydra looked at Scarlet. "We will need her eventually, and for her sake as well as ours, I pray she pulls through this."

# Chapter Fourteen

*Fortress of Fire's Hearth*
  *Country of Utara*

It took nearly three weeks, but Nasya did, in fact, pull through the sickness that grabbed hold of her. By the fourth day, the fever broke and she settled into a restful slumber. By the fifth, she was able to eat two bowls of broth a day, and by the second week, she was fully conscious and able to resume her studies. She was still physically exhausted, and not wanting to trigger a flareup of the sickness, Mother Hydra insisted she remain in bed for another week, with only small excursions around the fortress to build her strength. Once the three weeks had passed, Nasya was back to her usual self. And though she was healthy again, Scarlet remained at Fire's Hearth, and no one spoke of her returning to Passing's End.

With each day, Nasya waited for Scarlet to bring up their argument, but the moment never came. She could see that Scarlet wanted to mention it, she could even tell when she was close to doing so, but the words never passed her lips. Nasya didn't want to be the one to initiate the conversation, nor did she even know how. She was still hurt that Scarlet had not trusted her. It seemed they were both willing to let the anticipated conversation pass away, though neither could deny that, even unspoken, it hung between them like a silent truth neither wanted to admit.

Nasya's training with Mother Hydra took a turn as well. Although she was not a necromancer herself, Mother Hydra taught Nasya everything she could to help her control the ability and learn to use it to her advantage.

"What do we know of the afterlife?" Mother Hydra asked her as she moved through the forms of hand-to-hand combat.

"Precious little, Mother," Nasya replied, "but what we do suggests that the realms of life and afterlife run parallel to each other, sometimes intersecting and disconnecting randomly."

"And what causes these interminglings?"

"Magic, Mother."

"And what is magic?"

"A gift. A force. And a weapon."

"And what are you?"

"A gift. A force. And a weapon."

"Which means?"

"I am the connection between the realms of life and afterlife."

"Which means?"

"I can see, hear, and touch what others cannot."

Mother Hydra stood and watched Nasya's movements, her eyes squinted together in thought.

"Why is it dangerous for you to have this connection?" she asked.

"Because the spirits of the dead are unpredictable and uncontrollable."

"Which means?"

"I cannot control the spirit or spirits I am connected to. I can only control myself and how deep I allow myself to go within the connection."

Mother Hydra nodded. "Very good. And what happens if you go too deep?"

Nasya hesitated. She didn't know the answer. As far as she knew, there wasn't an answer because it had never happened before, or at least had never been recorded.

"The zenith?" she asked, unsure if this was correct or not.

Mother Hydra shook her head slowly. "Not technically, no. Necromancy is a form of death magic that impacts the body and the mind differently than any other type of magic. Going too deep into the connection with the realm of the dead will prove fatal, yes, but not because there's too much magic inside of one physical form."

She was quiet, clearly waiting for Nasya to try and answer again. Nasya thought for a moment, continuing to move through her forms.

"Because life can only look so far into death before becoming death itself," Nasya said.

Mother Hydra nodded. "Yes, very good. This is why you will need more than meditation to control your magic. Spirits of the dead have been known to cause mischief, to tease and prod at necromancers, to lure the souls of the living into the land of the dead like sirens. You must be aware of these things at all times. You must have control of your power, to know how to turn it off once you've made the connection, and how to keep it off once you've disconnected."

Nasya nodded and continued through her forms. There was a question in the back of her mind, one that she wasn't sure she wanted the answer to. But before she could stop herself, she spoke.

"Is it common for only a half-fae to be born with this magic?"

Mother Hydra took in a deep, slow breath.

"Common? No. But nor is it unheard of."

"I did read once that life and death magic are reserved only for the most powerful of beings," Nasya said. "Shouldn't the human half of me dilute that power?"

"There's still much we do not know about your heritage," Mother Hydra said. "In fact, I continue to be surprised at just how much magic flows through you. It shouldn't be possible with human blood, and yet it is made evident in your growth and strength."

Nasya stopped her forms. She was breathing deeply and sweat was dripping down the sides of her face.

"What does that mean?" Nasya asked.

"It means, fledgling, that whoever your real parents were, at least one of them was an extremely powerful fae, and their blood is your blood."

"The power is in the blood," Nasya muttered.

Days turned to weeks and things between Nasya and Scarlet began to improve. The awkwardness dissipated. The two girls found their footing with one another. They sparred together, took meals together, studied together, and made their way through the woods to the hot spring together, as though nothing had been amiss between them. Nasya still thought of Scarlet being a lycan, and she often wanted to jump into the conversation and get it over with, but the more time passed, the harder it was to discuss. Weeks and months carried them from season to season and the argument was forgotten.

Nasya completed the regular training for recruits and focused entirely on the magical elements of her training. Mother Hydra wanted her to be as prepared as possible for graduation, since she was now one of the remaining six recruits. Of all the girls who came to The Order for training, they were the ones who had lasted the longest, and they would be the new Sisters. Unsurprisingly, Scarlet was among them. Nasya couldn't help the thrill she felt at knowing that she and Scarlet had both nearly made it to the end, as had Florynce, Kassra, Maeve, and Briony.

Nasya wasn't particularly close to any of the others, but nor did she have any grievances against them. They weren't friends, but nor were they enemies. They were, as Nasya saw it, allies in the future that would impact them all.

"What will happen with the current Sisters?" Nasya asked Mother Hydra at supper one day. "Will they take over as Mothers? And will you go on to be Elders?"

Mother Hydra did not look at Nasya or acknowledge her question at first. Nasya cast a confused look at Scarlet who shrugged, and the two waited in silence for her answer.

"That has been the usual order of things," she said at last, still not looking at either girl, "but as there currently aren't any Sisters, there's no one to take our place as Mothers, and so the only change will be that you will graduate and become Sisters of The Order."

Nasya furrowed her eyebrows. "Why aren't there any Sisters currently active?"

Mother Hydra cleared her throat. "They died."

Neither Scarlet nor Nasya were prepared for that answer.

"All of them?" Scarlet asked.

Mother Hydra nodded.

"That seems peculiar," Scarlet added.

"It is," Mother Hydra said, taking a sip from her ale.

"How did they die?" Nasya asked.

Only then did Mother Hydra lift her gaze to meet the girls'.

"That is not information you need, fledgling," she said. "Suffice to say, their deaths were unexpected."

Neither Nasya nor Scarlet inquired further. They sensed the subject was a tender one and did not wish to anger Mother Hydra. But there was something odd in the tone of her voice, a tension that indicated she still felt keenly the loss of the former group of Sisters. Nasya couldn't help but wonder what had happened. It seemed impossible that six highly skilled and well trained assassins could all die unexpectedly. What could it possibly mean? And why was Mother Hydra holding the truth of it so close to herself? Nasya resolved to uncover the truth on her own.

She waited several weeks and then looked in the library for any texts on the event, but found nothing. In fact, she could find no instance of all six Sisters dying unexpectedly in the entire history of The Order. This only piqued her curiosity for it must have been something very particular to have happened at all. She wanted to try and access the realm of the dead to see if any answers awaited her there, but she didn't trust herself to control the connection yet, so instead opted to induce a dream-filled sleep. It was a far less intense version of necromancy, usually reserved for those who were not inherently necromancers, but it could do the trick.

Nasya studied the spell closely for over a week. She memorized it inside and out, backwards and frontwards, until she could practically perform it in her sleep. The spell had two parts: one was the liquid concoction she had to make that would put her to sleep, and it required exact measurements of each ingredient to ensure that she would only sleep for a certain amount of time; the second was the incantation that would use her dreams as a means of accessing the realm of the dead. This also had to be precisely executed so that she only went so far into the afterlife, and would disconnect from the realm of the dead once she awoke. Nasya studied both parts of the spell until she knew for certain the measurements were correct. Then, on a calm, quiet night with a full moon to balance the connection, she drank the potion and climbed into bed, ready to receive whatever information she could.

The first thing she heard was the sound of a river. Light enveloped the darkness so brightly, she had to close her eyes and slowly open them to adjust to the golden sun shining down onto the rushing water. She stood in an open glen surrounded by forest. Everything was green and warm with summer. It was beautiful and, for now, quiet. Birds chirped in the trees and a gentle breeze shook the leaves. The river water smelled of fresh mountain runoff.

But in only a few seconds, things changed. Something was wrong. Very wrong. The first indication was the suddenly overwhelming scent of blood that filled her nostrils. It was intense and made her heart begin to race faster. She couldn't move much of her body at first, and nothing in her direct line of sight explained the smell. Then, the sound of teeth crunching bones came from behind her. She willed herself to move and slowly turned. She had to swallow the scream that swelled in her throat.

The ground was covered in blood and dismembered body

parts. It was impossible to tell how many bodies there had originally been, they were so unrecognizable. But in her heart, she knew that these were the bodies of her Sisters. Five werewolves were before her, their teeth crunching down on flesh, muscle, bone. Walking among them was a figure she couldn't quite make out, but she had the voice of a woman.

"Remember to gather the hearts," she said, "and place them in the boxes you were given. We will need them before the night is over."

Nasya watched as the wolves continued to feast. As their bellies filled with blood and meat, they began to shift back into their human forms. They each reached into the bodies of those they had killed, grabbed the hearts, and placed them in identical wooden boxes. The woman who had spoken to the wolves came over to the body Nasya was in and reached deep into her chest. It was then that Nasya and the woman both realized the Sister was not yet dead. Nasya gasped as The Sister gasped, feeling a hand wrap around her heart as its pulse slowed. The woman stared down into the dying Sister's face. Nasya was both Sister and observer in this moment as the realms of life and death began to blur together.

"They didn't save you, did they?" the woman asked, holding onto the Sister's heart, but not yet pulling it out of her open chest. "Not a single one came to your aid." She squeezed a little tighter, causing Nasya and the Sister to gasp and groan. "If you think they didn't know, then you are sorely mistaken." The woman leaned in closer. "They left you here to die."

She tore the Sister's heart from her chest and placed it in a box just like the others. She laughed as life drained from the Sister's face. Nasya forced herself to take a deep breath as she felt the life of the Sister drain away. She watched, incredulous, as the woman stood to her feet and turned away from the Sister she had just killed. The edges of her vision blurred and then went dark entirely.

She awoke with a gasp and sat up in her bed. She didn't know how long she had been asleep, but all was quiet outside of her bed chamber. The fire in her hearth had not yet died out, so she couldn't have been asleep for very long. And yet, what she saw in her dream was no more helpful than Mother Hydra's explanation had been. She already knew the Sisters had been unexpectedly killed. Nasya let out a frustrated sigh and grabbed a piece of parchment and a quill. She wanted to write down the details as she remembered them. They would be her primary point of inquiry in the coming days. And already she knew she would need to induce yet another dream-filled sleep if she was going to arrive at any definitive conclusions. It occurred to her that she might very well be toying with information she was not ready to hear, but she couldn't help it. There was something strange about this turn of events, something that wouldn't al-low her to ignore it. And despite the risks, she was determined to find out the truth.

Weeks passed and nothing changed. She tried inducing other dreams to connect with the spirits of the Sisters who were killed, but none of them offered any further information. Most of the dreams showed the same event over and over from different Sister's perspectives, and one had been nothing more than a Sister sitting in the cold and the rain by herself watching for someone or something to come up the path towards Passing's End. Nasya was frustrated at her inability to focus her dreams on the point in time she most wanted to see, but after many failed attempts, she realized that the reason she wasn't getting any new information was likely because the Sisters themselves hadn't known who was attacking them or why.

Nasya poured over the details she'd written of every dream, anxious for a clue, or even the quietest whispers of one. She had seen the slaughter of the Sisters from four different perspectives. The dream by the river was where the remaining four Sisters had been cornered and attacked. Nasya had hoped this meant she could see the first two murders, believing that they might offer insight the other deaths couldn't, but no matter how hard she tried, the first two spirits eluded her. Nasya knew this was a possibility. Even necromancers weren't able to channel the spirits of every dead person. The spirit had to consent to the connection first.

Scarlet noticed Nasya's quiet dedication to this experiment, though she didn't know precisely what Nasya was attempting to accomplish. Sometimes she watched Nasya work, pouring over scrolls and other texts looking for clues on how to hone her focus on a specific spirit. Nasya enjoyed her company, but wasn't entirely sure she wanted her to know what she was trying to do. If Mother Hydra found out, Nasya was sure she would put a stop to it.

The friendship between Scarlet and Nasya had reverted back to what it had always been, and while this made Nasya content, she couldn't deny that she was also saddened. She remembered overhearing conversations between Scarlet and Mother Hydra; she remembered what Scarlet had said, and it pained her to know that, now her life was no longer in danger, Scarlet no longer felt an urgency to put words to her feelings and her regrets. Nasya knew she could always be the one to initiate the conversation, but her pride wouldn't let her. She was the one who had been hurt. She should not, now, have to be the one to repair the damage done.

Yet, something else lingered beneath the pain that made Nasya's stomach flutter, a truth that she could neither deny nor give a voice to. She knew that she had overreacted to Scarlet not telling her that she was a werewolf, and yet the unspoken truth was what led her to overreact. It was what filled her heart with confusion and turmoil, knowing that her best friend in the entire world didn't trust her enough to confide in her. Even if they were to discuss the argument, unless the unspoken truth was spoken, nothing would actually be repaired between them.

And for her part, Nasya wasn't prepared to cross that line. Not yet. Not now.

# Chapter Fifteen

*Capital City of Sun River*
*Country of Utara*

Hundreds of the wealthiest Utaran citizens, and hundreds more from foreign shores, made up the occupants of the room, all dressed in their finest. They wore gowns of the brightest silks and the richest velvets trimmed with gold, silver, and pearlescent ribbon, and tunics of equally bright linen trimmed in shimmering thread. Chandeliers hung from the ceiling, each covered completely with lit candles to illuminate the room. Tables lined the walls covered with plates, goblets, elaborate dishes, and dozens of bottles of wine and kegs of ale. It was apparently King Tavin's intention to display just how little he cared about his own financial straits in the sight of such wealthy guests, for he had spared no expense. Nothing was too good for his youngest son.

Nasya Ember stood in the back corner, pretending to sip on her goblet of wine. She had been in the ballroom for only an hour, not wanting to be the first or the last to arrive. She watched the other guests with mild interest, noting those which looked the most out of place; they were usually from the lands farthest away from Utara, and their fashions were intriguing. She watched the guests mingle, eat, drink, flirt, and after several minutes, dance as the orchestra began to play. This was, if she was honest, her favorite part of her occupation: the waitin, and the watching. It gave her the best thrill.

At the other end of the ballroom sat King Tavin with his two sons, High Prince Mael, heir to the throne, and Prince Xaran. Nasya's silver eyes watched them curiously. They were each clad in deep purple and gold tunics, evidence of their royal heritage and family bloodline. Crowns of gold sat atop their heads. High Prince Mael, the eldest by eight years, looked grave and serious. He had long brown hair that hung in loose waves over his shoulders. He wore a white mask that covered everything but his eyes and the lower portion of his face. He was clean shaven and seemed to be purposefully ignoring the two women seated on either side of him as they attempted to make small talk. Instead, he stared over the dancing couples, clearly unamused by the proceedings and, perhaps, irritated at the massive expense.

Nasya had read a lot regarding King Tavin and his two sons. High Prince Mael was known to be a grave fellow devoted to his duty as the heir to the throne. He had done what he could to lessen his father's expenses and had tried to find a way to end the war with Hevean, but it had all been to no avail. His father was still king, after all, and the man was helpless when it came to the amusements and desires of his youngest son. Watching the High Prince now, Nasya couldn't blame him for his disinterest in the party.

Her eyes flitted to where Prince Xaran sat, goblet in hand and eyes alight with laughter. He was not as tall as his brother, nor quite as intimidating, though he was considered the more attractive of the two. He had a head of short, blonde curls and eyes of an intense chestnut-brown. He wore no mask at all. Nasya grinned to herself as she watched him interact with the individuals around him, most of whom were women. Unlike his brother, he couldn't seem to get enough attention. It was known that Prince Xaran was the womanizing romantic who wasted his days drinking and falling in and out of love, while High Prince Mael worked to better Utara. It was unfortunate that he had been able to accomplish very little due to his father's and brother's efforts to bankrupt the country. The brothers could not have been more different.

Nasya looked around the room and wondered at the guests. They all must have known King Tavin's financial position, and yet they were here all the same, eating food he couldn't afford, the cost of which could have fed everyone in the capitol for months. It was an absolute spectacle, the likes of which Nasya had never seen before in all her thirty years of life.

Nasya had made her own costume for the masquerade. It was a gown of charcoal colored satin which, in certain lighting, appeared to be a deep, dark blue. It was long and flowed elegantly as she moved. From her back extended her two enormous black wings. Her feathers matched the gown and looked as though they were part of her costume. Her mask, adorned with black feathers and matching the color of her gown, covered her eyes and spread out from her face in the shape of wings. Her hair was pulled back into an elaborate braid, dark from the ink she had run through it. Her shadowed appearance contrasted against the silver of her eyes. Perhaps the most intriguing component of her costume was the pair of crystal-like slippers. They were made of dragon glass, a rare form of crystal made from the heat of dragon's breath kissing the sands of the earth. It was a feature of her costume that she hoped to use to her advantage. The front of Nasya's gown was shorter than the rest, revealing the fantastically glittering slippers. Those who would not have noticed her otherwise suddenly found themselves staring throughout the evening, once Nasya decided she was ready to begin attracting attention.

Among those staring were High Prince Mael and Prince Xaran.

Nasya walked slowly along the line of tables, picking up little pieces of food and chewing them absent-mindedly. She watched the dancers and kept track of the two princes in her periphery. Her success in this moment would depend greatly on how she played to the princes' desires, weaknesses, intentions. Patience was her greatest asset.

She was asked to dance by a number of men and women, all of which she accepted. She made only the briefest attempts at conversation with each partner as they led her across the ballroom floor. Her eyes fell on the two royal sons more than once and each time she found them staring at her, even as other women attempted to distract them both. In High Prince Mael's eyes she saw fascination, desire, and jealousy. In Prince Xaran's, there was focus, lust, and amusement. Which of them would ask her to dance first, she wondered.

# Chapter Sixteen

*Fortress of Passing's End*
*Country of Utara*

Nasya stared out the window of the room she shared with Scarlet. Mother Hydra, Nasya, and Scarlet had all returned to Passing's End earlier that morning. Soon, Scarlet would be taking her final test, determining her graduation from training. Nasya would take the same test, but hers would be different. Where Scarlet and the other recruits had merely to prove they'd completed their training through a series of questions and some randomized physical challenges, Nasya's test would be more personal. She was the only recruit with magic, and so could not be tested in the same way as the others.

It had been years since she'd last set foot in this room. It was amazing to think that the room itself hadn't changed at all while she had changed entirely. The girl she had been when last here was no longer; now, she was eighteen, a young woman filled with fire and excitement. It had been a long journey, one of complications and contradictions, but the person she was now was worth all of it.

Footsteps behind her caused her to turn. Scarlet walked into the room and smiled.

"I figured this was where you'd gone," she said, sitting on the edge of her bed.

"I didn't plan on coming here first," Nasya replied, walking to her own bed and sitting down. "I just found myself here."

"It's incredible, isn't it?" Scarlet asked, "Thinking of all the things we shared in this room."

Nasya grinned. "This was where we first met," she said, recalling the moment as if it had been just the day before.

"All of the nightmares I had to wake you from."

"The jokes you made at night to make me laugh and calm me down."

"The secrets we shared."

"Your smelly sock."

Scarlet turned wide eyes filled with amusement toward Nasya. The two young women laughed.

"When is your test?" Scarlet asked.

"In a fortnight," Nasya replied. "Apparently, I am to be the last recruit tested."

Scarlet nodded slowly. "Apparently, I am to be the first. Mine is in two days."

"Unsurprising. You've always been their favorite."

Scarlet rolled her eyes. "It was never a privilege I wanted."

Nasya shrugged. "Is it really so bad? Knowing that you are liked and respected among the Mothers?"

Scarlet sighed and stood to her feet. "No, not at all, but being singled out is never fun."

Nasya couldn't help but laugh out loud. "You don't have to tell me, darling."

Scarlet grinned. "I mean that having such high expectations placed on you doesn't leave room for anything else." She walked to the window. "There's no normalcy, no margin for error. Everything I've done has been analyzed and dissected since the moment I arrived here." She sighed heavily. "I'll be glad to have a moment's peace when I can finally leave this wretched place behind for good."

Nasya furrowed her eyebrows. "Well, Passing's End might fade away, but we will be just as much a part of The Order as we are now."

Scarlet said nothing.

"Do you know what your cover is going to be?" Nasya asked, suddenly uncomfortable with the silence between them. It had become their habit of moving on from the discomfort and awkwardness whenever it arose, neither of them willing or able to give voice to their deepest, most urgent questions and concerns.

Scarlet turned away from the window. "I do. Mother Fornax said I am to be a bounty hunter."

Nasya grinned. "Oh, how tantalizing."

Scarlet blushed and looked away. "What about you?"

Nasya leaned back on her elbows and began to speak in a melodramatic and teasing tone. "I am to be part of the oldest profession, an added member to that long tradition of women taking up their own livelihoods to make a living-"

Scarlet laughed. "Oh gods above and below, just get to the point!"

"I'm to be a whore," she said with a heaving sigh. "Every few years I'll move on to a different town or city, and when I'm in between assignments, I'll be earning a living in a brothel."

"I think Briony received the same cover."

"I'm surprised more of us haven't. It's really the only option for women that doesn't draw too much attention."

"Can you believe that Florynce is to be a political advisor in Hevean?" Scarlet asked, her eyes wide and bright. "After all the focus on stealth and drawing attention away from ourselves, they're sending a member of The Order to be an advisor to the cousin of the queen! It's the least stealthy cover I think they could have given her."

"And Florynce already attracts so much attention from how beautiful she is," Nasya added, "how is she to maintain a rigorous schedule with political issues in one of the largest countries in the west and manage to sneak away to assassinate people without drawing even more attention to herself?" Nasya shook her head. "It is utterly counterintuitive."

"It seems they're setting her up to fail."

Nasya sighed. "I suppose of the six of us, Florynce is the most regal and the least likely to be suspected of being an assassin," Nasya said. "She's meek and gentle and quiet. Perhaps that's why they chose her for that cover?"

"I don't deny that, but it is still strange. And, as far as I know, has never been done before."

Nasya shook her head. "No, that's not true. Mother Lynx was a political advisor to a count in Utara when she was a Sister. It's not completely unprecedented. Although it is still odd, to be sure."

Scarlet didn't respond. Nasya's information clearly didn't alleviate her concerns and, truth be told, Nasya didn't like where her own thoughts were leading her. Everything the Mothers did up to this point made sense. Drawing one of their own so openly into the public eye where she would have tremendously important duties while also a secret member of The Order did not make sense. Nasya could think of no explanation for it, even though Mother Lynx had been put in a similar situation decades before. What was to be gained by it when there was everything to lose if someone were to follow her? Nasya had no answer. She determined within herself that it was not her place to question the Mothers. For all they knew, this was a particular choice made with specific intentions by the Elders and had a perfectly reasonable explanation.

"Where will you set up your practice first?" Scarlet asked, changing the subject.

"For now, I am to travel to the city of Garden's Hem. It's on the eastern Utaran coast," Nasya said.

"That's quite a distance," Scarlet said, moving to lay down on her bed.

Nasya nodded. "I believe they want me to go back and forth between Utara and Hevean, see what pieces of intriguing information I can pick up from my clients."

Scarlet shook her head. "It seems we're to be spies as well as assassins," she said, her voice low.

Nasya couldn't deny that things were not as they had envisioned them when they were younger. She wasn't sure when they'd all realized what they were being trained for, but when the moment came, none of the recruits had been surprised. What else could they possibly be training for? Yet, even as they learned, it was clear that something else was brewing beneath the surface. Everything they imagined as their training intensified was different in actuality than what the Mothers had described, sometimes in small ways, and others in much greater disparities as to be entirely different.

Now, the remaining six had reached the end of their training, had surpassed all expectations the Mothers had held for them for years, and the lives they had planned for were about to come to pass. And at every turn, the unexpected never ceased to reveal themselves.

"How long do you think it will be until we see each other again?" Scarlet asked, breaking the chain of thoughts rushing through Nasya's mind.

Nasya turned and looked at her. "What do you mean?"

Scarlet rolled onto her side and lifted herself onto her elbow. "You're going to Garden's Hem. I will be on the opposite side of the country to make a living in the western woods." She looked down at her hands. "I just...can't help but wonder when we'll be able to see each other once we've graduated."

"You can always visit me," Nasya said, sitting up and facing her. "Utara is relatively small in comparison with its neighbors. Traveling from west to east shouldn't take more than six weeks on foot. Faster still if you travel by post."

Scarlet didn't respond or lift her gaze to look at Nasya. The two sat still and in silence for some time. Nasya wasn't sure why but she began to feel annoyed. Were they truly going to act as if the events of the previous two years hadn't changed their friendship? Were they going to graduate and go their separate ways without talking of it? The silliness of it all struck her as absurd and before she could stop herself, she spoke.

"Unless, of course, you don't wish to see me after all of this."

Scarlet furrowed her eyebrows and looked up at Nasya. "Why wouldn't I?"

Nasya shrugged. "I couldn't say. Perhaps you're worried I'll keep making everything about myself."

Recognition glossed over Scarlet's eyes, and after it, anger. She sat up, her eyes wide.

"I never said you make everything about yourself."

Nasya nodded. "Except that you did. In almost as many words, too."

"You're choosing to do this now?"

"I wanted to do it before, but you clearly didn't and so I kept quiet."

"Why can't you continue to keep quiet?" Scarlet stood to her feet. "We don't need to have this conversation."

"I think we do," Nasya replied, standing to her feet. "Nothing has been the same between us since I encountered you in those woods. I've tried to ignore it, tried to give you space, and still things are awkward. And I don't know what I'm supposed to do with you asking if we never see each other again. Are you trying to tell me that's what you want?"

"No!" Scarlet exclaimed, not quite yelling, but no longer speaking softly. "Of course that's not what I'm saying I want."

"Then what did you mean? Why even ask the question?"

Scarlet ran her hands through her hair and let out a deep breath. "I can't believe you're doing this now."

Nasya felt her chest constrict. She wanted to cry. To scream. To run away and pretend that none of this had happened. But she couldn't unspeak the words that had fallen off her tongue, and now couldn't bury the emotions that were exploding inside of her.

"It hurt that you kept such an incredible secret from me," Nasya said. "Perhaps it shouldn't have hurt as much as it did, but it cut deep. And when you came to help Mother Hydra watch over me when I fell ill, I thought perhaps we would finally talk through it all. But we never did."

"And you're blaming me for that?"

"No, I could have brought it up too and I didn't. I was scared.

And a bit prideful, I admit. I thought you were in the wrong and should be the one to initiate the conversation. If I could make a different choice, I would. But right now I need you to understand how much it hurts that you kept an enormous truth about yourself from me when it never would have occurred to me to keep anything from you." Even as she said the words, she knew they weren't entirely true. She had, in fact, kept things from Scarlet. She hadn't told her of some of the dreams, their specifics. She hadn't told her of her true feelings for Scarlet. A pang of guilt pierced her chest as she realized she had blatantly lied.

"Yes, Nasya, I know," she replied. "And that's why I didn't tell you."

Nasya frowned. "I don't understand."

"Everything about this place and my role in The Order has revolved entirely around you. I wanted one thing that was mine and mine alone. For a little while, anyway. I was going to tell you. I had planned to tell you that day, but I wanted to do it on my own time. It was my truth to tell and I wanted to choose where and when to tell it."

Nasya didn't respond.

"I'm sorry that it hurt you to find out the way you did, but I'm not sorry for keeping it from you."

The pain in Nasya's chest gripped tighter. Her heart felt as though it were being squeezed. Tears threatened to fill her eyes.

"Why didn't you just say this?" she asked.

"Because I knew you wanted me to say that I was wrong,

that I should have done things differently, and I wasn't going to lie and give you an apology I didn't mean. I let the matter drop because I thought we could both move through it and get back to the friends we were before." She shrugged. "But I was wrong. Clearly, you've been holding this against me all this time, resentment and bitterness making it impossible for us to ever reconnect fully."

Nasya felt as though everything in the room was suddenly much too bright and far too warm. Her head began to swim. It took a moment before she realized that Scarlet was grabbing all of her things.

"What are you doing?"

"I'm going to ask for a different room."

Nasya's heart slammed in her chest. She rushed forward and took Scarlet's hand in her own.

"No, please don't."

Scarlet pulled away. "I'm not prepared to deal with any of this right now. I need to focus on graduation. And so should you."

A moment later, she walked out of the room. Nasya was left standing alone in the place where she had first met and bonded with Scarlet, and now she held nothing but the brokenness of their connection. She ran her hands over her face and let out a deep groan. The conversation had not gone the way she'd intended. Though, she wasn't sure what she had hoped to gain by any of it. Perhaps Scarlet was right, and they just needed some time apart. As much as that hurt for her to admit, she knew she had to take the time to think over everything Scarlet had said.

And, right now, it was more important for her to prepare for the coming weeks. Graduation would be upon her sooner than she knew, and she had to pass. It was with a heavy heart that she accepted the distance between them, but she resolved not to bother her or speak to her until Scarlet initiated.

Two days passed. Scarlet took her test and left Passing's End without speaking to Nasya again.

Nasya stood tall, her back straight and her eyes forward. Though the summer sun was in her eyes, she did not squint or blink. Before her, Mother Hydra looked her up and down, walked slowly around her and examined her clothes. She wore a gown of many shades of blue trimmed with silver and white. She had made it herself for this exact moment, the final stage of her ascension. The Mothers of The Order would come and study her, examine Mother Hydra's recordings of her progress, and determine if she was ready to graduate.

"Are you nervous?" asked Mother Hydra.

"No, Mother," she replied.

"They will sense it if you are." Nasya said nothing. In truth, she wasn't nervous for the examination. She was confident in her own abilities enough to know the other Mothers would be impressed. She was nervous for what came after this, for what her life would become from this moment forward. Did she have the necessary dedication to this life? This career? This identity? And no matter how hard she tried to focus, she couldn't stop thinking about Scarlet. They still had not reconciled. It had been two weeks since Scarlet left Passing's End, and Nasya didn't even know where she'd gone, or if she'd see her again.

"Really, Nasya, I can practically smell how nervous you are," said Mother Hydra, standing before her once more. "Calm down. Remember to breathe."

"It's not The Mothers I'm nervous for," she said. "It's…"

"Everything after this," Mother Hydra said quietly. "Take heart, fledgling. You have been trained better than most who enter into our Order. It is one thing to hold the appropriate respect for the life you have earned; it's another to doubt yourself. Be careful which one you entertain."

Nasya looked at her teacher and nodded. "Yes, Mother."

There was silence between them for a moment. Nasya stared into her eyes and felt something in her chest soften towards the woman who had trained her, supported her, challenged her. They could not love each other, that much was clear. Neither had they been able to like each other, for in Mother Hydra, Nasya saw a stoicism that could not be shaken; in Nasya, Mother Hydra saw a desperation for acceptance and belonging that disgusted her. However, in between the lines of their mutual dislike was a mutual respect that ran deep and had only intensified with time.

"I do not say this often, child," began Mother Hydra, "but before the other Mothers arrive, I want you to know…I am proud of you."

There was no elaboration, no display of emotion. The tone of her voice did not even fluctuate. But it was honest, and that was one thing Nasya had come to realize about this woman: she was honest to a fault. She never said something she didn't mean. Which was hard to take when she was being cruel, but moments like these meant she was expressing her truest feelings. It was enough to make Nasya swell with pride. A less disciplined student might have even smiled, but Nasya held her bearing.

A moment later, the other Mothers arrived. They all wore the same style of robes in different shades of red. Mother Hydra greeted them all with a customary curtsey and embrace. Nasya watched as they performed their greetings and tried to keep her heart from beating faster. The Mothers' ability to sense her nervousness was a communal sixth sense developed by their connection to one another over time. It started with their training, and continued as they each moved from Sisterhood to Motherhood.

They studied her closely once their greetings were through, walked around her, touched her dress, even leaned close and smelled her hair. It was not the typical examination of those recruits who completed their training and became Sisters. It was more intentional, more intimate. Nasya would become a Sister today, that much she believed, but would The Mothers agree with Mother Hydra's assessment of her abilities?

Mother Cassiopeia was the first to speak. "It has been a long time since I have seen your face. I hardly recognize you."

Nasya knew this required no response, and so remained quiet. She was not happy to see her again. Of all the Mothers, she held the most of Nasya's hatred. Nothing Nasya did had ever been good enough. She worried the same would be true now, but did her best to remain calm and focused.

"To hear Mother Hydra's praise of you, one might think you were the strongest and most talented recruit we've had in decades," Mother Cassiopeia said. "What say you to that?"

It was hard to keep her bearing now. She did not know that Mother Hydra had praised her at all, let alone in such a way. She almost turned and looked at Mother Hydra, but kept her gaze forward. Nasya continued to focus on her breathing and when she spoke, did so calmly and without emotion.

"I'm sure I still have much to learn, Mother."

"She has recommended you as her replacement, when the time comes," said Mother Fornax from behind Nasya. "An honor we are not sure you have yet earned."

Nasya now had to exert all of her strength not to turn surprised eyes to where Mother Hydra stood in the corner, silently observing. This was the examination: to see how deeply her discipline ran. The Mothers could have been lying, for all Nasya knew, but even if not, even if these things were true, they were intended to elicit reactions, to distract her, to get into her head. Nasya hated how much it was almost working, and yet managed to maintain her composure. But she couldn't remain quiet about such a statement.

"I am grateful to Mother Hydra for her confidence in me,"

she said, quieting her mind of everything outside of this moment.

"Apparently Mother Hydra believes you have overcome a great deal since your arrival to Fire's Hearth," said Mother Fornax. "And I must admit, you are a far cry from the clumsy little wretch you were when we last saw you."

"But then, it is always easier to mold the exterior to hide the interior," added Mother Lynx.

"Perhaps you want to hide?" said Mother Cassiopeia. "Disappear? Blend in?"

"It is part of a Sister's job to blend in, Mother," replied Nasya.

"We know you were offered a chance to return home to your family," said Mother Corvus. "And we know you almost took it."

Silence fell between her and The Mothers, thick and heavy. She had not been asked a question, and so she remained silent.

"Why didn't you take it?" asked Mother Cassiopeia, staring directly into Nasya's eyes.

Nasya thought for a moment, remembering that day, that horrible afternoon. It had been on her mind a lot since the completion of her formal training, in her dreams even, and she didn't know why. It had been a prominent moment for her, a defining one, even. She had chosen, once and for all, to dedicate herself to this life, to try and make something of herself. But she had never really considered what it was that had kept her here. Not since that day when the portal to her past was closed once and for all.

"Going back would have meant accepting that I would never be anyone," Nasya replied truthfully. "I stayed for the chance to be someone."

"You mean you stayed for the chance to kill," said Mother Corvus, stepping closer to her. "For that is what all Sisters are: killers."

"I stayed to make a difference," Nasya responded.

"You stayed to kill," Mother Corvus insisted.

"Killers make a difference," Nasya rejoined.

Mother Corvus smiled brightly, her eyes twinkling in the light of the setting summer sun. "Tell me the process of The Order. From here, from today, where will you go? What will you do?"

"I will go where The Order sends me, and I will do as I am instructed."

"And then?"

"When The Order decides it's time, I will be sent to the Isle of Renewal with the six other Sisters to prepare for our role as the new Mothers."

"And then?"

"We will remain on Renewal until the Mothers before us retire. Then, we will come back here to Passing's End and begin training the new Sisters."

"And what becomes of the old Mothers?"

"They join the highest rank of The Order."

"Which are?"

"The Elders."

"What do they do?"

"They receive requests for hire and decide which to take and whom to assign them to."

"These positions must work together or they cannot function at all," said Mother Lynx. "Which means, Sister Ember, that you must be reliable. You will be given ample time between assignments to live within your cover. This time will be your own to do what you please, but how you utilize it will determine whether or not you are successful as a Sister. Do you understand?"

"Yes, Mother."

"Mother Hydra is a difficult woman to impress," said Mother Phoenix. "She recommends you highly, which is an unprecedented amount of praise. But time is what will prove her either right or wrong. Bear this in mind, young one: your success or failure reflects back on her, and on the rest of us. We do not take kindly to having our reputation tarnished." She stared into Nasya's eyes. "And should you ever abandon your post or lose a target or otherwise fail to complete an assignment, you will be punished accordingly."

"No amount of praise will save you then," said Mother Cassiopeia, her eyes alight. It was almost as if she wanted Nasya to fail.

"Yes, Mother."

As the ceremony continued, Nasya was put through a series of tests. She was asked to prove that she knew all of her forms of fighting, which she executed perfectly. As she did so, she was asked to repeat the six Rules of The Order in various degrees of repetition. These she had memorized within only months of being brought to Passing's End, and she knew them so well now that they were as natural to her as breathing: to keep hold of her cover; to observe everything within sight, sound, or touch, whether on assignment or not; to obey all instructions given from the Mothers or the Elders; to attach herself to no one; to never reveal her identity or betray the location of The Order's outposts; to do whatever must be done to ensure elimination of every target, and to never leave a trace of herself behind. She said them over and over, in order, in backwards order, in jumbled order.

From there, she entered into Mother Hydra's magical tests. She proved her abilities with fire, with water, and with healing. These were the three most essential forms of magic she would wield as a Sister, though they weren't her most powerful ability. She had nearly finished Mother Hydra's tests when Mother Cassiopeia interrupted them.

"I must say, I'm disappointed, Mother Hydra. Based on your accounts, I expected an unprecedented amount of talent," she said, taking a step towards Nasya. "I am heartily underwhelmed," she said, shaking her head. "Manipulating fire and bending water are not, after all, so very difficult."

Nasya stood still, breathing slowly. She had not anticipated this interruption, and judging by the look on Mother Hydra's face, neither had she.

"Remind me, Mother Cassiopeia, what kind of magic you wield?" challenged Mother Hydra.

Mother Cassiopeia said nothing. She simply glared at Nasya, her eyes bright with determination. Nasya knew that look well. It was pleasure in anything she could do to make Nasya suffer.

"Then, forgive me, but I do not believe you are capable of judging Nasya's abilities in this matter."

Nasya wanted to smile, but she forced herself to remain stoic and controlled. Whatever their misgivings between one another, it was clear she had Mother Hydra's support, and that meant more than she could ever express. Moreover, she had never seen a Mother side with a recruit, especially not when it meant contradicting one of their own. Mother Cassiopeia let out a slow breath. "I may not be able to wield my own magic, but I can see when someone isn't living up to the expectations I was told to have. And I remain unconvinced."

"Mother Cassiopeia, Nasya is no longer a recruit. She does not have to prove herself to you alone, but to all of us," said Mother Phoenix.

Mother Cassiopeia turned and faced the others. "And are you satisfied?"

The silence that filled the courtyard was so loud, it rang in Nasya's ears. She turned her eyes to Mother Hydra. This wasn't how the examination was supposed to go. She had completed every step of her training. She had satisfied Mother Hydra's standards, and yet her abilities were openly questioned? It did not make sense.

Mother Hydra was already looking at her. Mother Cassiopeia had begun speaking again.

"The Order has over valued magic for far too long," she was saying, "so much so that it has blinded all of you to the facts that Nasya, far from being an exemplary recruit, is actually little more than a failure." She looked at Nasya as she spoke, clearly wishing to exact a reaction. "For even with magic to aid her, she has accomplished nothing of renown."

While she was clearly prejudiced against Nasya, her words seemed to have an effect on the other Mothers. They began to murmur, Mothers Lynx and Fornax quickly agreeing with Mother Cassiopeia. Mother Hydra held Nasya's gaze for a moment, and then nodded her head once. Nasya didn't know how, but she knew what Mother Hydra meant.

If the Mothers could break the system in place for the final examination, then she could, too. Nasya breathed in a deep gulp of air and then closed her eyes. If Mother Cassiopeia wanted to be impressed, Nasya would do her utmost to provide.

Everything in Nasya's mind was dark. She drowned out everything around her: every voice, every smell, every brush of the wind in her hair. She pushed it all away until there was only the hollowness of darkness. She waited patiently, but it only took a moment for an unfamiliar face to come into view. It was that of a young girl. Nasya's body began to twitch, her muscles overcome with little spasms of energy as all the sounds around her which had faded to nothing began to penetrate her consciousness. The little girl's lips opened and moved, and slowly her voice filled Nasya's ears, overlapping with the sounds of the courtyard. The girl was crying out, reaching out, repeating the same words over and over. Nasya cleared her mind of every worry, every fear, every emotion and opened herself to the little girl.

The small spasms in her muscles turned to convulsions. She grunted as the little girl's spirit overlapped with her own, their consciousnesses blending through time and space. Nasya's eyes opened. Mother Cassiopeia's back was towards her, but the other Mothers could see her. Their eyes were wide, unblinking.

"Again, Odele," Nasya said, her voice blending with the little girl's. "Please sing the song again."

Mother Cassiopeia spun around mid-sentence, her eyes wide and her face pale. "What did...what did you say?" There was anger in her voice. And fear.

Nasya swayed back and forth at the waist. The spirit of this girl was strong, but Nasya remained upright, her feet planted firmly on the cobblestones of the courtyard. "The song, Odele. You know I love the song. Again, please sing it again."

Mother Cassiopeia's mouth gaped open. She blinked and looked at Mother Hydra.

"This is your doing!" she shouted, pointing a shaky finger. "This is all your doing!"

Mother Hydra said nothing.

"Odele," Nasya said again, her voice growing louder, deeper. "Please sing. Why won't you sing?"

Mother Cassiopeia shook her head. "No. It's not real. This is not real! She's dead!"

"Why won't you sing?" Nasya's voice was guttural now, a

veritable growl that came more from her chest than her throat. "Is it because you've forgotten the words? You wrote the song, Odele. You wrote it for me, remember? How could you forget? How?"

It was then the spirit of the girl emerged from within Nasya's body, a green and brown translucent shape with yellow eyes. Mother Cassiopeia fell backwards, her hands covering her face. She lost all composure and screamed. The girl took only a few steps towards her, cocking her head to the right. She opened her mouth and moved her lips, but her voice came out of Nasya, so low, so loud it sounded as though a giant were speaking.

"Did you forget me, too?" she asked. "Did you forget your Odette?"

The girl stood for a moment, staring at Mother Cassiopeia, her yellow eyes slowly growing dark until they turned as black as the abyss of death. The next moment, the girl's jaw unhinged and as she screamed, screeching shadows flew from her mouth and dove towards Mother Cassiopeia who fell to her knees and covered her head with her arms. Slowly, the girl faded away. The connection was broken. Nasya blinked as their spirits were severed. Her head swam and she fell to her knees. She felt she would be sick, but refused to let her body release the acid churning in her stomach. She wrapped her arms around her abdomen and sucked in sharp breaths to relax her muscles as they spasmed uncontrollably.

Nasya looked up at Mother Hydra. She was smiling brightly. Pride filled her eyes. The other Mothers stared, their mouths gaping. But no one's surprise was greater than that of Mother Cassiopeia. She was trembling from head to foot, speechless. Nasya took a moment to compose herself, to catch her breath, and then stood to her feet.

"Your little sister says hello," she said.

The examination was over. She had passed. She was sworn into The Order and pronounced an official Sister. Nasya was then instructed to pack her things, what little she had. The dormitory was empty, save for the beds that she and Scarlet had slept in. Nasya's clothes, books, and writing utensils were packed in her trunk. She stood in the center of the room and looked around at the place that had been her home for so many years. Yet, it had never felt like home except when Scarlet was there. Tears stung her eyes but she blinked them away. She hated how things had been left between the two of them. She hated how guilty she felt, how angry she was at the person she loved most in the world. And she was scared that they would never have a chance to make amends.

She carried her trunk out to the carriage that was going to take her to Garden's Hem, a small, forest town on the eastern coast of Utara. The trunk was tied to the back of the carriage. She was given money enough to live on until her first assignment would come in, and wished well by The Mothers.

And for the first time since she'd come to Passing's End, it was Mother Cassiopeia couldn't meet *her* gaze.

Mother Hydra shook hands with her, her eyes still alight with pride. Nasya thanked her for her instruction, and then climbed into the carriage. She did not look back as the carriage began toward Garden's Hem. Passing's End was behind her, now. Her training was over. She was a Sister, a powerful, magical assassin and necromancer.

It was more than she had ever thought possible. Nasya was quiet and introspective for some time as the carriage drove on, probably hours. She didn't know when it was she began crying, but somewhere around the fourth hour of their journey, she realized her cheeks were covered in tears.

# Chapter Seventeen

*On the road to Garden's Hem*
  *Country of Utara*

Utara was not a large country, and yet the journey from Passing's End to the city of Garden's Hem took nearly three weeks. This was due in part to the treacherous terrain that Passing's End was situated within. The pass was not easy to navigate, full of cliffs and narrow roads, and though the snow and ice had melted, loose rocks and mud meant they had to be extra cautious.

Nasya was in the carriage for a whole three days before they made it out of the pass. And as there was no village or inn nearby, they had to camp each night. They were able to make an easy, if not quite comfortable, encampment to rest. They built a fire each night and cooked a hearty dinner of pork sausage with bread and butter and ale to wash it down. When night fell, Nasya was given her own small tent, complete with a cot to keep her off the muddy ground, and blankets that kept her warm as she slept. And though the cot was certainly not nearly as comfortable as her bed in Passing's End had been, Nasya found herself unconcerned as she lay awake in the darkness thinking of how much her life was changing. Each of the three nights, she struggled to drift into a peaceful slumber, her mind running wild with images of her new life and all of the freedoms that would come with it.

Morning on the fourth day came. Nasya climbed back into the carriage that was to take her onward and away from Passing's End and its haunts. Her mind was occupied with questions, nervousness, and regret at how she and Scarlet had left things between them. She'd hoped that Scarlet might write to her before her graduation, but she had not. And now Nasya was leaving. She didn't know if she would ever see or speak to Scarlet again. The one person for whom Nasya carried the most affection; the closest friend she'd had during training; a true ally, and for all Nasya knew, she might never see her again. It made her heart ache to think of it, and she wished she knew what to say to make things right again. If that were even possible. But even if she had the words to say, she wouldn't know where to send them, or if Scarlet was interested in receiving them in the first place. She hated feeling so disconnected from such an essential person in her life, but it couldn't be helped. This was how the cards had fallen, and they both must learn to accept it.

The rest of the journey, the carriage stopped at different inns along the road, providing far more comfortable lodgings. Nasya found travel both interesting and lonely. She enjoyed watching the land pass by her, to visit these villages and towns and eat foods she'd never seen before. She had seen so little of the Utara, let alone the whole world, so that even the smallest things captivated her. Different accents and dialects among the people she met, the changes in terrain as they moved farther east, different fashions; all of it reflected just how little she had lived up to this point, and just how much life was now at her fingertips. It was also lonely because there was no one with whom she could converse, no one to point things out to, no one to enjoy the beauty of the landscape with. She assumed this was what her life would be from this point forward. Lonely. Isolated. And she couldn't strike up a conversation with anyone she didn't already know unless it was related to her cover as a whore. She couldn't risk raising suspicions. The Mothers had made this abundantly clear.

At last, after weeks of riding in a carriage through thousands of miles of forest, fields, hills, and moors, they came to the entrance of Garden's Hem. It was a large, rural city built into the dense woods that lead to Utara's only eastern port. The primary parts of the city were on the forest floor, like the main hall, the sheriff's abode, and the community ballroom. All of the public houses and inns were also on the forest floor, as were the different farms that made up the primary trade of Garden's Hem. But the personal lodgings of the city's citizens were built up in the trees and connected by bridges and ladders. It was surprising to see when Nasya first arrived. She had never encountered such architecture before, and she wasn't sure how it worked. But the people had all adapted to its strange structure.

When Nasya arrived, she climbed from the carriage and looked around at the center of the city. She had been told that the brothel was situated near the two public houses and that the madam, a woman named Thelasse, was expecting her. Nasya grabbed her bag and made her way through the city towards the brothel called The Lusty Lion. It was a large building three stories high and clearly well frequented. Nasya tried to ignore the nerves building in her gut. She was still a virgin and, while she knew the physical aspects of sexual intercourse, she didn't know if she would be any good at it. It seemed a little thing in comparison to her real employment, but she also knew she wouldn't last long as a whore if she weren't a skilled and pleasing lover. For now, she told herself, she needed to introduce herself to Madam Thelasse and settle in. She took a deep breath and stepped into the brothel.

The foyer was large and filled with the bustle of patrons and prostitutes. Although Garden's Hem was a rural city, the brothel seemed to be frequented primarily by upper class citizens and travelers from other countries. Nasya looked around for anyone who seemed to be in charge, and her eyes fell on a tall woman with bronze skin. She spotted Nasya and walked over to her.

"You must be the new girl," she said, her voice deep and somewhat raspy.

"Yes, ma'am. I'm N-"

Madam Thelasse held up her hand and shook her head. "We don't use our real names here. That information is yours alone. We all have professional names and those are the ones we go by."

Nasya nodded. "Very well. Do I pick this name or do you?"

She shrugged. "Doesn't matter, really. I think the names fit better if the workers choose them, but I can assist in this if it's something you're not comfortable coming up with yourself. Now, let's get you to your room."

She motioned for Nasya to follow, and follow she did. They went up two sets of stairs.

"The first floor is for cheaper experiences. The rooms are small and the patrons usually only stay an hour or two. The second floor is where most of our work occurs. It's for those patrons who can pay for more than only a couple of hours. Most of our regulars frequent the second floor. The workers on the first and second floors are called companions." They came to the third landing and Madam Thelasse led her to a door that was open. "The third floor, however, is where the money is really made. Patrons have to pay extra to reserve one of these rooms. The experience is typically overnight and includes food, wine, and ale. The workers here are called courtesans. Your lodging is on this floor."

Nasya entered the room and was surprised. It was large with a bed that was much nicer than any she'd ever slept on, a table near one of the windows for eating, a large hearth, a wardrobe, and other such amenities. She looked around the room with a faint grin. "This is a very nice room, Madam Thalasse. But, if I may be so bold, may I ask why I am being put in here when I'm entirely new to this profession?"

Madam Thalasse grinned ever so slightly. "I was offered a great deal of money to take you on," she said, "and the stipulation of your employment was that you not be treated like the others. You're to have complete control over your clientele, your comings and goings, and I am not to inquire as to the details of anything you choose to do or not do in the entirety of your employment here. Usually, I would start a new worker on the ground floor, but given the circumstances, I thought it best to give you a room up here instead."

Nasya nodded slowly. She offered the woman a smile. "Thank you. That is very kind."

Madam Thalasse did not smile in return. She merely bowed her head. "You have two days to settle in here before I will start expecting you to work. Your schedule is yours to set, but this is not a charity. You must pay a certain percentage of all your earnings to the house. This will cover your room and board, and this fee is paid weekly. As long as you pay on time, you and I will get along well." Madam Thalasse walked to the door. "There's a dressmaker farther into the city where you can buy clothes more fitting for this climate, as well as for work. You'll notice the others here like to dress to impress. I suggest you study their example, especially since you will be a courtesan. Customers expect courtesans to look noble. Your attire should reflect that. And now, I will leave you to settle in. Remember, two days.

Then work."

She left, shutting the door behind her and Nasya was left to ponder her first moments in Garden's Hem. She pulled up a chair close to the hearth, grabbed a slice of bread that was on her table, slathered it in butter, and ate it. She held her feet up to the fire to warm them. Garden's Hem was not cold like Passing's End had been, but she still found herself chilled. She attributed it to exhaustion. But, not wanting to waste her two days, she finished her slice of bread and took herself out into the city to search for what she might need to begin her life in Garden's Hem.

She found the dressmaker's shop within only a few minutes. She had enough money to purchase at least a dozen dresses, but decided instead on purchasing only three. One would be a casual day dress; it was made of dark green cotton with white embroidery on the bodice, the ends of the sleeves, and the hem of the skirt. One would be a casual work dress; it was much more form fitting than the other dress and made of a light blue linen trimmed in silver. It was a striking gown that exemplified a certain status in the intricacies of its design. The third would be a special work dress; it was sultry red satin that clung to her body like a second skin, with a very low cut down the front that reached down to her abdomen. She also purchased two new pairs of shoes, and then wandered around Garden's Hem to see what else there was for her to enjoy. To her great pleasure, she found an enormous library filled with books and scrolls. She couldn't help herself and checked out three books before she made her way back to the brothel where she put her three new gowns in the wardrobe, and then sat near the fire to read.

The next day, Nasya awoke at sunrise. It was natural for her to be up early, even though no one was banging on her door in the morning to ensure she was awake. She rolled onto her back and snapped her fingers, igniting a fire in the hearth in a single moment. It was still early spring, and while not freezing, it was not yet warm, either. She climbed from bed and wrapped her thick, wool robe around her before sitting near the fire.

She had learned from Madam Thalasse that the other prostitutes typically breakfasted together. Attached to the brothel was a large public house where delicious meals were served all day and most of the night. Breakfast was later in the morning, closer to 9:00 am, so Nasya had time to relax and reflect on what she needed to do today to be ready for the coming week. She would have been lying if she said she was ready for any of it, and yet deep in her fingers she felt a kind of buzz coming to life, as though this were the beginning of everything she'd hoped for.

She would also have been lying if she said her family had not been constantly on her mind since leaving Passing's End. The Mothers had impressed upon her and the other Sisters the importance of remaining out of contact from anyone from their former lives. And while she had promised to do so, she also felt keenly that she would not be satisfied with anything until she could see her family again. She didn't want it to be so, and yet it was. She needed to see them, talk to them, to understand why she'd been given up. It annoyed her that after all this time, she still needed those answers, but it couldn't be helped. No matter how hard she tried to deny it, ignore it, work through it, the need, the urgency, would not desist.

The morning passed in quiet reflection. After some time by the fire, Nasya stood and dressed in her casual day gown she'd bought the day before. She pulled her wavy red hair back into a simple braid and made her way down the stairs to the main level where the brothel joined with the public house. Three people were already there. One was Madam Thalasse, one was a woman, and one was a man. Nasya offered a small smile and sat at the table with them.

"So you must be the new one," said the woman, leaning back in her seat. She was older than Nasya by some years and not particularly beautiful, and yet she carried herself with a confidence that made Nasya's palms sweat. She eyed Nasya up and down. "No way you've even touched a cock yet," she said.

The man next to her nearly choked on his milk. "Heavens above, Almandine, let her have her breakfast first before you go pecking for secrets." He was older too and his hair and beard were flecked with silver. "There was a time when you and I had also never touched a cock before."

The two of them laughed. Nasya slowly began to help herself to the food on the table. There were boiled potatoes, thick slabs of bacon cooked crispy, plates filled with fruit, and at least three different types of bread. Nasya filled her plate, suddenly realizing how hungry she was. The woman, Almandine, sat across from her and raised her eyebrows.

"Don't fill up too fast, kitten. You might put something else in your mouth before the day's end," she said.

"This one will not start working until tomorrow," Madam Thalasse said, her dark eyes sparkling with amusement at the conversation taking place at the table.

A few more people came and sat and filled their plates. No one was properly introduced to Nasya, and she was grateful for it. She wanted to eat and observe. Not participate. Not yet. She wanted to see how these people interacted with each other to know best how to mold her behavior to match their own. Nasya studied the faces of those who sat at the table. They were all extremely different from one another. People of every gender, every skin color, every age and body size sat communed together as they broke their fast. It was the most diverse group of people Nasya had ever encountered, and as they talked and laughed and teased one another, she found herself envying their connections, their friendliness.

"Alright kitten," Almandine said, leaning forward and picking up a slice of bacon with her fingers. "Tell us truly...have you ever been with a man?"

All eyes were on Nasya. From her right, she heard someone say under their breath, "Of course she hasn't. She still has hope in her eyes."

The others chuckled.

"No, I have not," Nasya said.

Almandine nodded. "What about women? Have you been with women?"

Nasya shook her head. "No, I have not."

"Have you even been kissed?" Almandine asked.

Nasya's cheeks flared with heat. She shook her head. "No."

Almandine turned towards Mother Thalasse. "She's the most virgin of virgins," she said, a wide smile on her face. "You know what that means."

"Oh, here she goes," said one of the others at the table.

"It's tradition!" Almandine exclaimed. She looked at Nasya. "It's called The Awakening."

Even Madam Thalasse smiled and shook her head. "It isn't even ten in the morning. Gods, you're such a slut."

Everyone laughed. Nasya waited for someone to explain The Awakening to her and Almandine, too, seemed willing to wait and hear someone else explain the tradition. The man who sat next to her, the one with the beard flecked with silver, sighed and rolled his eyes.

"The Awakening is a ritual of sorts. Each room is decorated in different colored sashes and loads of candles are lit to give a seductive ambiance. There's food and a lot of wine. It's a party of revelry and debauchery of the finest and most exciting sort. After a while, the virgin is brought out in a white gown and veil, and the patrons all have to bid on which one gets to be with her for the night."

Almandine rolled her eyes and pretended to snore. "For fucks sake, Jasper, could you make it sound any more boring?"

Nasya shrugged. "It doesn't sound boring to me."

Jasper held out his hands as if to prove a point. Almandine shook her head. "No, kitten. No. It's an all day affair. It starts at noon and goes until midnight. By six o'clock, the virgin is brought out in gown and veil and the bidding begins. Then, once the bidding starts to slow, the veil is removed and the bidders see precisely what they've been bidding for, and that is when the money rolls in."

"The best part," said a woman next to Nasya, "is that all of the bids are recorded. The winning bidder's money goes to you, but all of the other bids are paid to the house and split among all of us."

A man from the other end of the table spoke next. "And then, those who didn't win the bid, are so drunk and ready to fuck, they'll pay whatever to whomever they can, and we walk away even richer."

"It seems a very profitable tradition," Nasya replied. "When would this be?"

Madam Thalasse sighed. "We would have to plan it today so that everything is ready tomorrow."

Almandine turned her whole body towards Madam Thalasse. "I can lead the preparations, Madam. You wouldn't have to lift a finger."

Madam Thalasse smiled. "Oh, go on. If you can get it done by tomorrow, then we shall, indeed, have The Awakening."

Everything burst into a bustle of excitement. The first thing to be done was hanging a sign to the door of the brothel announcing closure for the day as they prepared for The Awakening. Then, all of the workers began to list out duties and assigned them to one another. Nasya watched with wide eyes, surprised that merely her presence in this town could be enough to excite her fellows to this extent. But then, money was money, no matter how they came about it.

That day passed quickly and Nasya hardly knew how to process any of it. She was left out of most of the planning, as the event was meant to be a surprise for her as well as the guests. The two things she had to do were find an appropriate dress, and come up with her pseudonym.

As for the dress, she went back to the dress maker and gave a verbal description of what she was looking for. They brought out a stunning gown made of flowing white linen trimmed in gold. It fit her perfectly, as though made for her body, and was the right blend of innocence and seduction. Nasya bought it and an all white veil, and then went back to the brothel where she hung the dress in her wardrobe.

The rest of the day, she was left to herself. Madam Thalasse came to her room in the early evening and practically thanked her for going along with Almandine's plan as morale had not been this high in ages. It was not often they found virgins who were willing to be part of The Awakening in a rural city like Garden's Hem. Nasya nodded and smiled.

"I'm happy to be of any assistance," she said.

Madam Thelasse shut the door of Nasya's room behind her. "Are you nervous?"

Nasya nodded. "I didn't think I would be, but yes, I am."

"If it's any consolation, we have rules for all of our patrons. We may be a rural city, but we hold each other to a high standard out here. All of our workers are to be safe at all times. Any specific acts are to be agreed upon beforehand, or foregone entirely. Violence of any kind is not tolerated. There are other brothels for that and we are not one of them. We have hired hands who enforce these rules. It's been decades since our last incident."

Nasya listened intently, feeling relieved at every piece of information the woman offered her.

"Most of our patrons are regulars. They have their specific workers they pay for, and they seek an intimate experience. And those who will be bidding for you know that part of The Awakening is not merely their pleasure, but yours as well. This is why we make such a big deal out of the bidding."

Nasya nodded slowly. "I understand, Madam."

The woman offered her a gentle smile. "I'm assuming you...know the...physicality of it? You understand how...it's done?"

Nasya nodded. "Yes, I do."

"Good. That will help you a great deal. Now, tonight I want

you to rest. Tomorrow you will bathe and prepare." She turned to leave and then stopped. "Oh, I nearly forgot. What would you like to be called?"

She let out a slow breath, and settled on the name that had been running through her mind all day.

"Cinderella."

The next day dawned and Nasya awoke with excitement and nervousness. There was so much she didn't yet understand about what her life was becoming, but the newness of it hooked her. She was eighteen and had seen hardly anything of the world or of people, and now it was all washing over her at once. She climbed from her bed and put on her casual day gown. Unlike the day before, she would be taking her breakfast in her room. She was not to stir out of her chamber until The Awakening. That was paramount. No one could see her before the bidding started. It added to the mystery of the experience, and that was precisely what would lead patrons to bid enormous amounts of money for her.

Though she spent the day mostly by herself, she was not discontented. She read a great deal from the books she'd taken from the library. They were mostly histories of the lands around Garden's Hem. Since this was going to be her home for at least a few years, she thought she should know as much as possible about the area. Uataran's eastern coast and the country of Hevean were separated by the Utaran channel, a stretch of ocean only a mile wide at the smallest point. Ferries came and went periodically throughout the day all along the coast, allowing citizens from either country to pass over into the other.

Nasya found herself daydreaming of her Sisters, wondering what they were doing now. Only Scarlet and Nasya had been kept in Utara. The other Sisters had been sent to other countries. She wondered if the Sisters were acclimating well to their new lives, or if they were struggling. Deep down, she knew these thoughts primarily stemmed from her unresolved feelings regarding Scarlet. As much as Nasya admired and respected her Sisters, it was Scarlet with whom she had always been the closest, and it was agony to not know where she was or how she was doing.

At the very thought of Scarlet, Nasya stood to her feet and began to pace. She wished she weren't confined to her chamber. She needed a few moments in the air with her wings outstretched, the wind in her feathers. She needed to soar above the trees, above all of her concerns and responsibilities that tethered her to the ground. She needed space. She couldn't fix the rift between her and Scarlet right now, so what good did it do dwelling on it? But no matter how hard she tried to shove the thoughts away, the more they dominated her consciousness. If she'd known where to send a raven, she would have simply written a note and sent it, unburdening her mind and heart at once. But she had no idea where Scarlet was or would be.

She told herself to put Scarlet out of her mind. She had things to do, to prepare for. Nasya decided to meditate to try and focus her energy. She sat on the floor in front of her small fire, closed her eyes, and focused on her breathing. She cleared her mind of everything but her body – the feel of her dress against her skin, the warmth of the fire, the flutters in her stomach at the thought of The Awakening. In only a few moments, she felt her mood and emotions regulate. She continued to meditate until her supper was brought. By that point, The Awakening had begun. Nasya could hear the bustle of patrons arriving. It would still be a few hours before she was brought out, so she ate slowly and simply listened to the activity occurring downstairs.

Madam Thalasse came up a couple of hours later and helped her prepare. Nasya put on the white gown she had purchased. The fabric clung to her and was sheer enough that her body could almost be seen through the fabric. Madam Thalasse styled her hair in an elegant braid and then hung the veil over her face. It was long and came almost to the hem of her skirt.

"You're going to do extremely well tonight," Madam Thalasse said. "There are already dozens of patrons downstairs, all eating and drinking happily. You look stunning in this dress. Remember to breathe. Try to relax and enjoy yourself."

Nasya nodded, suddenly far more nervous than she thought she would be. Madam Thalasse stayed with her until it was time for them both to descend to the main floor. The woman seemed to be very concerned over Nasya's comfort and wellbeing, and for that Nasya was grateful. She was accustomed to managing her feelings alone, and now someone besides Scarlet was doing their utmost to take care of her. It was strange, but also welcome. Even if Madam Thalasse's primary motivation was the money she was about to make.

The time came for her to leave the room. Madam Thalasse went first and announced the arrival of Cinderella, The Virgin. Nasya let out a deep breath and made her way down the stairs.

The brothel was full of people. Companions and courtesans wore their nicest outfits. Tables covered in wine, ale, and food lined the outer walls. Candles were everywhere. It was beautiful, and yet Nasya could practically smell the lust as she made her way down the stairs. She stood next to Madam Thalasse and the bidding began. Men and women alike called out prices that made Nasya's eyes widen. She hadn't anticipated the bidding would start out so high, and yet for nearly thirty minutes, it continued, escalating ever higher. Nasya remained still most of the time, except when Madam Thalasse told her to spin, showing off her figure.

Finally, the bidding started to slow, and Nasya was instructed to remove the veil. A silence fell over the brothel that made Nasya's stomach flutter, and just when she thought no one was going to continue the bidding, a voice from the back called out, "15,000 florens." It was the highest bid yet, and from there they continued to climb, even more enthusiastically than before. Another forty five minutes passed and Nasya felt her head begin to swim. She didn't know how these patrons could afford to make such offers on just one night with a woman, but she couldn't help the smile that lit her face at the thought of being considered that desirable.

That was when another voice called out, "50,000 gold crowns." The room fell utterly silent. Nasya's heart thudded in her chest. She knew that voice.

"Good heavens," Madam Thalasse said, "we have a bid of 50,000 gold crowns. Anyone want to raise?" When no one replied after several minutes, Madam Thalasse nodded. "Very well. Winning bid goes to the woman at the back. Please come forward and Cinderella will lead you to her room."

Nasya could barely breathe. She saw her moving from the back clad in trousers, a loose shirt, knee-high boots, and a leather vest. It was Scarlet. She handed a large pouch to Madam Thalasse and then turned her hazel eyes to Nasya who felt dizzy. Her heart raced. Her breathing fluctuated. She was here; Scarlet was actually in Garden's Hem. She had come to see her. Nasya could have cried for joy, but she controlled herself. It was neither the time nor the place. Instead, she offered a sweet smile, pretended not to know this woman who had just won the bidding, and then turned and walked towards the stairs. She had so many questions. She was confused and excited and even more nervous now than she had been earlier. They walked up the stairs to Nasya's room. Once inside, Nasya shut and locked the door and then faced Scarlet. They stood several feet away from each other. Nasya wanted to run to her, embrace her, but she couldn't move.

"I don't even know where to begin," she said, wanting to ask every question in her mind all at once, and not knowing where to start or how.

Scarlet shrugged. "I wasn't about to let someone else have you."

Nasya's heart dropped into her stomach and then surged up into her throat. She didn't know what that meant, but it made her feel as though her legs would turn to liquid any moment. Her head swam with confusion and excitement and worry. She now had a chance to make amends with Scarlet, but she was afraid of saying the wrong thing, like she had the last time they saw each other. She wracked her brain to think of what to say, but nothing got to the heart of what she most wanted to express.

"What are you even doing here?" Nasya finally asked.

Scarlet was pacing slowly. "I couldn't stop thinking about our last conversation. It...bothered me. Once I had concluded my first bounty hunting job, I decided to come here and talk everything over with you."

"How in the name of heaven did you come up with that much money?"

"My first client was a very wealthy count. I found what he wanted, and he paid me what I asked for."

Her voice was tight. Emotionless. And she avoided Nasya's gaze. Nasya didn't know if Scarlet was nervous or still angry or both. She didn't know which one was better or worse than the other. She told herself to speak, to open her mouth and say the words she had wanted to say since their argument back at

Passing's End, but she couldn't. There was too much to say and not enough space to let the words breathe.

"I knew you'd be thriving, wherever you were. Whatever you were doing," Nasya said at last, her voice quiet.

"Me? What about you, miss virgin queen of the night?" Scarlet asked, finally lifting her gaze to meet Nasya's. "You look absolutely incredible in that gown. No wonder the bidding was so high."

Nasya felt her cheeks flush with heat. Under any other circumstances, she'd have been thrilled for Scarlet to think her beautiful. But her stomach flipped as nervousness coursed through her body like a second heartbeat. Silence fell between them for a moment. Not wanting to let the moment pass, Nasya spoke, her voice tight and shaky. "I'm sorry for what I said when we last spoke," she said. "I'm not entitled to every detail of your life, and it was selfish and inconsiderate of me to act as though I was. What you choose to share and with whom you choose to share it is entirely up to you. Not me." She gave a sorrowful, regretful look. "I'm very sorry."

Scarlet's eyes stared steadily into Nasya's. She didn't speak for a moment, and then suddenly walked over and wrapped her arms around her. "Thank you," she whispered, her breath warm against Nasya's neck. They held each other for several long moments and Nasya felt every concern, every fear, every worry fade away. She closed her eyes and breathed in Scarlet's scent. It was a mixture of pine and rain, exactly the same as when they had shared a room at Passing's End.

They pulled away a moment later.

"I actually came here hoping to explain everything to you," Scarlet said.

Nasya shook her head. "Please don't, unless you actually want me to know. I don't want you to tell me anything you're not comfortable with."

She smiled. "I understand. But I really do want to tell you. And I think it might actually help me find the answers I've been looking for."

Nasya walked over to the table. It was laden with fruits, cold meats, cheese, bread, and several casks of wine. She motioned for Scarlet to sit, and they filled their plates while Scarlet began.

"My mother was a lycan. My father was an ordinary werewolf, or at least that's what my mother told me. I never knew him. My mother raised me until I was about nine years old. We lived deep in the heart of a forest, alone and disconnected from everyone." She let out a slow breath. "One day, I went to a nearby apple grove to pick apples." Her eyes became distant as she recalled the memory. "I was only supposed to be gone for a half an hour or so, but I lost all track of time. I don't know how long I wandered lazily through the woods, but it was at least a couple of hours. When I finally came home, I walked into the scene of a gruesome murder."

Nasya stared at Scarlet as she spoke.

"A lycan had killed my mother. It was standing over her body when I walked into the hovel, its eyes as red as the blood on its snout. I dropped the basket of apples and turned to run. It followed. I would have been killed if not for a hunter who had tracked the lycan to our home. He managed to graze its face with a bolt from his crossbow. That must have scared it enough that it ran into the woods." Scarlet paused and took a large gulp from her goblet of wine. "I've always known that I would try and get revenge for my mother's death. The first time I shifted into my lycan form, and every time I've shifted since, I was reminded of my mother's slaughter. I can't talk about shifting without immediately thinking of her and the lycan that took her from me. Keeping this information to myself was just...a way for me to handle the memories."

Nasya reached across the table and took Scarlet's hand in hers. "Scarlet, I am so sorry. I had no idea."

"I know. I wanted it that way."

"How did you keep this from everyone? Even the Mothers?"

"I didn't. Mother Phoenix actually found me once in the woods as I was shifting back to my human form. She helped me shift in secret from that moment forward and she swore she wouldn't tell anyone." Scarlet took a bite of bread. "I don't know if she did, but no one ever confronted me about it."

"I'm assuming you'll be looking for the lycan now that we've graduated?"

Scarlet nodded. "Every chance I get."

Nasya watched Scarlet as they ate. She would never have guessed that she had witnessed her own mother's murder at such a young age. She carried herself so confidently, so detached, it seemed, as though she hadn't a care in the world. "I hate that you've had to carry this alone," Nasya said.

Scarlet looked up from her plate. "It wasn't anyone else's burden to bear."

"You said you hoped I'd be able to help you?"

Scarlet nodded. "I was...hoping you might be willing to find my mother's spirit? Maybe ask her who attacked her that day?"

Nasya blinked in surprise. "Uh...I...I suppose I could try," she stammered. "But I cannot guarantee any results."

"I don't expect guarantees. It would just mean a lot if you could try."

Nasya looked down at her plate of food. Emotions filled her chest, bubbled up into her throat, tightening it. She frowned, feeling as though she might cry at any moment. "Is...Is this the real reason you came here?" she asked, looking up at Scarlet. "Not to reconnect or mend fences but...to use my necromancy to find your mother's killer?"

Scarlet sat silent and motionless. "Cannot it be both?" she asked, her voice soft.

Nasya shook her head. "No. It cannot."

"Why?"

Nasya stood to her feet. "Because your coming here was a pretense to gain access to my magic," she said, walking towards the hearth.

"It's not a pretense," Scarlet said, standing to her feet. "I came here because I missed you and I wanted us to be friends again."

Nasya scoffed. "Only because you knew you couldn't ask a stranger to look for the spirit of your murdered mother. But someone who loves you would want to help in any way they can."

"What was I supposed to do?" Scarlet asked, holding her arms out wide. "I don't know any other necromancers. If I did, I would have asked them."

Nasya guffawed. "Is that supposed to make me feel better? Knowing you would have continued to avoid me if I didn't have a potential solution to your problem?"

"No, that's not what I meant –"

"But it is what you just said." All she knew in that moment was anger. "I've thought of you every single day since you left our dormitory," she said at last, tears glistening in her eyes. "And I know that I was wrong for how I made you feel. But I have spent every single day thinking of you and wondering if I would ever even talk to you again. I didn't know if you would even want to hear from me, and I had no way of asking. And now you're here and all I want is to embrace you and remember how things used to be between us, but I can't because you're not here *for* me. You're here to *use* me."

Scarlet looked down at the floor.

"And you paid a hell of a lot of money to do it," Nasya added.

Scarlet looked back up at her. "That isn't why I bid on you."

"Then why?"

Scarlet walked around the table up to Nasya, took her face in her hands, and planted a kiss onto Nasya's lips. Nasya gasped with surprise. She didn't know what to do. She'd never been kissed before, and she certainly never expected that Scarlet would want to kiss her. She didn't know what was happening, but when Scarlet broke the kiss and moved to pull away, Nasya grabbed her face and pressed a kiss to her lips.

The moments blurred together. Scarlet's hands were all over her and Nasya felt her body come alive with flutters. In seconds, they were on the bed. Nasya's lips parted, her tongue meeting Scarlet's, and a fire took hold of her body. Scarlet cupped her breast with one hand and held herself above Nasya with the other. Nasya's heart was pounding and an ache built suddenly between her legs that she had never felt before. It was more than a tingle; it was a pulse of heat, of desire, of love. After a while, Scarlet trailed kisses down Nasya's neck, pulled her skirt up over her legs, and pressed kisses on the inside of her thighs. Nasya writhed beneath her lips, desperate for something to touch her between her legs where she was hot with desire. One touch and the tension would release. She felt certain.

Suddenly, Scarlet wrapped her lips around her and Nasya let out a sharp gasp as a jolt of pleasure shot through her body.

"Did that hurt?" Scarlet asked, looking up at her.

Nasya shook her head. "No. Do it again. Please."

Scarlet did and Nasya let out a moan of pleasure. Scarlet's tongue began to slide back and forth and Nasya felt her head spin. Nasya could do nothing but cry out in pleasure as the ache continued to build. Scarlet seemed to be in no hurry. She spent time pleasing Nasya with the gentlest and slowest movements, stopping every so often to press kisses against her legs. It was heaven, being here with her. When the release did finally come, it was beautifully slow and long. Nasya cried out and arched her back, every part of her body tingling with pleasure.

The next morning, Nasya awoke after the sun had already risen from behind the horizon. She blinked slowly as sleep left her and smiled, remembering the events that had taken place between her and Scarlet. Their lovemaking had gone on well into the night, each of them urgent in their desire for the other. They took turns teasing, pleasing, and fucking one another. The passion had been palpable, as though everything between them had been leading to that moment. It had been unforgettable and Nasya felt herself overwhelmed by a feeling of contentment entirely unknown to her. She let out a slow, deep breath and rolled over to greet Scarlet. But she wasn't in the bed.

Nasya frowned and sat up, casting her gaze around the room. Scarlet wasn't there. Nor were any of her belongings. Nasya wondered if she had gone to retrieve something to eat, but a glance at the table and the food left over from the night before quickly put an end to that. Had she left? Nasya tried not to jump to any conclusions as she climbed from bed and began to dress. She rushed down the stairs to see if she was elsewhere in the brothel, but to no avail. Madam Thalasse met Nasya in the hall with a knowing smile.

"I assume you had a good time last night, considering how

late the morning is and you're just now waking," she said with a smile.

Nasya turned towards her. "Have you seen the woman I was with?"

Madam Thalasse squinted her eyes at the frantic expression on Nasya's face. She nodded. "Yes. She was up very early this morning. Said to give you this." She handed Nasya a rolled up piece of parchment.

Nasya took it. "But she left?"

"She said she had somewhere to be."

Tears sprung into Nasya's eyes. She moved away, not wanting Madam Thalasse to see her crying. She rushed back to her room and shut the door before allowing the tears to fall down her cheeks. Her chest was heavy with emotion and she felt as though she might lose her ability to breathe if she couldn't regulate herself. She shook her head and rolled open the parchment. It was a short letter and did nothing to offer Nasya any comfort.

*Dear Nasya,*

*I am sorry to do this so abruptly, but I had to leave. It was wrong of me to come here expecting you to drop everything to help me connect with my mother's spirit. I am very sorry for it. Please understand, I must find who killed my mother. And I now see it's something I must accomplish on my own.*

*As for last night...I do not wish you to believe it came from anything other than my intense feelings for you. I hope that we will meet again soon.*

*Scarlet*

Anger rushed through Nasya. She crumpled the letter into a ball and tossed it into the hearth, lighting it and the wood still in the hearth on fire. She stood still with her back against her door, breathing heavily. She had not expected this. Any of it. Tears fell steadily down her face. Part of her understood Scarlet's plight; she couldn't imagine what it must be like for her having such a deeply rooted need for vengeance burning within, and Nasya wanted Scarlet to find the justice she sought. But she couldn't deny the pain of each new rift that tore them farther apart. Scarlet was everything to Nasya, and the night before had manifested every truth that she had never allowed herself to feel. Moreover, Scarlet had indicated that she reciprocated those feelings, only to leave without even saying goodbye or offering an opportunity for real reconciliation.

Nasya walked to the table and poured herself a large goblet of wine. She drank it in one gulp, needing something to help numb the pain and the confusion that filled her. None of this was what she wanted, and she had no recourse to change it. She felt helpless. She felt pathetic. She sat and ate slowly, allowing herself to cry and mourn the loss of the first love she'd felt since being taken from her family all those years ago. By the time she'd finished eating, she felt numb. It was good. She needed to focus. She needed to keep herself prepared for her first assignment, whenever it might come.

It was only then she noticed a large purse on the table next to her. And with it, a note from Madam Thalasse. The note read:

*Here are your earnings from last night. I've already taken out your room and board for the week. Last night was our most profitable Awakening yet. The others have been singing your praises all morning. When you wake, come see me. I have a letter for you.*

*M. T.*

Nasya opened the purse and saw the golden crowns Scarlet had paid for her. It gave her some comfort, knowing that she was wealthier than anyone in her family had ever been. It was her goal to provide for her family as much as she could, though she didn't know why she felt such an impulse or responsibility. She counted out an amount she thought would get them by for some months, put it in her own purse, and set it aside. The next time she was sent anywhere close to Terrace, she would be sure to give them the money.

Weeks passed and Nasya heard nothing from Scarlet. Not that she expected to. But she couldn't deny the hope, the wish, the longing in her heart for something from her. Alas, nothing came. Nasya continued to work in the brothel, taking clients more often than she needed to so that she could begin saving as much money as possible. Moreover, it was a good impression on Madam Thalasse to see her working more often than necessary, so that when the time came and she had to leave for assignments, Madam Thalasse knew that Nasya would return and pay her what was owed.

Nasya found she enjoyed the work. Men and women came to her often. And if she was unavailable, they went to the other companions or courtesans of the brothel, as was protocol. Prostitutes couldn't be available all of the time, and in those moments, it was customary for others to step in instead. This made Nasya popular among the other workers, for she was among those with the highest paying clients. If she couldn't pleasure them, the others could, and they would be paid handsomely to do so. Nasya liked the feeling of popularity, of belonging. It was new and exciting, and it helped to fill some of the emptiness she felt from Scarlet's absence.

Two months after her arrival in Garden's Hem, she received her first assignment from The Order. And it was Mother Cassiopeia who sent her the instructions. Nasya opened the scroll and found it held three pieces of parchment. One was a map of where she was to go. One was a numbered list of instructions in the exact order and timeline they were to be completed, and the last was a letter outlining the identity of the person she was to eliminate, as well as the amount of compensation she would receive upon completion. She would be traveling outside of Utara, which meant she needed to book passage on a ship to Lorzo, the country south of Hevean. It would be a two week journey by ship, and then another three day journey by coach to the palace where her target lived.

Nasya began to make preparations that day. It would be her first trip outside of Utara.

# Chapter Eighteen

*Capital City of Sun River*
*Country of Utara*

High Prince Mael moved from his place at the royal table and made his way onto the dance floor. It seemed he would be the first to make the plunge. He approached Nasya as her dance with one man ended, bowed, and without expression asked her if she would allow him the honor of the next dance. She graciously accepted, feigning embarrassment at being so singled out. The music began to play and the floor cleared of all other couples. Nasya had never danced with a prince before. Under any other circumstances, she might have been a little giddy.

The music played and the dance began, the High Prince leading elegantly, if not passionately. He was quiet and grave, and Nasya wondered why he had asked her to dance at all if he did not intend to converse.

"You are quiet, your majesty," she said, risking a glance up into his face.

"I never talk when I'm in the middle of studying," he said, his voice gruff and deep.

"And what are you studying, precisely?" she asked.

"You," he said matter-of-factly, smiling ever so slightly.

"Am I so interesting?" She smiled suggestively in return.

"You don't belong here," he said, "you are out of place, and I want to know why."

She was alarmed, unsure of exactly what he meant. He didn't appear to be flirting, but then, would anyone know if he was? He was not expressive at all. Like her, he masked his real emotions. But the tone in his voice made Nasya wonder if, perhaps, he was more observant than he let on.

She maintained an innocent, flirtatious attitude. "The invitation was sent to all of the eligible women in the city," she said. "I may not be royal or even noble, but I was invited to this party all the same."

He grunted. "My father's attempt to please my brother, no doubt," he mumbled. "Surrounding him with women who are all little better than peasants." He shook his head. "It's absurd, if you ask me."

Nasya raised her eyebrows. "You certainly know how to flatter a girl, sire," she muttered.

"Forgive me," he said. "I do not count you among them. You are an outsider, I'm just not sure what kind yet."

She grinned. "And what happens when you solve this mystery?"

His eyes narrowed, staring into hers. "Then, you will be unmasked."

Nasya said nothing in response. Did he suspect her? Did he know of the threat she posed? If so, how? The Order operated anonymously. No one knew who anyone was. All meetings between The Elders and potential clients were kept secret. The Elders veiled themselves whenever they met with clients so as to maintain anonymity. The Mothers and Sisters were given aliases so that their real identities wouldn't be traced or remembered. Every assignment was carried out with the utmost secrecy and caution.

The silence that settled between them was awkward and heavy, but Nasya pretended not to be disconcerted. As far as she was concerned, it was one dance among several. She glanced to where Prince Xaran stood, and his eyes were ever on her. He seemed more intrigued by her now that his elder brother had chosen her as his fist dance partner of the night.

Nasya flashed a small smile to Prince Xaran and watched as his eyes sparkled. He would ask her to dance next, she was sure of it. She waited in anticipation as her dance with the High Prince continued through its revolution, casting her gaze up to meet his every now and then. Every time, she saw his eyes on her, staring deeply into her face, as though attempting to see through her mask. Nasya almost felt as though he was searching for something - someone - in particular. It wasn't only the way he stared, it was also the intensity of his gaze. It was the tension in his hands around her waist, sometimes so loose she thought she would spin out of his embrace, and sometimes so tight she thought she could feel his fingernails digging into the fabric of her gown. It unnerved her.

The dance continued and as the music slowed and came to an end, High Prince Mael pulled her in close, his face mere inches from hers. He held her there, his eyes searching hers for whatever it was he was so anxious to find. Then he bowed briefly, dipping his head rather than bending at the waist. Nasya curtsied low as his rank required, though he barely waited around long enough to see it. To her astonishment, the High Prince left her on the dance floor, rather than escort her back to the tables. Under any other circumstances, Nasya would have laughed, but everyone was staring, whispering.

"Excuse me miss," came a voice from behind her.

She turned and found Prince Xaran standing close. She curtsied.

"Will you dance with me next?" he asked, holding out his hand.

She smiled. "A woman who refuses the offer of a prince is, indeed, a simpleton," she said, accepting his hand.

# Chapter Nineteen

*City of Tenderness*
*Country of Lorzo*

The Palace of Lost Tears was the central landmark on the south eastern coast of Lorzo. Nasya had been within the palace walls for two days disguised as a passing traveler, and few had taken any notice of her at all. She had been given food and drink as she waited for the return coach to take her back to the ship that would return her to Utara, but no other attention had been paid to her. It was exactly as she desired. She was allowed to traverse most of the palace, save the east wing, which made her time there incredibly useful. She had seen her target a total of two times, and based on his movements throughout the day, she determined that the best time to eliminate him would be in the early hours of the morning. If she killed him at night, there was too much of a risk that his body would be found before morning, and all of the palace residents would be held for questioning. Killing him in the morning meant he likely wouldn't be missed until she was on the coach headed back to the ship.

That meant she had to wait until the next morning to make her move.

Her target was a gruff, unpleasant man of large stature and a mean nature. She watched him physically beat the stable boys and verbally accost the maids for no reason at all. Nasya heard the other servants talk and it was clear the man was a brute disliked by everyone, including his employers. Apparently he was the son of someone renowned for their ability managing an estate, which was the only reason he was kept on. And though Nasya knew the morality and likeability of her targets was irrelevant to her purpose, it gave her some satisfaction to know that she would be ending the life of someone who made the lives of others miserable.

The afternoon of her third day passed slowly and with ease. Nasya spent much of her time in the palace library, immersed in the almost drunken-like stupor the sheer number of books filled her with. The Duke of Balesburry, the man to whom the palace belonged, was known for his love of literature, history, poetry – all forms of the written word. It showed in not only the size of the library, but the well kept and safely preserved condition of the books and scrolls. Nasya found herself particularly drawn to the enormous poetry section. She had not had the luxury of reading much poetry throughout her life, and now that she was free to read what she liked, couldn't seem to get enough of verses.

She stood in the library holding a poetry book open in her hands, her silver eyes scanning the pages with such fervor, it was as though her mind was starving for words. A faint smile curled the corners of her mouth upwards as she read. She didn't think anything had ever brought her so much pleasure as reading poetry. Or, at least, nothing solitary. Her night with Scarlet was still like its own form of poetry and she often thought of it, especially when she was alone with her thoughts and ached for Scarlet's presence. She still didn't know what that night had meant, if it had meant anything at all, and she was hard pressed to understand her own feelings of what had occurred. There was still so much of life she didn't comprehend. She wondered if any of it would ever make sense.

Nasya had been in the library for quite some time when the light of day faded and the room fell too dark to read by, even with the torches lit. She returned the book to its place and made her way to the dining hall where supper was to be served. The duke never appeared at these meals, though his wife did, and so did Greck, the man who was her target. The meals were excellent moments for her to study him, learn his manners and his habits. He was not an attentive man. In fact, there were times when she thought he spent most of the day too drunk to pay attention to much of anything.

The dining hall was less full tonight than it had been. Several roast chickens had been placed on the long table with boiled potatoes, brown bread, apples, herb butter, and many casks of ale. Nasya sat and filled her plate and ate quietly, content to listen to the conversation around her. She didn't want to stand out in any way, didn't want to say anything that would draw attention or cause anyone to remember her afterward. She needed to be nothing more than the mere whisper of a presence. Still, she enjoyed the voices and the talk around her. Lorzo citizens seemed far less inhibited in their conversations with each other compared to Utarans, revealing what seemed to Nasya to be incredibly personal pieces of information to complete strangers.

Across from her, two women were talking in not so quiet tones about how many affairs they'd had and how their husbands had no idea of any of it. Nasya knew that if she heard their conversation, others at the table had as well. It struck her as enormously risky to be so open about something that could impact their lives grievously should their husbands become aware of their indiscretions. And yet they continued to talk, going so far as to outline in detail the whos, the whens, and the hows of almost every extramarital encounter.

Nasya took mental notes of those pieces of information that seemed as though they might be useful in the future. Among all of the bustle around her, she was able to pinpoint several details that struck her as either odd or interesting. To her left, a man was talking loudly and with animation about what he called "a ferocious beast" that had been stalking the livestock of farmers on the outskirts of Lorzo's cities. He claimed to have seen it himself, describing it as an almost bear-like creature that stood at least six feet high on all fours and had the deepest red eyes he'd ever seen. Most of the men around him openly defied his tale, telling him that they didn't believe his story, that the creature he described could not possibly exist.

He shook his head. "Then you're damned fools," he said, tearing into his bread. "I saw it sure as I see you now."

"I'm a professional hunter," said one of the others, "and I've hunted every kind of creature you can imagine. Ain't never seen anything like that before. If it existed, I'd know."

"And you ain't never left this valley either, has you?" asked the first man.

The hunter didn't respond.

"That's what I thought. I've been all over in Lorzo and in Hevean, especially up in the mountains and those woods that are so dark, sunlight barely reaches the ground. You'd shit yourself if yous seen half of what I has up there."

"If you're shitting yourself, Folsheth, then perhaps you should see a physician?" said a third man farther down the table.

Folsheth glared around at everyone. "None of yous will know until you sees it for yourselves. I know what's out there. It's evil, and it's coming for us." Then, he grabbed his plate and stood up from the table, clearly intending to finish his meal elsewhere.

Nasya watched him walk away and looked back at the other two men who snickered and chuckled as he left. Some of the women around them were whispering among themselves. The men assumed it was fear over what Folsheth had said and tried to offer comfort, assuring them that there was no such beast, could not be such a beast without it being known worldwide, and said that Folsheth was a poor soul who had lost his family in a tragic accident and had been making up wild tales ever since. Nasya turned her eyes to where the duchess sat to see if she had seen any of these interactions, but the woman merely stared blankly at her plate. She had touched little of her food, by the looks of it, and seemed entirely uninterested in the conversations going on around her.

By the time the meal was over and everyone was heading to their bed chambers for the evening, Greck was completely drunk. He stumbled away from the table mumbling inarticulately as he walked away, carrying a pitcher of ale with him. Nasya already knew which room was his so she let him walk away and made for her own chamber. The palace would be quietest after midnight. That's when she would make her move.

When she reached her room, she shut her door and locked it. She went through her luggage, the little she'd brought with her, and changed out of her day dress into an all black frock made of cotton. It looked like a sleeping robe, but really it was to make her movements through the palace quiet and keep her blended in with the shadows. Then, she sat on the floor in front of the hearth and meditated. She needed a clear mind and intense focus on the task at hand. It was her first assignment from The Order and while she knew she was entirely prepared for this, she also knew that if she weren't careful, things could go incredibly wrong. She couldn't afford that.

Nasya spent the better part of two hours meditating and focusing on her breathing. Soon, the sounds of the palace began to diminish until the entire place was quiet. The night ticked on and Nasya prepared for her first kill. She imagined the route to Greck's room. He was on the main floor of the palace, while she was on the fourth. It would take careful movements, but she could get there in just under three minutes. She had already walked the route several times.

"You can do this," she said to herself. "You will do this."

Midnight came. Nasya crept into the dark hallway, shut her door behind her, and began to walk down the hall. She was barefoot so as to limit the sound of her steps against the stone floor. With the palace so quiet, every noise was amplified and she didn't want anyone hearing her. Only a handful of paces away from her door was a staircase. She took it. She rushed down the stairs quickly, the red velvet carpeting soft against the soles of her feet. She made sure to keep to the shadows as she reached each subsequent floor, just in case a servant was around the corner preparing to take the same stairs. In moments, she was on the main level and only fifteen paces from Greck's chamber.

No one was within eyesight as she came out of the stairwell and crossed to his room. She could hear him snoring heavily. Nasya opened his door quietly, went inside, and shut the door behind her. He was sprawled out on his bed, passed out from drinking. She reached into her pocket and pulled out the mushroom she had plucked from the woods behind the palace. She went over to his sleeping form. His mouth was already open. She dropped the mushroom into his mouth and then forced it shut and held it there. He struggled against her for a moment and she thought he might wake up. But he didn't. It took a minute, but he finally swallowed the mushroom. Nasya stepped back until she was pressed against the door and watched. She couldn't leave until she saw its effects.

It seemed ages before the impact became visible, but it had only been less than a minute. It started with a cough, and then the choking set in. He foamed at the mouth and began to convulse. Then, the foam turned to blood and the choking turned to a deep gurgle as blood filled his lungs. It was then that Nasya decided to leave. She rushed away quickly and quietly, her feet barely touching the carpet as she ran back up the stairs. She made it back to her room, shut and locked the door, changed out of the black robe and into her nightgown, and climbed into bed. She knew she wouldn't sleep, but she had to be in bed so that when her breakfast was delivered in the morning, nothing would look amiss.

Nasya lay awake, her mind reeling. He was most certainly dead by now and when he was found, it would look as though he had finally drank himself to death. Which, considering how drunk he had been at dinner, would not surprise anyone. The night and early morning rolled on in silence. Nasya could hear her own pulse in her ears, her heart was beating so heavily. Now, all she had to do was get through the morning without incident, and she would be on her way home. This was the part she had dreaded most. She knew she would be able to complete the kill. It was the getting back home that was less certain.

A maid came by with her breakfast a little after dawn. Nasya ate what she could, dressed in her day dress, packed her few belongings, and made her way down to where the coach would be waiting. No one said anything to her or anyone else about Greck. She wasn't even sure his body had been found yet. She gave the coachman her trunk, climbed into the coach, and only a few moments later, they were on their way to the harbor to catch the next ship back to Utara. What she had thought would be the hardest part, getting away, turned out to be as easy as the assassination itself. Either Greck's body had not been found, or if it had, no one cared much. The coach made its way to the port without incident, and Nasya soon found herself sailing home.

Nasya had been back in Garden's Hem for only a day when a knock sounded at her door and Madam Thalasse entered.

"You have a visitor," she said, and from behind her walked Mother Hydra.

Nasya stood to her feet and waited until Madam Thalasse had shut the door, leaving the two to talk alone.

"I didn't expect to see you here in person," Nasya said.

Mother Hydra placed a pouch on the mantelpiece above the hearth. "Your payment for your journey to the Palace of Lost

Tears."

Nasya nodded slowly. "I take it this means I was successful."

"Very much so. The client was most pleased with the outcome."

"Are you here to deliver a second assignment?"

Mother Hydra shook her head. "No. We would like for you to be more settled here before you leave again. Don't want to pique anyone's curiosity too much." She walked slowly around the room. "No, I'm here because I have a favor to ask of you."

Nasya furrowed her eyebrows. "A favor? Me?"

Mother Hydra faced her. "It's about Scarlet."

Nasya's skin ran cold and the hairs on her arms stood on end. "What about her?"

"She has been...unruly and unpredictable since graduation. At first it seemed she couldn't be given enough assignments. She refused to take any time in between the jobs we gave her, except for a highly profitable bounty that she insisted on completing. Now, though, we can't get her to take a single one."

Nasya snapped and a roaring fire came to life in the hearth, warming the room in mere moments. She didn't like the cold she felt in her body.

"It has been some time since she last responded to any of our letters. We were hoping you might talk to her. See if you can get to the bottom of what's going on," Mother Hydra said.

"I already know what's going on," Nasya said, facing the fire and holding out her hands. She was chilled to the bone to hear Mother Hydra speak of Scarlet like this. "She's trying to find the lycan that murdered her mother."

Mother Hydra stepped forward. "You know this for certain?"

Nasya nodded. "I do. She was here not even a month ago asking for me to connect to her mother's spirit. She thought it might help her identify the killer."

"Nasya, I hope to the high heavens you did not –"

"I didn't do it," she said. "She left angrily and I haven't seen or heard from her since."

Mother Hydra nodded slightly and let out a deep breath. "I wonder that she didn't come to me for help," she muttered under her breath.

"Would you have offered it?"

Mother Hydra shook her head. "No, but I might have been able to help her see the error in this obsession. However tragic her mother's death was, however painful it may be to carry, it is in her past life. It might as well not even exist. That is how this must be for all of you."

Nasya said nothing. She knew all too well that it was easy enough to say that their past lives were gone and should be forgotten; it was something else entirely to actually give up those memories, those people, those loves. Nasya thought of her family far more often than she cared to admit. She didn't tell Mother Hydra of her plan to see them again as soon as she had the opportunity. And for the first time, Nasya felt she understood Scarlet's inability to let go of her need for vengeance.

"Well, if she is this determined to find her mother's killer, it seems we are to go on without her until she succeeds. If, indeed, she ever does," Mother Hydra said. "If you do happen to see her again, would you mind passing on this note for me?"

Nasya turned and took the rolled up piece of parchment. "I doubt she will come back here," Nasya said. "But if she does, I shall pass this along."

Mother Hydra offered a faint smile of gratitude and made her way towards the door. There, she hesitated. "I know you struggled in training," she said, facing Nasya once more, "and I know you weren't always given the help you needed." She paused for a moment, seemingly trying to find the words for what she intended to say. "I would wish you to believe me when I say that none of what we did was done with malice."

A tingle moved slowly down Nasya's spine.

"And as far as The Order is concerned, we are all extremely proud of how far you've come, and how dedicated you have been."

It was said softly, but with conviction. Nasya gave a singular nod to Mother Hydra. She would have thanked her, but emotions caught in her throat and she feared she would cry if she tried to speak. Mother Hydra returned the nod, and then was gone. Nasya looked down at the parchment in her hands. She placed it on the mantelpiece and sat down at her table with a heaving sigh. This wasn't what she'd imagined her life would be after graduation. It wasn't what she wanted. But she couldn't deny how very fulfilling it was to hear one of the Mothers – any of them, really – tell her they were, collectively, proud of her. She already knew Mother Hydra was proud of her. And she guessed that Mother Corvus was as well. But the others had barely taken any notice of her at all, so to hear that she had impressed them meant more than she was willing to admit.

"Deep down, you're still that little girl trying to prove your-self," she said aloud in the quiet of her own room with only the flames to hear her.

# Interlude: Kyndra

*Tears stung Kyndra's eyes.*

*"I do not believe you," she said, her voice cracking under the weight of the emotion in her chest.*

*Rhaean laughed. "It matters not."*

*"Please," Kyndra said, "let her go."*

*"I do not listen to you. I do not even listen to her."*

*The room had become almost blisteringly hot as Rhaean continued to build the flames to the point of raging on the torches and in the hearths. Kyndra turned and looked at Ygritte. She was crouched on the ground trying to cast a spell. Kyndra's heart panged for the girl, her bravery, her selflessness.*

*"Ygritte!" Kyndra shouted, "Get out of here!"*

*The fifteen year old shook her head. "Not without Rhaean!"*

*Kyndra felt rage, heartbreak, and fear build inside of her. The tears that stung her eyes fell down her cheeks. How could she have done this? How could she have thought bringing her daughter here was a good idea? How could any of the Mothers have brought any of the girls here? Suddenly, everything was abundantly clear to her: the brutality of their way of life, the cruelty of separating children from their families merely to bring them up as efficient killers, and the sheer arrogance of their belief that they were doing any good in the world.*

*She looked up at Rhaean. She didn't know if her daughter could hear her or not, but she knew that she had to face the reality of her own choices.*

*"I'm sorry, Rhaean," she said, "I'm so sorry for ever bringing you here. I'm sorry for taking you away from your siblings. I'm sorry for placing so much on your shoulders that you were not ready to carry. I was wrong. For all of it." She let out a deep breath. "Please, if you must take someone, take me. Leave everyone else." She was talking to the spirit inside of her daughter now. "Leave Rhaean. She deserves better than this, but I don't."*

*"You poor woman," Rhaean said, "you stupid woman. Don't you realize yet that I am your daughter now?"*

*Kyndra's heart began to race.*

*"She invited me in, and I am here to stay. Well, at least for the next few minutes."*

*"Don't, please," Kyndra pleaded, "Take me instead. I am willing. I'm inviting you in!"*

*"Tell me, Mother Andromeda, do you know what happens when too much magic floods a weakened vessel?"*

*Kyndra's eyes widened and she shook her head. "No, please, I'm begging you!"*

*The black and orange of Rhaean's eyes suddenly cleared and she looked down at Kyndra. "I am sorry mother," she said, her voice returning to normal. "This is how it must be."*

*"My darling, please!"*

*But it was too late. It took only seconds for it all to end. The fire on the torches and in the hearths began to move towards Rhaean's body. The flames burnt away her clothes and she breathed them into herself, lighting her entire form ablaze from the inside out. But it wasn't the flames that destroyed her. As they went into her, something else came out and covered her body in a bright flame-like essence. Kyndra turned and ran back to Ygritte, quickly casting a protection spell over the two of them. A second later, Rhaean let out an agonizing scream as magic ate away at her body, reducing her to nothing more than silver flames. Kyndra looked up only when the screaming died away. The room was dark. All of the flames had disappeared and all that remained of her daughter was the smoke left behind from the magic that consumed her.*

*Beside her, Ygritte trembled violently. "What...what happened? Where did she go?" she asked. Kyndra choked on her tears.*

*"She zenithed," she said.*

# Chapter Twenty

Myssa was the capital city of the country of Lorzo. It was large and sprawled across a vast expanse of open plains and grassy hills for miles. It was known to be the largest city on earth. Nasya had been in Myssa for several weeks preparing and planning for her next assignment from The Order. This target was not an estate manager who would be easily eliminated. No, this was someone of great importance who would be difficult to get to. Nasya had been watching her for some time, taking note of her movements, her habits, her secrets – anything she could use to her own advantage.

The woman was Queen Mar'lina.

Nasya had initially been livid over this assignment, not knowing how she would ever manage to assassinate the single most powerful woman in the country and escape the largest city in the world without being noticed. But her objections to the Mothers went unacknowledged. She was merely told that she could reject the assignment and it would be given to one of the other Sisters. This was unacceptable to her and insulting. She felt that her reliability and her dedication to the life she'd been brought up in had earned her more respect. To disregard her worries and then offer to give the assignment to one of the other Sisters implied that she couldn't handle the assignment and was making an issue out of nothing. Not wanting to seem disloyal or incapable, Nasya accepted it, despite her objections.

The queen was a woman of habit. Every morning she took a stroll through the city, surrounded by armed guards and at least two of her ladies in waiting. She would pass out alms for the poor, taking care to give generously, as far as Nasya could observe. It was one of the primary things about the queen that the people of Myssa spoke fondly of. Queen Mar'lina was always generous.

Halfway through her walk, she would enter a small establishment that seemed to be a dress shop, and she would be inside for some time. This wasn't unusual except for the fact that when she would emerge, she never carried a new dress or a parcel or any indication that she'd purchased anything at all. In fact, it took a few days before Nasya was able to determine the real cause of her visits to this dress shop.

The Queen of Lorzo was having an illicit affair with one of the king's guards, and the dressmaker was the facilitator of their liaisons.

After her morning walks, the queen would return to the palace and there she would stay. It was like this every single day, a risk that had likely led to The Order sending Nasya to put an end to it. She guessed that the client was, in some way or another, connected to the king. It was not uncommon for royal men to have their wives eliminated under even false pretenses, and this was certainly not a false pretense. The sheer lack of discretion in the queen's behavior was, in all likelihood, intentional and, believing herself free from retaliation, had continued for some time. Kings did not like to be disrespected and embarrassed.

Nasya knew that her best chances of completing her assignment would be when the queen was outside of the palace, which meant she would have to make her move when the queen was in the dressmaker's shop. Nasya didn't like this as it would be in broad daylight at a time when everyone expected the queen to return to the palace by late morning. It was far more risky than Nasya was comfortable with, but going into the palace to complete the assignment was out of the question.

Nasya spent the rest of the several weeks trying to plan out her attack. She could sneak into the dressmaker's store easily enough and wait for the king's guard to arrive. As far as Nasya could tell, he was always inside the dressmaker's before the queen which would give Nasya plenty of time to incapacitate him and then wait for the queen, who always went into the dressmaker's alone. It was a sound plan and as safe as she could possibly make it. Now, all there was to do was execute it, and then get out of Myssa as quickly as possible. She resolved to complete the assignment the next morning, and so threw away anything she would not need on her journey back to the port. She ate a hearty supper that night and put herself to bed early. She needed to be well rested and clear headed if she was going to successfully commit regicide the next day, and live to tell the tale. She fell asleep in minutes, drifting into a deep and dream-filled slumber.

All she heard at first was the loud crunching of teeth on bone. The pathway leading up to the door of the hut was stained with blood. Her heart pounded in her chest and everything within her small body told her to run as fast as she could in any direction, to get away. But her feet compelled her forward. Each step towards the hut produced even louder crunches and sounds of skin and muscle being torn away from a body. She didn't know how she knew what the sounds were, but she did.

The door to the hut was open. She was only a couple of yards away and she could see inside. Her heart stalled in her chest and breath caught in her throat. Blood was everywhere. And just inside the doorway, she saw a beast larger than anything she had seen before tearing into the lifeless body of her mother. Even though she was young, she knew what death was. Her mother's eyes were open and still. The shining light of life and love were gone from them. They didn't even look blue anymore, but a dull gray that made her skin crawl.

She wanted to turn away, but her eyes were frozen on the horrific scene before her. She wanted to rush forward and save her mother, but there was nothing to save. Not even her body was whole. It had been torn into pieces and the beast was feasting on her as if she had been nothing more than a pile of meat. Tears stung her eyes. She tried not to cry. She sniffed and tried to calm herself, but to no avail. The beast had heard her. It stopped crunching down on the newly torn flesh and lifted its head. Its brown fur was thick and slick with blood. Saliva dripped from its snout.

It snarled as its red eyes stared into her own and she knew she was next.


Nasya gasped as she awoke and sat up. It had been years since she'd had a dream like this, though this one was new. She blinked and looked around her room. At first, she didn't know where she was, and then slowly everything came back to her. She was in Myssa. She was staying at the Eagle Point Inn. She was here to complete an assignment and take out a target. Whatever had been in her dream, that's all it had been: a dream. Nasya knew this wasn't necessarily true, but she couldn't afford to let the dream unnerve her.

She climbed from bed and walked over to the basin near the window. She poured some water into the basin and splashed it onto her face. It was refreshing in the darkness of the early morning. She closed her eyes and let out a slow breath. She hated how her dreams affected her, hated how they made her feel. It was like a kind of disorientation, as though her mind wasn't sure who she was anymore. It was temporary, of course, but it got under her skin and seemed to crawl around until she felt as though her skin wasn't hers.

Nasya shuddered and splashed water on her face a second time. She needed fresh air. She wasn't going to get back to sleep, so she grabbed her cloak and made her way outside. It couldn't have been any earlier than one in the morning. The late spring air was cold, but not frigid, and the streets of Myssa were utterly empty. Lit torches lined the walls, illuminating the streets enough for her to see in the dark. She walked slowly without paying much heed to where she was. She knew the city well enough to find her way back to the inn. Right now, she needed peace and quiet. She needed focus. She needed to get back inside of herself.

She walked down the city streets and alleyways, her mind reeling with too many thoughts. She chewed on the inside of her lower lip in frustration and anxiety. The dream had unnerved her more than she originally thought. Even with the cool night air in her face, she couldn't shake the images, the sounds, the smells. It was as if they were still with her in that moment, transposed across consciousness. Her heart simply would not slow. She tried to breathe deeply, tried to focus on nothing but her body and its movements through the city, all to no avail. After some minutes, she ducked into an alleyway, leaned against the stone wall of a building, and let herself feel everything she'd been trying to bury and ignore.

The dream reminded her of Scarlet. Nasya wasn't entirely convinced the dream had not been about Scarlet and the day her mother was killed. How much of the dream was true and how much of it was merely her own thoughts and feelings, she didn't know. But somewhere inside of her, something had called out into the vast expanse of the dreamworld, and she had been answered. It was the same feeling as when she was a child as Passing's End and the dreams had first begun. She hated this feeling then, and she hated it now. Tears were on her cheeks. Nasya didn't even realize that she'd been crying since the moment she'd ducked into the alleyway. She was so out of sorts, she didn't hear the footsteps approaching her from farther down the alley.

"Nasya?" a voice said suddenly.

Nasya spun towards the voice. The alleyway was dark and unlit, so she could only make out the silhouette of a person in the darkness.

"Show yourself, stranger, or else I cannot guarantee your safety," Nasya said.

The figure moved closer. Nasya made out a red hood and cloak, and then all at once realized who was before her. "Scarlet?" she asked, her eyes wide.

Indeed, it was so. The young woman let down her hood and offered a sheepish smile to Nasya.

"What on earth are you doing here?" Nasya asked.

"I could ask you the same question," Scarlet said, moving closer.

"I'm here on business."

"As am I."

Nasya gave Scarlet a doubtful look. "I'm here on The Order's business," she said. "And I'm guessing you are not."

Scarlet shook her head. "No. I am not here for The Order. I was hired to kill someone."

Nasya frowned. "You were hired to kill someone, but this assignment did not come through The Order?"

Scarlet raised her eyebrows and winked.

Nasya ran her hands down her face. "You do realize that the reason we don't communicate with the clients is that it allows the Elders to vet those who would hire us?"

Scarlet rolled her eyes. "Yes, Nasya, I am aware of how The Order operates. But as a bounty hunter, I can take jobs directly from my clients because they're *my* clients. And usually they're too poor to seek assistance from The Order."

"Am I correct in assuming, then, that you are no longer a Sister? Since you're taking on assignments entirely on your own, without The Order's facilitation?" The bitterness and judgment in Nasya's voice was too strong to be missed. She could see the hurt in Scarlet's eyes, but at this moment, Nasya couldn't say that she cared much. Scarlet had left The Order, their way of life, everything they had worked to build since they'd been taken to Passing's End. Although it wasn't that on which Nasya's bitterness was founded. It was that in leaving The Order, Scarlet had also left Nasya. It had been months since they'd last written to one another, and longer still since they'd spent time in each other's company. Scarlet knew she was the closest thing Nasya had for a family, and yet she stayed away. Didn't write. It was as though she didn't matter to Scarlet anymore.

"It has been some time since I've taken an assignment from them, if that's what you mean," Scarlet replied.

Nasya didn't respond. She didn't even know what she should do now that Scarlet had shown up. She came out into the streets looking for peace and a renewed sense of focus, and instead she found the one person responsible for her lack of focus to begin with. The world certainly had a shitty way with things, Nasya thought to herself.

"Who are you here to kill?" Scarlet asked after a few awkward moments of silence.

"Queen Mar'lina," she muttered.

Scarlet raised her eyebrows. "That's who I was sent to kill."

Nasya stared at her. "Are you joking?"

She shook her head.

"You were hired to kill the target I was hired to kill?" Nasya asked, refusing to believe it.

"It seems so."

It beggared belief. Nasya felt as though she could scream for anger and frustration. She ran her hands through her hair, feeling more angry than she had in years, though she wasn't entirely sure why. "We cannot both seek to eliminate the same target," she said.

"Why not?"

Nasya looked at Scarlet incredulously. "Because of the risk.

The more people involved, the more likely we are to be discovered and stopped."

"Or the more likely we are to succeed," Scarlet suggested. "What if we worked together? We both want the same outcome."

Nasya furrowed her eyebrows. It wasn't a bad proposition. She was already distracted – would it be so bad for them to help each other? She wanted to think of an excuse to say no, but her mind was blank. She sighed. "Fine. But you will follow my lead."

Scarlet gave her an odd look, one that Nasya didn't like. It was a look of stubbornness and irritation. Scarlet, who once could have done no wrong, no longer liked taking orders. However, she nodded and waited for Nasya to continue. Nasya motioned for Scarlet to follow her, and they made their way back to the inn. They were quiet the entire walk. Nasya was too annoyed to make any conversation, and she was angry at herself for being so annoyed and preferred to keep to her own thoughts. She didn't know why Scarlet's presence should aggravate her. If anything, she thought she would be happy to see her again. Was it the manner in which Scarlet had disappeared when they last met? Was it the way in which Nasya felt as though Scarlet were simply toying with her feelings? Or was it misdirected anger? Nasya felt it could be any or all of the above, and she didn't know how to calm herself.

They walked into the room and shut the door. It was still very early in the morning. No one else was awake. All was quiet.

"Make yourself comfortable," Nasya said. "Breakfast won't

be served for several hours yet."

"I assume you have a plan in place?" Scarlet asked, sitting in a chair near the fire.

Nasya nodded. "I do."

Scarlet waited a moment. When Nasya didn't continue, she said, "Are you going to share it or leave me in suspense?"

"Queen Mar'lina walks through the city every morning. She stops at the dressmaker's for a liaison with one of the kings-guard. If we can sneak into the dressmaker's early and incapaci-tate him, then we can ambush her when she arrives, kill her, and then escape out the back, leaving her body to be discovered by others," Nasya said.

Scarlet nodded slowly. "And what of the kingsguard? He would certainly see us. He would know who we are."

"Are you suggesting we kill him, too?"

"I am, actually."

Nasya didn't respond right away. She thought it over and though the death of the kingsguard was not in the scope of this assignment, she also saw that it would likely be necessary to ensure their ability to leave the city afterward. Killing a queen was no small thing, and doing it in such a way that her lover might see who committed the act was reckless, at best. Nasya agreed that the kingsguard should be eliminated too, and the women settled into an uncomfortable silence. Nasya was not in the mood to discuss their last meeting, or how Scarlet snuck off in the night without even saying goodbye. She wasn't in the mood to discuss anything at all, and instead stood at the window and stared out into the darkness of the morning. Scarlet must have sensed this because she didn't try to keep any kind of conversation going. She simply sat near the fire and stared into the flames.

The morning passed slowly, but the time came for them to leave the inn. They agreed to walk separately and come from different directions. On their own they would be more likely to blend in with the other citizens of Myssa. Nasya decided she would be the one to sneak into the dressmaker's from the back and find somewhere to hide and wait for the kingsguard. Scarlet would go in the front and find somewhere else to hide. It was not a flawless plan, but it was one the two women felt confident they could carry out.

Nasya reached the dressmaker's and found the back door unlocked and ajar. She entered and shut herself in a small closet. She would be able to see anyone who entered or exited from the back of the shop. This was the part she hated most. The waiting. Things could go very wrong and she wouldn't know. She told herself to trust the process, to focus, to breathe.

It wasn't long before Nasya saw the kingsguard enter the back of the shop. She snuck out of the closet and cast a muting spell on him. If he was hard to subdue, she didn't want him crying out for help or warning off the queen. Then she went up behind him, grabbed the metal iron to her left, and hit him over the head with it, knocking him unconscious. He was a tall man, but not large. He was rather lanky. Nasya found some fabric and bound his hands and feet. He was not her target, therefore she could not be the one to kill him. That had to be left to Scarlet.

Just then, Scarlet appeared. She came from the front of the shop and shut the door behind her. In one swift motion, she pulled out her knife and slit the kingsguard's throat. It was over in an instant. Once his throat was slit, he gurgled for a moment, his body twitching in pain as life drained from his eyes. Then he was still. Blood pooled around his body.

Nasya and Scarlet exchanged glances at one another. They had never worked together before. At least, not outside of training, and Nasya suddenly felt the close proximity of their connection. It had lasted throughout training and now beyond, though she wasn't entirely sure if that was good or bad. It seemed neither of them could do right by the other. And for Nasya's part, she wasn't sure what doing right by Scarlet should even look like. Helping her find her mother's killer? Encouraging her to give up the obsession and return to The Order? Both of them leaving The Order entirely?

Nasya was brought out of her conflicted daze by Scarlet snapping her fingers in her face.

"Focus!" she whispered harshly. "The queen will be here any moment."

Nasya nodded and moved to hide behind the door that connected the back of the store to the front, where the queen would be coming from. The kill would have to be swift, just as Scarlet's had been. The shop keeper would likely keep a close watch on the two lovers, especially as one of them was part of the royal family. There would be no time for lollygagging, as Mother Corvus once put it.

They waited for less than ten minutes. Queen Mar'lina rushed into the back of the shop, her eyes looking around excitedly for her lover. Scarlet had hidden his body under a large piece of fabric. Nasya waited until the door was shut before she cast another muting spell over the queen, and then rushed forward and grabbed her hair with one hand. With the other, she lifted the knife that had been on the kingsguard's hip and struck down hard on the queen's chest three times. It was over in seconds, and for that Nasya was grateful. Then, she slowly laid the dead woman's body on the floor and placed the knife in the hand of the dead guard. It would look like the guard killed the queen and then killed himself. It wasn't much of a cover, but it was what they had.

Nasya stared at the bodies for a moment and then rushed out the back, careful not to make any noise. She had blood stains on her clothes, her hands, and her neck, but she didn't have time to wash. She and Scarlet had to get far away from the dressmaker's shop, and quickly. The bodies would be discovered soon and anyone in the vicinity would be under suspicion. Nasya grabbed a cloak that was hanging on a clothesline and wrapped it around herself as she and Scarlet walked quickly through the city.

The inn was a fair distance away, but they took the longest

route possible down alleyways and up streets that were well out of the way. They wanted to ensure they would not be followed. It took them over an hour to get back to the inn, but it had been worth it. They returned to Nasya's room without incident. Nasya immediately changed out of her dress and tossed it on the roaring fire in the hearth. No evidence would be left behind. Only cinders. She put on a different day dress, packed up her few other belongings, and then prepared to leave.

Scarlet stepped between her and the door to her room. "Wait," she said.

Nasya looked at her. "The sooner we get out of this city, the better," she said. "We have a limited window before they close the city gates, and we've already used up too much time."

Scarlet nodded. "I know. But...I was hoping you might come with me instead of going back to Garden's Hem."

Nasya furrowed her eyebrows. "I don't have time for this," she said, shoving past Scarlet and rushing down the stairs.

She stepped out into the sunny spring morning and quickly made for the city gates. Her heart was pounding in her chest. The amount of time it had taken them to return to the inn had eaten up the time Nasya had intended to use to get out of the city without drawing suspicion. Now, she walked quickly down the streets towards the gates. She knew she could fly away if the gates were closed before she got there, but she didn't want to do this. It would be too distinct. People would remember her, and that would make returning to Myssa at any point entirely out of the question.

Nasya didn't check to see if Scarlet was with her until she had passed through the gates of the city without interruption. She looked over her shoulder, but Scarlet was nowhere to be seen. A pang of guilt cut through her. Perhaps she should have gone with Scarlet? Or, at least, heard her out? But there hadn't been time. That was a fact. Nasya shook her head before continuing down the road towards the port. Guards would be patrolling the road outside of the city come nightfall. And though there was nothing on her that would link her to the death of the queen, Nasya didn't think anyone would believe that she had been murdered by the kingsguard, which meant they would be looking for the real killer. She intended to be back in Utara by then.

Nasya had only made it a couple of miles down the road before she heard footsteps in the underbrush around her. She stopped and looked around, careful to discern from which direction the steps came. "I know you're there, Scarlet."

From her left, Scarlet emerged. She was still wearing the bright red cloak Nasya had seen on her the night before.

"You could have come with me out of the city gates, you know," Nasya said, continuing to walk down the road.

Scarlet didn't respond. She fell in line next to Nasya. "You never answered my question," she said, her voice quiet.

It was true. Nasya had hoped Scarlet would drop the subject.

"I don't know what you want me to say," Nasya said. "The Order is my life, as it was meant to be yours."

"But are you happy? Are you fulfilled?"

Nasya looked over at her and found Scarlet's large eyes staring at her anxiously. "What are you suggesting we do?" she asked.

"We could run away together. Find somewhere in Nynivri to live and provide for ourselves."

Nasya considered her words. It sounded like a glorious life, if she were honest. But she knew Scarlet well enough to recognize what she wasn't saying. "If I'm to give up The Order, would that mean you would give up your journey of vengeance?" she asked, though she knew the answer.

Scarlet seemed surprised by the question. "Well, no. I wouldn't need to give it up. We'd be searching together."

Nasya let out an unsurprised chuckle. "I thought so."

"Why are you so against that?" Scarlet asked, moving to stand in front of her. "Would it be so bad?"

"Yes, Scarlet," she said, staring into her eyes. "Yes, it would."

Scarlet looked exasperated. "Why? We would be together!"

"Do you honestly think giving up my purpose to traverse the earth in search of one specific lycan would actually make me happy?" Nasya asked. She knew her words would hurt Scarlet, just as they hurt her to speak them. Deep down, she reveled at the idea of a life with Scarlet away from The Order. A quiet life in a small town. A settlement, land of their own to work. But in every vision, every daydream, Scarlet was absent, too consumed with lust for blood to stay in one place for long. "Our lives would never be about just us. Nothing has ever been just us. And I will not abandon a life that gives me stability and purpose to be your partner in revenge."

Scarlet shook her head. "Partner in *life*, Nasya." She took Nasya's hands in her own. "That life would include continuing my search, yes, but you would not just be my partner in that search. You would be my partner in everything else, too."

"Then you would be receptive to my wants and desires? My dreams and goals for us?"

Scarlet nodded. "Yes! Of course I would."

"And if my dream was for us to live a simple life, a settled life without revenge or hate or killing? Would you be receptive to that?"

She hesitated. Eventually, she nodded. "Yes, I would. Once I've completed my search –"

Nasya pulled her hands away and walked by her, anger flaring in her chest. Scarlet grabbed at her hands again, but Nasya wrenched away.

"Nasya, please!" Scarlet pleaded.

She turned around to face Scarlet again, tears in her eyes. "I have never been anyone's first choice!" she exclaimed. "Even my own parents chose money instead of me. Since that moment, I have played second fiddle in everyone's story. And now you present me with the image of a life that I would grab at the first available chance, but it's one I can have only after you've completed your search for your mother's killer. *After.* I can come along with you, but the things that would fulfill me would be suspended until after you've gotten what you want." Tears were on her cheeks now. She was closer than she had ever been to admitting the truth of her feelings for Scarlet.

The woman across from her stood still, her eyes wide. She said nothing.

"And what if you never find her killer? Will there ever come a time when you can lay aside your need for vengeance? And even if you do, will you ever be fully with me? Or will you live each day in regret and anger and distraction?" Nasya asked. "Because Scarlet, if I thought there was even a chance that you would actually give up this obsession, I'd drop everything and leave with you in a heartbeat." She shook her head. "But I know better."

"I'm not wrong for wanting revenge, Nasya," Scarlet said, her voice quiet but hard.

"And nor am I for wanting to be my lover's first priority," Nasya said. She wiped the tears off of her cheeks and walked around Scarlet. She continued down the road, hoping that Scarlet would rush after her, apologize, and promise that yes, they would be together and yes, she chose Nasya first above all things. But she didn't. And Nasya didn't look back.

# Chapter Twenty-One

*Capital City of Sun River*
*Country of Utara*

The music began again and, moments before Prince Xaran swept her across the dance floor, she met High Prince Mael's gaze. He was as stoic as ever, though now his anger seemed to have swelled to rage. She didn't know if it was that he was being upstaged by his younger brother, or if his general disgust with the evening's proceedings had simply turned sour, but his emotions were evident. He gave her a knowing look, his dark eyes intensely focused on her. Nasya couldn't tell if he felt rebuffed, or if he was still suspicious of her. Either way, it made her uneasy. She didn't like the look in his eyes.

The dance with Prince Xaran was long and intimate. Where High Prince Mael was quiet, Prince Xaran was pleasant and easy to converse with. He smiled and laughed and teased and flirted. It was everything one would expect from a dance with a prince. Nasya gave him the sweetest smiles she could muster, laughed at every joke, and asked him as many questions as she could think of. It wasn't that she was particularly interested in his answers, but she was struck by the stark difference between the two brothers, and what she knew to be true about the younger of the two.

"I am surprised that you have yet to take a wife, your highness," she said, testing out the subject that was most assuredly on the mind of every other woman in the room.

Prince Xaran smiled. "Yes, as is my father. He has tried his hardest to work the necessary political magic to make a betrothal of some kind solidify between myself and someone. Almost anyone would be enough for him it seems."

"But you will not be so easily satisfied," she said.

His blue eyes sparkled. "Precisely. I need more than a large dowry and a plot of land to satiate my appetites."

Nasya smiled. "Is the prince determined to marry for love, then?"

He laughed heartily. "I'm not nearly that sentimental. I know that love is a myth in the royal world. No matter how hard some like to pretend that they love their spouse, it's simply not a reality for royalty." There was almost a hint of sadness in his voice. "My father tried to convince my brother and I that he loved our mother. And even though she died when I was young, I remember enough of their relationship to know it was a lie."

"Well, relationships are bound to look differently to children. Maybe he did love her, just not in a way that would make sense to a child's mind?"

He shook his head. "They rarely spoke to one another. They had separate bed chambers on opposite sides of the castle. And when she died, he never shed a single tear." He sighed. "She was a means to an end, just like my wife will be, and just like I am."

Nasya said nothing.

"No, I do not need love to be happy. I do not even need friendship or respect with the woman I marry," he said, holding his head up.

"Then what do you need, sire?"

"A face I find pretty enough to fuck every once in a while," he said, looking back at her. "And a mind wise enough to hold her tongue when I seek out physical pleasures with others."

Nasya felt her skin go cold. She didn't have to pretend to be caught off guard and even repulsed. She stopped smiling.

"I've offended you," he said.

"Surprised me would be more accurate, your highness."

"Am I wrong to know what I want?" he asked.

"No, sire. But when what you want is so superficial and does absolutely nothing to better any connection between yourself and a woman, I wonder how much harm would be caused for all involved if you should marry under such pretenses."

He chuckled. "Pretenses? I've offered no pretense."

"You've offered no decency, either."

She could see the increase of his interest. There weren't many who would openly oppose a prince as she just had.

"Some might say the real indecency is in living a lie," he replied.

"And others might say that marriage is precisely what you make it."

He blinked slowly as their dance ended. Nasya was prepared to walk away, but he took her hand.

"Will you dance another with me?"

She furrowed her eyebrows. "I don't see the point in it."

He leaned in closer. "Please? It is my birthday, after all."

She agreed, though the idea of being close to him for yet another dance was repulsive. Still, this was what she needed: to pique his interest, to make a mark. Like everything in her profession, her desires and wishes were of the least importance.

The dance began and for a while, it seemed they would only dance in silence. His eyes were ever on her, as though willing her thoughts to penetrate his own mind. Their hands intertwined in intricate spins and turns, their bodies facing and then turning away from each other at intervals. Under any other circumstances, it might have even been called romantic.

"I know my attitude towards marriage is disappointing to most," he said finally. "And I acknowledge that it is shocking, but I see no point in deceiving myself. Royals do not have the luxury of hoping to even like their intended. I will, in all probability, have no say in who I marry. And I will be lucky if I meet my future bride more than once before the wedding takes place. It is simply the order of things. I choose to try and find a way to make the most of it."

Nasya said nothing.

"Do I have none of your sympathy?" he asked.

"No, sire. None at all. Your father put on this celebration at great expense to the people of your country who are already starving to death. You are surrounded by luxuries of incalculable value, and yet you complain over a life that will banish you to a loveless marriage, as though you have no control over how you choose to exist as a husband?" She shook her head. "I cannot sympathize with that at all."

He stared at her, but he did not speak. They continued the dance, his movements drawing her body ever closer to his. She kept her gaze cast down, focused on one of the buttons of his tunic. Her posture was tall, her movements rigid. She didn't entirely resist his pull to bring her in close, but she didn't make it easy for him either.

He had riled her, and he knew it. The longer the dance went on, the more he tried to get her attention, to raise her gaze to meet his own. He ran his hands along her bare arms. She allowed his hands to dip low on her back, pressing her into him, holding her close enough she could smell the wine on his breath. He wanted her to relax, and she refused.

At last, she could resist him no longer. She blinked and slowly met his gaze, but she did not relax her body. She remained rigid. Defiant. His eyes were steady. They held the rhythmic pulse of his heart, a beat she could feel in her chest as he pulled her up against his. Her skin tingled with excitement. She was a whore -

she loved to be touched and teased. But she had also won more than his interest, his curiosity. She'd won his desire, precisely as she'd intended.

Her heart raced with what she knew was coming. In only a minute more, the dance ended and the spell between them snapped. She curtsied, he bowed, and they walked away from each other. Nasya walked to one of the tables that lined the ballroom, grabbed a goblet of wine, and took a sip. The younger prince had gotten under her skin, and she wasn't sure why. Even despite his insulting views of marriage and women, he had been far more pleasant than his older brother. Of course, a friendly demeanor didn't negate or justify what he had said. But why should she care what a total stranger believed about marriage and women anyway? It was unexpected, this response, this anger she felt. It came from somewhere deep inside of her, someplace she had not allowed herself to look for a long time. Coupled with the sudden rush of desire in her body, she felt herself blush.

She took another sip of wine, unsure of what to do. She was here for a reason, and she knew the consequences if she failed. She'd been a Sister for years, and in that time, she had never failed an assignment.

"You didn't find my brother charming?" asked a voice from behind her.

She turned quickly and was face-to-face with High Prince Mael. Startled, she choked on the wine she was drinking. He reached out an awkward hand as though to help, though there was nothing he could do as she began to cough and sputter. It took her a moment to compose herself.

"He...was a very pleasant dancer," she said, evading his question.

The High Prince nodded slowly. "He must have been for you to dance with him twice. But by the end of the second, you seemed...disillusioned. May I ask why?"

"You're inquiring as to the nature of a private conversation?" she asked, suspicious of his interest.

"I'm seeking answers as to why you, unlike every other woman here, aren't fawning over my brother, even after he paid you such special attention as to ask for a second dance." When Nasya didn't answer, his eyes narrowed. "You realize this is quite atypical?"

"It might have felt more like special attention if he hadn't admitted that he sees women only as pretty faces to look at." Nasya said, annoyed at both brothers now.

High Prince Mael furrowed his eyebrows. "I'm sure he didn't mean it that way, whatever he said."

"He was explicit, your majesty. He said that he only needs a face pretty enough to stomach while fucking."

High Prince Mael stared at her a moment and then said, "I can see the indelicacy of such a statement, but, forgive me, since you are not the one he is going to marry, I can't see how any of it concerns you," he said.

Nasya raised her eyebrows. "I didn't realize you were responsible for choosing your brother's intended," she said, her gaze drilling into his.

He shook his head. "I'm not."

"Oh, then pray tell, what qualifies you to determine who your brother may or may not marry?"

A faint grin tugged at the edges of his lips. "I can see why he asked you for a second dance."

Nasya looked away and took a sip of her wine.

"I only meant that since you are not, as of yet, his betrothed, then his reasons for marrying can be nothing to you."

"Only a man would isolate another man's words from his actions," she said, turning her back to High Prince Mael.

"And only a woman would see herself as the subject of any conversation about the weaker sex," he replied.

Nasya glared at him over her shoulder. If he had known how many men she had single handedly killed in her lifetime, he might have reconsidered his use of the words weaker sex.

"I may not be the woman he will marry, but he will marry someone," she said, "And the very nature of his attitude towards women will affect how he interacts with my sex throughout his life. What if he should have daughters? How will he treat them? How will he raise his sons to view women? This is not a moment isolated in time. It will extend far beyond today."

He only stared at her, his gaze steady. She hadn't intended to say all of that, and she wasn't entirely sure from whence it had come. And judging by the look on the High Prince's face, he was just as surprised as she felt.

"And besides," she said, picking up another goblet of wine

and leaning closer to the heir to the Utaran throne, "how do you know I won't be the one he chooses to marry?" Her voice was barely a whisper now.

He did not respond immediately. When he did, he cleared his throat, visibly uncomfortable with the thought she'd posed.

"My brother has been indulged and enabled his entire life," he said, choosing to ignore her last statement. "He has yet to experience any consequences to his actions, and my father does little to instruct or guide him. Xaran was an affectionate child, but he has grown into a willful, impulsive, and entitled adult. He has caused an enormous amount of grief for many, and I have done what I can to show him a better path. But, he does not want a better path. And I am left picking up the pieces he leaves behind." He sighed. "I sincerely apologize for my brother's behavior."

Nasya took another sip of wine.

"Well, at least one of you pretends to be well bred," she said.

She watched as his interest was piqued again. A smile still tugged at the corners of his mouth. She imagined that he was probably a decent man, even a pleasure to be around if he could manage to relax a little. Never one to miss an opportunity to flirt, she was about to speak when Xaran approached.

"Did I overhear you apologizing for me?" he asked, standing next to the High Prince. "No need, brother. I am capable of making amends myself," he said.

High Prince Mael said nothing, but nor did he move away. Nasya assumed that he wanted to watch the anomaly of his younger brother apologizing. Prince Xaran stared down into Nasya's eyes, every bit of his flirtatiousness pouring out of them.

"You were right," he said, "I have been born into luxury and privilege and while I cannot bring myself to rejoice over the life I am doomed to, I can see the ignorance of my words. I humbly apologize and ask for your forgiveness."

"Doomed?" Nasya asked, raising her eyebrows. "You make it sound like indentured servitude, your highness."

"What else would you call it?" he asked, clearly annoyed that his halfhearted apology had meant nothing to her.

"I would call it a life you should be grateful to have."

He scoffed.

"You do realize, sire, that you have every choice in the kind of relationship you build with your intended? That you both can choose how you treat one another? If, indeed, you are doomed to a life of misery with your spouse, it's because you want it to be so."

Both High Prince Mael and Prince Xaran stared at her in silence. In the elder brother's eyes she saw hints of admiration and awe. In the younger's, she saw a mixture of confusion, anger, and intrigue. She had nothing else to say, and so stood in silence with them.

"I can't decide if I want to have you thrown out, or if I want to ask you for another dance," Prince Xaran said.

"I will not allow you to be thrown out," said High Prince Mael, looking at his brother. 'It's about time someone spoke some honest sense to your face. Someone other than me, that is."

Nasya grinned.

"It was refreshing to be so bluntly addressed, I'll admit it," said Prince Xaran. "No one else ever speaks to me that way. Not even my own father." He looked at his older brother. "Well, no one but you, and you are far too miserable to be taken seriously." He grinned and looked back at Nasya. "I rather enjoyed it, if I'm honest."

"I'm glad I could oblige you both," she said.

"Will you do me the honor of another dance?" the two brothers asked at the same time, both of them holding out their hands to her.

They looked at each other, both of them clearly annoyed. Nasya could only chuckle.

"As flattered as I am by both of your offers, I don't think I can dance anymore. I've spent the entire evening spinning in circles, and after two goblets of wine, I'm not feeling quite steady enough to attempt it. But I heartily thank you both."

Prince Xaran stepped closer.

"Well then, what if I wanted us to go somewhere...more private...would you...be interested?" His eyes sparkled with lust that he didn't try to hide. "You could rest your legs and...let me do the work."

Nasya watched as High Prince Mael stared with wide eyes at his brother. She was surprised that Prince Xaran was still capable of shocking him. It was almost amusing, but then the High

Prince turned his gaze to her to see what her answer would be. She looked up at Prince Xaran and cocked her head to one side.

"Tell me, your highness, did you mean the apology you gave me a moment ago, or was it also a *means to an end*?" she asked with emphasis.

"I did mean it. Completely. But I also cannot deny -"

"That mine is a face pretty enough?"

She held his gaze steadily, though she could feel High Prince Mael staring at her intensely.

"I know how this looks. I acknowledge I am a rascal -"

"That's putting it lightly," High Prince Mael muttered.

Nasya held up a hand and they both fell quiet. She gave one final glance to High Prince Mael, and then turned her eyes to Prince Xaran once more.

"Well, it is your birthday, isn't it?"

He smiled, his eyes alight with excitement.

"There's a room just at the end of the hall where we can go," she said, leaning forward. "Meet me there in two minutes."

She didn't wait for his response, nor did she allow herself to look at the elder brother. She simply walked away and out into the hall. Her heart was racing. The night had not gone at all as she'd thought it would, but then the intricacies of getting to this part were never set in stone, and nor could they be planned in the first place. Her body hummed with excitement. She focused on her breathing and kept mindful of her surroundings.

It was almost over.

# Chapter Twenty-Two

*City of Garden's Hem*
*Country of Utara*

Nasya was twenty-five years old. She had been in Garden's Hem for several years. Life moved quickly in the Ashland Woods that bordered Utara's eastern coastline. In that time, she had become a prolific Hand of the Order. She had even received a letter with the signatures of all the Mothers highlighting her achievements. Her continued success and dedication to The Order had earned her distinction among those with whom she had graduated. Hardly one Sister of every graduating class was likely to receive such a letter. It had been mailed to her from Passing's End and she carried it with her everywhere, a reminder of all she had overcome.

It was Mother Casseiopea who had written and sent the letter communicating this honor. When the letter arrived and Nasya saw Mother Casseiopea's signature leading the others, she sat and stared with wide eyes for a full ten minutes. She had expected Mothers Corvus or Hydra to have sent it, not Mother Casseiopea. Never her. Not in a hundred years. It meant more than she was willing to admit seeing her signature there and knowing she had signed it of her own accord. The Mother who nominated the Sister would sign the letter first.

Nasya was also beloved and respected by all of those who worked at the brothel. In her time there, she had never received a single complaint from a customer, nor from any of the other companions or courtesans. Nasya played her role perfectly and, truth be told, enjoyed it immensely. She loved the pleasure she brought to those who sought her company, and she even enjoyed most of her clients. Aside from a few travelers who were disrespectful and abrasive, none of her clients were violent or rude or entitled. They treated her well. Madam Thalasse was beyond pleased with the atmosphere of the brothel in the years since Nasya had arrived. No one directly attributed this pleasure with Nasya's presence, and yet it was an unspoken truth that things had not been quite this good before her. And in all of this, Nasya had hidden away a small fortune. She wore the finest clothes. She ate the finest foods. She drank the most expensive wines, and still had more than enough to put by to support her for the rest of her life, should she decide to leave The Order. There was almost nothing she would have changed, almost nothing she regretted.

Except one.

It had been years since Nasya had heard from or seen Scarlet. The Mothers wrote to her and inquired about Scarlet's whereabouts from time to time, but Nasya had nothing to offer them. Not even the slightest hints of where to look. It was the one blight on an otherwise beautiful life that Nasya relished. At times, thoughts of Scarlet weighed on her so heavily, she could barely think of anything else. Sometimes she woke screaming in the night from horrific nightmares about her, unable to breathe or calm herself for some minutes. She missed Scarlet terribly. She feared for her safety. She wondered if she was even still living. And if she had known how to contact her, she would have done so without hesitation.

But even the pain and the loneliness she felt for her was not enough to make her regret leaving Scarlet in the woods those two years ago. As hard as it had been to walk away, she knew it would have been harder competing with Scarlet's need for revenge. Nasya respected herself too much to put herself in that position. Instead, she tried her best to live contentedly away from the woman she loved. It was hard. She missed Scarlet more than ever, but chose to focus on her accomplishments and the little beauties in her life.

One summer afternoon, Nasya was in her room reading when a knock sounded at her door. "Come in," she called and through her door walked Mother Phoenix. Nasya stood to her feet. "Mother Phoenix. This is a pleasant surprise."

The woman looked much older than the last time Nasya had seen her. Her pale skin was worn thin and sallow. Her eyes were sunken and in them she saw the remnants of a great deal of stress.

"I'm here to deliver another assignment," she said, holding out a rolled up piece of parchment.

There was a curt tone in her voice that made Nasya hesitate. She took the parchment slowly and unrolled it. Her eyes scanned the writing and she quickly saw the potential reason for Mother Phoenix's tone. "The deed is to be public?" Nasya asked, raising her eyes to look at Mother Phoenix. "Are you joking?"

She shook her head. "Unfortunately, no. I am quite serious. As is the client."

Nasya looked back down at the paper and finished reading the instructions. There weren't many and they weren't as detailed as she would have liked. "Did they give any justification for why it has to be done in public?" Nasya asked.

Mother Phoenix gave her a hard look. "You know that we do not require our clients to justify their preferences."

"Yes, and that's usually because they want everything to be as quiet and secret as possible. For a client to demand the deed be committed in public, I think justification is necessary. Dare I even say mandatory."

Mother Phoenix stared at Nasya for a moment, as though judging how much she should and should not reveal. "It is not the practice of The Order to require such communication from our clients, although in this case we did attempt to discuss their reasons for wanting the death to be public. They declined our request and we were forced to let the matter drop."

Nasya raised her eyebrows. "And I am expected to hold to these instructions? As vague and dangerous as they are?"

Mother Phoenix nodded. "Yes."

Nasya tossed the paper onto her table and ran her hands through her hair. "You realize that this greatly increases the chances of my failure?"

"We understand your concerns. The Mothers know the risks involved here, which is why I was also instructed to give you this." She pulled another rolled up piece of parchment from her robes and handed it to Nasya, who read it eagerly.

Nasya scoffed. "You think this is sufficient?" She read from the paper, "A reassurance that, as the Sister carrying out this assignment, all aspects of its execution ultimately remain at my own discretion and that, should things deviate off course, I will be supported in whatever actions I deem necessary to complete the assignment and remove myself from the location safely." She looked up. "That's all?"

"What more would you have liked us to say?"

"Considering that the most important part of my job is ensuring an assignment is carried out according to the instructions I am given, this reassurance feels hollow."

"Our hands are tied too, Nasya. We did what we could to alter the instructions, even if only a little in your favor, but the client was adamant. Death must occur in public."

"And if I were to kill any normal citizen, the situation might not be as treacherous. But they're asking for the death of a holy man!" Nasya cried. "What cause could there be for such a thing?"

"It is not our place to question the motivations of our clients, Nasya. They offered a lot of money for us to carry out this assignment, and we would not have given it to you if we didn't feel you were more than capable."

At this, Nasya burst out laughing. "Yes you would. Even if you knew I couldn't pull this off, you still would have given it to me. That's what you do. It's your role in this game. And mine, apparently, is as the unwitting pawn."

Mother Phoenix did not respond, but she did not miss the implications of Nasya's words. The two stood in silence and stared at one another. Nasya was angry, livid even, but she would not defy The Order.

"If you're really asking me to take this assignment, then I will do so," Nasya said after several moments. "But when I complete it, and I shall, I will be paying all of The Mothers a visit to discuss the absolutely unacceptable bullshit that is this list of instructions," she said, tapping on the parchment she had tossed onto the table.

Mother Phoenix turned and left. Nasya shook her head and poured herself a glass of wine. She had never been a favorite of Mother Phoenix's, and neither had she been a favorite of Nasya's. But still, Nasya thought the woman might have conjured a little more concern for the safety of one of the girls she had known for over a decade. It was incredible what she was being asked to do. For any of the other Sisters, it would be a mission of suicide. Luckily for her, she had magic and would have to use it if she was going to complete this assignment. And though she was filled with many conflicting emotions, she was resolved to do it, and do it well. She hadn't missed a target yet, and she didn't intend to start now.

The new assignment took Nasya deep into the heart of Hevean, to the country's capital city, Zillah. It was, in fact, the farthest away from Utara she had ever been, and for the longest amount of time. In an attempt to limit the almost certain amount of suspicion that would arise once she had completed the assignment, Nasya opted to live in Zillah for some months before attempting to kill the holy man she had been sent for. His name was Brother Caspian. He was the High Priest of Zillah and, as far as Nasya could see, was well loved and respected. He walked among the citizens daily, offering comfort, wisdom, teaching, and alms. Every morning and evening, he led the townspeople in prayer, gathering them at the steps to the entrance of the temple just outside of the palace. The rest of his time was spent indoors serving the members of the court.

Nasya had set up a small shop in the town square selling natural remedies and tinctures. She could make these easily enough and they sold well. She listened to Brother Caspian's teachings every day, hoping there would be some sign, some hint at his corruption or hypocrisy that would make what she had to do more palatable. But every interaction she observed only confirmed what seemed to be true at once: he was a genuine servant of their gods, and he took to heart his responsibility to the people. Why anyone wanted him dead, Nasya could not ascertain.

She had been in Zillah for three months when she decided it was time to fulfill her task. It grieved her, but she knew it must be done. Not only for her sake, but for the sake of The Order. Brother Caspian's routine was highly consistent, making it easy for her to plan the assassination. He gave three sermons every day, one mid-morning, one in the afternoon, and one after dark. She decided she would wait until dark, and then slowly move into the crowd. She would cast a small illusion spell to make herself temporarily invisible.

The day of the assignment came. It was early morning and Nasya had just finished setting up her stall for the day when a deep and familiar voice greeted her good morning. Nasya returned the greeting and looked up from her bottles. It was Brother Caspian. He was standing at her stall, his dark eyes drilling into hers as if he already knew what she was planning to do. Nasya blinked, caught off guard by his sudden presence. "C-Can I help you find anything, m'lord?" she asked.

He smiled. "No, I am not here looking for remedies. I'm here to offer you one."

Nasya's heart began to beat hard. She knew there was no way he could possibly know or even suspect what was coming, and yet the tone in his voice gave her pause. She offered a small smile and cocked her head to the side. "Offer me one?"

He nodded. "We all walk a dark and dangerous path, though for some of us, the path is darker and more dangerous than usual." He paused, as if for effect. "I hope you know you are allowed to choose differently."

Nasya's gaze was caught in his and in his eyes she saw her own reflection. But it wasn't her reflection as she was now; it was different, though she wasn't sure in what ways. Was it her as she could be outside of The Order? Was it who she would become if she remained a Sister? She didn't know. Maybe it was neither. Maybe it was both simultaneously. What she knew for certain was that she was seen, perhaps more clearly than she ever had been before, and it unnerved her. She broke the link between them and looked down at her items for sale.

"Having permission to choose is not the same as having the opportunity," she said, though she immediately regretted the words.

"It is so for us all," replied Brother Caspian, "and yet some of us take the leap of faith anyway. We all must decide which paths of darkness we can live with."

Nasya chanced another glance up at him, but whatever she had seen before was now gone. She just saw a man before her, one dressed in a plain, black robe with a leather belt around his waist.

"And which path of darkness do you live with, Brother Caspian?" she asked.

He smiled then, a bright, glorious smile full of amusement. "I am one who must walk the paths most shrouded in shadow so that I may reach the souls of those others deem to be lost." He shrugged. "It is my blessing and my curse, but it is the one I choose every day."

Nasya's skin began to tingle. This wasn't about her, she realized. The hair on her arms and on the back of her neck stood on end. "And which souls are those?" she asked.

He did not speak. He simply turned and looked up at the palace behind him. Then he turned his gaze back to Nasya. "Are there any souls more lost and in darkness than those who possess the greatest power and influence over so many?" he asked. He held Nasya's gaze, as though trying to see into her very soul.

Then, as quickly as he had appeared at her stall, he walked away, and Nasya was left alone to ponder the implications of his words. How much he suspected, how much he knew of her plan, she truly didn't know. But it took some time for her pulse to slow enough that it no longer thudded in her ears. She had not lost her resolve to complete her assignment, but it did increase the amount of regret she held over taking this particular life. Still, as he had said, she had choices to make, and this was one she was determined not to shy away from, however much she wanted to.

Night fell and with it, an eerie, ominous feeling, as if the very air anticipated what was to come. Nasya had spent the day selling her vials, making sure to be as forgettable as possible. She made little conversation with her customers, but that didn't stop them from talking endlessly at her. She heard rumors and tales of creatures living amongst the citizens of Zillah, changing into and out of various beastly forms. She heard of dark magic contaminating the city, leaking out of the castle, tempting the innocent. And while Nasya paid little heed to these chatterings, something in the back of her mind told her they were not entirely unfounded. For her own part, she had sensed magic emanating from the castle. This wasn't strange on its own; many rulers kept mages in their employ. It was practically an expected practice at this point. But there was something different about the magic here, something not quite ordinary that made Nasya wonder what was actually going on inside.

The later the evening got, the fewer customers approached her stall. Before she knew it, Brother Caspian had reappeared in the square and taken his usual place on the steps just outside of the palace. Nasya waited until a small crowd had formed in front of him before moving from behind her stall. As he spoke to the crowd, offering words of wisdom from his scroll of scriptures, Nasya inched her way closer. She was careful not to draw too much attention to herself. She had already cast the illusion spell, but it only worked to maximum effect when she was mostly still. She settled into position only a yard or so away from Brother Caspian, far to the left of the crowd where she would not be as noticeable. She waited several minutes, letting the stillness of her body erase any outline of her form.

In her hand she held a thin tube made of wood. In it was an even thinner blade dipped in a fast acting poison. Slowly, she lifted the tube to her mouth and prepared to blow the dart from her place in the shadows into Brother Caspian's neck. Seconds before she let the missile fly, Brother Caspian's gaze turned and locked onto her. Nasya froze, holding her breath. His eyes were on her, his gaze connected to hers.

"Remember, my children," he was saying, "the darkness may feel safe at times, but it will always betray, always steal, always deceive." Nasya began to tremble. "It cannot satisfy. It is not loyal. And only you can choose to leave the darkness and embrace the light."

Nasya let the breath in her lungs fill the tube and propel the blade forward. It struck Brother Caspian in the neck, just where she had aimed. He sucked in a gasp of pain. His hand came up to grab where he'd been struck. He felt the missile and pulled it out of his flesh. Blood began to spurt out of the wound and the people in the crowd screamed. Nasya knew she should move, but she was transfixed, her feet practically nailed to the ground where she stood. Brother Caspian had not averted his gaze and now stood, unblinking, staring at her in utter calmness as blood poured out of his body. "What have I done?" Nasya thought as a chill of dread slithered up her spine.

"There!" a voice shouted.

It was then Nasya realized she was at least somewhat visible to the others in the courtyard. Panic began to set in. She had not expected to be seen, and she didn't understand why her spell wasn't working. Had it worked at all? She didn't have time to find out. In a moment, she unfurled her wings and leaped into the air. It wasn't the extraction she had planned for herself. She had meant to leave Zillah only when she could guarantee that she would not be followed. But she couldn't afford that luxury now..

Nasya cursed as she flew. This was precisely what she'd feared would happen, though she had not anticipated that her magic would mysteriously fail her. It made no sense. She would have to ask Mother Hydra about it when she got back to Utara. If she got back to Utara. She might have made it out of Zillah, but they would certainly send scouts to look for her. They knew what she wore, what she looked like. If she didn't make it to the port in time, she might not make it onto the ship at all.

She flew as far as she dared before landing deep in the heart of the woods. Everyone had seen her fly away. Any scouts they sent ahead to look for her would know to search for a woman with wings. She guessed that she had flown at least five miles away from Zillah and that she had a good week's worth of walking to get to the port. She stood in the woods, breathing heavily, bent over at the waist. She shook her head, unable to get Brother Caspian's eyes out of her mind.

"Fuck!" she shouted, retracting her wings.

She had nothing with her but the clothes on her back and some money in her purse. She hadn't left much back in Zillah, but if she had been able to pack up her stall, she might have been able to sell some vials in any cities she came across between here and the port. She had also left behind some food, but it would have been better than having nothing on hand at all. Anger and frustration built within her, but she did her best to quell them. She had to focus. She had to keep calm. It was the only way she would make it back to Utara.

Nasya began to walk through the woods. She knew in which general direction to go and made her way through as quickly as she could without exhausting herself. It was midsummer, so the night air was warm and humid. Having spent so much of her life in the cold and the snow, it was refreshing not to battle the frost. But she quickly found that the heat came with its own setbacks. Thirst, for one. In less than an hour, Nasya was parched and she had no way of carrying water with her. But she also dared not make her way into any villages just yet, not that there were any close by anyway.

She considered unfurling her wings and simply flying to the port tonight, but her wiser self prevailed. It was many miles between there and where she now stood and she had never made such a journey by flight before. She didn't know if she could carry herself that far without sustenance. At the very least, she would need water before even attempting such a thing. Though it irritated her, she resolved to find herself a source of freshwater and spend the night there. In the morning, she would look for something to eat nearby, and then evaluate her options.

It took her about fifteen minutes to find a freshwater source. She drank until she had slated her thirst, and then drank some more, before falling into a restless sleep among the leaves and bushes of the forest floor.

Three days passed and her magic still did not work. At least not as it had before coming to Zillah. She had used her magic successfully to lure a few rabbits to her to skin and cook, but none of her other spells seemed to take. It was as though she was back in training, struggling to get a candle to remain lit.

She didn't understand what had happened or why. Nothing had negatively impacted her abilities in years, not since she had made her choice to stay at Fire's Hearth. Why would they suddenly break down now? And why could she do some things but not others? Had the rumors about dark magic in the palace been true? Nasya didn't know. She hoped that the farther she got from Zillah, the more her abilities would strengthen and return to what they had been before. For now, she was stuck making the most of her situation. Not that there was much to make anything of.

It was late evening on her third day walking through the woods. On her hip she carried the dead bodies of two rabbits she would skin and cook for her dinner when she stopped to rest that night. She was tired of roast rabbit, but she was grateful she had anything to eat at all. She had nothing with which to carry water. Luckily it seemed as though there were several rivers and streams winding through the woods for her to follow. And it seemed they, like her, were making their way to the ocean. She was in good company, then.

Nasya had never been this deep in the woods of Hevean. She was used to the woods of Utara where there was minimal underbrush and the land was mostly flat until the woods sloped up the mountain ranges. The woods here were different, darker, and more eerie. It wasn't that the Utaran forests were entirely safe, but there was something about the woods in Hevean that made Nasya feel as though she was always being watched. She couldn't shake the feeling.

The night had grown quite dark by the time Nasya stopped to make camp near the river. She built a small fire, skinned the rabbits, and hung them on sticks above the flames. It would be a while before they were ready to eat, but as she watched their small, slender bodies cook, her stomach growled. She thought of her bed back in the brothel and the hearth where she always had a fire to keep her warm. Mostly she thought of the delicious foods she ate; the braised pork, boiled duck and quail eggs, freshly baked rye bread with the creamiest butter, roasted vegetables with garlic and lemon, and so many other foods. She smiled, telling herself that she would prepare a mighty feast for everyone at the Lusty Lion on her return.

A sudden noise from deeper in the forest jolted her out of her daydream. It was a loud shriek, a cry of pain, coming from somewhere distant in the darkness. Nasya was on her feet in a second, her eyes wide and staring into the forest. She had yet to encounter any beasts or other creatures in her trek through the woods, and now felt certain that whatever was out there was not friendly. The shriek continued. It sounded like a woman in a tremendous amount of pain, and yet the tone of voice was ethereal and otherworldly. It filled Nasya with a desire to find whatever made the noise and put an end to its suffering. However strong the impulse was to leave her campsite, Nasya had the wherewithal to resist. Her gut told her not to move from where she was. A few minutes passed. The voice faded, leaving Nasya in the darkness alone without any idea of what or who it had been, or if they would be back.

# Chapter Twenty-Three

*The woods outside of the Capital city of Zillah*
  *Country of Hevean*

Slumber faded in and out. Every rustle of leaves in the wind, every crackle of the fire, and every scurry of critters on the forest floor jostled her from sleep. The shriek had set her on edge. She didn't trust the woods. She didn't feel as if she were in danger necessarily, but she knew she was not alone, and that unnerved her. She was a wanted woman in a kingdom not her own, a country she didn't know. And she still did not know what had cried out from the darkness as she roasted her rabbits. These thoughts filled her mind every moment she awoke in the night, and they remained in her subconscious as she drifted back to sleep.

The light in the room was bright. Too bright. It was filled with people. Too many people. Something was wrong, but she didn't know what. She stood at the back of the room and watched as others continued to file in. The queen's guard stood against the walls of the stateroom, hands on the hilts of their swords, unmoving. Everyone was quiet. The throne sat empty. No one knew why they had been awoken at such a late hour.

"I assume you know what this is about, Lady Florynce" said a voice to her right.

It was the queen's chief advisor.

"You assume wrongly," she replied. "I haven't the slightest idea why we're all here. It must be a matter of great importance to be pulled from our beds at this hour."

The man did not respond. His dark eyes watched her closely, as if trying to read her thoughts. Even if he could, he wouldn't find the answers he sought for she had spoken the truth: she did not know what was happening or why. Everyone was still in their night clothes. She had been attentive enough to grab her robe on her way out of her chamber, and now was glad of it. The room was not cold, but she was chilled to the bone with anticipation. Something was not right. That much was apparent to everyone. But she sensed something else bubbling beneath the shroud of mystery that lay over the palace, and it wasn't good.

Several minutes passed before the large door at the head of the room swung open and the queen entered. She, too, was in her nightgown, an all black robe made of satin and trimmed in silver. Her black hair was pulled back in a loose braid. On her head she wore a large crown. Everyone curtsied as she moved to sit on her throne. Her already pale skin looked even whiter in the brightly lit room as the flames gleamed from the torches that lined the walls. Her eyes flashed with a fire of their own as she scanned the room.

"Thank you all for making your way here so quickly. Your haste and cooperation are much appreciated, I assure you," the queen said, her voice deeper than one might anticipate. "I am sure you're all wondering why you've been summoned. Rest assured, I will not leave you in suspense any longer."

At this she stood to her feet and let out a harsh breath. "Last night, our anointed Brother Caspian was assassinated in the square."

A murmur spread through the crowd. Florynce felt her throat tighten. She did her best to maintain her composure, but a sinking feeling of dread had begun to tighten in her chest.

"It seems a poisoned dart was shot into his neck by someone attending his nightly sermon," the queen continued. "Many tried to save his life, but the poison acted quickly."

The queen stepped down from her throne and began to walk slowly about the room.

"The person who committed this act was not apprehended, but she was seen fleeing the city," the queen said.

"I beg your pardon, your majesty, but did you say she?" asked the man standing next to Florynce.

"I did, Sir Gwilym. The assassin was a woman. She escaped by flying over the city walls. It seems she had wings, or at least that's what witnesses claim."

Florynce's heart beat wildly in her chest. She instantly knew who had done the deed. She knew the woman with the wings. All at once, it seemed imperative that Florynce make it out of Zillah as quickly as possible. She couldn't leave now. Not yet. She would have to wait for the opportune moment, but it was simply no longer safe for her here. The Mothers would be angry, but she would worry about that later.

"You may be wondering what any of this has to do with the lot of you," the queen said, moving further into the center of the room. "And that is a fair question. To speak plainly, I believe that one of you knows the identity of the woman who killed our Brother Caspian. I believe one of you aided her arrival in the city, provided her information regarding Brother Caspian's schedule and movements throughout the day. I believe one of you is a traitor to the throne, and to me, your queen."

The room was eerily silent. No one dared speak for fear of calling attention to themselves. Florynce kept her gaze lowered. She prayed that they would be given a warning and let go to return to their rooms. She would leave tonight. She would sneak out the servant's passage and take the long road to the port. She would bring only what provisions she absolutely needed. She would make her escape.

"Lady Florynce Lyric," the queen said then, her voice loud and demanding. "Step forward."

Florynce gasped and lifted her eyes from the floor. The queen was staring at her, staring right through her as though seeing her most intimate and secret thoughts. Next to her, Sir Gwilym stood, his eyes wide with shock.

"Bring her to me, Sir Gwilym," the queen demanded.

He did as instructed and grabbed her arm, his eyes staring into hers with confusion, concern, and pity. Florynce was trembling. He pulled her away from the wall and stood her before the queen. Florynce curtsied and kept her eyes lowered to the ground. "I am your humble servant, your majesty," she said, her voice quavering, "Tell me what I can do to aid you and I shall do it."

"Good," the queen said, "that is what I like to hear." She placed a finger under Florynce's chin and lifted her gaze to meet her own. The queen's eyes stared deep into hers. "Tell me the identity of the woman who killed Brother Caspian," she said.

"Majesty?"

"If you are in earnest in your desire to assist me, you will tell me the name of the woman who was here. You will tell me how you know her. And you will tell me where to find her."

Florynce's heart sank. She shook her head. "Majesty, I am your loyal servant in all things. If I knew the name of the person you seek, I would give it to you, but alas, I do not. I am sorry. But I do not know."

The queen's eyes darkened. She stared down at Florynce in silence. She leaned forward until their faces were only an inch or so apart. "I can hear your heart pounding in your chest," she whispered, "and I can taste the lies on your tongue."

Tears filled Florynce's eyes. She couldn't. She knew she couldn't. "Please, your majesty, have mercy. I cannot give you what I do not know."

A glimmer of fury passed over the queen's eyes. "Then you are of no use to me," she said. A second later, the shimmer of a blade flashed in the firelight and came down hard, and her world faded to red, and then black.

Nasya gasped as she awoke and sat up quickly. Her breathing was fast and shallow. Her entire body trembled as though cold, and yet she was drenched in sweat. She looked around herself, unable to get her bearings. Where was she? Who was she? What had happened? It was still dark, though a pale twilight loomed behind the horizon in the distance. She could barely see it through the trees. Slowly, she oriented herself, but she could not calm the rapid beat of her heart. The dream had been so vivid, she couldn't say for sure that it hadn't been real.

Just then, the shriek from the night before filled the air, only much louder this time. The creature was close. Very close. Nasya stood to her feet and scanned the trees for any sign of something approaching. It didn't take long for the creature to come into view. She was a woman with short brown hair. She wore a white cloak and hood. Tears streamed down her cheeks and her eyes were red and puffy. She looked normal, except for when she opened her mouth to scream; her jaw became unhinged and stretched open like a snake, and the sound she belted into the darkness was dreadful.

"She's…she's gone, isn't she?" the creature said, moving from behind the tree where she'd been peering out at Nasya. "She's left us!"

Nasya frowned and stared, unsure of what to do or say.

"The one in the nightgown…" she said, her words bleeding into another cry of agony and despair. "She should not have lied!"

An icy chill rushed over Nasya's skin like a brisk winter breeze. Every hair on her body seemed to stand on end. "I don't…I don't know w-what you're talking about," she said, trying not to shiver.

The figure stomped her foot hard. "Yes you do!" she screamed. "You saw her! I know you saw her! And now she's gone!"

The shriek was shrill and loud and high pitched. The person before her was no human. Nasya didn't know what she was, but she wanted her to go away.

"She's gone, just like the others will be soon…" she said, her voice quieting a little.

"What? What do you mean? What others?"

"The others!" she screamed, and her face changed into something fierce and terrifying. Her eyes disappeared into their sockets. Her skin stretched thin across her face and turned a sickly blue. Her teeth lengthened into sharp points. It caused Nasya to step backwards and put her hand on the knife she carried on her waist. "All of the others!" Her screams turned to sobs and then to wails. "All of them!" She looked over at Nasya. "You will lose them."

Nasya nodded slowly and took a step closer to the creature. "I understand," she said.

The creature's face turned back to what it had been before. Her cheeks were tearstained and she looked at Nasya with a deep-rooted fear. She watched each step Nasya took towards her.

"What can I do to prevent that?" Nasya asked.

But the creature shook her head and cried. "No preventing," she said, heartbreak in her words. "No changing course."

"I must try," Nasya said softly. "There must be something I can do?"

The creature stared at her and sniffled. She moaned as though she were about to cry again, but this time the moan turned to laughter. Loud, sickening laughter that rumbled deep from within her. "Nothing! Nothing *you* can do! Plenty you *will* do! Plenty! Plenty!" She was practically hysterical, her head thrown back in a high-pitched squeal of delight that shifted back to a shriek of pain and despair. "Nothing and plenty! Nothing and plenty!"

She cried again, but they were merely whimpers. Nasya still didn't understand what the creature was saying, and she didn't have time to clarify. The creature turned and made her way back into the woods. She disappeared in only a few seconds, and her cries faded into the wind. Nasya stood where she was, unsure of what she had just seen and heard. Regardless, she needed to get back to Utara as quickly as possible. She couldn't afford to waste any more time. As risky as it was, she decided that she would fly during the night and rest during the day. She hoped it would mitigate some of the risk and keep her anonymity intact. Urgency was in her bones like a prophecy. Something horrible had happened, or was going to happen, to one of her Sisters. She could feel it.

It was time for her to fly home.

Morning came and she spent the daylight hours hunting and hydrating herself. She didn't know how her body would fare flying so far for so long, and the least she could do was ensure she had eaten her fill and drank as much water as she could. Then, she rested. Where she was in the woods, the canopy was thick and the forest floor was covered in shade. She slept as much as her mind and body would allow. The dream she'd had and the creature she had encountered still weighed on her. Her worry would have kept her awake if she hadn't forced herself to meditate. She needed sleep if she was going to fly through the night. The meditation did not immediately push her into slumber, but it did relax her body and allowed her mind to wander aimlessly, which was restful enough.

Morning turned to day, day to noon, and noon to evening. By the time the sky began to darken, Nasya was restless and ready to begin her first long distance journey of flight. She unfurled her wings and used them to help her climb above the canopy. She stopped at the top of the trees and stared out at the vast expanse of wilderness before her. The sky was not yet fully dark, but she couldn't wait any longer. If she stayed high enough in the sky, she would be out of sight for most people. And even if they saw her, at that height she would look like nothing more than an enormous bird. With one last slow exhale, Nasya leaped into the air, flapping her wings hard to rise higher into the sky. She quickly found an updraft and it carried her up, and up.

The flight had begun. She did her best to reserve as much of her energy as possible, and for the first hour or so, had no difficulties. Part of her training had included longer flights in harsh weather to help build her endurance. But even those flights had been incredibly short in comparison to the distance she had to fly now.

The hours passed slowly in the sky. It seemed as though ages had gone by before all light faded from the horizon and the sky was engulfed in darkness. Clouds had rolled in, blotting out the silver light of the stars and moon. Nasya was grateful for this as it provided her more coverage. No one would be able to see her now. And as time ticked on, Nasya found herself surprised at how little energy she seemed to use in flight. She had expected to be tired early on, but even after several hours had passed, she felt perfectly fine. Her wings were strong and agile and her body seemed to take on a lighter form with the air beneath her wings. She tried flying faster to see if that might tire her out, but found that she had more speed in her than she thought. She flapped her wings harder and harder and watched as the earth below sped by. She could hardly help the fascinated grin that tugged at her lips.

By the time dawn began to peer from behind the horizon, Nasya had only just begun to feel fatigued. She found a glen to land in and laid on her back for some moments, breathing deeply. She was, indeed, very tired, but nowhere near as severely as she had anticipated. She lay there, her neck cradled by the tall grass, and stared up at the brightening sky. She had flown much farther than she had hoped she would. With any luck, she would reach the port by dawn the next day. She had not yet determined if she would fly across the sea to Utara or take a ship, but it was comforting to know she was that much closer to home. Though she did not relish the conversation she would have with The Mothers once she returned.

Nasya slept. It was deep sleep, dreamless, and resful, the kind of sleep that can only come after intense physical exertion. When she finally awoke, it was from the intense hunger that caused her stomach to growl. Based on the position of the sun, she guessed it was late morning, and set off into the woods for something to eat. She caught three rabbits, made a fire, skinned the rabbits and cooked them. As she bit into the roasted meat, she realized just how ravenous she was. She ate the three rabbits in a matter of minutes and immediately went looking for more. She spent over an hour hunting and when she returned to her makeshift camp, she had another four rabbits ready to skin and cook. She had also found a grove of mushrooms and carried as many of them back with her as she could. She ate the mushrooms as the four rabbits roasted over the fire.

As Nasya waited for the rabbits to cook, she laid back and stared up at the afternoon sky. It was peaceful here, deep in the woods where no one else lived or wandered. Even the forest itself seemed to be happier here than it was closer to the treeline where humans had built their villages. If she hadn't been, literally, fleeing for her life, she might have stayed in these woods and just enjoyed the peace and the quiet for a change.

When the rabbits had finished roasting, she ate until she couldn't eat any more. She found a source of freshwater and drank until her stomach felt too full for another drop. Then, she forced herself to sleep some more. Night would fall fast and she didn't want to waste a single second of the time she had to rest. Especially if she was going to try and make it all the way to the port before dawn. She did sleep, though not nearly as heavily as she had that morning. At times she awoke and simply laid still in the grass, her eyes closed, her body connected to the earth. Rest was rest, even if she never fully fell asleep.

Finally, the evening sky began to darken. Nasya leaped from the floor of the glen and made her way high above the forest canopy. She flew swiftly. Her wings felt even stronger than they had the night before, and she decided to push herself harder. Under any other circumstances, she would have relished the power and strength she carried in her body, and the speed at which she could fly for long intervals. It was not something she had expected. Except under very specific circumstances, Nasya lived her life as though she was entirely human. She used her magic in small ways and only, ever, used her wings when she had to. It bothered her to be neither human nor fae, and yet exist as both simultaneously. She had been unable to reconcile the truth of her identity with her everyday life, and as such had chosen to keep the bulk of her fae blood concealed.

Now, soaring above the earth under the cover of darkness, with the wind and clouds for company, she wondered if she had made the wrong choice. Was this not better? Did this not feel like precisely what she was meant to do? To be? Mother Hydra had always hinted at her embracing a life outside of The Order one day; though Nasya had given it little thought, she couldn't help but see just how many choices she had before her. If she could do this, fly hundreds of miles at once without tiring, what incredible things could she accomplish with her magic? What else might be lurking inside of her?

"Focus, Nasya," she muttered. "You can think about all that later."

She determined that she would bring the matter up with Mother Hydra and see if, perhaps, it would be beneficial to connect more with the fae blood inside of her. Maybe even seek out the fae to try and attain some of their wisdom regarding magic. It struck her as odd that this idea had never occurred to her before, and that Mother Hydra had never mentioned it.

Nasya knew very little of the fae. No one knew much about them. They kept to themselves deep in various different woods, caves, and mines. They were not friendly, that much was apparent, and aside from the different types of fae (royal, woodland, perennial, dark, and blood), no one knew anything else about them except that they were inherently magical. Nasya wondered what type of fae blood flowed through her veins. Who had her real parents been?

She had many questions and no means of answering them until she arrived back in Utara, and that would still take many hours of flying. But the thoughts themselves were enough to excite her. It was strange, this surge of curiosity regarding her heritage. She had never cared about such things before and wasn't entirely sure why she cared so much now, but, as was her way, once her interest was piqued, there would be no satisfaction until she found answers. She was, after all, the most prestigious assassin among her Sisters; perhaps there was more for her to accomplish?

# Chapter Twenty-Four

Nasya waited in the room she'd chosen for Prince Xaran to arrive. So long as no one other than his brother saw him leave the ballroom, she figured all would work out fine. Truth be told, she would have rather the High Prince not have been privy to their conversation, but it wasn't as though he knew who she was. He had not seen her face. He did not know her name. They might have seemed like trivial pieces of information, but it was astonishing how much one could conceal so long as those two pieces of information remained hidden. Her eyes, being silver, were quite distinctive. If the High Prince made note of them (and she had to assume that he had), it could come back to bite her later. But there was nothing she could do about that now.

Within a moment, he arrived, entering the room quickly and then shutting and locking the door behind him. He faced her, his eyes wide and fierce with desire. They stared at each other for only a moment before he moved towards her. He covered the distance between them in seconds and pressed his lips to hers. His hands wrapped around her waist, pulling her hips towards his.

"What is your name?" he asked, his voice low and tense.

Nasya did not respond. Her body was hot with anticipation. Her skin practically came alive at his touch, his eagerness. Having lived her entire adult life as a whore, she loved this feeling, the burning, the ache. Had she been there for any other purpose, she might have let him slide inside her and satisfy the longing that built within. She had certainly never fucked royalty before.

But more than anything, she could feel the rush of the kill that was to come.

"Please," he said, clawing at her skirt, trying to lift it high enough for him to feel her skin. "Your name. I must have it."

His hands were practically shaking as though he had never undressed a woman before. His breath was hot on the skin of her neck. She let him fumble with the skirt around her legs. It gave her time to slide one of her slippers off of her foot. She held it behind her back and snapped off the heel, revealing a jagged, glimmering edge. His eyes opened at the sound of shattering glass. Before he could look down at the blade she held, her other hand waved through the air, her fingers moving too quickly to see, as she cast a muting spell over him. It was only temporary, but it would be long enough.

He felt the spell take hold and took a few steps back, confused. He tried to speak, and when he realized he couldn't, he looked back at her, his brows furrowed. That was when he saw the blade in her hand. Every bit of passion and lust evaporated from his eyes. He stared at her with wide, angry, fearful eyes as he continued to try and speak. She stared back, unmoved. He turned and made for the door, but she intercepted, slicing down against his leg, causing him to stumble.

She lunged forward again and tried to stab him in the side, but he managed to leap out of the way. He faced her and jumped sloppily, his arms outstretched as if to subdue her. She cut one arm open above the elbow as she moved aside, allowing him to pass, and then cut open a deep wound in his side after he moved by her. Blood streamed from both wounds, for they were deep. He shook with hatred. He was calculating his chances of survival. Nasya guessed that his next move would be toward the door again. She was right. He ran for it, his only chance to escape mere feet away, and she used her wings to land between him and his reprieve. She swiped the blade downward across his face, cutting into the flesh.

She waved her hands and cast another spell, one which brought him to his knees. He was before her in helpless desperation, tears streaming down his face, as if pleading for mercy. In one fluid motion, she used the heel of her glass slipper to slice his throat open. He fell to the floor, writhing and sputtering blood. She watched life leak from his body and then, using both hands, snapped her fingers, igniting his body. The flames were dark blue and burned with great intensity. In mere seconds his form was reduced to nothing but a pile of smoldering cinders. She watched for a moment longer before she ran to the window, swung it open, and leaped into the night.

She landed gently on the ground just outside of the palace walls. No one was around, thankfully. She furled her wings closed and took off the gown and mask she'd worn. There was blood on them and she didn't want anyone to find her with the dress. They would surely remember the mystery woman who danced with Prince Xaran at the ball. She stuffed them in a crate with moldy bread and tossed in the slipper she'd used to kill the prince. Only then did she realize that the other slipper had fallen off her foot. She spun around frantically, hoping to find it among the dirt. It was nowhere in sight. It must have fallen off as she left the room.

Her heart thundered in her chest. How had she not felt the slipper come off her foot? She cursed under breath. There was nothing she could do now. She had to go back to the inn, and fast. She couldn't be seen looking around outside for the slipper, and the guards wouldn't leave the Prince alone with a mysterious young woman for long. She let out a frustrated breath and walked away in just her undergown. She hurried through the city, careful to keep to the shadows. Once she got back to the inn, she ordered a bath to be drawn quickly. The servant girl filled the tub in her room with hot water and gave Nasya a bar of soap and a towel. Nasya slipped into the steaming water.

Her thoughts were immediately on the lost slipper. Could she, perhaps, sneak back into the palace and retrieve it? Even as she entertained the idea, she knew the answer was no. There was no telling how long it would take for Prince Xaran's absence from his own party to be noticed, but she didn't think it would take long at all. Even being around the palace when his burnt up body was found increased her chances of being caught. Not to mention, she had no idea where she'd lost the slipper. She couldn't very well wander around the palace looking for it. And if she was found with it...that was something she could not risk, no matter what.

She allowed the hot water to soak into her body. It calmed her after the rush of the kill. Even after all these years, she never got used to how it felt to take a life. Mother Phoenix had always said everyone was so focused on the importance of creating life, that they missed the power of eliminating it.

"The gods grant life, they create. But we snuff it out, we undo. We are the opposite sides of the same coin," she'd said.

Given the immense power Nasya felt with each kill, she understood what Mother Phoenix had meant. It was unlike anything else she had ever experienced. Nothing could compare.

Nasya washed the ink out of her hair, blackness fading from the fiery red waves which covered her head. She lathered soap into it and scrubbed. She rinsed herself off and then climbed from the tub, all remnants of her presence at the masquerade gone. No one would know she had been a part of anything amiss. She put on the plain dress she'd worn earlier that day, and tied her hair back in a long braid.

Then, she sat on the bed, closed her eyes, and meditated. As exhilarating as the kill was, and as much as she enjoyed the feeling of accomplishment, she needed to calm herself. Peacefulness was the antidote to murder, and it was the only way she would keep her cover. At the ball she had been Cinderella, the assassin. But now, she was Nasya, the whore, and she was simply waiting for customers to solicit her.

She didn't know if the man she'd met earlier from the square still intended to stop by, but if he did, she wanted to be prepared for him. A woman intoxicated by a fresh kill was not who he intended to fuck, and so she needed to be the same as she had been when they met. She breathed deeply, her eyes closed, and centered her attention on her body: her fingers, her arms, her legs, her toes. She allowed herself to feel them as deeply as she could, forcing her consciousness to dig deep into every muscle, every bone. Then slowly she pulled herself back to the room, to the crackling fire, to the smell of the soap she'd bathed with.

Nasya opened her eyes and let out a final breath. She called for the servant girl and ordered some bread and cheese, and asked for a bottle of wine to be brought up to her room. The girl brought the food and drink only a few minutes later, and with her was the merchant from the square. Nasya smiled as he dipped his head.

"I was beginning to wonder if you were going to show," she said, holding the door open for him.

He grinned. "So was I, if I'm honest." He walked towards the fire and rubbed his hands together near the flames. "I've never actually...well, you know..."

"Paid for it?" she asked, pouring them both some wine.

He chuckled nervously, his eyes scanning the room. "Exactly."

She smiled. "Well, shall I tell you what's involved?" she asked, handing him the glass of wine.

He took it and nodded nervously. "Please."

Nasya walked back to the table and grabbed her glass of wine. She took a sip.

"We can go as slow or as fast as you like." She gave him a knowing look. "Obviously, longer will cost more."

He smiled.

"I can start with a massage, or a kiss. Or if you prefer to lead, then you can tell me what you'd like to do. I only have two boundaries that I demand be respected: leave my ass alone, and nothing violent. Some whores like it rough, but I don't."

He raised his eyebrows. "Not even if I'm willing to pay extra?"

"Not even if you could offer me a palace of gold and jewels."

He nodded. "As you wish."

"Does this sound agreeable to you?" she asked.

"It does," he said, throwing back the rest of the wine and swallowing it in one gulp.

Nasya finished her wine, too, and set the glass on the table.

"How should we begin?" she asked.

He stood still and quiet for a moment and then walked towards her. He stopped mere inches away and reached behind her, slowly and gently untying the strings of her bodice. She could feel his hands shaking. Nasya gave him a gentle smile. His hands slid up to her shoulders as he tugged the dress down, revealing her bare chest. The dress tumbled to the ground in a heap of fabric. He let out a deep breath at the sight of her naked body and then looked back up at her face.

"What should I call you?" she asked.

"Don't call me anything," he said, leaning forward and pressing his lips against hers. "Just...let me touch you."

His hands found her breasts and gently pressed against them. She let out a moan as his lips pressed against hers once more. She wrapped her arms loosely around his neck. He smelled differently than she thought he would. Most merchants were dirty and didn't bathe often, but his skin was smooth, clean, and his clothes seemed fresh. It was a pleasant change from her usual clientele. His black hair was soft. She slid her fingers through it.

His lips trailed from her lips down the side of her neck to her shoulder. Nasya's fingers began to work at his trousers, untying them quickly, but his hands dropped to hers and he stopped her.

"No," he whispered. "Not yet."

She looked up into his face, somewhat confused. Typically men liked her to be eager, full of lust. She had never had one stop her from undressing him before.

"Sit," he said.

Nasya gave him a coy smile, but did as he instructed. She

lowered herself onto the bed. He knelt before her and slowly spread her legs open. He licked two of his fingers, and then slid them gently between her legs. A jolt of heat and pressure shot through her and she gasped. He smiled.

"Is this alright?" he asked.

She let out a deep, quick breath. "If you weren't the one paying to be pleasured by me, I'd ask you to do that again…and again…and again."

He held her gaze for a moment and then slowly brushed his fingertips against her again, and then again, and then again, causing her to gasp with each stroke. The pleasure was overwhelming, and was only ever something she had experienced with women. Never men. He pulled his hand away and let out a deep, slow breath.

"Did you enjoy that?" he asked.

She smiled and nodded, looking down at his lust-filled eyes. He nodded.

"Good," he said, and then leaned forward, pressing his tongue to where his fingers had been.

Nasya sucked in a deep breath and let out a loud moan as every inch of her body began to tingle. His hand slid up her abdomen to her chest and found one of her breasts. As his tongue slid back and forth, he took her nipple in between his fingers and began to play, tugging, pinching, brushing. She longed for more, and yet reveled in the teasing nature of her partner. She laid back onto the bed and closed her eyes.

He stayed there until she cried out with pleasure, and then

pressed a trail of kisses up her body, eventually landing on her lips once more. Nasya lost all track of time as their bodies tangled together, their breath hot and urgent as they moved, thrusted, and tossed about on the mattress. This man surprised her in many ways. He was strong, his muscles large and toned, and yet everything he did with her was gentle. Even his strong thrusts, his hips pounding into her, held a feeling of tenderness. He kept his gaze locked with hers, one hand cupping her face as he propped himself up on the other. And never did his focus on her waver. If she expressed a feeling of pleasure at something he did, he repeated it over and over until she was, again, in the throes of ecstasy. Again and again he brought her there to the edge and then slowly, gently, intimately, lead her into one climax after the other. It was as though he was making love with her rather than merely fucking. She had never had that with a man before. Not even with her best male customers.

Nasya didn't know if one hour had passed or three, and nor did she care. The more time ticked on, the hungrier her body became. The ache inside of her became insatiable. She rolled him onto his back and straddled him, tossing her hips forwards and back, pushing him as far into her as she could. She stared down at him, a teasing, passionate smile lighting her face. He moaned, quietly at first, and then louder as her hips steadied, rhythmic with their breathing. Under other circumstances with other partners, she might have teased him, left him desperate, but he had taken such tender care of her pleasure that she would not deny him his.

His breathing quickened. "Oh gods, yes," he muttered, keeping his eyes locked with hers.

She grinned, slowing her hips enough to draw out his orgasm, but not so slow as to ruin it. His breaths sharpened and groans escaped from his lips in brief, loud bursts until the climax came. He pushed himself into her, deep, and cried out one last time, before settling back into ecstasy. Nasya rolled off of him and laid on her side, her eyes bright with passion. They both glimmered with sweat. He looked over at her and smiled. Neither of them felt the need to speak. In only a matter of moments, sleep overcame them both, and Nasya drifted off into a restful slumber wrapped in his embrace.

# Chapter Twenty-Five

*Southeastern Port of Benevolence*
  *Country of Utara*

Nasya arrived at the port just before dawn the next morning. She had flown so swiftly that no one from the palace had arrived yet to either find her or keep the ships in port. She quickly made inquiries to discover which ship would be leaving first. A small ship, The Sea Diamond, was preparing to leave for Utara that morning. She had only to wait an hour or so. She paid the captain for a place on his ship and he obliged. The hour passed by in no time at all. Nasya stood on deck and waited until the ship was far enough out of the port to be safe from royal interception, and then immediately went below deck, laid down in an empty hammock, and fell fast asleep.

All she knew was a searing hot pain that covered every inch of her body. It was as though scalding acid had replaced the blood in her veins and was burning her alive from the inside out. She could only scream as the pain intensified. She tried to pull away, tried to resist, tried to end the pain but she was frozen. Not restrained, she didn't think, but stuck, unable to move either from the intensity of the pain or by some other means.

"Please," she managed to speak, her voice strained and hoarse, "make it stop."

"Stop," a voice said. "We're done. She can't take it anymore." The voice was not quite familiar, but also not entirely strange.

"We cannot stop now," another voice said. "Once it has begun, it will run through her until the end."

"And how will we know it's the end?" the first voice asked. It sounded as though they were irritated, perhaps angry.

"She will either survive the fever or she won't," the second voice said. "That is when we will know."

She didn't know if the pain was worse when she held still or when she moved. She didn't know where she was or whom she was with. She didn't know anything but the pain. She opened her eyes to try and identify her surroundings, but her vision was blurred by an endless stream of tears. Somewhere, a voice told her to breathe, to try and keep herself relaxed. She would have laughed if she didn't feel as though she were seconds away from death. Her head felt as though a knife were being sliced through it; every muscle clenched as tight as it could, her body was full of fever and she was drenched in sweat.

"Can't...any...more..." she said, barely even able to put those three words together.

"Is there nothing we can give her for the pain?" asked a third voice.

"If there were, don't you think I would have given it to her by now?" replied the first.

She was shaking violently and she couldn't stop.

"Oh gods. What's happening?" asked the second voice.

"Shit!" Something was taken out from under her neck and she was rolled onto her side. "Get me that basin of water."

The voices were blurred together. Her vision had gone completely dark. Still, she shook. The convulsions did not stop or slow, they only intensified. And as she lay unable to discern what was happening to her, her mind came alive with images. One by one, they flashed before her: landscapes, castles, oceans, lakes, mountains, fire, rivers of blood, teeth, decay. On and on they went. In the distance, someone was shouting, screaming, crying.

She looked down at her hands. Every vein emanated a brilliant, golden light. It turned to silver, then to green, then to red, and back to gold. Her skin burned. She didn't care. The world around her faded to ash. She didn't notice. Darkness took hold of her mind. She didn't fight it.

Nasya gasped as she awoke. She was disoriented and filled with terror. She looked down at her hands. They were normal. No light. No fever. No burning. She was still on the ship. By the sounds from outside of the lower deck, she assumed they were docking. Nasya let out a deep breath and rested her head in her shaking hands. The dreams were getting worse. She assumed it was due to the lack of rest she'd had over the last few days and decided that before she made her way to Passing's End to meet with The Mothers, she would take at least two days to rest and recover from her stressful journey.

She stepped out onto the deck of The Sea Diamond and was greeted with the familiar sight of the Utaran port. The captain greeted her with a smile. She thanked him for letting her travel with him and his crew, and then she made her way off the ship and into the surrounding woods. Garden's Hem was only a couple of hours from the port. She would be home before nightfall. She thought of her bed and blankets and felt that she couldn't reach them soon enough.

However, the more she thought about it, the more she felt she should bring her concerns to The Mothers sooner rather than later. It wasn't just a matter of what had happened in Zillah. The dream she'd had, the banshee she'd encountered, were ominous and not to be taken lightly. If her suspicions were correct, then The Mothers needed this information as quickly as possible. It would only take her a few hours flight to reach Passing's End. She stood on the docks and stared into the woods. She wanted to rest, but the urgency in her gut wouldn't let her. She cursed under her breath and made her way into the woods. She waited until she was out of sight and then unfurled her wings and began to fly, weaving around the trees. Nasya made her way up and through the canopy before turning and heading into the mountain pass.

It had been years since she had traveled this way. She had not been back to Passing's End since her graduation. If she were honest, she did not relish returning to the place where she had suffered through her entire childhood. Passing's End had shaped her into who she was now, it was true, but she held no affection for the place and did not want to see it again. But the events of the last few days urged her forward. Fear for herself and for Florynce urged her forward. She flew fast through the late summer air, the warm breeze a soothing balm against the feathers of her wings.

She landed in the courtyard at Passing's End only a few hours later. It was empty and quiet. She walked through the large doors at the fortress's entrance. The foyer was empty. The stone floor was not nearly as clean as it had been when the recruits had lived here. In a second, she saw herself on her hands and knees scrubbing mud and dirt from in between the stones. She heard Mother Casseiopea's voice chastising her, mocking her, laughing at her, ridiculing her. Her stomach flip-flopped with anxiety. Other memories rushed over her, but she pushed them away and walked forward. She was no longer a recruit. She was a Sister, a Hand of The Order. She had nothing to fear from this place or its inhabitants. Not anymore. She heard voices down the hallway and followed them into the large dining hall.

Four of the six Mothers were there. They turned as she entered the room, their eyes wide and brows furrowed.

"Nasya," said Mother Corvus, stepping away from the dining table where the Mothers were all gathered. "What on earth are you doing here? We thought you would be in Hevean for another week at least."

"As did I," Nasya replied, stepping forward. "But after my assignment went wrong, I barely had the chance to escape the country." She didn't bother hiding the anger in her voice.

The Mothers exchanged looks, but did not speak.

"Did you complete the assignment?" asked Mother Lynx.

Nasya guffawed. "Yes, Mother. I killed the holy man. Of course, that is of the utmost importance here."

"It *is* important, Nasya," said Mother Corvus. "We want to hear what happened, but it is good to know that the assignment is complete."

Nasya did not respond. She merely glared quietly at all of them.

"Tell us what happened, Nasya," said Mother Casseiopea.

"Where are Mothers Hydra and Fornax?" Nasya asked. "They need to hear this."

"They are not here at present," said Mother Phoenix.

It was all the answer she was given. Nasya shook her head, already feeling as though nothing she had to say would be heeded. She let out a frustrated breath and began. She explained all she had observed while selling vials in the courtyard of Zillah. She described her plan for assassinating Brother Caspian. She told of her encounter with him, all of what he had said, how she had prepared for the assignment, and all that had gone wrong.

"You're saying he saw through your invisibility spell?" asked Mother Lynx.

"He looked right at me, Mother," Nasya said. "As did others in the crowd. Somehow, the spell did not take."

"That is strange," muttered Mother Casseiopea. "And you're sure you cast it correctly?"

Nasya glared at her. "Do not insult me, Mother," she said. "I am in no humor for it."

"What do you think happened?" asked Mother Phoenix.

"I do not know. But I think there was something about Brother Caspian that negated most of my magic."

"Like what?" asked Mother Corvus.

Nasya shrugged. "I really do not know. I got the sense that he knew what I was there to do, as if someone had told him.."

The Mothers were quiet for several minutes.

"You think the client set you up?" asked Mother Corvus.

"Them," Nasya said, looking each of them in the eye, "or you."

The surprise in their expressions filled Nasya with satisfaction.

"You don't honestly think we would betray The Order when we have devoted our lives to it?" said Mother Lynx incredulously.

"I don't know what to think," Nasya said. "All I know is that I was sent into a country where I knew no one and had no support, and somehow the target knew who I was and why I was there."

"You don't know that for certain," said Mother Casseiopea. "It could have been a coincidence."

"You taught me never to believe in coincidence," Nasya said.

"Is this why you've come here?" asked Mother Phoenix. "To complain about how your assignment went? If so, your complaint is noted."

Nasya shook her head. "I also have reason to believe that Sister Florynce might be in danger."

The Mothers all started at this and exchanged glances with one another.

"What makes you say that?" asked Mother Corvus.

"I had a dream," Nasya said. "A vivid one wherein the queen of Hevean killed Florynce for not giving up the person who killed Brother Caspian."

Silence fell over the room.

"This is why you think you were set up," said Mother Lynx. "You think that your assignment was meant to expose Florynce."

Nasya didn't respond. She simply waited.

"This is what happens when Mother Hydra takes dreams too seriously," said Mother Casseiopea. "Sister Florynce is fine, Nasya. Mother Hydra spoke to her just yesterday."

"That's why Mother Hydra is not here," said Mother Lynx. "She and Mother Fornax are using magic portals to arrange meetings with all the Sisters."

Nasya's heart thudded hard in her chest. They did not see the urgency she did. "I encountered a banshee in the woods after I awoke from the dream," Nasya said. "And she spoke of Florynce's death."

The Mothers did not respond.

"It was a bad omen," Nasya insisted.

"Banshees are tormented creatures, Nasya," said Mother Corvus. "They wail about death constantly. It doesn't mean anything."

Rage flared in Nasya's chest. "I take it this means you're not going to do anything."

"What do you expect us to do?" asked Mother Phoenix. "Sister Florynce is alive. Her cover is intact. And you stand before us no worse for wear."

"The only reason I made it out of Zillah, indeed the only reason I made it out of Hevean altogether, is because I can fly," Nasya said. "If I had made the journey on foot, I would have been intercepted."

"Do you even know if the queen sent riders after you?" asked Mother Casseiopea.

Nasya couldn't answer. In fact, she did not know. She had not seen any riders from the capital. "No, Mother. I do not know."

"Then there isn't anything we can do, Nasya," said Mother Lynx. "We will make sure that your concerns are noted, and we will discuss everything with Mothers Fornax and Hydra once they return to Passing's End. Aside from that, I'm not sure what you expect from us."

"And what of the fact that my magic was negatively impacted by Brother Caspian or some other power in Zillah?" Nasya asked. "Does that not seem strange to you?"

"Not particularly," said Mother Corvus. "Holy men and women often wear talismans and runes and other magic-resistant items to keep themselves protected. Perhaps he was wearing one such item?"

Nasya was speechless. She had made this journey for nothing. It did not matter what she said, they were determined to dismiss her. She looked at each of them, hoping for something more than what they were offering, but they said nothing. Even though her life and the lives of her Sisters were on the line, the Mothers were unconcerned. Nasya shook her head slowly.

"When Sister Florynce turns up dead, remember that I warned you," she said before turning and walking out of the room.

The Mothers called after her, but she ignored them. Something was wrong. She could feel it, but she didn't know what it was. She did not think that all of the Mothers were against her or the other Sisters, but she was disheartened at how unconcerned they were by all she had related. It was as though they couldn't see what she saw. Or that they chose not to see. It was unlike them. Had they told the truth about Sister Florynce? Was she really alive? It wouldn't be the first time that Nasya's most vivid dreams came to nothing at all. Mother Hydra had said once that sometimes, when magic flows too strongly in someone, it manifests as dreams that taste of prophecy when, really, they're just dreams. Nasya wondered if perhaps this was what her dream about Florynce had been?

She walked out into the courtyard and wanted to scream. She didn't know what was real. She suddenly thought of Scarlet and her obsession with her mother's killer, and how it blinded her to everything else in her life. Nasya's heart panged as she thought of their last conversation. Scarlet was too consumed with revenge to see the truth in front of her. Nasya couldn't help but wonder if the same could be said of her? She was so used to being cast aside, she wondered if perhaps this had all stemmed from her belief that everyone would betray her eventually? Was it possible that the Mothers were actually on her side and that all that happened in Hevean really was just coincidence?

She couldn't accept that. Not yet. She decided she would be more cautious now than she had been. She would take note of everything and everyone around her. She would watch and listen. She would wait. If there was something untoward going on within The Order, she would find proof of it sooner or later. She also determined that she would not take any other assignments in Hevean or Lorzo. She would stay in Utara. It was the only way she could ensure her safety.

Nasya returned to Garden's Hem and allowed herself several days of relaxation. She was not satisfied with how her meeting with the Mothers had gone, but she couldn't sulk. She had work to do and clients to please.

Several weeks passed. Nasya continued her work in the brothel, taking on only a few new clients and tending to those who saw her repeatedly. Most of those were travelers and merchants coming to and from Hevean and Lorzo. Garden's Hem was on the main road to Utara's only eastern port, and it meant the brothel saw many familiar faces throughout the year, but especially in spring and summer when the weather was clear for travel and the ocean was calm.

Nasya relished the busyness, the consistent flow of work. She hated to be idle. It left too much time for thinking, and she hated being in her own mind. Her thoughts too often drifted to Scarlet, and once hooked on her, she couldn't think of anything else. Nasya didn't know where Scarlet was or if she was even alive. As hard as it was to admit, she knew she needed to let her go. She couldn't do that if she thought of her everyday, remembered the one night they had spent together, and recalled the words they had spoken to each other in those moments of ecstasy. It was one thing to know her heart belonged to Scarlet. It was something else entirely to allow herself to feel that love, to focus on it, and to yearn for Scarlet's company. The former was simply fact. The latter meant heartbreak and torment.

But as the summer faded into autumn and the travels of merchants lessened, Nasya found herself with far too much leisure time. It weighed on her and made her irritable. Madam Thelasse had noticed and came to her the day before to see if she was alright. Nasya had insisted she was, but Madam Thelasse had not been convinced.

"You are too often by yourself," she had said, looking at Nasya with eyes full of concern. "If you're not working, then you're shut up in your room pouring over books and maps. You take no time for yourself."

Nasya had been unable to meet her gaze. "I enjoy the time alone," she had lied, hoping to end the conversation. Madam Thelasse was persistent.

"Or, perhaps, you're too used to giving all of your time away to others that you now no longer know what it means to enjoy yourself," Madam Thelasse had said.

Nasya had been unable to reply.

"Is there no one you care for?" Madam Thelasse had asked. "No one whose company fills you with joy and pleasure?"

Nasya grinned bitterly. "There is, but she has chosen her own path, and it does not lead back to me." She looked at Madam Thelasse. "Until I can forget her, until I can disconnect her from my soul, there can be no one else."

"And what would that take?"

Nasya shook her head. "Death," she said, before she knew what she was saying. "Hers or mine. Nothing else is strong enough to tear her out of me."

It wasn't until that moment that Nasya had even realized how much of her heart belonged to Scarlet. It was her first admission of the intensity of her affections, and now that the words had been spoken, she knew they would only ring truer. It was Scarlet. It would always be Scarlet. Madam Thelasse had left her in silence.

Now, she sat and stared at the fire in the hearth, tears on her cheeks. She wondered if any of the other Sisters felt as lonely as she? Did they long for something else? Something more? Did they love as deeply as she did? Did they feel it in their very bones and in every beat of their hearts? What did they do about it? Perhaps they had built secret lives, secret loves outside of The Order and their covers. If so, she envied them.

A knock sounded at her door and jolted her out of her thoughts. She quickly wiped away her tears and called, "Come in."

The door opened. Mother Hydra walked into her room. Nasya stood to her feet. "Mother Hydra...I did not expect to see you."

The woman shut the door behind her. "I decided it was best not to announce my coming," she said. "I wanted to discuss your meeting with the other Mothers at Passing's End."

Nasya let out a slow breath. "I'm not sure there's anything to discuss," she said, sitting back down. "My concerns were completely dismissed or explained away."

Mother Hydra sat in the chair next to her. "Yes, they told me all of what was said. I thought you should know that I don't agree with their conclusions."

Nasya laughed. "When have you ever agreed with them when it comes to me?"

"What is that supposed to mean?"

Nasya felt exasperated. She was tired of this neverending back and forth. "It means that your own colleagues no longer respect your opinions regarding me, my magic, my dreams. It means that, whatever your opinions are about the issues I presented to them, they will change nothing. I was heard, and I was dismissed, and that was the end of it."

"Do you really have so little faith in yourself?"

Nasya looked over at her.

"I am not perfect, Nasya. I have made many mistakes, especially with regards to your magic and how it has manifested. But I also have my reasons for seeing things the way I do. Besides Mother Corvus, I have always seen more in you than has anyone else. And I came here because I want you to hear my perspective of your most recent assignment, as well as your dream and your encounter with the banshee."

Nasya took a deep breath and nodded. "Very well."

Mother Hydra adjusted her position in her chair so that she could face Nasya more directly. "Firstly, the complications of your assignment. You said you felt you were set up by either the client or the Mothers because the holy man seemed to know what you were doing in Zillah. I can promise that the Mothers did not intentionally or knowingly set you up, but that doesn't mean that the client didn't manipulate the rules of The Order to lessen your chance of escape."

Nasya furrowed her eyebrows but said nothing.

"I cannot speak to the client's intentions, but given the instructions they provided for how the assassination was to be carried out, it would not surprise me if they did, in fact, intend for you to be captured."

"Mother Casseiopea said it was merely coincidence," Nasya mumbled.

"Yes, well, if the client's purpose was to set you up, then it would be an unprecedented event. Mother Casseiopea, like the others, was probably trying to hold onto what's familiar. It's why they so often dismiss anything that they cannot immediately understand or process. It's why they refused to see how magical you were until literal wings sprung out from your shoulder blades. Sometimes the truth is too hard to accept."

Again, Nasya remained quiet. There was truth in Mother Hydra's words, but Nasya wasn't sure how she felt about them.

"I believe you also said the holy man, Brother Caspian, looked at you during the assassination and saw through your invisibility spell. Is that correct?"

Nasya nodded. "Others saw me, too. It was as though my magic was suppressed by something. Or someone."

"It probably was," Mother Hydra said. "Those who belong to religion often wear talismans, runes, and other such items to protect themselves from magical influence. Brother Caspian was the queen of Hevean's own minister. It would be imperative that he protect himself from being manipulated by magic to harm the queen."

"Then you agree with the others that this, too, was a coincidence," Nasya said.

"I agree with their assessment of why your spell didn't work as it should have," Mother Hydra replied, "but I agree with you that this, too, could have been intentional by the client. If it was information they possessed, it could have played into the instructions they passed on to us."

"And my dream?" Nasya asked. "Of the queen of Hevean uncovering Sister Florynce's identity? And then the banshee appearing the exact moment I awoke from that very dream?"

Mother Hydra sighed. "You're a necromancer, Nasya. Death is your magic. You are going to dream of things that both have and have not happened, things that may or may not happen. It's what magic does. Sister Florynce is alive, but that does not mean we should ignore your dream, or the omen of the banshee. I have ordered that Sister Florynce be removed from Zillah and brought back to Utara. Perhaps your dream was a premonition, or a warning, or maybe it was induced through stress. Regardless, the safety of all of you is paramount."

Nasya was relieved to hear that Florynce had not been left in Zillah to fend for herself, but she didn't know what to do with the rest of Mother Hydra's explanations. "Am I really nothing more than the sum of my abilities?" Nasya asked. "Am I nothing more than a necromancer and an assassin? Do I mean anything else to anyone?"

Mother Hydra did not respond. She stared at Nasya, her eyes sparkling the way they did whenever she felt strongly about something. "You're referring to Scarlet," she said.

Nasya felt her heart pang. She could have cried, but she held back her tears.

"You know that she is no longer part of The Order?" Mother Hydra asked.

Nasya looked at her, eyes wide. "What?"

"She wrote to us some time ago communicating her desire to leave The Order, and we granted it."

"Then, you don't know if she's…"

"Alive?" she shook her head. "I'm afraid I don't."

Nasya turned her gaze back to the flames. She was glad of the fire. A coldness had fallen over her, the kind of chill that sank deep into the bones and froze from the inside out.

"The Mothers and I have come to a decision," Mother Hydra said, standing to her feet. "We think it would be best if you moved to Armistice."

Nasya looked up at her, surprised.

"There is a small brothel there. The madam has already agreed to accept you. You would be closer to other cities, other people. We think it would do you good."

Nasya scoffed. "Are you worried about my personal life now?"

Mother Hydra sighed. "Under normal circumstances, I wouldn't care. But you're…different…for me." The words were stiff as they were spoken, but Nasya could see the emotion in Mother Hydra's eyes. "And for Mother Corvus. You have thrived in many areas, but without some kind of support, we fear that you will begin to falter."

"And you think moving me to a new town where I don't know anyone is the best solution?"

"We think a change of atmosphere will do you good. Armistice is situated in the plains on the way to Sun River. You will meet more people. You will see other ways of life. Here, while you have been popular, you are too isolated." Mother Hydra took a step towards here. "Pack your belongings. A coach will be here tomorrow morning to take you to Armistice." The woman turned and walked towards the door, where she stopped and faced Nasya once again. "I know that it's none of my business," she said, "but if Scarlet were to ask you to leave The Order and travel with her a second time, I think you should accept."

Nasya raised her eyebrows. "Are you telling me to quit The Order?"

"I'm telling you to choose what will make you happy."

She shook her head. "I can think of a hundred different things that would have made me happy as a child, a teenager, but you didn't care about my happiness then. Why do you care now?"

"Because now I can actually give you what will make you happy."

Nasya was angry. She had worked harder than any of her Sisters to be successful, to thrive in the life she was given, and now Mother Hydra, the only woman who had even come close to being a mother figure in her life, was telling her to give it up.

"I don't know how you know the details of that conversation with Scarlet, but it means you also know why I refused her offer. The only time I have ever been anyone's first choice, has been since you honored me as a distinguished Hand of The Order. I carry that letter with me always as a reminder that I am, at least, wanted by this organization. I won't give that up just to be Scarlet's shadow as she tries to avenge her mother."

Mother Hydra sighed. "It's your decision, obviously. And only you can choose what's best for you. But I think that's the wrong choice, for what it's worth."

Nothing more was said. Mother Hydra left, and Nasya found herself back in a flood of tears. She was furious, but not with Mother Hydra. In fact, she was grateful for the words she had spoken. They held wisdom and, if Nasya was honest with herself, the truth of her own regrets. She was proud of Scarlet for getting out of The Order, and she wished she could find the strength to do the same. But her words to Mother Hydra had also been the truth; she couldn't give up the one part of her life that filled her with any sense of purpose or identity. She knew Mother Hydra saw a future for her outside of The Order. She had since Nasya was in training. But her guidance there had been minimal, and Nasya knew it was because it had to be her own choice, free of influence. Whatever she did outside of The Order had to come from her own desires. Nasya Ember's entire life had been about what The Mothers wanted from her. Leaving The Order, then, had to begin and end with her, and no one else. She wasn't prepared for that.

Nasya cried for several minutes. She would move to Armistice as she had been instructed. She would try and heed Mother Hydra's words, however irritated she was by them. And she would think on what she wanted for herself, though she already knew part of the answer. Her thoughts shifted to Scarlet as they always did, and she wished for nothing more than to see her again, to talk to her, to try and find common ground on which to build a life together. She didn't know if her chances with Scarlet were gone, or if Scarlet was even alive, but if she was and if there was any hope for them, Nasya decided she would not let that hope die.

# Chapter Twenty-Six

*Town of Armistice*

*Country of Utara*

Armistice was smaller than Nasya had anticipated. Most of the populace was made up of farmers who lived on the outskirts of town. The heart of it was made up of a butcher's shop, a dressmaker, a few other small stores, a public house, and the brothel where Nasya was to work. Her trunks were taken into the brothel where she was greeted by the Madam, a woman named Brygitte. She was a beautiful, large woman with olive-toned skin, dark eyes, and black hair streaked with silver. She was dressed in yellow satin and, to Nasya's eyes, was far too elegant to live in such a rural place. She smiled as Nasya approached.

"And you must be Cinderella," she said, holding out her

hands to Nasya.

Nasya took them. "Yes, madam."

"I'm Brygitte," she said, "and this is my brothel. We are a small establishment, but we are well known for our talent and high quality experiences."

She led Nasya inside. It was built with wood and stone, but it carried the look of a palace. Linens and satin fabrics hung from the rafters in purples, blues, and golds. Fresh flowers hung in vines from the ceiling and wrapped around posts of wood. Hundreds of candles lit the inside. The air was filled with the fragrance of vanilla and other spices. It was beautiful. Nasya couldn't help her surprise.

"It's not what you expected, is it?" Madam Brygitte asked.

Nasya shook her head. "No, it isn't. But it is beautiful."

"I take it that the brothel you've come from is more...rustic?"

Nasya smiled. "That would be an accurate assessment, madam."

Madam Brygitte nodded and showed Nasya the rest of the building. "We have only four other companions, so there will be plenty of work available for you. The house takes a five percent cut of everything you make, and that pays for your room and board. Everything else is yours to keep."

Nasya was shown to her room. It was smaller than her room in Garden's Hem, but it was far nicer. All of the furniture had been made from the finest wood. The curtains and blankets were made of expensive fabric and well maintained. She was left alone for the rest of the night to recover from her journey, and to prepare for her first day of work. As she sat in her room and stared at the fire, she considered Mother Hydra's words. Nasya knew she had kept mostly to herself in Garden's Hem. The other companions and courtesans had been welcoming, kind, and friendly, but Nasya had kept them at a distance. She wondered if, perhaps, it had been a mistake to do so. If Mother Hydra was right, then she needed to make some friendships here in Armistice that would add something more to her life than just work and money.

It also was not lost on her how close Armistice was to Terrace. She knew that she couldn't reconnect with her father and sister, but she saw an opportunity to pass along the money she had been saving for them. She had been sending them money in smaller amounts, hoping they would write back to her, but they never had. She had planned on making a trip specifically to Terrace to meet with them face to face, and now was determined to do just that the first chance she had. Whatever her feelings about her family, whatever anger she held towards them, she couldn't let them starve. Not when she had the means of providing for them.

That night, Nasya ate supper in her room. It was a simple meal of bread, cheese, and sliced ham, but it filled her. She resolved to introduce herself to at least one of the other workers the next morning. She wasn't sure she knew how to make friends anymore, but she would try. If she could fuck strangers and leave them satisfied, she should be able to make a connection with another person. That night, she fell asleep early to the sound of flames crackling in the darkness of her room.

Darkness and silence faded into a blinding red light and fierce gusts of wind. She couldn't see much at first, but as her eyes adjusted, she saw she was in a clearing in the middle of a forest. The clearing stretched out towards a rocky cliff face where an entrance to a cave was located. At the entrance stood a group of people facing the cliffs, their arms outstretched towards the mountain. She could hear their voices. They spoke a language she didn't know.

A moment later she was standing among the crowd. The air around them was charged with anticipation, wonder, excitement, and dread. The wind continued to blow and groan as it circled the group, as though it, too, was speaking an unknown language and crying out to the earth. Above them, the sky was filled with the red of a blood moon. Each second that passed, the faces of the people around her came into focus. She knew none of them. And yet, she also knew all of them, somehow.

Only then did she see the form of a woman tied up at the entrance of the cave. She was squirming, as though trying to free herself from her bonds, but her movements were slow and sluggish. She didn't seem fully conscious. Tears flowed down her cheeks. Her dark skin looked as though she had suffered burns from an intense heat.

She stared at the tied up woman, her heart suddenly filled with concern and compassion. Her face was the last to come into focus and when it did, her heart stalled in her chest.

"Scarlet?" she said, trying to take a step towards her.

Her feet wouldn't move. She was stuck. She pulled and tried to move closer to her, but it was no use. At that moment, a loud, deep roar came from inside of the cave. In seconds, the entrance was engulfed in flames and a figure emerged that was terrible to behold. It stood at least seven feet. The lower half was that of a goat, while the upper was a beast with enormous horns and a face that resembled the skull of a bear. Its entire body was engulfed in flames. It screeched as it stepped out of the cave and into the light of the blood moon, unfurling its impossibly large wings. It was a demon, a being of intense malevolence and cruelty. Scarlet moaned and tried to roll onto her stomach to crawl away, but she was tied down too tightly.

"Scarlet, move!" she shouted. "Wake up and move!"

As much as she tried to get to Scarlet, she couldn't. She could only watch as the creature looked down at Scarlet. It fell onto all fours and sniffed her. It stuck out its forked tongue and licked the side of her face. Scarlet looked away.

"Stay the fuck away from her you fucking monster!" she screamed. Tears were streaming down her own cheeks now.

The demon lifted one of its hands and brought it down hard onto Scarlet's chest. It sunk into her body. Scarlet gasped. Fire shot into her body and began to illuminate her from the inside out.

"No!" she screamed. "Let her go! Scarlet! Let her fucking go!"

No one heard or saw her. She was there to watch, to see the ultimate end of her heart's one and only love. In seconds, what had once been Scarlet was nothing more than a burnt up pile of ash. The demon removed his hand from Scarlet's body and with it, her heart. It was still red. It was still beating. The people around her fell to their knees and bowed low to the ground. The demon held the heart above its head and let out a terrible cry. It lowered the heart down to its own chest and placed it inside of its body.

The heart glowed. With each heartbeat, the fire around the demon grew dimmer and its form shifted. Hooves were replaced with feet. Fur was replaced with skin. The bear skull changed to human and in only seconds, the demon's form fell away. It was a woman with pale skin, red hair, large, black wings, and silver eyes. Breath stalled in her lungs as she came face to face with the person who had destroyed the woman she loved.

It was herself.

Nasya awoke to the sound of her own screams. She looked around herself and found she was no longer in her room. Indeed, she wasn't inside at all, nor was she in Armistice. She was in the woods somewhere. She must have wandered there in her sleep. She hadn't sleepwalked in years. Her heart was racing. She fell to her knees and sobbed. Her hands shook and her body ached. She didn't know what she had just dreamed, but it horrified her. She tried to tell herself it was just a dream, like the dream about Florynce had been. She tried to tell herself what Mother Hydra had said about excessive magic creating vivid dreams that seem real, but don't mean anything. Over and over, she tried to explain it away, but in her gut she knew that she had been shown something important. Something about her future.

She didn't know how long she had been crying, but when the tears finally subsided, she allowed herself to look around. She needed to find her way back to Armistice. She was in a forest, and in the distance through the trees she thought she could see the lights of a village. Armistice wasn't located near a forest, so Nasya assumed that she must be near the outskirts of a neighboring town. As she emerged from the treeline, she saw at once that she was near Terrace. She would need to walk back through the trees.

Or fly.

She opted for the latter. It took less than an hour to make it back to Armistice. It was still dark outside, so she crept quietly into the brothel and back up to her room. She still didn't know how she had managed to get all the way to Terrace in her sleep. She had sleep walked before, but never like this. Never had she gone so far. She shut her bedroom door behind her and crawled back into bed. She tried to relax, tried to focus on the comfort and warmth of her bed, but it was no use. She knew she wouldn't be getting any more sleep tonight. Not after the nightmare she'd had.

Nasya climbed out of bed, lit a fire in her hearth, and sat at the table up against the wall near the only window in her room. She grabbed a piece of parchment and wrote down every detail of the dream she'd had that night, and then worked backwards to do the same for every other dream she'd had in the last few months. She wondered if there were any connections, similarities, or overlapping themes that could illuminate the meanings behind them. But even as she wrote them down in heavy detail, she could see nothing to connect them.

Nothing but the person who had dreamed them.

She didn't stop writing until the sun began to rise above the horizon some hours later. She watched the sun stretch its light over the land and wished it was strong enough to reveal to her the truths of her dreams. How they came and went inconsistently; how they always foretold death and destruction; how she was always at the center of them. Mother Hydra and the other Mothers had decided long ago that her dreams were nothing more than that. Vivid, yes, and perhaps disturbing at times, but they were still only dreams. Nasya felt this was a convenient determination, for it left all the responsibility for uncovering the truth behind her dreams entirely to her.

Nasya wondered if there was a way for her to understand the meanings of her dreams without the Mothers' help? Certain types of witches had been known to interpret dreams. How accurate they were, she didn't know, but it was better than nothing. She decided that she would begin searching for a witch. And if it came to nothing, then at least she would have tried.

The hovel was small and nestled deep in the thickest part of the forest. It had taken Nasya weeks to find where the witch lived. No one in Armistice wanted to discuss her presence. She was an undesired citizen. And even though, as far as Nasya could tell, she kept to herself, the very mention of her name was enough to end an entire conversation with the other citizens of Armistice. Everyone knew where she lived, but no one wanted to pass that information on to her. Luckily, Nasya was an excellent sleuth.

Now, she stood in front of the hovel and let out a slow breath. She knocked on the door. Seconds passed. The door opened and a middle aged woman with brown skin and blonde hair stood before her.

"Took you long enough," she said, leaning against the door post.

Nasya raised her eyebrows. "I beg your pardon?"

"I've been waiting for you for some time," the witch said.

"You...knew I was coming?"

The witch rolled her eyes. "Of course I knew. You'd best come in," she said, moving aside.

Nasya entered the hovel. It was dark, save for the light from the fire in the hearth. The forest canopy was thick in this part of the forest. It was the middle of the day, but the forest floor was dimly lit, hardly any lighter than if it had been midnight. The witch shut the door and walked over to the table that sat in the middle of the hovel.

"My name is -"

"Nasya, yes, I know. I'm Cypress. Now, please sit."

Nasya did as instructed. "If you know my name, then I assume you also know why I'm here."

Cypress nodded. "Yes, I do. You want me to interpret your dreams."

"That's correct."

"Then you've come to the right witch."

Nasya stared at the woman before her, unsure of what to expect from this meeting. She had not anticipated that Cypress would know who she was or what she wanted, and now wasn't sure what else would surprise her.

"Should I describe the dreams to you?" Nasya asked.

Cypress shook her head. "I already know of your dreams, Nasya. For they have been my dreams, too."

Nasya's eyes widened. "You've had the same dreams as I have? I...I don't understand..."

"I don't either, I'm afraid. Magic is unpredictable that way. But, I can tell you what they mean."

A chill crawled over Nasya's skin. Despite sitting next to the fire, she was suddenly very cold and could hardly stop her body from trembling. Cypress let out a deep breath and stared into Nasya's eyes.

"I should warn you...most people do not like the interpretations of their dreams. Most wish they hadn't come here, once the meanings have been given to them. This is your chance to walk away with your ignorance still intact."

Nasya shook her head. "I appreciate that, but I must know what these dreams mean. Especially the most recent one."

Cypress nodded and began, keeping her eyes locked with Nasya's.

"You want to know the meaning of the demon who takes out the heart of the woman you love," she said, "and you want to know why the demon had your face."

Nasya nodded. Cypress stared into her eyes and continued to breathe steadily. The chill on Nasya's skin sunk deep into her body, growing colder from the inside out. A moment later, she could see her breath on the air inside of the hovel.

"Your dreams have been a blend of the past and the future," Cypress said, "sometimes they are literal, and sometimes they are metaphorical. You already know the difference between them."

"And the demon?"

"You already know the answer to that."

A tingle in her chest began to engulf her entire body. "I must hear it from your lips," she said, her voice cracking as she spoke.

"The demon is both literal and metaphorical. It is a culmination of the past, the present, and the future."

"Then...what I saw...myself do...will it really happen that way?"

Cypress watched her for a moment. "Dreams are complicated, Nasya. You are the demon in the dream, but the context of the circumstance is withheld. It could mean many things."

"That's why I came here," Nasya said, her voice sharp with irritation. "To find out the meaning."

"Without context, I am limited in what explanations I can offer."

"You just said the dream is literal and a metaphor."

"Yes, but how much of the dream is one or the other, I cannot say. I only see what you see."

Nasya scoffed. "Then what good is in my coming here?"

"Because there is something I know that you do not."

"And what is that?"

"It's about the woman in your dream. The one tied up at the entrance to the cave."

Nasya swallowed nervously. "What about her?"

"You love her?"

Nasya nodded.

"And she loves you?"

"I think so."

Cypress nodded slowly. "Be wary," she said. "Love is not always a source of freedom. Love, like any other force on earth, can corrupt and mislead."

Nasya blinked. "What are you saying?"

"The turmoil that plagues your mind and soul is rooted in your love for Scarlet le Ve, yes? Because she will not give up her revenge to be with you?"

Nasya nodded slightly. Her heart was pounding hard. She did not like where the conversation was going.

"Broken hearts are the most dangerous weapons, particularly

when the heart that has been broken belongs to a powerful fae like yourself," Cypress said. Her bright eyes had darkened until they were almost black. The little light inside the hovel had dimmed as well, making it nearly impossible to see in the darkness. "Love does not always set us free," she said, her voice deepening. "Sometimes it is the shackles that bind us to our innermost shadows."

Nasya didn't know what to say. She was freezing now. Her body trembled violently. "H-How do I know..."

"...what type of love you have?" Cypress paused. "You won't know until it's too late. That is the metaphorical warning of your demon. And its answer will determine the meaning of your literal demon." She leaned forward. "Love often leads people to do horrible things. The demon you saw could very well be the love you carry for Scarlet."

Nasya shook her head. "No. I would never hurt her. I couldn't possibly."

Cypress smiled sadly. "Everyone thinks that until faced with the truth of their feelings." She placed her hands on Nasya's. "You carry a great deal of pain, child. Abandonment. Betrayal. Rejection. These are all potential catalysts for the violence you have seen in your dreams." She gave Nasya's hands a squeeze. "You must be careful, fledgling. Pay attention to the details, the little things that seem unimportant. Most of all, you must remain in tune with yourself and your desires."

Nasya's head swam. The room was thick with magic. She could practically taste it. "What about my other dreams?" she asked, desperate to think of anything else other than Scarlet. "Do you see any meanings in them?"

Cypress nodded. "You are gifted with powerful magic," she said. "Your dreams have been its manifestation within your psyche."

"Then...they don't mean anything? Just magic reaching into my dreams?"

"I wouldn't say that, no. Some of the dreams have connected you with souls of the dead and shown you visions of their most vulnerable moments. And some of them are warnings of potential deaths to come."

"How can I know the difference?"

"You can't."

"How am I to stop them from coming true?"

"You can't."

Nasya stood to her feet. "This is nonsense! I came to you for answers!"

"These are the answers, Nasya. Some things are already written on the pages of the future and cannot be altered, no matter how hard you try." She stood to her feet, compassion in her eyes. "I told you that most people regret asking for answers. That is because they want to know they can change what they have seen, and that is almost always impossible."

Tears filled Nasya's eyes. She shook her head. "I cannot accept that."

Cypress's eyes filled with sadness. "Then you will reap the consequences of your actions, whatever they may be."

A second later, Nasya was back outside surrounded by trees, and the hovel was gone.

# Chapter Twenty-Seven

*Capital City of Sun River*
  *Country of Utara*

Blood covered the ground at her feet. It stained the snow with steaming crimson. The wound was fresh, only a few minutes old. Nasya was crouched low, her silver eyes studying the prints in the early winter snow. They were enormous, at least as round as her entire head. She knew of only one creature that could make marks like that. The forest around her was unusually quiet. Eerie. It meant the beast was close. The hair on the back of her neck stood on end.

She had to keep going. There was no turning back. Not now. Nasya stayed low, bent at the waist and the knees, and took slow, deliberate steps through the underbrush. There was no telling how close the beast was, no telling if it was already watching her, already waiting. Nasya was not afraid, but nor was she foolhardy. She was strong enough to take on this creature, but she was also wise enough to know there could be more lurking in the shadows.

And last night there was a blood moon. They would still be bloodthirsty, eager for as many kills as they could find. Her feet crunched as she stepped through the snow. In the silence of the pre-dawn woods, the almost undetectable sound seemed as loud as a gong. She breathed slowly, focusing on her senses. She would not allow herself to be this beast's next victim. Not after the amount of money she had been paid to kill it. Yet, even as she moved steadily through the forest, she couldn't ignore the feeling deep in her gut that something was wrong. She tried to ignore it. She tried to bring her focus back to her breathing, but it wasn't her own fear that bothered her. She wasn't afraid.

It was outside of her, this feeling, this sensation. As though she had walked into it, like an atmosphere.

Nasya stepped into a grove where the underbrush had been cut away. No, not cut. It had been dug up, pulled out of the ground. Hundreds of holes remained empty, their former plants lying next to them, roots exposed. She had never seen something like this before. Who would dig up hundreds of ferns and bushes and saplings, and then leave them to be buried in the snow?

A flash of crimson appeared in her periphery and she spun towards it, ready to strike, but froze. She furrowed her eyebrows.

"Scarlet?" she asked.

Nasya sat up quickly. She was covered in sweat. She was still in her room. The fire that had burned brightly the night before crackled with the last few embers of wood. She let out a slow breath, relieved it had been a dream. She didn't like that she had grown so used to strange dreams that now she hardly had much of a reaction to them. But it was better than losing sleep or accidentally enacting spells in her sleep. She shook her head and looked to the place in the bed next to her.

It was empty. Nasya cast a glance around the room but saw no trace of the man she'd been with the night before. She sighed and climbed from bed to dress. It was not uncommon for her customers to leave before she awoke. The morning after could be awkward and embarrassing, especially if they were seen leaving her room. Nasya slipped on her plain dress and then walked to the table where the bread and cheese was still out.

That was when she realized he had not paid. At first she thought perhaps he had left the money somewhere inconspicuous, but the more she looked around the room, the more positive she became. He had gotten her services for free. She shook her head, incredulous. The audacity. She was thinking that perhaps he had left the money with the owner of the inn madam when she heard commotion outside her window. She peered through the open shutters, certain that the bustle had to do with Prince Xaran's death. It was still early, the morning sky filled with purple twilight, but it had been long enough for what remained of him to have been discovered.

Guards were moving through the streets, shouting and shoving and causing a ruckus. Some were going into homes and pushing people out in their night clothes. At the center of the group of guards was a tall man clad in armor with the royal seal on the breastplate. He was shouting orders and waving his hands. He motioned towards the inn where she was staying and shouted, "And search in there! Bring every woman out!"

Nasya backed away from the window, wrapped her cloak around her shoulders, slipped into her boots, and was about to sneak out the back when the door to her room swung open. A guard entered and motioned for her to follow him.

"This won't take long, miss," he said, clearly uncomfortable with the task he had been given.

Nasya cursed under her breath and followed him outside. She wanted to flee, to run, to unfurl her wings and fly away to a safe place, but she knew she could only do so under the gravest of circumstances. For now, she had to play the part of ignorant wench. She followed the guard outside and was placed in a line against the wall of the inn. On either side of her were dozens of other women. The commotion had drawn an enormous crowd of people who stood a few yards away, watching with curiosity at what the king's guard was doing.

"Last night," began the tall guard who had been giving the orders, "Prince Xaran, the youngest son of our most gracious king, was slain!" Murmurs spread throughout the crowd. "No one saw it happen, but one piece of evidence was left at the scene!"

Nasya felt her heart begin to race. The guard pulled out her slipper.

"This shoe was found next to the prince's dead body. It remains the only clue to his murderer's identity. The foot on which it fits will belong to the person who killed our prince!"

With that, he motioned for the guards to begin sitting women down and holding out their feet. Nasya was panicking. The slipper was magic and would fit only her foot. She looked around to see if she could sneak away unnoticed, but doing so would be risky. The very act of running would confirm her guilt. Chances were that guards were stationed behind the inn in case of an attempt of escape. She knew she could always fly away, but that would draw far too much attention. There weren't many young women with retractable wings flying around these days, and that piece of information alone could lead them to seek out The Order. Moreover, she was already wanted in Hevean for that very thing. She couldn't risk the same in Utara.

If she was going to escape, she had to do so without drawing further attention to herself. She wracked her brain to think of a spell she could perform that would enable her to sneak off, but hesitated. The last time she had tried that, the spell hadn't worked. She either had to sneak away unseen, or face whatever was about to come.

One by one, the captain of the guard tried fitting the slipper on each woman's foot. And one by one, women were eliminated. The longer it took, the more people gathered around to watch, probably excited to know what would happen to the one whose foot fit in the slipper. Nasya tried to keep herself calm and focused, tried to keep her breathing slow and smooth. She still couldn't believe she had made such a novice mistake as to leave her shoe behind. It was an unacceptable amount of recklessness.

Moments later, commotion grew within the crowd. High Prince Mael made his way through the onlookers riding atop a black stallion. He dismounted and handed the reins to a nearby guard.

"Which are the women from the inn?" he asked the captain of the guard.

He motioned for the rest of the women up against the wall. "They are, sire. We've already tried the slipper on a dozen women or so."

High Prince Mael nodded slowly and looked at all of the women standing and waiting to be called over. Nasya kept her gaze cast to the ground. Her silver eyes would give her away to the High Prince. She could feel her chances of escape eeking away like the ink she had washed from her hair the night before. She would be seen by him, she was certain, and then what would she do?

She was right. High Prince Mael motioned for the guard to grab her and sit her down. Nasya felt herself begin to lose control of her emotions. Her heart was racing. Her breathing quickened. Her hands trembled. She was afraid. Truly afraid that she was about to meet her end. This couldn't happen. Not to her. Not here. Not now. She resisted the guard, but didn't speak. She didn't make a noise at all. A second guard walked over and shoved her down onto the bale of hay up against the wall of the inn. The High Prince walked over and knelt in front of her.

He slipped the shoe onto her foot with ease. He grinned and looked up at her. "I told you I'd unmask you."

Nasya didn't speak.

"You left quite a mess," he said. "I would have thought the renowned assassin known as Cinderella would have been more...delicate."

Nasya's mind whirled with confusion. How did he know who she really was? The slipper was enough to reveal her identity from the ball, but nothing else. He knew her name. He knew she was an assassin. It didn't make sense. To make it worse, he was teasing her, mocking her, laughing at her expense. It made Nasya's stomach churn.

He must have seen her confusion because he leaned forward so that only she could hear. "I'll make sure The Order knows you did as you were instructed, that you completed the assignment precisely as I planned."

Nasya's eyes widened. He had hired her to kill his own brother?

"I wasn't about to be the impoverished king," he whispered.

Anger flared in Nasya's chest. He hadn't done this for the greater good. He hadn't done it for the betterment of his country or the wellbeing of his people. It had all been for his own ambition, his own wealth.

He laughed as the realization dawned on Nasya's face. "See,

this is my favorite part, when all the pieces fall together."

The Order had been deceived, used as pawns to bring about his own selfish gains. She felt rage and hatred flooding through her. She began to tremble. The sides of her vision turned red. She and The Order had been puppets to his greed, and they had executed his will exactly as he wanted. He had killed his brother for money. And now she would take the fall for it. Nasya's hands began shaking and her vision blurred.

It wasn't just her own anger she was feeling.

"How could you do this?" she asked, her voice dropping deeper than normal.

Mael's eyes narrowed. Nasya rolled her head backwards, feeling as though something was moving through her bones, pushing out of muscle, tissue, tendon. It was like an itch clawing from behind her flesh, trying to get out. She was shaking violently, her muscles spasming.

"Tell me, brother..." she said, her voice deeper still, and raspy, "how could you do this to one who loved you? Idolized you? Worshiped you?"

Mael's eyes darkened. "I will not fall for your illusions, witch," he said.

Nasya laughed, her voice loud and deep and heavy with the echo of many voices behind it.

"Do you remember when you saved me from the river?" She wrenched free of the guard's hands and stood to her feet. Her silver eyes had turned black. Around her pupils was a thin red circle. "Do you remember the promise you made that day? To always watch out for me? To protect me?"

Mael was on his feet backing away. His face was pale. His eyes were wide.

"Kill her," he said to his guards.

The three closest guards brandished their spears and thrust them at her. But they stopped six inches short, as though they'd hit a wall, even though nothing was there that they could see. No amount of striking or thrusting would break through the barrier.

"I said kill her!" Mael shouted.

"I call your bloodline cursed!" Nasya screamed, holding out her hand towards the High Prince. "Fear, poverty, and sickness will fall upon your head from this day until your last day! Long and miserable will be your life, for you have taken the life of one you should have cherished!"

Nasya stood still, her feet planted firmly on the ground, but something else moved, something wispy and red. It was as though it was coming out of her body: a spirit in the shape of a man, flesh falling away from the bones. The people watching had all begun screaming and rushing away to hide. Mael stumbled backward as the spirit moved towards him, its form coming together to reveal the soul of Prince Xaran.

"No," Mael said, falling backwards and frantically trying to crawl away. "No, you're dead, you're not real. This is not real!" His voice elevated to shouting as the spirit moved closer.

Nasya smiled, and so did the spirit whose eyes glowed a hot red. They laughed, their voices mingled and shrill.

"The woman!" Mael shouted. "Destroy her!"

Every guard that hadn't yet abandoned their post moved to try and take Nasya down, but none could get any closer to her than half a foot. They were stuck in place, unable to lift their feet to move any direction other than backward. Slowly, they all dropped their weapons and backed away, unwilling to risk their own lives. Nasya cackled, her voice made of many voices echoing through the city. She could feel the power of magic rushing through her. It was unlike anything she had ever experienced before. It was thick and left a sugary taste in her mouth. She couldn't describe the sensation, not even to herself.

The look on Mael's face when he realized that he was completely at the mercy of the woman who had not only killed his brother at his behest, but was also the one who now conjured his dead spirit, was enough to make Nasya bend over laughing in glee. The spirit of Prince Xaran laughed too. Mael rolled onto his hands and knees and made to run away, but Nasya stretched out her hand and stopped him, magic holding him in place.

"Not yet, brother," said Nasya and Xaran. "We are not quite finished."

Mael tried hard to get away. He clawed at the ground and dug his feet into the dirt. He was strong, but no match for the combined anger of Nasya and Prince Xaran. The two of them were simultaneously connected and acting on their own volition. It was as though Nasya was the vessel through which Prince Xaran's anger was channeled, and her anger was what allowed the connection to be made.

"Please," Mael pleaded. "I only did what I thought I should."

But Xaran was silent. He moved closer to Mael, reached out a bony finger, and pressed the tip to Mael's forehead. A shape that looked like an X with a long line down the center glowed red as it was branded into Mael's skin. The High Prince let out a grunt of pain as the mark was seared into his flesh. It was the last step to the curse upon his house.

Prince Xaran's spirit faded back into Nasya. Her vision returned to normal. She felt as though she would faint, but forced herself to remain awake. She had only a small window of time to escape and she couldn't squander it. She unfurled her wings and lifted herself into the air. High Prince Mael screamed for her to be shot down, but she didn't wait for his guards to try. She flapped her wings hard and fast and took off to the north, away from Sun River. She flew until she reached the forest. The cover of the trees would keep her concealed.

Nasya landed on the carpet of moss and leaves. She let out a deep breath and gave herself a moment to reorient herself. Her body shook from the remnants of her connection to the dead. But this one was different. She had never conjured the spirit of one she had killed, and even now, though Prince Xaran was gone, she could feel the sensation of his soul inside of her as though he still existed beneath her skin. She wanted to be sick, to purge her body of every last ounce of him, but she couldn't afford to lose any time. She had to get away from the city as quickly as possible.

"Impressive," said a voice from behind her. Nasya spun

around, ready to attack, but froze when she saw it was the merchant from the night before. The one who had not paid her. "I've never seen a fae's wings before."

"You," she said, still dizzy and disoriented. "What are you doing here?"

"I was sent to find you," he said, "and bring you to a safe house."

Nasya frowned. "You were sent to find me? By whom?"

"Scarlet," he said.

Nasya's heart skipped a beat. "Safe houses are only for members of The Order, which Scarlet is not any longer."

He nodded. "I'm aware, but it was an emergency. She had nowhere else to go."

"What emergency? Why did she need somewhere to hide?"

"I'll explain everything, I promise, but we must move if we're to get back before they find her."

"They?"

"Please, Nasya. I know we don't know each other, but you must trust me."

Nasya crossed her arms over her chest. "I have no reason to trust you."

"She said you'd say that. She said to show you this." He reached into his pocket and pulled out a scrap of red cloth. It was from Scarlet's cloak. "She said you would see this and know that I'm telling the truth."

It wasn't much, but it proved that he had, at least, met with Scarlet at one time. And if he was telling the truth and Scarlet was in danger, Nasya knew she couldn't walk away or ignore it. She felt something trigger a warning in the back of her mind, and she made note of it, but she wasn't going to change her mind. She knew that this could very well be the path to her undoing, but she couldn't ignore the woman she loved. Not when she might be in trouble and was asking for her help. If it was a trap, she would be ready for it.

She nodded. "Very well. Let's move."

# Epilogue

*Kyndra stared down at the memorial she'd had built to honor Rhaean's death. She was alone in the autumn darkness. She had placed the memorial deep in the woods around Passing's End. Fire's Hearth was somewhere she didn't think she would ever be able to visit again. Not after all that had happened, all she had lost. She ran her hands over her face and fell to her knees, allowing herself to cry. She couldn't stop playing over the events of the days leading up to Rhaean's zenith, wracking her brain to think of any signs she might have missed, hints that her daughter was struggling more than usual. But the truth was that she'd had no way of knowing what would happen, and that made the grief all the worse.*

*And Ygritte, poor thing, had suffered acutely. She had been the first to find Rhaean in the dining hall. She had not known what it was she was facing. She had tried to stop her, tried to keep her concealed inside a protection spell, but Rhaean had already been too far consumed by magic to be controlled. By the time anyone came upon her, the zenith was imminent. Ygritte had blamed herself, despite the Mothers all assuring her that she had done nothing wrong. In fact, Ygritte had likely been responsible for saving the lives of everyone in Fire's Hearth. If she hadn't come upon Rhaean when she did, chances were the zenith would have consumed the entire fortress.*

*But even that knowledge was not enough to calm Ygritte's mind or alleviate her guilt. Kyndra shook her head and cried. This was all her own fault. No, not hers alone. It was the council of Elders. It was the other Mothers, too. It was the entirety of The Order, its function, its very existence. For the first time, she felt she saw the truth clearly. She had been part of the problem, and she had enabled the rest of it, but the real issue was The Order itself. And had not that been Rhaean's very argument? Had she not said almost those very words to her once before?*

*Her tears stopped. She looked at the stone memorial; it had been carved into the shape of a phoenix to honor the spirit of her daughter that, she hoped, had arisen from the ashes of her zenith to embrace the peace of the afterlife. Kyndra knew what her life's focus needed to be, now. If she was going to really honor her daughter's sacrifice, then there was only one thing she could do.*

*"I swear to you," she whispered, "I will make this as right as I can."*

*"Are you still so naive?" came a voice behind her.*

*Kyndra stood to her feet and spun around. She saw nothing, no one. "Hello?" she called. "Who is there?"*

*A voice above her laughed. She looked up but saw no one. The laugh came from behind her, but when she turned no one was there, either.*

*"I grow tired of your games," she said, her voice rigid and thick*

with anger. "Show yourself!"

A second later, a flash of silver ahead of her gleamed in the midnight darkness and from the shadows emerged a figure. She emanated a kind of light that sometimes looked like flashes of lightning under her skin. Kyndra's eyes widened.

"Oh dear gods above," she said, taking a step forward. "R-Rhaean?"

"Aye, that was my name before," she said, disappearing and then reappearing right beside Kyndra. She stared down at the memorial and grunted. "A phoenix? Really?"

Kyndra faced her. "You...you always loved them," she said, wondering if she was dreaming or hallucinating.

"Did I?"

Kyndra studied the figure before her. "You're not a ghost," she said. "You're not merely a spirit, either."

"What gave it away?" Rhian asked mockingly as she faced Kyndra.

"But...zeniths...they're supposed to be fatal..."

The figure before her looked like her daughter, sounded like her daughter, but there was something else in her eyes, something she didn't recognize. She turned away from Kyndra and began to slowly spin in circles, humming an unfamiliar tune. "They're supposed to be, yes," she muttered.

"Then...how are you...here?" Kyndra asked confusedly.

"You're the one with all of the answers, remember?" she said, crouching down and staring at a fern. "What did you always tell me about zeniths?"

"That they're...uh...they're when too much magic consumes a body."

Rhaean didn't respond and she didn't need to. A thought came to Kyndra, an idea that clicked in her mind and made sense of how she could see this spiritual manifestation of her daughter. Fear gripped her heart like a hand plunging into her chest. She wanted to deny it, explain it away, find any other answer, but she knew there wasn't one. It seemed impossible, and yet she couldn't deny there was a sense of truth in it, of logic. However impossible it was, however unlikely, it did, at least, make sense.

"You...you're a...a fury?"

Rhaean clapped her hands. "Good job!" she said, as though speaking to an annoying child.

It was unbelievable, and yet she believed it. She wanted to tell herself she was hallucinating or dreaming or that her grief was playing with her vision, but she knew none of that was true. Instead of resting in peace, her daughter's spirit was set loose, chained to magic, doomed to exist forever but live no longer. Her soul was gone. Her body was ash. Tears fell down Kyndra's cheeks.

"I am so sorry, my love," she said, her voice cracking.

Rhaean glared at her, flashes of light and fire running up and down her arms, across her face, into her eyes, all underneath her skin. "This is what you and The Order did to me."

Kyndra shook her head. "I did not want this for you."

"But this is what you caused," Rhaean said, her voice deep and loud, growing bigger. "You could have taken me away. You didn't."

*"If I could do it over again –"*

*"Oh," she said, pouting, "but you can't. It is done now. And there is only one thing that can make this right."*

*"What do you wish me to do?" Kyndra asked, her heart sinking into her stomach.*

*"Anything you can," Rhaean said, turning away. "Anything and everything you can."*

*She was gone. Kyndra called out her name, asked her what she meant, begged to know what it was she needed to do, but she was met with silence.*

*Rhaean was a fury. It was almost too unbelievable. Such a thing had not happened in centuries if, indeed, it had ever really happened at all. Zeniths producing furies had been all but completely discounted as a myth for as long as she could remember. What made it happen now? What was different with Rhaean's zenith that led to the creation of this incredibly powerful, terribly hostile creature? Kyndra didn't have any answers. Nor did she know where to find them. She considered asking the Elders, but then thought better of it. If furies could come from zeniths, she didn't want anyone else knowing about this but her. There was no telling what the Elders might do to eliminate all that remained of her daughter. They could no longer be trusted. She would find answers on her own. And they would not be ready for what would happen when she did.*

# Acknowledgements

This book would not have been possible without the support, encouragement, advice, and feedback from some incredible people:

*Dark Fire Fiction* – for publishing my short story "Masquerade" that this novel is based off of. You gave a home to my work. You gave it space to breathe, to exist, to be. And now it's become this novel. Thank you.

Eric – if you hadn't urged me to expand my short story into a novel, this book wouldn't exist. Thank you for giving me that push. Thank you for reading each iteration. Thank you for giving me such honest and encouraging feedback.

Angelee – not just for designing my cover, my maps, my concept art, and the interior of this book, but for being excited about the story and these characters. You're part of what kept me working on this when I thought it would never come together.

Rachel – words can't describe how much your enthusiasm and support have meant to me. You didn't know it, but you kept me going when I wanted to give up. I count you among the best blessings in my life.

<u>Jaime, Nicole, and Nastashia</u> – our writing retreats have been so helpful and motivating; just being around you three writing powerhouses inspires and motivates me to keep pushing myself. Thank you for your insights, your support, and most importantly, your friendship.

<u>My beta readers Eric, Angelee, Jessa, Ashley, CJ, Kayla, Amber</u> – your feedback was tremendously helpful to the continued revision of this manuscript. Thank you for allowing me your time and creative energy. I honestly can't say thank you enough.

<u>My extended writing community on Facebook, Twitter, Instagram, TikTok, Clapper, and Lemon8</u> – I can't list all of you by name, but I need to tell you how much I appreciate every last one of you. I would have given up on this book long ago if not for your posts, your videos, and your willingness to support and uplift all independent authors. You make so much magic happen! Thank you.

<u>My partner, James</u> – thank you for always encouraging and supporting me, no matter what my endeavors are. Thank you for letting me read this novel out loud to you while I revised and edited it. Thank you for listening as I rambled on and on about my world building. Thank you for helping me resolve some big plot holes. And mostly, thank you for being who you are. I love you with my whole self.

# Excerpt from book 2 of The Hands of the Order:

Excerpt from book 2 of The Hands of the Order:

Scarlet loved coming here. She had named all of the trees and spent time talking to each one as she carefully picked only those apples that were ripe and ready to be picked. She told them stories, she imagined their responses and made up entire conversations with each of them. When she had finally filled her basket, she set it on the ground and made her way into the forest again. There was a river nearby where she loved to sit and watch the wildlife. It was only a few minutes walk into the treeline.

Summer sun shone against the river as the water slowly flowed through the heart of the forest. Nine year old Scarlet sat and stared at the water, fascinated by the many species of living things that seemed to mold their entire existence around the river. There were many such currents of water that flowed, connected, and disconnected throughout the forest, but this one was her favorite. It wasn't full of rapids like some, nor did it dry up in the summer like others. It was steady. Constant. Dependable. And Scarlet had come to know its personality intimately in the years she'd been visiting its banks.

Black and yellow butterflies with large wings filled the glen around the river. They loved the fragrant, ripe scents of the flowers that grew around the river and on top of it. Lillypads floated on the water's surface, moving slowly as the current carried them farther down river. Crows, finches, flickers, and hummingbirds all mingled in the shallows, feasting on the flies, mosquitos, and other insects that made their homes in grasses covered by the river. Scarlet thought of these creatures as her friends. She loved the birds. Even named those that stayed in the glen year round.

The river, her mother had taught her, was the beating heart of the earth. It fed every living thing, both plant and animal alike, and provided homes for fish, frogs, and others. She taught Scarlet to always hold profound respect for the river, and Scarlet had taken those words to heart. She spoke to the water often, expressed her love and devotion by ensuring it and every living thing around it was tended to. She was its guardian, its self-appointed protector.

She had been out at the river for several hours that day, drinking in the humidity and the heat. Summer was her favorite of the four seasons. She loved the rays of sun on her skin, the taste of the air on her tongue, the feel of the warm summer breeze in her curls. There was so much life and beauty in the summer. Not that there wasn't in the other seasons, but Scarlet felt more akin to the summer months, the longer days. They filled her with a sense of life and longing that couldn't compare with the other three seasons of the earth.

As the sun began to set, she made her way home, full of joy

and adoration. She always regaled her mother with stories from the river. She loved seeing her mother's eyes alight with joy and amusement. Scarlet rushed through the forest, her bare feet soft on the moss that covered the dirt. Her dark eyes sparkled with pleasure at everything around her. This was home. This was life. This was her joy.

Scarlet and her mother lived alone in a small cottage in the woods. It was only a ten minute walk from the river, clustered among a thick grove of trees. It was the only home Scarlet had ever known, and she loved it with every ounce of affection her small body held. The last few yards were her favorite. A dirt path led from the glen up to the front door of the cottage. It was lined with all of her mother's favorite flowers, but mostly lilies and gardenias. Their scents mingled in the air, creating something altogether luxurious and calming. Scarlet couldn't think of any smell she loved more.

But today, her walk up the path was different. The path looked much the same, but something felt off, felt wrong. The front door was ajar. While that alone was not unusual, she couldn't deny that it looked odd. She wasn't sure why at first, but then it occurred to her: everything was quiet. There were no birds chirping. No bees were buzzing around the flowers. All was eerily quiet. It made her hesitate.

She stepped slowly towards the front door and that was when the smell of blood wafted towards her.

Book 2 of The Hands of the Order Series is coming June 2024!

www.ingramcontent.com/pod-product-compliance
Lightning Source LLC
Chambersburg PA
CBHW022020300726
48970CB00003B/971